Bernard Treves's Boots
A Novel Of The
Secret Service

by

Laurence Clarke

Double 9
BOOKS

Bernard Treves's Boots
A Novel Of The Secret Service
by Laurence Clarke

ISBN: 978-93-59951-52-2

Published by

DOUBLE 9 BOOKS

2/13-B, Ansari Road
Daryaganj, New Delhi – 110002
info@double9books.com
www.double9books.com
Tel. 011-40042856

ABOUT THE AUTHOR

"Bernard Treves's Boots," Laurence Clarke's literary masterpiece, will always be remembered as a super paintings of writing. Clarke tells a gripping story that appears into humans's lives and how complicated existence may be through his beautiful writing and deep knowledge. "Bernard Treves's Boots" is a thrilling journey thru the characters' hearts and minds that makes you consider the complex nature of relationships, feelings, and time. Clarke's fashion of writing suggests how nicely he is aware of a way to use phrases to weave a colorful web of emotions, settings, and people that readers from all walks of life can relate to. "Bernard Treves's Boots" is a must-read for all people who loves excellent literature because it indicates how correct a storyteller he's through having complicated characters and frightening testimonies. With this book, Laurence Clarke solidifies his popularity as a famous writer, giving readers a deep and enlightening enjoy that remains with them lengthy after the remaining page is turned. "Bernard Treves's Boots" is a masterpiece of writing that shows how properly Clarke is at telling tales and what kind of he is aware of approximately what human beings experience.

CONTENTS

CHAPTER I

"Are you sure your name is Manton?"

Captain Gilbert looked keenly across the table. The light in the little room was not good, and the expression on the Captain's face was one of intense interest and bewilderment.

"Quite sure, sir—John Manton," answered the man standing at the further side of the table.

Manton was one of a number of recruits who had that day presented themselves at the Ryde Recruiting Office—a tall, well-poised man of twenty-six, dark-haired, blue-eyed, firm-lipped and vigorous-looking, despite the fact that his countenance was somewhat pale. He wore a well-brushed blue serge suit, noticeably the worse for wear. His bowler hat, too, had seen long service.

Captain Gilbert, still looking at him, drew forth a sheet of paper, and took up his pen.

"John Manton," he wrote, then his eyes lifted, and he looked once more and with a peculiar expression into the tall young recruit's face. For a moment he paused. "Manton," he said, "I should like to see you privately after the office closes."

The young man steadily returned his gaze.

"Very good, sir," he said, with an air of docility. "At what time shall I come?"

"At eight o'clock," returned Gilbert. "Wait for me outside." His eyes followed the other as he turned and left the building, but the moment the door had closed Captain Gilbert plunged once again into his work.

"Next," he called to the line of men seated on the far side of the room; and the man at the end of the line rose and advanced towards the table.

Manton in the meantime paced the streets until eight o'clock, then turned his steps towards the recruiting office.

"I wonder what he wants," thought the young man.

Possibly Gilbert guessed he had been in the army before, and wished to question him upon that point.

"Whatever he wants," thought Manton, somewhat wearily, "does not much matter. If he refuses to take me, and manages to find out everything, I can enlist somewhere else."

As the clock struck eight Captain Gilbert, with an air of haste, closed his desk, left the office and came striding along the street.

"Ah!" exclaimed the Captain, catching sight of Manton, "we'll come up here to the left; it's quieter."

He led the way as he spoke towards a deserted side street. It was already almost dark, and the dimmed street lamps had been lit. They had proceeded some distance together in silence, when Gilbert halted suddenly, and laid his hand on Manton's shoulder.

"Treves," he said, "so you had the grit to do it, after all?"

Manton turned and stared in wonderment.

"Do what, sir?" But he suddenly felt his fingers seized in a cordial grip.

"Gad," went on Gilbert, "that'll make a man of you—eh?"

"I'm afraid I don't understand a word of what you are saying, sir!"

"You don't understand a word! Why, of course you don't! I like you for it—and I'll be frank, I thought I never could like you. Somehow," he went on, looking into Manton's face, "you are the same and yet different, but I'd know you anywhere, despite this shabby old suit and your battered bowler. You knew me, too, when you came into the office."

Manton, still bewildered beyond measure, shook his head slowly.

"I have never seen you in my life before, sir!"

"No, of course not," laughed Gilbert, who was jovial and good-natured. He slipped his arm through Manton's. "Come along now, and we'll talk about it!" Something in the situation of the moment seemed to exhilarate him. "So you've decided to make good after all? Well, all I can say is—I'm delighted. For your own sake, for the old Colonel's sake, for everybody's sake!"

Again he paused and looked into his companion's face.

"I'll admit, Treves, I didn't think you had it in you. I thought——"

Manton freed his arm from the other's grasp.

"I am sorry, sir," he said, "but you are evidently making a grievous mistake. My name is Manton——"

"I don't care what your name is," retorted Gilbert, irritated a little by what he believed to be the other's unnecessary reserve. "You can get rid of your name and call yourself Manton or Jones or Smith or Robinson or anything you like for all I care! But I know you to be Bernard Treves, and——"

But this time a note of firmness appeared in Manton's voice.

"My name is not Treves, sir!"

Gilbert shrugged his shoulders.

"You needn't keep up that note with me," he said. "I'm delighted to find you have the grit to try to make some sort of reparation."

Manton moistened his lips.

"I still don't understand you," he said slowly. "But all I can do is to assure you I am not Treves. If you know some one who resembles me and whose name is Treves, perhaps you would look at me again. To my knowledge, sir, I have never met you in my life before."

As he spoke he took off his hat and turned his face fully towards the Captain.

For a moment there was silence.

"In this half-darkness," said Gilbert, "you look absolutely like Bernard Treves to me. You looked like him in the office. I could see that you had been in the army the minute you stood at my table." He paused, and for the first time a slight doubt crept over him. "The only thing that seems changed to me," he went on, "is your manner. Come, now, Treves, you know me well enough to confide in me; that's why I asked you to speak to me out of the office. Anything you care to say will go no further. I will accept it as unofficial, and if you intend to make good I'm prepared to be a good friend to you. But in the first place admit that you are Treves; it will make matters much easier."

For some moments Manton remained silent. Gilbert believed that at last he was about to admit his identity.

"I will tell you my history for the past three months, sir," said the young man.

"I shall respect your confidence," Gilbert answered.

"I am sorry to disappoint you, sir, but my name is really Manton, and, as you guessed when I came into the office, I have been in the army before. I was at Scarthoe Head, Battery A. I was a sergeant, and, being a public school man, was made book-keeper to the acting adjutant." He fell into silence again, and went on after a pause. "Something went wrong in regard to the delivery of stores to the fort. There was a hundred and forty-five pounds deficit in the accounts. I was held responsible, sir."

There was an intensity and a genuineness in the ring of the stranger's voice that gripped Gilbert's attention. He listened with the closest attention, and as Manton narrated in detail his life during the past six months, Gilbert's convictions faded and gradually vanished. It was impossible that the man could have invented the story, a story so easy of verification. It was some time, however, before he let Manton perceive his change of view; then he drew in a deep breath.

"Gad!" he exclaimed, "then you are not Treves after all!"

"No, sir."

"Go on with your story."

Manton obediently resumed his discourse, bringing his history down to that afternoon and his visit to the recruiting office.

"It's amazing!" exclaimed Gilbert. "I could have sworn—— But, after all," he went on, as if communing with himself, "there's something in your eyes that's different."

"My one ambition in life," concluded Manton, "is to repay that hundred and forty-five pounds. I wanted to do it for the honour of the battery. But when three months had passed and I found I couldn't manage it, I decided to enlist again."

Gilbert, when his first surprise had departed, began to feel an unusual interest in the young man, and as the two strolled back towards the Captain's hotel, he dropped his slight tone of authority, but was quite uncommunicative as to the mysterious and evidently delinquent Treves.

"If you could come to the office in the morning," he said at parting, "I think we can get round any difficulties there may be in regard to your re-enlistment. Do you mind if I make inquiries about you, merely as a matter of form?"

"Not in the least, sir."

A few minutes later Captain Gilbert put through a trunk call to Scarthoe Fort. The commandant of Battery A, who was known to Gilbert by name, happened to be on duty. Gilbert explained that a man giving the name of John Manton, lately of his battery, had that day attempted to re-enlist at Ryde.

"I'd like all the information you can give me about him," Gilbert asked.

"One of the best," came back the prompt answer from Scarthoe Fort. "Manton was a favourite here, and quite unofficially, although matters got a bit muddled, and the case went against him, none of us believed him guilty. A first-rate gunner and white clear through. I shall be glad to know that he's back in the army again."

Gilbert rang off, and all that night the amazing resemblance between his friend Treves and Manton occupied his thoughts. As a result of this preoccupation, and some time during the small hours, a startling idea came to him, first as a nebulous, vague possibility, then as an entirely practicable and simple solution of a difficulty. The thought was this: why should not the singular resemblance between Treves and Manton be turned to good account? Manton had said he wanted more than anything in the world to repay the money due to the battery. Treves, on his part, wanted— — Gilbert broke off here, but his thoughts continued to pursue the new, startling idea that had come to him.

"Gad!" he exclaimed, as the morning broke, "I believe the plan would achieve miracles. If Treves got away under another name he might rouse himself. He might become a man again." ...

In the morning Manton came into the office looking bright, vigorous and full of vitality. Gilbert rose and examined him. Yes, there was a difference, a slight, almost undetectable difference. Something in the eyes—nothing more than that.

"Are you convinced now, sir?" asked the young man, smiling and standing at attention.

"I am quite convinced, Manton, and I have a proposition to make to you."

He took his visitor into an inner room, and, seated there, he unfolded a little of the plan that had come to him during the watches of the night.

"Manton," he said, "I must get authority before I can accept you as a recruit, but in the meantime," he went on, "I have been thinking of our talk of last night. I like you for trying to earn that hundred and forty-five pounds, and they gave a good account of you at Scarthoe."

"I don't know who had the money, sir, but I'd do anything in the world to pay it back for the honour of the battery."

Captain Gilbert paused, then took a letter from the pocket of his tunic. The envelope was addressed: "Lieutenant Bernard Treves, 15, Sade Road, Lymington."

Gilbert had written this letter earlier that morning. With a certain air of formality he handed it to John Manton and instructed him to deliver it to Lieutenant Treves that evening after dark.

"I have a plan in regard to you, Manton, that I think will work out to your entire satisfaction. I won't tell you what it is until you have seen my friend Treves. But when Treves has read this letter he may, or may not, think it worth his while to pay you the money you need. If he doesn't, please come back to me to-morrow, and we will go on with the matter of your re-enlistment."

"In case Lieutenant Treves decides favourably, sir, what must I do to earn the money?"

"You will learn that from him," answered the Captain. "Go to-night, as unobtrusively as you can," he said. He rose, held out his hand and gripped Manton's fingers cordially in his.

CHAPTER II

That evening, when John Manton stepped off the boat at Lymington, a heavy summer rain was falling. In the town itself the streets appeared to be deserted, and it was some minutes before he encountered a workman hurrying home, with upturned collar. He inquired the way to Sade Road, and five minutes later came upon a row of small workmen's cottages with little gardens in front. Counting the houses until he came to number fifteen, he entered the garden gate, and, striking a match, discovered that he had halted at the right address. A woman came to the door in answer to his knock, and stood in the dark, looking out at him, opening the door only a few cautious inches.

"What do you want?"

Manton, with collar turned up and hat drawn over his brows, answered that he brought a letter for Lieutenant Treves.

"You'd better go up to him, then," said the woman, drawing open the door. "It's the front room at the top of the stairs."

There was a candle at the stair-head, and Manton passed her, ascended the single flight of steps and halted at the door. The smallness of the house, the shabbiness of the woman who had admitted him, depressed his spirits. He liked Captain Gilbert, with his sleek and buoyant confidence. This plan of his suddenly struck Manton as the wildest piece of quixotism.

He lifted his hand and knocked quietly upon the door. A voice from within instantly invited him to enter. A moment later he stood in a small lamp-lit bedroom. The room was littered with trunks, suit-cases, boxes and a general confusion of other articles. The close air reeked with the smell of Turkish cigarettes, and at a table near the window, with a lamp before him, sat a young man, busily occupied scribbling figures on a sheet of paper.

Bernard Treves, whose back was towards the door, wore mufti, and Manton, in the moment of entering, noticed that he was well dressed and that his hair was smooth and dark.

"If that's my supper, Mrs. Dodge," said Treves, "put it on the bed." He spoke without looking round, took a drink of whisky from a glass at his side, then went on with his figures.

Manton, standing near the door, coughed to attract his attention.

"Hallo!" exclaimed Treves, and turned swiftly. In an instant at sight of Manton his expression changed. He sprang to his feet in what appeared to be a state of terror, and stood staring at his visitor without uttering a word. With brows drawn together, he passed a hand over his eyes, then he turned, and, lifting his lamp from the table, held it aloft.

"Who are you?" he demanded savagely, "and what the devil do you want?"

John Manton took the letter from his pocket.

"I have come with a letter from your friend, Captain Gilbert," he answered quietly.

With his eyes still fixed on Manton, Treves lowered the lamp and replaced it on the table.

"A letter," he repeated, "from Gilbert? Give it to me." He held out his hand. "God!" he exclaimed, as he snatched the envelope, "coming in like that, you gave me a devil of a start. I thought that I was looking into my own face! Come nearer; come into the light."

Manton advanced farther into the room.

"I suppose these figures I've been poring over," went on Treves, "have made my eyes a bit wrong, but I've never seen anything like it." His nerve was gradually returning, and his astonishment was turning to amusement at the intensity of the resemblance between them.

"Look into the mirror there," he said. "Don't you think the likeness is amazing?"

Manton looked into the mirror, and then again at the young man, who had replaced the lamp on the table, and was tearing open Gilbert's envelope. As he scrutinised Treves's face and figure he, too, was astonished. He began to understand now something of Captain Gilbert's strange behaviour of the day before. But Manton had never been occupied over much with his own appearance; he took himself for granted, and after the first momentary flash of curiosity he thought no more of the resemblance. Besides, there was, after all, a difference. Treves wore a black moustache; his complexion was flushed, whereas Manton, as a result of gas poisoning at the Front, was still pale. Treves's eyes, moreover, were evasive and furtive in expression. Nevertheless, it would have been difficult to tell the two men apart.

"Sit down, Sergeant," Treves said. "Help yourself to a drink." He waved towards the whisky bottle and a siphon on the table. Upon Manton refusing the drink, Treves pushed towards him a box of cigarettes. Then read Captain Gilbert's missive through a second and a third time, and seemed to be considering it deeply with brows drawn together. "Do you know what is in this letter?" he questioned at last.

"No."

"Captain Gilbert told you nothing?"

"Nothing whatever, beyond saying that you might be willing to make some sort of offer."

"Well, he makes an extraordinary suggestion," went on Treves, leaning back in his chair. "It's all brought about by your resemblance to me." His eyes sought the letter again. "He tells me you are a public school boy and all that, and gives me here an outline of your little trouble at Scarthoe Head. Well, for certain reasons known to himself and to me, he thinks you may be able to make yourself useful to me. That is," he added, "if you are willing to undertake a somewhat delicate piece of work."

Manton looked inquiringly at Treves; he was not sure of the young man.

"Perhaps you will let me know the nature of the work."

"The fact of the matter is, Manton," Treves resumed, dropping his voice confidentially, "I am in want of help. Owing to certain peculiar circumstances, I want somebody to make use of my name and my personality for a short time."

He took up his whisky and Manton observed an almost imperceptible tremor of his fingers as they closed about the glass.

"Now, your extraordinary likeness to me, and the fact that you are in need of cash—well, do you see the point?"

"I'm afraid not," remarked Manton quietly.

Treves made a gesture of impatience.

"It's pretty plain, I should think. You need cash, I need some one to step into my shoes; somebody who must take the name of Bernard Treves. Now, do you understand?"

"Your suggestion is that I should pass myself off as you?"

"That's it exactly!"

His visitor stared at him in amazement.

"But I don't see," said he, "any advantage in that for either of us."

"Perhaps not. How much money are you in need of?" Treves inquired pointedly.

"Nearly one hundred and fifty pounds."

Treves whistled.

"Lot of money," he said.

John Manton agreed with him, and for a space there was silence. John's hopes that had risen fell to zero.

Then Treves poured himself another glass of whisky, and drank it down. He wiped his lips with a silk handkerchief from his breast pocket.

"All right," he said at length; "carry out my wishes and you shall have it."

"Then you are serious?"

"I was never more serious in my life. You are to take everything that is mine, and in return you shall have the money you need."

A vague doubt stirred in Manton's mind; then he thought of Gilbert. The Captain was most obviously a man of honour.

"If I accept, can I still enlist?"

"Enlist by all means."

"It seems to me to be an easy way of earning the money, but what about your rank in the army?"

Treves flashed a suspicious glance at him; there was a questioning expression in his eyes.

"If you accept my offer we can go into details later, and as regards my rank, I—I happen to be leaving the army."

"In that case," said Manton, "I am much obliged to you; the money will be a great boon to me."

"You accept?"

"Like a bird!" smiled Manton. "But there is one thing I would like to ask."

"Well?"

"The terms are generous enough," he said, "but what is to happen to my name; is that to disappear too?"

Bernard Treves lit a cigarette, and looked at him with the expression of one from whose mind has been lifted a heavy burden. He made an expressive gesture with his hand.

"For the time being," he answered, "the name of Sergeant Manton will vanish into thin air."

CHAPTER III

Six days later Manton found himself once more in Lymington, alone in Treves's lodgings, in the crowded room, littered with that young man's desirable possessions. Those possessions were, for the time being, his own; even Treves's name was his, for, carrying out his bargain, Treves had vanished from the scene. Again Manton fell to wondering why the other had been so anxious to dispossess himself of name and identity. There was nothing criminal in the matter, he was assured of that, otherwise Captain Gilbert would not have had a hand in it. The idea that the Lieutenant had suffered from shell-shock, and desired to hide himself from all who knew him for a time until he had recovered, came to Manton, and struck him as feasible. He had himself known quite a number of peculiar manifestations of this particularly mysterious disease. In any case, whatever Treves's reasons, it mattered little to Manton at that moment.

"I have simply got to make myself act as Treves, and to do the best I can in Treves's shoes for the time being."

A few days earlier the young man had written him a letter in which he had said: "Use everything of mine as if it were your own. It is only fair if you get the kicks meant for me, you should get the ha'pence as well. I have few relations, and none of them are likely to bother you. When we shall meet again I do not know, but, in the meantime, *au revoir*. I wonder what you will feel like this time next year?"

Manton, in the quiet of the room, took some considerable time trying to realise his new circumstances, and gradually the sense of strangeness and mystery that enveloped him began to fade away. In all his life Manton had been used to the buffets and hard knocks of Fate; he began to wonder what his immediate future in Treves's shoes held for him. Both parents having died in India, he had been educated from a small fund in the hands of a guardian, first in Germany, and later at Rugby. After that he spent two years at Bonn. His resources were at an end, and the guardian, feeling that he had done his duty, left him to fend for himself. A period of hard going had followed, until the war broke out, whereupon he precipitately enlisted in the first hundred thousand. If he had waited a little longer a commission would have been thrust upon him as it was upon all public school men in any way eligible. Treves's past, Manton surmised, had not been of that nature, for despite the poorness of the young man's lodgings, all his belongings were of the costliest order. And all these belongings were now his, Manton's, to do with as he liked. The idea came to him to write to Captain Gilbert, thanking him for the amicable intervention that had wrought this change in his circumstances. He sat down, drew forth a sheet of Treves's notepaper, and had taken up a pen when a knock came at the door, and the landlady appeared.

"You'd like some tea, sir, wouldn't you?"

"Yes, thank you," answered the young man.

"I've dusted the room every day, sir, since you've been away," said the landlady.

"It's exactly as I left it," responded he truthfully. She was looking at him across the width of the little room, but there was no doubt or curiosity in her gaze; she had accepted him instantly on his arrival that day as Bernard Treves, and even now, looking at him full and closely, no thought of deception entered her mind. "I wonder what she'd think," he pondered inwardly, "if Treves were to come in behind her now."

But no such dramatic event occurred; the landlady brought up his tea, and later furnished him with a bottle of whisky, a siphon of soda, and a glass.

Next morning, when she cleared these things away, she was surprised to find that no more than one peg of whisky had been taken.

"Wasn't you feeling well, sir, last night?" she asked.

"Quite," answered Manton, who was busy with an excellent breakfast.

She went away wondering. Until that day she had never known Mr. Treves to drink less than half a bottle of whisky in the course of an evening.

During the morning John went for a stroll in the town, and on his return the landlady handed him a letter which had arrived by the post in his absence. Manton took it up to his room, and noticed that the handwriting was sprawling and shaky. Twice he read the superscription, "Bernard Treves, Esq., 15, Sade Road, Lymington." He hesitated several minutes before breaking open the envelope. He felt as though he were stepping beyond the pale of decency in opening the letter addressed to another man, then he recalled Treves's admonition, "Everything that is mine is yours." He tore open the envelope. Within was a single sheet of paper headed, "Heatherfield Grange, Freshwater." Manton quickly scanned the contents.

"Dear Bernard,—They tell me you are in hiding, as well you may be, but if you have a spark of decency left in you, you will come here to me at the first opportunity. There are things I have to say to you.

"You have dishonoured and disgraced the family name, but I have still a faint hope that you will retrieve yourself at the last moment.—Your affectionate father,

"R.T."

For many minutes John Manton sat staring at this letter, staring from the stiff, sprawling writing out into the little street and back again.

All that day he pondered upon the missive he had received from Treves's father. He wondered what it was Treves had done, and why he should have been skulking in hiding at that address? A sense of uneasiness swept over him, and was succeeded by a violent curiosity. For the first time he felt vividly interested in Treves and Treves's history, and at the same time doubtful and uneasy. Unpleasant and difficult situations presented themselves to his mind.

Next morning, as a result of a decision he had taken, he was on his way to Freshwater by midday. At three o'clock in the afternoon he walked through the town and out to Heatherfield Grange, which he discovered to be a large, many-chimneyed, many-windowed Elizabethan mansion, standing in a spacious, heavily-wooded park. The mansion itself was approached by a long carriage drive, too much overshadowed by trees, and when Manton reached the lodge gates a bent old man, who was sweeping leaves from the path, hurried forward and drew open the gate for him to enter. The man drew himself up and saluted.

"Good day, Master Bernard."

Manton nodded and smiled. As he walked along the drive towards the grand old house, his pulse-beat quickened. After all, had he a right to act the part; was it honourable and fair that he should thus step into another man's shoes? The under-gardener had taken him for Bernard Treves; the whole world evidently was prepared to believe in the deception. But there was Treves's father to face. Naturally Treves's father would detect an impostor in a moment. But was he an impostor; was it not probable that the elder Treves also was aware of what had occurred?

The broad front door of the mansion was opened to him. A white-haired butler, with pouches under his eyes, and a general air of world-weariness, looked at him from the threshold, and slowly lifted his eyes in surprise.

"Good afternoon, sir," said the butler. He took Manton's hat and stick, and deferentially stood aside. "Your father will indeed be pleased and surprised to see you, sir," he said, as he closed the door. His manner was studiously civil, and yet somehow Manton felt a lack of cordiality towards himself in the butler's tone.

"Possibly he's a privileged servant," he thought, "and does not like Mr. Bernard."

"Where is—is the Colonel?" he asked after a moment's hesitation.

"In the library, sir, as usual. Will you go up at once?"

"Yes." He wondered consumedly where the Colonel's room might be, and experienced a pleasant thrill of impending event. He attempted a little harmless finesse to discover the way. "Perhaps you will go first and tell him I am here."

"Very good, sir." The butler looked at him meditatively for a moment, then went to a side-table and took up a silver salver containing three letters and a telegram. Manton seized the moment to survey the heavy splendour of the dark antique furniture, the wide spaces of the hall and the richness of the rugs scattered over the polished floor. High above the mantelshelf hung a portrait in oils of a personage in eighteenth century costume. Descending to the middle of the hall was a wide oak balustraded staircase, carpeted in scarlet, a single flight ascended to the first floor, then branched to right and left.

"Your letters, sir." The butler was standing at Manton's elbow with the silver salver extended. John took up the three letters and the telegram. A renewed and intensified disinclination to pry into Bernard Treves's affairs seized him. He was about to put letters and telegram into his pocket when the butler spoke in his firm, polite voice. There was a note of reproach in his tone, however, "The telegram came two days ago, sir."

"Oh!" exclaimed Manton. And under the bleak eye of the butler he disinterred it from his pocket, tore open the envelope, and read the contents. The telegram had been dispatched from Camden Town, and ran:

"*Wire when you can come. Of course I will forgive you.*—ELAINE."

He was conscious, as he read the words, that the butler's eyes were fixed steadily upon him.

Then the old servant turned and preceded him towards the broad staircase. They ascended to the first landing, and here the butler wheeled to the right and halted before a double green baize door. The elderly man knocked, paused for a moment, then pushed open the door, and stepped into a room lined with books, a spacious, luxuriously furnished apartment, with two mullioned windows overlooking the park. John, following him, saw him cross to a deep, high-backed arm-chair near the hearth.

"Mr. Bernard's here, sir," he announced, standing before this chair.

There was a movement in the chair, then a tall, soldierly, grey-haired man revealed himself, leaning on a stick, and looked across at Manton. He looked at him with a cold, inimical gaze, and until the butler had closed the door and departed, did not utter a word, Then he spoke:

"So you've come, you dog, have you!" The almost savage intensity of dislike and contempt in his tone struck the young man like a blow in the face.

"I got your letter——" he began.

"Oh, yes, I found out where you were. Well," he went on, harshly, "there is no need for us to waste compliments on each other. We will settle the business that is to be settled at once."

He moved shakily towards a desk in the middle of the room, using his stick as a support. Manton, seeing his frailty, hurried forward to assist him, but the old man drew himself erect, raised his stick, and flashed a look at him of utter repulsion.

"Do not dare to lay a hand on me," he said violently.

When he reached his desk he seated himself in a big swivel-chair, drew out a drawer, and flung certain documents on the table. From under his eyebrows he glowered at Manton.

"Sit down," he commanded.

John moved to the table side and occupied a chair near his elbow. Among a pile of documents Colonel Treves searched for a certain typewritten sheet. He found it at length, a long, yellow piece of official paper.

"Listen to this," he commanded. From the table beside him he took up a square reading glass, and deciphered the typewritten paper with faded grey eyes. "This," he vouchsafed, raising his eyes, "is from my old, good friend, General Whiston." He paused a moment, and John seized the opportunity to intervene, "May I say a word, sir?"

"No," thundered Treves. Then he read aloud in a voice vibrant with emotion:

"My dear Treves,—Your boy had every chance.... It was the merest fluke in the world that he escaped as easily as he did. He is not of the right stuff, and my condolences are with you. I wish I could suggest something, but I cannot. I know, old friend, what a tragedy this must be to you——"

The Colonel stopped abruptly, flung down his reading glass, and looked into Manton's face. "Well?" he demanded. "What do you think of that?"

Manton said nothing.

"Can you read between the lines?" questioned the elder man.

"It suggests," said John, after a moment's hesitation, "that the punishment meted out to—to me, was a light one."

"I see you are as evasive as ever," retorted Colonel Treves. He turned and smote the open letter twice with the back of his hand. "In this letter, General Whiston," he measured his words slowly, "tells me, by implication, that you are guilty of cowardice in the face of the enemy—you, a Treves!" Then in a moment the anger that had vivified him seemed to fade; he appeared to Manton to become suddenly old, bowed, and pitiful, the expression on his face was one of anguish. The dishonour that had befallen his name was no less than torture to him, but once again he recovered himself, and gripped the arms of his chair with both white-knuckled hands.

"You know the just punishment for cowardice in the face of the enemy?" He was leaning towards Manton now; his mouth twitched, but there was a blaze in the old grey eyes.

"I know it, sir," said John quietly.

The Colonel drew in his breath slowly and sat erect.

"Ah, you know. And, having escaped that punishment, and knowing yourself to be guilty, you skulk in hiding! You fail to seize the one chance that is open to you to redeem the past!"

"What is the chance?" inquired Manton, forgetting himself for a moment.

The Colonel stared at him in astonishment.

"The chance of re-enlistment, of course. Instead of doing that," he went on, "you write me a whining letter, saying you can't stand the trenches, you can't face it, your nerves—bah! nerves, my God, and you a Treves!" He hurled these words forth with a contempt and loathing that was like a blow in the face. But Manton noticed that he was breathing heavily. The emotional intensity of his feelings was wearing on him, and the younger man felt a sudden tenderness towards this old, stricken, bitterly disappointed father.

"Is it too late now, sir?" he asked quietly.

"Eh?"

"Is it too late for me to make good?"

"Talk!" exclaimed the Colonel, in bitter derision; "always talk with you. You don't mean that any more than you meant any of the lying promises you made to me in the past. You have always been a liar! A liar, a spendthrift, and a fool—and now, added to all these things, to your gambling and your profligacy, you've finished as a— —"

He paused, and Manton ventured:

"In regard to a way out, sir?"

The Colonel looked at him with renewed ferocity, then his expression slowly changed. For some seconds he was silent, and, without a glance at Manton, he began to fumble at a drawer. He drew it open at length, and groped in its interior. His hand shook visibly, but there was something in his attitude, some strange intensity of purpose, that riveted Manton's attention. Presently the Colonel discovered the object he sought, and revealed from the depths of the drawer an automatic pistol.

"If you have a shred of honour left you will know what to do," he said grimly. He reached out, and laid the weapon on the corner of the desk at the young man's side.

CHAPTER IV

Then Colonel Treves rose slowly to his feet, took up his stick, and moved towards the door of the room. With his hand on the door knob, he pointed his stick at the weapon on the table. Manton had remained motionless; utterly at a loss. Now the old soldier's meaning gradually revealed itself.

"You want me to take this and — —?"

"And," broke in Colonel Treves, "use it to recover such shreds of honour as are left to you."

He drew open the door.

"Thanks," said Manton, taking the pistol from the desk. He slipped the weapon into his hip pocket. The Colonel halted, looking back at him in surprise.

"What are you going to do?"

"I am going to use it," answered John, "if occasion arises."

He saw the Colonel hesitate. Some deep emotion seemed to stir within him. Then with an effort he turned swiftly, and was about to hurry from the room. Manton strode towards him.

"There was another way out?" he questioned, rapidly.

"There was, and you failed to take it. You whined that you couldn't face the army again—you, a Treves! In the past, before my time and yours," went on the Colonel, suddenly violent again, "there have been Treves who have been fools and spendthrifts; there may have been Treves who kept their honour none too clean—but never in our long line has there been a coward until you came, until you grew up to be a curse to my existence, and made my life a shame to me!" His lip trembled, the old, proud head was held aloft, but a world of desolation dwelt in the faded eyes. On a sudden impulse, John gripped him by the hand; he could feel the old man resisting him, seeking to free himself.

"I want to make you a promise, sir," he said. "I am going to Ryde the first thing in the morning. I have a friend there who will help me to get back into the army."

The Colonel narrowed his eyes and tried to read the expression on his face.

"There is a new ring in your voice, Bernard," he said, after a moment's pause, "but I cannot trust you."

He turned and walked away. John saw him go, using his stick for support, and felt a renewed pity for the old, broken father. He spent that night at an inn in Freshwater, and took the first train next morning for Ryde. Here at the recruiting office he presented himself before Captain Gilbert. This plump and comfortable officer was busy at his work when John stepped into the office. His shadow fell upon Captain Gilbert's desk, and the elder man looked up quickly.

"Great Scott!" he exclaimed. He stared wide-eyed at Manton for a moment, and John broke into a smile.

"I see you mistook me for Treves."

"I did," said Gilbert, leaning forward and looking into his face. "The resemblance is really closer than I thought at first. Well," he said, "you've done your part of the bargain splendidly. You earned the money you needed, and you've lifted a great load off the minds of several deserving persons, including myself."

"I should like to know how I've done that," said Manton. "It seems to me the only service I have rendered has been to myself."

"You forget the battery at Scarthoe Head. You made up the deficiency, and the Colonel's delighted with you, Manton."

"Thanks to you—and young Treves—I was able to put matters straight there."

"You have probably saved young Treves from going utterly to the devil," said Gilbert. "I'll tell you about that later; I'm busy till one o'clock, but come to my hotel then and we'll have lunch together."

"But I am here on business myself!" protested Manton. He was feeling cheerful and particularly satisfied with the course of events so far.

"What is your particular business?" inquired Gilbert.

"I want to get back into the army."

Gilbert looked at him for a moment.

"Of course—of course," he said hastily. "I'd forgotten that; we will discuss the subject at lunch time."

Until lunch time Manton was free to stroll upon the pier and consider his situation. He felt a deep curiosity to know what had happened to the man whose clothes he was wearing; to Treves, whose money he was jingling in his pocket, whose excellent cigarettes he had smoked.

At a quarter to one he threw his cigarette end over the rail into the water, and turning, made his way to the hotel where Gilbert was staying. He found the Captain already there, busy mixing a salad at a table in the corner of a small dining-room. There were half a dozen tables in the room, none of which were as yet occupied.

"Sit down, Manton," invited Captain Gilbert, as John entered. "I always mix my own salads. What will you have? There's the menu."

John chose a dish and accepted his host's invitation to divide with him a bottle of Chablis. During the meal Captain Gilbert talked on general matters. But at length the conversation appeared to drift round to the subject of Treves.

"Old Treves took you for granted, eh?" asked the Captain.

"His eyesight isn't good," answered John, "but he suspected nothing."

"And Gates, the butler?"

"He called me 'Mr. Bernard' the moment he saw me. Also, he gave me Treves's letters and a telegram. I didn't read the letters, but the telegram — —" Manton put his hand in his inner pocket. "Perhaps I'd better hand them all over to you now."

"Not so fast," Gilbert said, pushing the letters and the telegram back across the table towards Manton. "As a matter of fact, I can't hand them to Treves just now, as I have persuaded him to go to a nursing home for a time. A very good friend of his father's, General Whiston, recommended that something of the sort should be done with him months ago."

"Treves did not give me the impression of being actually ill," Manton observed.

"He wasn't, but his nerves were all to rags. He was in such a state of acute neurasthenia that I expected him to lay hands on himself any minute. Anyway, where he is he will be safe for a while; he will be out of his father's way and the discipline of this particular nursing home may pull him together."

John lit a cigarette and smoked thoughtfully. There was evidently something on Gilbert's mind, something of which he wished to unburden himself. John waited, and at last the elder man broke the silence again:

"Manton," he said earnestly, "I want you to do me a particular favour."

John inquired the nature of the favour.

"I want you," went on the Captain, "to sustain Treves's personality for a little longer. He is in good hands in the nursing home, and for the time being has vanished from the public gaze." Gilbert paused, and again appeared to hesitate. What he had to say was very difficult to frame in words. He wished to hint at something that was the merest suspicion in his own mind. Two or three times he was on the verge of putting his thoughts into words, and each time the effort appeared too much for his gift of expression. Finally he leaned back in his chair. "Manton," he said, "I cannot tell you all I think and suspect, but I will give you such confidences as I can."

He paused for a moment, then went on: "Since Treves came back from France, he appears to have got into the hands of undesirable company. One of his rooted ideas, possibly the result of his drug habit, is that some one is watching him, and that, for some reason or other, his life is in danger."

John listened quietly; then, when the other had finished, he observed seriously: "So far as I see it, you want me to continue my impersonation of Treves until he is cured and comes out of the nursing home."

"That is it, exactly," said Gilbert.

"You are putting a good deal of trust in me," answered John.

At that Gilbert stretched out his hand and gripped John's fingers heartily.

"Manton," he said, "you and I are in this together for the good of the Cause. Not only for Treves and the old Colonel, but perhaps for bigger issues."

"I don't get your meaning," said John.

"Don't ask it, trust me as I trust you. And now to get back to the matter in hand," he said, resuming his ordinary tone. "Perhaps it would be worth your while to open those two letters."

As John obediently tore open the envelopes and read the contents of the letters, Gilbert called the waiter and paid for the two lunches. One of the letters was a typewritten screed from a quack doctor in which he claimed to cure any victim of the drug habit within the space of three months. John experienced a real feeling of pity for Treves as he read the quack's fraudulent promises. The second letter contained two lines only on a single sheet of paper with the printed heading: "208, St. George's Square, S.W." The letter ran:

"Dear Treves, — I must see you at once. You understand; it is essential that you should come to me without delay. To-morrow night at nine o'clock I shall expect you. — Yours, G. MANNERS.*"*

Manton handed both letters to Gilbert, who studied them carefully.

"I haven't a notion who G. Manners is," mused the Captain when he had read the letter through a second time, "but he may be one of the friends Treves ought to get rid of, and for that reason I should advise you to call on him to-morrow."

Manton was thoughtful for a moment.

"What if he discusses matters I know nothing about? Treves's past life is a blank to me:"

"Come," said Gilbert, touching him lightly on the arm, "you are playing a part; you are not such a fool as not to play it well. I admit there are certain little precautions you may find it wise to take. In the first place, you might have a go at copying Treves's degenerate handwriting. You might also keep in mind that Treves is over-strung, lacking in will-power, and so much a victim of the cocaine habit that he would do anything, short of murder, to get the drug when the craving is upon him. As to Treves's past life, it seems to me that a victim of the drug habit can be afflicted with convenient lapses of memory when occasion arises."

Manton glanced at the Captain's pleasant, fat face, and the thought crossed his mind that there was a good deal more cleverness behind Gilbert's amiable exterior than he had at first realised. He forthwith decided to go to town that night. London always held a vivid attraction for him, and he had not had the pleasure of visiting it since his journey through its streets in an ambulance on his return from France. Some weeks in hospital had followed that visit, then had come his transference to the R.G.A. at Scarthoe Head. And now, with returned health and in new, strange and portentous circumstances, he was to visit London again.

Mr. Manners, the mysterious, imperative writer of the letter, had demanded to see Treves at nine o'clock. The hour of John's arrival was eight, and he was in a hurry. He was impatient to plunge into whatever adventure awaited him. Without bothering to engage a room for the night, he deposited his bag in the cloak-room at Waterloo Station, and set out to find St. George's Square. He arrived at the corner of the square, the Embankment corner, at precisely eight-thirty. The square's decorous, solemn-looking houses with heavy pillared porticoes struck him as gloomy in the extreme. The only individual upon the long strip of pavement which ran the length of the west side of the square was himself. His footfalls appeared to echo with inordinate resonance in the areas as he made his way towards Number 208.

It was not his intention to ring the bell immediately. In the first place he wanted to reconnoitre the house, to see if it were possible to judge of the house's occupants by its exterior. This thought occupied his mind, when a taxi sped into the square and drew to a halt within half a dozen yards of him. The taxi had stopped behind him, and its occupant had alighted.

"That's all right; half an hour," said a curt voice in a cultured accent.

The chauffeur nodded, and slammed the taxi door. The young man who had alighted hurried forward, passed John, and continued down the square. Without paying over especial attention, John noticed that he was tall, that he wore a morning coat of distinguished cut, that his light grey felt hat was of expensive quality, and that the pearl in his tie-pin was also, if genuine, of exceptional value. He was of John's height and age, fair-haired, blue-eyed, and with a slight tooth-brush moustache. His features were large and heavy-boned, without being harsh. Two things John noticed as he hurried past; one was that he carried a silk-lined light overcoat over his arm, and the other that he wore a "service rendered" badge on the lapel of his coat.

"Invalided from the army," thought John. "All the same, he doesn't look as if there was much the matter with him."

John continued to walk until he reached the corner of the square, then he turned, and as he did so he saw the tall young man flit up the steps of a house a considerable distance away. John fixed his eyes on the portico of this particular house and walked towards it. And as he neared the door he realised that the young man had entered the very house at which he also had an appointment—Number 208. For a moment Manton paused, hesitated, then passed on. Before making the plunge into whatever adventure awaited him, he wanted still further to consider the situation.

In the meantime the stranger, who had alighted from the taxi, was now within the hall of Mr. Manners's residence. He had opened the door with a Yale key and had admitted himself. The hall was narrow and somewhat dark, and the young man laid his gold-headed cane noisily on a little table, and began to draw off his grey gloves. A door at the back of the house opened noiselessly, and a sombre-faced, sallow-complexioned butler advanced.

"Mr. Manners is in, of course?" demanded the young man in a voice that rasped a little.

"Yes, Herr Baron, in the library."

The visitor nodded curtly, ran swiftly up the stairs, turned to the left, and opened a door on the first landing. He entered a room where the curtains had already been drawn. Two electric chandeliers, one on either side of the hearth, illuminated the apartment. A large bookcase occupied one wall of the room, and in the middle of the floor was a business-like table, scattered with papers. On the table was a green-shaded reading lamp, and by its illumination a man sat at work busily writing. He looked up as the stranger entered, then sprang quickly to his feet. He was a tall man of fifty, uncomfortably stout, with a fleshy neck that protruded over his collar at the back. The big man's iron-grey hair was short, his nose broad and short, and his lips thick and pouting. Despite his inelegance of figure, he was dressed, with an attempt at smartness, in a well-cut frock coat and newly-creased trousers. His heavy eyebrows shielded his eyes, hiding his expression from any but the closest scrutiny. For a man of his excessive bulk he showed extreme activity on his feet.

"I didn't expect you to-night," he said. He placed a chair near the desk for the younger man to seat himself.

His visitor, however, stood still and fixed him with a direct, cold stare.

"Well, Manners," he demanded, "what have you to say for yourself?"

Manners shrugged his heavy shoulders, and displayed the palms of his hands.

"Nothing, Herr Baron," he said, "except that I have done my best. Won't you sit down?"

The young man took a cigarette from his case, and lit it.

"Your best is damned bad!" he said.

"I exercised such judgment as I have," returned the other, in a tone of abasement.

"Judgment alone is of no avail," retorted the other. "What we want is aggressive action. We don't get that from you—you talk, and think, and scheme— —"

The other ventured a faint note of protest.

"I was chosen, Herr Baron— —"

"I don't want to hear your history," returned the younger man, coldly. "I want to know about this expedition that is being prepared by the Eastern Command, that has been under preparation for the past six weeks."

"I gave you such figures, Herr Baron, as I was able to collect."

The young man crossed to the hearth and stood leaning with his back against the mantelshelf.

"Doesn't it occur to you," he demanded, after a moment's silence, "that figures are only a detail? Figures are something any fool could gather. What Berlin wants to know is, what is this expedition's objective, where is it bound for, also what port it sails from, and when?"

The elder German—Gottfried Manwitz by name, though he figured in the London directory as Godfrey Manners—turned nervously towards his desk and began to search among the papers. An expression of relief crossed his face as he took up a particular sheet of paper.

"That is the date, Herr Baron," he said, "when the expedition will sail, and also the place of departure."

The young man took the sheet, scrutinised it with frowning brows for a moment, then lifted his eyes and looked into Manwitz's fat face with cold, contemptuous gaze.

"Excellent!" he said, cuttingly; "wonderful and utterly useless! You provide Headquarters with all this detail, and fail to give the one vital, useful piece of information—the sole item that Headquarters requires."

"It is very difficult, Herr Baron," apologised Manners.

"You and I, Manwitz," retorted the younger man, "are retained in London for the sole purpose of overcoming difficulties." He paused a moment, and looked complacently for the first time in the elder man's face. "For instance, I myself have overcome quite a number of difficulties."

"Indeed, that is true, Herr Baron," conceded Manners.

"I expect you to do the same. Since you let the *Inflexible* and the *Invincible* vanish to the Falkland Islands without any one of us being aware of the fact, Berlin doesn't think so highly of your attainments as before the war. For my part," he went on, "I find you too much of a dreamer." He paused; some one had knocked lightly on the door of the room. "Open it, Manwitz!" he commanded.

The big man crossed lightly to the door and drew it open. Upon the threshold stood the sombre-countenanced butler. The tall young man from the hearth called aloud to him:

"Well, Conrad, what is it?"

"Mr. Treves, Herr Baron, to see Herr Manners."

"Thank you, Conrad," said Manners. He closed the door and turned to his superior.

"This is one of my instruments, Herr Baron, arrived to-night from the Isle of Wight. You approved of him when I gave you his *dossier* a month ago."

"He is the British officer who was cashiered," returned the other, swiftly. "Takes drugs, and generally gone to pieces?"

"The same, Herr Baron."

"Is he quite" —he paused—"er, quite amenable to your orders?"

"I flatter myself that I can do a good deal with him," Manwitz answered, with pride. "He comes here for cocaine, but he is of good English stock, and there are moments when he tries to shake himself free of me. For the last three weeks, as a matter of fact, he has disappeared entirely. I had great difficulty, Herr Baron, rediscovering his hiding place."

"I don't like that!" returned the Baron. "How do you know what he has been up to in the meantime?"

He was silent for a minute; then he looked with his cold, pale eyes into his elder's face. "Manwitz!" he exclaimed suddenly, "this may be the man for our business!"

For the first time a flicker of triumph lit in Manners's eyes. He went to his desk, unlocked a drawer, and produced a single sheet of notepaper. "This is a letter in his own writing, Herr Baron, signed by himself. I think it is satisfactory, eh?"

The younger man took the sheet and fixed his keen eyes upon it.

"My dear Friend," ran the note, *"the s.s. 'Polidor' is due to leave H— — at four o'clock to-morrow, Tuesday afternoon. I had this on absolute authority; you can rely on it."*

The tall, fair-haired man came to the end of the brief note, and his hard mouth tightened; then he read the postscript: *"Don't forget the tabloids!"*

He looked up slowly, and fixed his keen gaze upon Manwitz's apoplectic countenance. Baron Rathenau, who had taken his degree at Oxford, who spoke English like an English gentleman, and possessed, on the surface, the manners of an English gentleman, was quite five years older than he looked. His brain was subtle and keen, and in the service of the Fatherland he was hard and ruthless as steel.

"You have done not so badly here, Manwitz," conceded the Baron. "This letter alone"—he folded Treves's note carefully—"this letter alone would bring our young friend, Lieutenant Treves, into the presence of a firing party within forty-eight hours." He paused a moment. "Our English enemies," he went on, "are unpleasantly hasty in regard to spies. But when it comes to traitors, the celerity with which they put a man face to the wall in their Tower of London, it is marvellous!"

He had folded the note carefully, and lifting his light fawn coat, he slipped Treves's note into the inner pocket, then he flung the coat back again on the chair.

"I'll see our young neurasthenic friend at once," he said. "You will leave him to me, Manwitz." He turned and pressed the bell twice. When the footman presently appeared at the door, Baron Rathenau was standing with his back to the mantelshelf, toying with a cigarette.

"Bring up Mr. Treves, Conrad," he said, briefly.

CHAPTER V

"Do I introduce you as Captain Cherriton, Herr Baron?" asked Manwitz, when Conrad had closed the door and departed.

"Yes," said the Baron. "I find the name of the poor, dead Captain Cherriton an excellent recommendation in even the best of homes." He smiled his somewhat derisive smile.

A moment later the door opened and John Manton stepped into the room. Manners rose and held out his hand.

"My dear Treves," he said, "you have been away from me a very long time." He was thinking to himself that Treves carried himself a little better than usual; his gaze was more direct, his handgrip firmer. However, there was no suspicion in his eyes as he turned towards the younger man at the hearth.

"Captain Cherriton," he said, "this is a young friend of mine, Mr. Treves."

For a moment Rathenau's light blue eyes widened, and then narrowed.

"We've met before, Mr. Treves?"

"In the square, half an hour ago. I saw you come in."

"Oh, yes, yes," returned the Baron. "My good friend, Mr. Manners, has been telling me about you."

"I hope he had something complimentary to say," smiled John Manton. He was thinking to himself: "There is no doubt at all in my mind that this big, fat man, Mr. Manners, is a German. His finger nails are cut neatly to a point." John recalled the habit of the Germans he had met at Feldkirch, of the masters of his school, who had trimmed their nails in that particular fashion. Rather a Chinese fashion, John thought. His eyes travelled from the fat man's face and took in the younger man's hard countenance. He was recalling something he had read of Captain Cherriton.

"I think I remember reading something about you, Captain Cherriton," he ventured.

"You mean my escape from the British officers' prison camp at Celle," replied the German, easily.

"Yes," returned John, "that was it. You had rather an adventurous time getting across the frontier."

"I had a pretty hot time," laughed Cherriton.

The conversation between the three became general after this, and presently Cherriton invited John to accompany him to his hotel in the Strand.

"Come along and have a drink and a smoke with me. I should much like to have a chat with you, Treves."

John considered the proposal for a moment, and then decided to go. He bade good night to Manners, and as he shook hands with the big man, a little phial of white tabloids passed from Manners's palm to his own. For a minute John felt inclined to ask a question, but caution saved him. He slipped the little cocaine tablets into his waistcoat pocket, thanked Manners under his breath, and followed Cherriton, who had taken up his light overcoat, and was moving towards the door.

It was quite dark in the square when they emerged, and in the distance, near the river, a taxi was moving slowly.

"That is my vehicle," remarked Cherriton, standing under the light of a shaded lamp, so that the distant taxi-man could observe them. A minute later the taxi drew to a halt. John stepped inside, and Cherriton followed him.

As the taxi door closed, a man, who had been standing in the darkness against the rails of the square opposite stepped out into the road and signalled with his arm. At that moment John was leaning back in the taxi, giving himself up to thoughts of the swift events of the last half-hour. Who was this Captain Cherriton, who appeared to have taken such a fancy to him? Was it possible— —? His thoughts received a jolt.

"Hey, stop!" a loud voice from the road echoed in his ears. John was projected forward almost upon his face. The vehicle came to a sudden halt; the door of the taxi was flung open; two men appeared in the aperture, and a heavy hand fell upon John's shoulder. He glanced at his companion, and saw that, from the other side, intruders were also laying heavy hands upon him. With a mighty wrench of his shoulder John snatched himself free. Scarcely knowing what had happened, he attempted to dash after his companion, who had been dragged out into the road. He was ignominiously pulled back by the leg. He heard a voice shouting:

"Don't bother about the other one—this is our man!"

Then, in a confusion of gripping hands, John was flung back on the seat of the taxi; a voice spoke firmly in his ear:

"You'll keep quiet, young man, or it will be the worse for you!"

John saw Captain Cherriton flitting like a shadow along the road and out of the square. He looked at the person who was seated beside him in the taxi, and was surprised to find a big, typical police officer in plain clothes. Opposite John two other officers, who had crowded into the vehicle, were seated, looking at him with steady, interested gaze.

"Your name's Treves?" demanded one of the men.

"What of it?" returned John.

"It's all I want to know," answered the man, coldly.

As the taxi glided along John strove to gather his scattered wits, but it was not until a plain, quietly-furnished room had been achieved in Scotland Yard, that any light broke in upon his senses. He found himself confronted by a tall, grey-moustached man in civilian clothes. The man was standing beside a table, and beside him stood a distinguished-looking staff officer.

As John entered the room, in charge of two detectives, his senses were still in a whirl from the swiftness of his adventure. The grey-moustached man, whom the detectives addressed as "Sir Robert," rose from his chair and looked at him with stern, brooding eyes; then his gaze turned to one of John's captors, who had entered the room and was holding Baron Rathenau's overcoat on his arm.

"Have you his papers?" he demanded.

"That is not my overcoat," intervened John.

"Silence," commanded Sir Robert.

The detective went through the pockets of the overcoat. He found a small time-table, two or three paid restaurant bills, and finally the letter Treves had written to Manners. The grey-moustached police commissioner took these articles, and laid them on the blotting-pad before him. Then, at a brief command, a second detective stepped forward and searched John's pockets, taking out the two letters that had been addressed to Treves and the telegram signed "Elaine." These also were laid upon the desk. The staff officer and Sir Robert read them carefully. When the officer, whom John observed to be a general of staff, read Treves's incriminating letter to Manners, he drew in his breath and whistled.

"My God!" he exclaimed.

The grey-moustached man took the letter from his fingers, read it, then held it forth towards John. His tone was utterly aloof, cold, and forbidding.

"It was unfortunate, Treves," he said, "that you should carry this letter in your pocket. For this, added to the information we have gathered about you during the past three months, condemns you absolutely." He paused a moment, then went on. "I can only say," he added ruthlessly, "that I thank God we have been able to lay our hands on you."

It was only in that moment that John for the first time realised the appalling danger that was sweeping upon him.

"I would like to make some explanation, sir."

"Your correspondence," retorted Sir Robert, with sinister meaning, "has made all the explanation we require! General Whiston here is quite satisfied, and so am I."

General Whiston, who had been looking fixedly at John, now passed round the table and walked towards him. He was a tall, bronzed man, with a clipped moustache, and a wide, strong mouth. John had recognised his name in a moment. He was Colonel Treves's old friend.

"Bernard Treves," said General Whiston, "you have broken your father's heart already; you must now make your peace with God. There is only one thing left for me to do for my old and dear friend, and I intend to do it—he shall never learn that his son died as a traitor to his country. Even now," he went on, "though I have had you watched for three months, I can still scarcely credit it, you—a Treves!"

He glanced towards the door. John felt a heavy hand fall upon his shoulder from behind.

"This way, please," said a polite voice in his ear.

As the detective's voice sounded in his ear and the detective's hand fell on his shoulder, John's scurrying senses seemed to gather themselves together. He became calm in presence of the greatest danger his life had ever known. When next he spoke his voice was steady, and his manner, despite its deep gravity, portrayed not the slightest trace of nervousness.

"Sir," he said, "may I speak merely one or two words before I am removed?" He looked into the bronzed countenance of Colonel Treves's old friend. There was no pity for him on that strong, handsome face. In General Whiston's eyes he had been guilty of the blackest of all crimes. The General answered in his deep-toned voice of authority.

"You will be permitted to make a statement, but not now."

"I have a very important declaration to make, sir."

Sir Robert, who was still scrutinising the incriminating letter that had been taken from Rathenau's overcoat, looked up now, then rapidly pencilled a few words on a slip of paper which he handed to Whiston. The General read the slip.

"Yes, perhaps so," he said; "I agree with you, time is everything."

Sir Robert looked into John's face.

"Are you prepared," he went on, "to give us the name of the person to whom this letter was written?" He lifted Treves's incriminating missive and held it for John's inspection. John had already been permitted to read the letter, though not to hold it in his hand.

"Certainly," answered Manton.

A slight flicker of surprise lit in Sir Robert's eyes.

"His name," answered John, "is either Manners, or Cherriton."

Sir Robert laid down the letter with an impatient gesture.

"That is no answer to my question. You wrote the letter yourself. To whom did you write it?"

"I didn't write it!"

"You suggest that it is a forgery?"

"Either you wrote the letter or you didn't write it," pursued Sir Robert. "Your statements contradict each other. You say, in the first place, that you did not write it. In the second place, you say it is not a forgery."

General Whiston now spoke, his stern gaze on John's face.

"This letter," he said, glancing towards the sheet, "is in your own writing, which I happen to know very well. Your attempt at mystification," he went on, "will be of no avail, either now or later."

John felt in his tones intense antagonism.

"If I might be permitted to speak to you gentlemen alone," he said, "I will in three minutes explain the mystery."

General Whiston glanced at the Commissioner of Police.

"It is for you to say, Sir Robert," he said. "To-night the affair is in your hands."

Sir Robert pondered the subject for a moment, then glanced at the detectives who stood behind John; with his hand he made a slow, significant gesture. John, who was standing at attention before the table, heard the detectives move away, and a moment later the door softly closed behind them.

He was alone with the Commissioner of Police and the General.

On his accusers' faces John read a stern and determined intention that the law should take its course, not the tortuous, long-drawn old law of pre-war days, but the swift justice which is meted out to traitors.

"You shall have three minutes in which to speak!" Sir Robert's voice smote John's ears.

Manton knew that if he held his peace and the law moved with its inexorable swiftness, he would by to-morrow have expiated the crime of another man. He was in another man's shoes. Innocently, he had taken up that other man's identity.

But he had not shouldered everything, he had not rendered himself liable for that other man's treachery. And yet, at the back of his mind, there was pity, even for Treves. He thought of the man's weakness, of his shattered nerves, of Manners's obvious power over him. Perhaps, even in uttering the truth to these two stern judges, he might put in a good word for Treves.

"The statement I have to make, gentlemen, is an amazing one."

"It will also have to be a brief one," retorted Sir Robert coldly.

"Well, out with it," interposed General Whiston.

John turned towards him.

"I wish to say, sir, that I am not Bernard Treves!"

A flash of anger lit in General Whiston's eyes.

"You say that, despite the fact that I am prepared to identify you as Bernard Treves."

"My statement," returned John, "is, I admit, an amazing one. Nevertheless, it is a fact, gentlemen. My name is Manton."

The Commissioner of Police pulled at his moustache.

"A statement of this kind," he said, "is ridiculous in presence of General Whiston, who knows you and recognises your handwriting in this letter." He leaned back in his chair and struck the letters that had been taken from John's pocket with the back of his hand. "These letters, taken from your person, this telegram addressed to you, and this letter conveying information to the enemy, are sufficient in themselves to identify you."

"There is nothing you wish to say, General?" asked Sir Robert of Whiston.

The General shook his head, and Sir Robert put his thumb on the bell-push at the corner of his desk.

John heard the whirr of a bell in the room beyond.

"I am prepared, sir," he said hurriedly, "to prove every word I say. My name is Manton, and I undertook to assume Treves's identity merely to please a friend who wished to help him."

"You are ready to give us the name of your friend, of course?" interposed General Whiston. He had been utterly unmoved by this statement of John's.

"His name is Gilbert, sir; Captain Gilbert, of Ryde, Isle of Wight."

General Whiston answered nothing; there was no softening in the harshness of his expression. For a moment he was silent. Then, with a glance at Sir Robert, he moved towards the door.

"Just a few minutes, Sir Robert," he said. "This is a matter easy of proof."

He passed out of the room. At the door, as he drew it open, John heard him speaking to two men outside.

"Sir Robert will be ready for you in five minutes," he was saying.

The door closed.

Sir Robert tapped his fingers upon the surface of his desk.

"You wish to affirm that Captain Gilbert is prepared to prove the truth of your statement?"

"I am sure he will be prepared to prove that my name is Manton," answered John.

In his long experience Sir Robert had come across many singular and dramatic events. The great police force of which he was the chief was dealing always in drama. In his experience he had interviewed every quality and degree of criminal, from affluent company promoters downward.

John's bearing and manner struck him as nothing unusual. John's statement that his was a case of mistaken identity, that Scotland Yard had for once made a mistake, meant nothing to the Police Commissioner. Such a statement was one of the commonest in his experience.

He felt no sympathy for John, and believing explicitly in his guilt, was determined to listen no further. He leaned forward and began to make rapid notes upon the writing pad.

Manton, in the meantime, stood motionless beyond the desk. Save for the movement of Sir Robert's pen, and the tick of a small travelling clock on Sir Robert's desk, no sound disturbed the heavy silence. Despite his calmness, John felt the tension grow upon him; the waiting seemed to draw itself out. He glanced at the clock, and observed that it was only a little after ten.

The whirl of events that night sped through his mind in rapid panorama, but of one thing he was certain—Manners and Captain Cherriton were either spies or traitors, and Scotland Yard in laying hands upon him, and allowing Cherriton to go, had made a mistake.

He had already guessed that General Whiston had gone to telephone Captain Gilbert. He recalled now the letter General Whiston had written to old Colonel Treves. The letter which said that he had done for Bernard Treves everything that was possible.

His mind then turned again to Gilbert. He wondered what the Captain would do when he heard of the extraordinary outcome of his visit to St. George's Square. He had gone there at Gilbert's own suggestion. He felt that the situation for himself at that moment was delicate in the extreme. But it was not yet fatal. A miscarriage of justice was impossible if Gilbert spoke up, as no doubt he would do. He knew that all Gilbert's sympathy for Bernard Treves would vanish the moment he heard to what depths that young man had descended. He recalled what Gilbert had said:

"Treves is afraid. He imagines that some one is watching him."

Then it suddenly occurred to John that at the back of Treves's mind there had been a subtle idea against himself. Treves had desired that he, John, should step into his guilty shoes and should not only wear those shoes, but should suffer for his crime.

"I stepped into far deeper water than I knew," mused John, and as the thought passed through his mind, the door opened and General Whiston re-entered.

The General walked behind John, then turned and looked keenly into his face.

"Treves," he said, "you will be examined again in the morning."

Sir Robert's finger was suspended over the bell upon his desk. In answer to his inquiring glance, General Whiston nodded.

Again John felt a man's hand laid on his shoulder, and for the second time a voice uttering polite words:

"This way, please!"

This time, however, there was no pause; he was led out into the corridor, with a tall, heavily-built man at his side and another walking behind him.

The door of Sir Robert's room closed with a soft click.

CHAPTER VI

The moment the door closed upon John, General Whiston flung himself into a chair beside Sir Robert's table. There was an expression on his face that puzzled the Police Commissioner.

"Well, Sir Robert," began the General, "it is an amazing thing, but Captain Gilbert corroborates our prisoner's statements entirely."

Sir Robert flashed a glance at the incriminating letters on the table.

"That's impossible!"

"Nevertheless, Gilbert, who is a very sound officer, corroborates every word this young man has said. I have ordered Gilbert to present himself here first thing in the morning."

Sir Robert was staring in utter bewilderment.

"You mean we have got the wrong man?"

"I don't know," answered the General, impatiently; "the thing is beyond my capacity. I've known this young blackguard for years. Only slightly, of course, but I would have sworn to him anywhere. Gilbert, however, tells me an extraordinary story. He says our prisoner is a thoroughly honest fellow, by the name of Manton. He gave me a minute history of the man, who was formerly at Scarthoe Head. I have ordered the adjutant from Scarthoe to report himself here to-morrow. We can then get to the bottom of this extraordinary tangle."

"But," protested Sir Robert, "these letters must be explained; and you have had this man watched for months."

"Precisely; that complicates matters enormously."

"Was Treves guilty of the crimes laid against him, or was this man guilty?" inquired Sir Robert.

The General shook his head in bewilderment.

"Don't ask me; I don't know," he said, "to-morrow will settle everything."

The night that followed was the longest that John had ever spent. What if by some awful mischance Captain Gilbert disowned him entirely? However, he could not think that of Gilbert. He was prepared to swear by the Captain's honesty.

A police officer called him early next morning. He dressed and was served with a satisfactory breakfast. A morning newspaper was brought to him, but at ten o'clock he was peremptorily summoned to present himself in Sir Robert's room. Under escort he made his way along various passages. The door was opened and he stepped into the room and stood at attention.

Sir Robert was not present. General Whiston stood at the window, and near him was a sleek-looking, smooth-haired, clean shaven man in a morning coat, well cut trousers and patent leather boots. John could feel the stranger's eyes steadily upon him.

Then Whiston turned from the window.

"Captain Gilbert," he said, "has been here. He has made certain statements on your behalf which are so far satisfactory."

A silence fell; the stranger moved to Sir Robert's desk, seated himself in Sir Robert's chair, and beckoned John to a chair opposite.

Dacent Smith was the head of a great branch of the Secret Intelligence Department, but there was no air of authority in his manner.

"Sit down, please," he said. His voice was smooth and agreeable. He glanced at the window, then again at John.

"Will you kindly tell me the name of your officer in command at Scarthoe Fort?"

John promptly gave him the name.

"How many men were in the fort?" The quiet gentleman, who possessed one of the subtlest brains in England, glanced at a slip of paper on his desk. He was putting John through an examination such as many a suspected person had failed to survive.

"One hundred and fifty, sir—eighty at the lower fort and seventy at the upper, exclusive of officers."

"Can you recollect the calibre of the guns?"

John gave the exact dimensions of the guns at both the lower and upper fort.

"Can you possibly recollect," inquired the other, "from your books, what store of six-inch ammunition there was?"

Fortunately John recollected the number of shells exactly.

"I see," commented the cross-examiner. "But your statement doesn't tally with my present knowledge."

"I am speaking of six weeks ago, sir; since then there would have been a heavy gun practice," John added promptly.

The elder gentleman leaned back in his chair.

"These are all details which a spy would make a great point of observing." He looked steadily into John's face, until John became conscious of nothing but his keen, grey eyes. They were kindly eyes, but the intensity of his glance was something that John had never before experienced. He looked back frankly into the elder man's face.

"I suppose they are, sir," he answered, "but they came to me in my ordinary course of work."

"How many fort candles were there in the storeroom?" asked the other, casually.

"Eight dozen, sir."

Dacent Smith nodded, as though satisfied.

"We will now come to another matter," he said. "You were educated in Germany?"

John admitted the fact.

"Have you been in Germany since your boyhood?"

"Never, sir."

"What is your opinion of Captain Gilbert?"

"I took a great liking to him."

"You trusted him when he asked you to assume another man's identity?"

"Absolutely, sir."

"So do I," said Dacent Smith, suddenly changing his tone. "I trust him absolutely. I will only try your patience just one moment longer." He pushed a clean slip of paper towards John. "Would you mind writing on that these three words, 'Deceive,' 'parallel,' and 'nursery.' Just scribble them quickly, without care."

John wrote the words and handed them across the table. The elder man took the sheet and immediately compared it with Treves's incriminating letter, and a pile of other letters in Treves's handwriting, which lay beside him.

He glanced up at the General, who stood near the window.

"The handwriting is totally unlike, General. Moreover, our young friend here can spell the words, whereas, from letters supplied us by Gilbert, Treves could not." He turned again and looked at John. Then he broke into a smile that John found charming.

"Well, Manton," he said, "you have come through the ordeal excellently. But as a matter of formality you must be identified both by Captain Gilbert and your adjutant from Scarthoe Head."

"Thank you, sir," answered John. "I am sorry to have caused so much trouble."

"No, not at all," protested the elder man. "Your desire for adventure placed you in a very nasty position. But such trouble as you have caused us may yet be turned to good account."

John hesitated a moment, then ventured:

"If I may, sir, I would like to make a statement in regard to the man Manners, at 208, St. George's Square, I am certain he is a spy, sir—a German spy."

"My dear Manton," said Dacent Smith, laying his hands on the desk, "we know that already."

"And the other man," continued John, "Cherriton. I don't believe he is all he pretends to be."

At the mention of Cherriton the lightness of mood vanished from the elder man.

"What name?" he inquired.

"Captain Cherriton, the man with the fair hair, who was in the taxi with me. The police officers allowed him to escape."

Beyond the table the great man of the Secret Service who had been cross-examining him, eased his spectacles. For, without knowing it, John had made a statement which aroused all his interest.

"This afternoon, Manton," he said, "you must come to my room. It seems to me," he continued, "you can be of very great use to my department."

"What is your department, sir?" asked John politely.

The elder man smiled.

"I think we need not give it a name, Manton. But perhaps you can guess. Perhaps, indeed, you are destined to make further acquaintance with my department and with your friend, Mr. Manners." He paused a moment.

"Captain Gilbert tells me that you wish to rejoin the army?"

"That is so, sir," answered John.

"An excellent intention," continued Dacent Smith. "But it has occurred to me that there is other work of national importance which may suit you better." He glanced at Whiston. "With General Whiston's aid I think we can arrange that you do not appear in uniform for some time. Another thing Captain Gilbert reported to me," he went on, quietly, "is that you are a young man with a taste for adventure."

John smiled.

Dacent Smith extended his hand in farewell. "You are a free man, Manton. But I shall expect you to come to my rooms at 286, Jermyn Street at three o'clock this afternoon." He gave John a card. "You will give this to my servant at the door."

The card read: "Mr. Dacent Smith, Savile Club"—that and nothing more.

*   *   *   *   *

At the time when John was undergoing his cross-examination at the hands of the great Dacent Smith, Manners and Captain Cherriton were seated in a back room at a house in Hampstead. Cherriton, who had read half a dozen morning papers, glanced at his companion.

"There is no word in any of them about our friend Treves."

"There was scarcely time for an announcement," Manners answered. "Perhaps it will be in the evening papers."

The two men waited till evening, but still the papers contained no line about Treves's capture. Cherriton was still not sure on what charge Treves had been arrested. If the charge had been an ordinary one, other than treason, there would already have been an account of some kind.

"We must find out some other way than through the papers."

"I have an excellent way of finding out," observed Manners.

"Well, put it into execution at once," returned his superior.

Manners looked at his watch.

"That way won't do until after six o'clock. After six o'clock, Herr Baron, I will take you into the presence of the most beautiful girl in England."

"I do not admire English beauty," answered Rathenau, caustically.

Manners lifted his hands.

"Ah, but this one, she is wonderful!"

"How will she know about Treves, any more than we do?"

Manners looked across at him.

"Leave that to me," he said, "I can assure you she will know." He took out his pocket-book and looked up an address. "If we go now," he said, "we shall get there a little after six, in time to interview the lady on her return from business."

Half an hour later a taxi sped along Kentish Town Road and turned into Bowles Avenue, Camden Town. The street was a particularly respectable one, with windows and doors freshly painted. Judging from the cleanliness of the curtains and the brightness of the door handles, the inhabitants of this thoroughfare each took a pride in his residence.

The taxi containing Manners and Cherriton drew to a halt before the door of No. 65. Cherriton paid the driver and dismissed him. The two men crossed the pavement, and Manners lifted the bright brass knocker. Three times Manners knocked.

He was that day attired with particular smartness in a grey, soft felt hat, a grey frock-coat, and light fawn linen gaiters. The Baron was wearing a navy-blue suit, made for him at the Army and Navy Stores. He also wore a grey felt hat, set well back on his head. In his hip pocket he carried a Mauser pistol, but this was always part of his apparel, as it were. Manners carried other little aids to his personal safety. But upon that evening their mission was pacific. They had only a desire to ask a certain lady if she had news of Treves.

Three times Manners applied the knocker; then footsteps came rapidly along the passage. The door was opened by a tall, brown-haired girl, wearing a white blouse and blue skirt, both of which Cherriton noticed were well cut. The girl's complexion was not pale, yet tended towards pallor. Her cheeks were softly rounded, her chin small, yet firm. Her eyes were grey, frank and steady in gaze. Cherriton, noticing her long, curved lashes and finely-arched brows, conceded that here, for once, he was looking upon a truly beautiful English woman.

"Good evening," Manners was saying. He had lifted his hat with extreme politeness.

"Good evening," responded the girl, looking with puzzled eyes from one man to the other.

"You have no doubt forgotten me," Manners spoke again, and then a faint recognition came to the girl's eyes.

"Oh, not at all," she said. "Will you come in?" She led the way to a little parlour, a bright little apartment, where she lived alone. She had made it as pretty and comfortable as possible with her small means.

The two Germans entered the room, and Manners closed the door. After some preliminary conversation he broached the subject of his visit, but artfully and cunningly hiding it in a veil of words.

"I have some business, madam," he said, "with"—he paused a moment—"with Mr. Treves. I have lost his address; I wonder if you could give it me?"

The girl looked at him a moment; an expression of reserve came into her face.

"I am afraid I cannot oblige you," she said.

"You have heard from him lately?"

The girl hesitated a moment, and pushed back the fine brown hair from her brow.

"Not lately," she answered.

"You will be seeing him again shortly, no doubt?" pursued Manners, smiling amicably.

"I don't know," said the girl. "I am afraid," she said, "I cannot give you his address, and if that is all you wish to see me about——" She rose quite politely, but firmly. And as she did so some one lifted the knocker of the front door and smote it thrice.

Manners started visibly.

"You have visitors?" he asked quickly.

"I don't know who it can be," said the girl. "I am expecting no one."

Manners sprang up and stood between her and the door. He looked into her face as she came towards him, then moved politely away. He felt that her candid eyes held no secrets.

When the door had closed he turned to Cherriton.

"She has heard nothing of him; she knows no more than we do."

"She is a beautiful woman, I'll admit," said Cherriton, who had been deep in thought. He raised his strong, supple hand and pointed towards the door. "Just open that," he said quietly, "and see who it is who is coming to visit her."

Manners, with his usual swiftness of step and dexterity of movement, approached the door and noiselessly drew it open. Quietly he put his head out and looked along the passage. Then he drew back and gently closed the door. His face, when he turned towards Cherriton, was deathly white.

"Who is it?" demanded Cherriton, who had come swiftly to his feet.

"Bernard Treves!" answered Manners, moistening his lips with his tongue. The thought that Treves had betrayed them blazed through his mind.

In an instant Cherriton sprang to the window and peered furtively up and down the street.

"He's alone," he said, with a note of relief in his voice.

"Gott in Himmel!" exclaimed Manners under his breath. "How did he get here?"

"Either escaped or acquitted," answered Cherriton, curtly. "Our business," he went on swiftly, under his breath, "is to express great delight when we see him. In the meantime I'll compose myself with a cigarette."

"I don't know why his coming back like this should make me feel so nervous," mused Manners. "I am more psychic than you are, Herr Baron."

Cherriton looked at the big, fat figure in the chair opposite him. He curled his lip in faint contempt.

Meanwhile John Manton, having knocked at the door of 65, Bowles Avenue, found, to his astonishment, that that door was opened by a girl of most extreme beauty. He had come there under orders from Dacent Smith to discover the identity of the sender of the telegram signed "Elaine." He had been given many instructions during that afternoon, but as he stood upon the threshold of No. 65 a swift admiration leapt into his eyes for the girl who confronted him on the doorstep.

"May I come in?" asked John.

"Of course," answered the girl. To his amazement, she seized his hand as she spoke. "Oh, how long you have been!" she said. She drew him into the hall and closed the door. Silence and caution were the parts John had been ordered to play. He did not withdraw his hand from her warm grasp. "You never came, you never wrote," continued the girl.

"I wasn't able to," John answered, truthfully.

"And yet I told you, Bernard," she went on, looking up into his face—he was glad that the light in the hall was not intense—" and yet I told you, Bernard, that if you confessed everything to your father he would forgive."

"He has forgiven a great deal," answered Manton, vaguely. He looked down at her—a little colour had come into her cheeks, and, as for her eyes, he had never seen eyes which evoked in him so much admiration. At that moment Manners put his face out at the door of the inner room; then swiftly withdrew it.

"Who's that?" John asked, quickly.

"It's a man who has come to see you, Bernard; but before you go in I want to say"—she laid her hand softly on the lapel of John's coat—"I want to say, Bernard, that I forgive you—everything." She was smiling at him, a smile of wonderful beauty. "After all, Bernard," she whispered, "I am your wife, and it is a wife's privilege to forgive."

"Yes," answered John. He could think of nothing else to say. Here was the most beautiful woman he had ever seen, holding his hand warmly in hers, and telling him she forgave him everything. The situation would have been delightful if he had only been the other man!

"Bernard, for my sake, you will try, won't you?" She paused, and this time he was obliged to frame some sort of answer.

"I'll do the best I can," he said, lamely, then added, to turn the subject, "Who is your visitor?"

"It's Mr. Manners, the big, stout man you brought here a long while ago. He has a friend with him, a younger man."

"Captain Cherriton?" asked John, lowering his voice.

The girl nodded.

"They came to ask where you were, and wanted your address, but I remembered what you told me and would not give it."

Then for the first time John looked keenly into her face. He had never seen her in his life before, and at any moment she might recognise him. But even with that danger hovering over him he could not help wondering if she loved Treves.

"Come, Bernard"; she took his hand in hers. "You must see your friends and get rid of them."

John walked with her along the narrow passage. At the door of the parlour the girl halted.

"When they are gone," she whispered, "I have whole heaps of things to tell you."

She pushed open the door and followed John into the room.

Manners, who was seated at the hearth, sprang up and rushed towards Manton.

"Come in! Come in!" he cried, drawing John forward. "It does my eyes good to see you again, eh, Captain Cherriton?"

Baron Rathenau, who had also risen, enclosed Manton's fingers in his hard, cold grip. "I, too, am glad to see you," he said, fixing his eyes steadily on John's.

CHAPTER VII

Things were not as they seemed. The situation in the little parlour was delicate in the extreme, and as John's gaze passed from the fat countenance of Manners to the cold forcefulness of Cherriton, whose strong hand but a moment ago gripped his own in greeting, he told himself that if he could creep from that situation with credit he could escape from anything. Both Cherriton's and Manners's welcome rang false. They were not pleased to see him. They were startled and puzzled, and Cherriton, at least, was more than puzzled. John knew that whatever occurred between himself and these two men must occur privately. Moreover, there was a second danger, which he knew to be ever present. The light in the bright little parlour was quite strong. The fact that he had dexterously placed his back to the window might not serve him for more than a few minutes. What if Elaine Treves suddenly discovered her mistake?

Somehow the teeming possibilities of the moment gave steadiness to John's nerves. He thought of a plan, and put it into execution on the instant.

"Elaine," he said—he used her name for the first time, and as he spoke he took her slender hand in his grasp—"I have business to discuss with Captain Cherriton and Mr. Manners."

"I promise we shall not keep your husband more than a few minutes," intervened Cherriton. "Yes, old Manwitz for once is right," he thought; "here is an Englishwoman possessed of beauty."

He made across the room, intending politely to hold open the door for Elaine to pass out. John, however, was quicker, and as he held the door wide Elaine lifted her grey-blue, beautiful eyes and searched his. Her expression, John thought, was one of surprise—surprise at what?

He closed the door, and instantly Cherriton laid a hand on his shoulder.

"Well," he demanded, "what happened to you last night."

"You were present at the beginning of the happening," returned John.

"The four men were police officers, were they not?"

"Detectives from Scotland Yard. They took me there, cross-examined me, and discovered that a mistake had been made."

Manners drew in a deep breath of relief.

"Ah—a—mistake!" he exclaimed.

Cherriton, who was busy with a cigarette, looked at John under his brows. He had retreated to the hearth, and was leaning with his back against the mantelshelf. "A very unpleasant incident for you, eh, Treves?" he inquired.

"Very," responded John.

"And my overcoat—my very excellent summer overcoat—what happened to that?"

From the moment of John's appearance in the room he had been leading up to this question—had his overcoat been searched, had Treves's incriminating letter been discovered? It occurred to him that if John, immediately after his arrest, had established his identity no search of his overcoat was probable. And yet caution was bred in him. His deeply subtle mind prompted him to probe the matter to its depths, and at the same time to convey no suspicion of his anxiety to John.

"Cherriton, your overcoat is quite safe," John said quietly. "I left it on your behalf in the cloak-room at Charing Cross Station." He put his hand into his pocket and drew out the ticket. Cherriton took it from his extended fingers.

"I am particularly obliged to you, Treves," he said. "I have a special fondness for that overcoat? So the Scotland Yard people were for once mistaken."

"Entirely," said John, with truth; "they mistook me for another man."

"Were you made acquainted with the charges against the real person?" probed Cherriton.

"He was wanted for misappropriation of military funds."

Both Manners and Cherriton exhibited increasing interest in the unknown culprit.

"You heard the person's name?"

"His name was John Manton. He was a sergeant at Scarthoe Fort."

"That is in the Isle of Wight?"

"Yes," John answered; "that accounts for them seizing me—they traced me from the Isle of Wight."

Cherriton and Manners exchanged glances; neither man felt at all comfortable. But Cherriton felt that he had pressed the matter enough. He suddenly assumed his air of bland amiability, but it sat ill on him.

"Well, Manners," he exclaimed, looking at his confrère, "you were mistaken—you assumed that our dear friend Treves had escaped, and were in a great fluster of anxiety on his behalf; whereas the little misfortune that occurred to him was all a mistake."

"All a mistake," repeated John.

"And now, I think," Cherriton remarked, taking up his grey felt hat and denting it carefully with his hand, "I think we will not keep you from your wife any longer."

For the second time that day he gripped John's hand in his, and John, looking back into his cold blue eyes, felt the steady, penetrating power of Cherriton's gaze.

"Here was a man," thought John, "used to command—a man possessed of exceptional powers of mind and physique. You are a daring fellow," thought John; "a subtle and cunning worker of evil, but for once in your life you are mistaken. I am not the man you think, either in name or in character."

Then a singular thing happened to John. On the very instant when his fingers slid away from the other's touch a flaming instinct ran through him—a passionate impulse to leap upon the other's throat and squeeze the life out of him came upon him as a definite and conscious wish. Though he had known Cherriton only for two days, he felt a great hate swirl up in him against this serenely poised, potent enemy. Against Manners, whom he knew, and whom Dacent Smith knew to be a spy, he felt nothing of this. That afternoon he had been instructed well and thoroughly by Dacent Smith. Dacent Smith had talked much with him, drawing him out, subtly examining him as to his aspirations and his powers. And gradually, during the talk of that afternoon, Smith had come to realise that in John Manton he possessed a keen and highly-wrought weapon. Here was a young man who had fought for his country, who was willing to fight for it again in any circumstances. And long before the end of that interview the chief of a great branch of the Secret Service had laid his hand on John's arm.

"Manton," he had explained, "you were wasted as a sergeant at Scarthoe Head. There are big things awaiting you. You have fought the enemy in the open; from to-day you shall fight him in the dark. You will find him more tricky and subtle and dangerous than he was in France"—then he had paused a moment, looking at John. "Accidents sometimes happen, Manton, my boy!"

"One must be prepared for accidents," John had answered, quietly.

"I have lost two or three splendid fellows during the past year. I am telling you this," the chief resumed, "that you may remain always on your guard. Fate or Providence has placed you in a wonderful position with the aid of your acquaintance, Manwitz. I have the complete dossier in that cupboard over there." He pointed to a cabinet against the wall. "Your acquaintance with Manwitz gives you a splendid start. You will use it to acquire such information as will be useful to the Department, but in the first place you must discover all there is to know about the amiable and unexpected Cherriton. We shall at the same time be working to discover things from our end."

John thought of this conversation as Manners and Cherriton took their departure.

"You will come and see me again soon, will you not?" Manners had remarked at the moment of departure. He looked cunningly and meaningly into John's eyes. In effect he had been saying: "You will come and see me again immediately those cocaine tabloids have been consumed." Bernard Treves's craving for cocaine, both Manners and Cherriton knew, held that young man as by bonds of steel.

"I'll come again soon," John had answered, slipping the new address Manners had given him into his waistcoat pocket. He watched the two men pass into the street, then closed the door, and re-entered the empty parlour. The daintiness, the cleanliness, and the perfect taste of the little apartment had already won his appreciation. He wondered when Elaine Treves would descend from above, and what would happen then. Until now only a few fleeting words had passed between himself and the beautiful girl who was Treves's wife. What was to happen now in the intimacy that would ensue when she re-entered the room?

John was smoking one of Treves's cigarettes, with his back against the mantelshelf, when the door opened and Elaine quietly entered.

"So you have got rid of them, Bernard?"

She looked at him, he thought, a little shyly, with something of reserve in her glance. He watched her as she crossed to a chintz-covered wicker arm-chair, with its back to the window. At her side was a small work-table. She took out a needle, a thread, and various bits of coloured silk. A silence drew itself out that became awkward. John moved from one foot to another; then he made an effort to pick up the thread of what he believed to be Treves's life in relation to the girl who was so industriously sewing, with bowed head.

"I am sorry I wasn't able to come in answer to your wire."

"I think, Bernard, you might have answered it," returned Elaine, quietly, without raising her head.

"Well, you know, I was not able to. Circumstances did not permit me to answer it."

"I was afraid of that."

She suddenly looked up at him with an expression of hopelessness in her fine eyes.

"Bernard," she said, "sometimes I think you will never, never be able to keep your promise to me!"

"Why not?" John asked, feeling his way cautiously. He could see that she was stirred, that something had moved her deeply. He was more than ever assured of this when she rose, stood before him, and looked steadily into his face.

"Oh! Bernard, if you could only, only fight!"

Under the close scrutiny of her eyes John felt extraordinarily uncomfortable.

"Other people have fought and have conquered," went on the girl. "Why should not you? Sometimes," she went on, "you are quite as you should be, just as you are now—the man who once won my love. And then, again——" She broke off.

Accidentally John had put his fingers in his waistcoat pocket. He felt the contact of the little bottle of cocaine tabloids Manners had forced upon him. He had guessed that Elaine was referring to Treves's enslavement to this drug, and he drew out the bottle, holding it in the palm of his hand. He saw the girl look at the tabloids with an expression of loathing; then something seemed to pass through her that drew her rigid and erect.

"I wonder," she said, "in our very short months together, how often you have promised, have sworn, to give it up!" Her manner suddenly changed again, and she held out her hand imploringly. "I wonder, Bernard, if you have the courage to give them to me?"

"Certainly," John said, "I will give them to you!"

He unscrewed the top of the little bottle, and poured the white tabloids one after another into the palm of her hand. She looked at them for a moment, then into his face. John was still standing with his back towards the small fire. He felt the girl's hand on his arm; she was thrusting him aside. A moment later she had flung the tabloids into the red embers, and before John knew it she was holding his hand in hers, looking up into his face.

"Bernard," she said, in a low voice, "I believe—I believe you have changed! I think strength is coming to you—you will win yet!"

"Yes," John answered, "I swear I'll win."

The words came from him almost without volition, and at the same moment an instinct came to him that matters were drifting too far. He turned the conversation with a laugh, and for some minutes they were discussing general topics. He helped her to prepare the supper, going into the little kitchen and bringing out plates and dishes, under her direction.

Daylight faded, much to John's relief. They took supper together in the little parlour; John noticed how deft and womanly she was.

"Our friend Treves is a lucky man, if he only knew it," thought he.

"I am afraid there is nothing to drink, Bernard."

"That doesn't trouble me," John answered; then saw her pause with the teapot uplifted in frank surprise. "I mean," said John, striving to recover the situation, "if you haven't got it, I don't mind."

The meal passed off in an air of general cheerfulness. Elaine's little clock struck nine, and when the meal was at an end John took the seat opposite Elaine and her little work-basket. She busied herself with her fancy-work, and occasionally John caught her eyes resting upon him with a thoughtful and somewhat puzzled expression. He strove to gather from her manner what her feelings really were towards her husband. "She can't love him," thought John; "he's too much of a brute and a waster for that. And yet women are strange creatures."

Elaine had been silent for some minutes, but presently she spoke, uttering something that appeared to have dwelt for long in her mind.

"Bernard," she said, "I am not so hard as you think, but I am sure the way I am acting is the only right way." She paused.

"I am sure it is the right way," answered John, looking into her candid, girlish face.

He noticed again the flicker of surprise. He was always making false steps. The situation was difficult beyond everything he had experienced. Dacent Smith had impressed upon him the importance of tact and finesse. Here was a situation thrust upon him requiring abundance of both.

"You seem to have changed your point of view?"

"Well— —" John began, cautiously.

"You were so violent with me," interposed Elaine.

"There was no intention on my part to be anything of the sort towards you," John answered.

He wondered what Treves had done, what Treves had said. He began to experience pleasure in the situation; he began to wonder what was to happen next. But very soon after that the clock struck ten.

Elaine put away her needlework and rose somewhat abruptly.

"You must go now, Bernard."

John looked at her for a moment in surprise.

"Oh, yes," he said, "I see—of course."

Then Elaine crossed the hearthrug and laid her slender hands on the lapels of his coat.

"To-night, Bernard," she said, "I have almost felt as if you were your old self again."

"Thanks," answered John, awkwardly; his position at that moment was awkward and utterly false; he was like a man who walks blindly on the edge of a precipice. He wondered if she was about to kiss him, or if she expected him to salute her in that way. This doubt was still upon him when Elaine reached up and touched his cheeks lightly with her lips. There was no passion, no love—nothing but a sort of sisterly affection in the embrace, but John was glad when it was over. If she had been a less beautiful woman the situation would have been so very much easier.

Elaine accompanied him along the passage, handing him his hat and stick as they went. In the darkness at the door, as they shook hands, John felt that the impression of her fingers was warmer and infinitely more cordial that the greeting she had given him upon his arrival. He could see her face only dimly. She had seemed surprised that he had departed so easily; he felt that he must say something, utter some remark that possibly might have been uttered by Bernard Treves.

"I am sorry to have to go," he said.

Then Elaine's voice came to him quietly in the darkness. There was a new note in her words.

"You must come again—soon, Bernard."

The door closed softly, and she was gone.

CHAPTER VIII

Dacent Smith, busy in his luxurious bachelor apartments in Jermyn Street, was going through a pile of documents, all relating directly or indirectly to the multitudinous activities of his department. He had continued his work for, perhaps, half an hour after his brief luncheon interval when the man-servant entered and announced a visitor. Dacent Smith's man-servant was discretion itself. He looked like a walking secret, and was a big, pallid man, with high cheek-bones and a grim, hard mouth. He was devoted body and soul to Dacent Smith, and no tortures ever devised could have ever wormed a word from him of his master's activities.

"Well, Grew?"

"Mr. Treves, sir."

"I'll see Mr. Treves at once."

Grew, the man-servant, departed, and a minute later John was ushered into the apartment.

Dacent Smith greeted him with brief cordiality, then indicated a chair.

"Well, Treves," he said, with a smile, "what is your news?"

"There is very little to tell you, sir, so far. The person who wrote that telegram signed 'Elaine,' is Bernard Treves's wife!"

Dacent Smith lifted his eyebrows; a twinkle of humour was detectable in his expression.

"What happened?"

"She was quite deceived, sir!"

"A piquant situation," smiled Dacent Smith.

"Very!" answered John, seriously.

"You see how quickly you find yourself in deep waters, my friend." Dacent Smith was looking at him with an expression of raillery in his keen eyes. Nevertheless he was saying inwardly: "I like you, Manton; you are a man after my own heart. There is a good deal of humour, as well as courage and intelligence, hidden behind that good-looking face of yours."

"Now, Manton," he said, "tell me about Manwitz. Are you in touch with him again?"

"I have his address, sir, and an invitation to go to him whenever I wish—that is, whenever the cocaine habit seizes me violently."

"I see," remarked the elder man. "Whenever the craving is violently upon you, you go to Manwitz and he supplies your want?"

John nodded.

"It is amazing," went on the chief, "the way these fellows manage to secure these drugs. Perhaps, later, Manton, you will be able to enlighten us upon that little matter; but in the meantime Cherriton is your chief responsibility."

"Cherriton showed a particular anxiety about his overcoat, sir, containing Treves's letter."

John gave a brief report of the events of the previous evening, and Dacent Smith made one or two notes on a slip of paper marked M. 15.

When John had finished, the elder man leaned back in his chair.

"It will take you some days—perhaps weeks," he said, "to get the hang of things with us. At present you are to play a lone hand. There is a chain of German emissaries working against us—some traitors and some spies—who pass information from all our dockyards to London, and thence to Germany. I want you to get into contact with one of the links of this chain—any link will serve our purpose. You must do all you can to keep the confidence of Cherriton and Manwitz. If they set you upon any task, carry it through absolutely. If papers or documents are given to you to be delivered elsewhere, don't fail to act absolutely according to their instructions. If you can get a sight of the documents, and memorise them during transit, do so, of course. This applies to letters or documents which may be handed to you by strangers—other German spies. Do you understand the importance of all this?"

John assured him that he did.

"It appears to me, sir," he added, "that by doing this I shall myself become a sort of link in their chain."

The great man looked at him with eyes of approbation.

"Exactly," he responded; "that is what you will be. Information is leaking out of England day by day, hour by hour—rippling along these chains of which I speak."

Half an hour later, John took his departure from the chief's sumptuous bachelor apartments. He had learned many things that amazed him, and one of these things, which filled him with fury and loathing, was that there were indeed traitors in unexpected places, that there were British-born people, few, but active, who were willing to sell their country into the power of the enemy.

"I hope it won't be my destiny to run across one of these gentry," thought John; "for even the chief himself would find it hard to make me keep my hands off him."

And yet that night, in a few brief hours, he was to find himself in contact with just such a traitor.

Reaching the corner of Jermyn Street, after his departure from Dacent Smith's rooms, John hailed a taxi and drove to Hampstead Tube at Tottenham Court Road. Here he took train to Hampstead, and made his way towards the address Manwitz had given him. The address was Cherriton's, and when John arrived there he found that the unamiable captain occupied a suite of rooms in a large, old-fashioned house near the Heath. The house was maintained by a retired butler, who received John at the door. The butler ascended to a handsomely furnished, spacious drawing-room on the first floor. Here Manners was seated at a grand piano, and Cherriton, deep in an arm-chair, was reading an English Pacifist pamphlet.

"Is that a telegram?" asked Cherriton, as the door opened.

"No, sir," answered the man; "it is a Mr. Bernard Treves called in to see Mr. Manners."

Two minutes later John stepped into the room.

"Did you get your overcoat?" he asked, shaking hands with Cherriton.

The fair man nodded.

"Many thanks," he said.

He had spent the earlier part of that day inquiring into the existence, status, and habits of John Manton. He was still not quite satisfied as to his visitor's release from Scotland Yard, and at that very moment he was awaiting a telegram from the Isle of Wight which would either increase his suspicions or remove them altogether. In the meantime, he preferred to trust John to a certain extent.

"You have come at an opportune time, Treves," he said.

John was seated now, and this time accepted a cigarette from the Baron's case. Suddenly, Rathenau looked him full in the face.

"You and I, Treves," he said, "have both been treated damnably!"

"Damnably!" answered John, wondering what was coming. The other continued:

"But there comes a time, Treves, eh, when the worm turns? You turned and I turned! You cast in your lot with our friend Manners, who knows how to appreciate loyalty! Manners," he continued, in the ironical tone that was his general habit, "fat and stupid and lazy as he is, is always willing to pay for loyalty!"

John looked into the Baron's thick-skinned, pallid face, into the steel-like eyes, and smiled inwardly. A pause came. John leaned forward.

"Cherriton," he said, "what are you leading up to?"

Manners, from the piano-stool, spoke up.

"Ah, you see, Cherriton—he is sharp, our friend Treves. Tell him what you want, Cherriton, straight out!"

He rose, came, for all his great bulk, softly across the room. He laid a fat hand on John's shoulder and looked down at him.

"Bernard," he half whispered, "you shall have all you want of everything. Money—and the other thing. I want you to throw in your lot with me as the good Captain has done. That note," he continued, still in the half whisper, "you gave me in regard to the sailing of the *Polydor* was well appreciated in certain circles."

"I am glad to hear that," John answered.

"That was good service," continued Manners, "but there are bigger things afoot." He paused a moment, then walked round John, and seated himself on a sofa quite near. "You have heard, no doubt," he continued, "of the *Imperator* — —"

"You mean the new Grey Star liner?"

Manners nodded.

"A monster ship—a wonder ship! Forty-eight thousand tons."

He uttered the words slowly, rolling them unctuously over his tongue.

"Nearly as big as the *Vaterland*," John said, and for the life of him he could not help looking across at Cherriton's face.

But Cherriton was quick as lightning.

"The *Vaterland*?" he repeated. "You mean the German ship?"

John returned his attention to Manners. He could feel the web closing about him—the web in which Dacent Smith had ordered him to entangle himself.

"The *Imperator*," said Manners, "is to sail one day quite soon, but your Admiralty has grown doubly cunning of late. As yet we know not either her port of departure or the hour of departure!"

John noticed that the fat man's tones deepened as he spoke; excitement gleamed in his eyes. He leaned forward and laid a fat hand on Bernard's knee.

"Treves, my boy, I trust you—eh?"

"Certainly!" answered John, truthfully. "I want you to trust me."

"Good!" exclaimed Manners, uttering the word thickly in his throat. "Now, you will understand Cherriton and I cannot appear in certain places, but with you—it is different with you—eh?"

"Quite," said John. "I can appear anywhere without suspicion."

Cherriton, who had remained silent, again took control of the situation.

"What Manners and I want you to do," he said, "is to stay a few days at the Savoy Hotel. A Dutch gentleman is giving up Room 104C. You are to take that room, and stay at the hotel at Manners's expense."

"Thank you," said John.

"There will be no need for you to stint yourself. What is more, you will have no duties whatever to perform!"

John lifted his eyebrows in genuine surprise.

"I don't quite see what help I can be in that case!"

"We are hoping that the matter will resolve itself," said Cherriton.

"Yes—yes!" intervened Manners, "everything will resolve itself beautifully. All you have to do now, my dear boy, is to say that you accept the——"

"The invitation," intercepted Cherriton.

John thought there was nothing easier in the world than to accept an invitation to stay, free of expense, at a first-class hotel, and with no duties to perform. He said as much to Manners, and two nights later found him the occupant of the room 1046, a delightful Louis Seize bedroom overlooking the Embankment. He had spent a day and a night at the hotel, and no incident whatever had occurred. On the evening of the second night, however, after dinner, John seated himself in the foyer and ordered coffee and cigarettes.

Presently, in the great crowd moving, laughing and talking near him, John observed a politician who at various periods in the past had loomed importantly in the public eye.

"He is even more ugly than his photographs," thought John, watching the important personage move among his friends. John did not like Beecher Monmouth's smile; altogether he disliked the man on the instant, and was the more astonished to notice that a strikingly beautiful woman of thirty, wearing a glittering diamond necklace and diamond ear-rings, moved towards him and slipped her arm through his. The woman wore a deeply decollété evening dress of a shimmering silk that looked to John now green and now blue. He noticed her flash a smile into Beecher Monmouth's face. He saw the politician put her hand into his. Then recollection came to John. The woman was Beecher Monmouth's wife, a beautiful woman thirty years his junior, who had appeared from nowhere and married him.

"She certainly is a beautiful woman," thought John. "A case of Beauty and the Beast!"

Then, to his utter amazement, Mrs. Beecher Monmouth's eyes met his. She slid her arm from her husband's, and made her way quickly through the crowd to John. He felt his heart-beat quicken. A moment later Mrs. Beecher Monmouth was holding out her hand towards him. She flashed a smile into his face.

"My dear Mr. Treves," she said, in a voice that was low and intimate, "I have been looking for you all the evening!"

A moment later she was shaking hands with John.

"I must fly now," she added, "but you must come and see me to-morrow—six o'clock."

A moment later she was hurrying back towards her husband, her gown shimmering and gleaming as she went. There was something in the palm of John's hand—something that had passed from Mrs. Beecher Monmouth to himself.

Holding his hand below the table and free from observation, John saw that the something Mrs. Beecher Monmouth had passed into his hand was a slip of paper on which was pencilled: "*Imperator*—three o'clock to-morrow. Route 28."

John was conscious of a quite definite thrill. His nerve was of the best; he had accepted the momentous slip of paper without any outward sign of disturbance. Indeed, he had smiled back into Mrs. Beecher Monmouth's eyes in a manner that had won that lady's sincerest approbation. Nevertheless, he was not inwardly calm. He felt that fate, or destiny, had seized him suddenly in its relentless grip. The slip of paper was still in his right hand, concealed beneath the level of the table. For some minutes he drew at his cigarette, then, carefully taking out the pocket-book, laid the slip in its leaves, and replaced the book in the inner breast pocket of his coat. For some minutes longer he retained his seat, leaning back in the delicate gilt chair. His gaze wandered among the brilliant and fashionable crowd moving about him. The gentle murmur of music mingled still with the chatter of voices, and twenty feet away he caught the gleam of Mrs. Beecher Monmouth's earrings, the scintillation of her superb diamond necklace. She was talking to her yellow-skinned and unprepossessing husband, but her attention was entirely and solely fixed upon John.

Their eyes met, and John was obliged to concede, for the second time, that she was a woman of exceptional beauty. The art of her coiffeur, and, possibly, the art of her complexion expert, had wrought its best for her. Nevertheless, she would have stood out among any assemblage of young and prepossessing women. Her husband quite visibly adored her, and every word she condescended to transmit to him was received with a quick, responsive smile on his part.

John was thinking rapidly, wondering and speculating. Was it possible that Beecher Monmouth knew of the existence of the little slip of paper that reposed in his pocket-book? Beecher Monmouth, who had sat on numerous committees, who had more than once stood in the running for an under-secretaryship? The thing seemed utterly incredible!

As these things flashed through John's mind, realisation slowly came to him that Mrs. Beecher Monmouth was observing him with close intensity, under slightly lowered lids.

John rose, and as he did so the lady flashed a brilliant smile towards him—an intimate, understanding smile, full of meaning.

"I wish I knew what you meant," thought John, as he made his way through the throng out towards the cloak-room.

The circulating door received him, and he passed out into the dim light of the Strand. There was a crowd, as always at that hour, and a young man who followed closely at his heels found difficulty in keeping him in sight.

John was burning once more to look at the information Mrs. Beecher Monmouth had conveyed to him. But caution forbade anything of the sort. He was determined that this, his first swim in deep waters, should achieve a successful issue. His chief desire in life was to make good in Dacent Smith's eyes, and, moreover, obeying his chief's instructions, he had already indelibly impressed upon his memory the portentous sentence: "*Imperator*—three o'clock to-morrow. Route 28."

The word "treachery" floated into his mind, and filled him with rage. Until now he had been outside—one of the public. But to-night the curtain had been drawn aside. He felt himself engaged in the secret fight which is for ever taking place beneath the surface—the fight between our own secret service and the spies and traitors in the pay of the other nations.

At Hampstead, John emerged from the Tube and made his way through the darkness of Well Walk. Presently he turned to the left, through an alley, crossed a square of shabby-looking houses, and ascended a further closely-built, narrow street, leading towards Cherriton's residence.

The young man who had followed him from the Savoy was still in his wake. At this point, however, he apparently ceased his pursuit, and vanished up a side alley.

John, who had been aware of footsteps for some minutes, halted and looked behind him. The road was empty, and the suspicion that had been growing on him vanished. Nevertheless, he laid a hand on his hip pocket, assured himself that he was prepared for eventualities and moved forward again.

"I'll give this nefarious bit of news to Cherriton, then hop down to Dacent Smith and report the fact as quickly as I can," thought John.

He reached the top of Christ Church Road and paused to recollect which turning was the right one. At that moment some one moved in the shadow of the church railings near him, and before John could turn his head a doubled fist smote him heavily. The attack was so sudden, unexpected and swift that before he could in any way retaliate a second blow had been delivered.

His assailant leaped through the air, clasped two strong hands round his neck, and fell into the road, still gripping for all he was worth.

The two struggled ignominiously, and John became aware that the stranger, who had released one hand grip, was groping for the precious pocket-book. For the first time John was able to aim a blow, then, with a violent twist, he drew himself uppermost, and plunged his knee heavily into the other's chest. In the dim light he observed that his opponent was young. John was already aware that he had met no mean antagonist, and he was taking no chances.

The downward blow he now delivered on the other man's countenance staggered him for a moment. He wrenched himself free and stood upright on his feet.

His enemy was prone, but only for a moment.

"You've got a good deal of spirit, my young friend," said John, through his teeth, "but you'll get nothing from me, except another punch like the last! Now, get up!"

"Thanks," returned the other.

He rose and began to dust his clothes carefully. John did not like the man's attitude. He was quite obviously preparing to make another attack.

"Now," commanded John, moving back a pace, "don't try that with me!"

He stepped back and reached for the Colt weapon that reposed in his pocket.

"I should hate to do anything drastic," he continued; "but if you make it a habit to leap at people in the dark, and to aim half-arm jolts at strangers, you must take the consequences."

"I am prepared to take anything that is coming to me!" responded the young man.

He spoke almost jauntily, and John admired his spirit.

"I evidently did not hit you quite as hard as I thought," John remarked.

"Quite hard enough," responded the other, "but please don't shoot, because ——"

Then, to John's amazement, and with the utmost daring, he leapt forward like a flash and seized John's pistol. There was a swift, fierce struggle. The moment was one for quick decisions. The stranger held the weapon by the wrong end, and John knew it. Unexpectedly he let go, and simultaneously landed a heavy left on the young man's downbent jaw. He followed with a right, and then another left. He was as busy as he had ever been, and he knew he was fighting for his entire future, possibly for his life.

"I've had enough," gasped the stranger.

He reeled away, and seated himself on the farther side of the narrow street.

John searched about, picked up the weapon from the middle of the road and pocketed it. Then he buttoned his coat, after carefully satisfying himself that the pocket-book was still in its place, and prepared to go.

"Good night," called the other, seated on the edge of the pavement, as he went.

Manton, however, was in no mood for persiflage. He took himself off, walking as swiftly as he could.

"He certainly doesn't lack pluck," mused John.

Five minutes later he reached the large house wherein Cherriton had his abode.

"I want to see Captain Cherriton at once," he said, when the door was opened to him.

He found Cherriton alone in the big drawing-room. He was in evening clothes, and was wearing comfortable house slippers.

"So it's you, Treves?" exclaimed the German as the door closed. "Come in, and I'll give you a drink of whisky; that is always acceptable, eh?"

"Always," answered John.

Cherriton was looking at him intently.

"There is a slight cut on your forehead."

"Is there? It must be a scratch."

John applied his handkerchief to the slight abrasion, then slipped off his overcoat and took a drink of whisky and soda.

"I have some news for you, Cherriton."

"News?"

The other flashed a swift glance at him.

John slowly drew out the pocket-book and produced the slip of paper.

"You wanted to know when the *Imperator* sailed out, and by what route."

Cherriton was suddenly and unfeignedly impatient.

"What is it you know?" he demanded.

"At the Savoy to-night," John said quietly, "this was handed to me."

He passed the slip of paper into the German's eager fingers.

"Gott!" exclaimed Cherriton, utterly absorbed. "You got this from——"

"Mrs. Beecher Monmouth."

"Three o'clock to-morrow," mused Cherriton. "There is not much time for us to act!"

He looked suddenly into John's face.

"What a woman she is!" he exclaimed. "Invaluable—invaluable!"

"Invaluable!" echoed John.

Cherriton laid a hand on John's arm.

"Keep your hold on her, my dear Treves. Your work to-night has been excellent!"

Excitement had brought an unusual gleam into his hard eyes.

"We will do great things for you yet!"

He crossed the room and rang the bell imperiously.

"My coat and hat," he commanded of the butler when the man appeared. "When Mr. Manners returns, ask him to wait up for me."

CHAPTER IX

The hour was eleven o'clock. Dacent Smith was, as usual, up to his ears in work. Very little of the real work, conducted by him on behalf of the Department, was dispatched at the office. If he possessed a weakness at all, it was a weakness for the luxury of his own suite of rooms and for the benign, competent aid of Grew. Servant and master were each equally devoted to the other, and yet even Grew was only vaguely aware of the greatness, of the importance of the stoutish, bland, keen-eyed gentleman who was his master.

At Dacent Smith's elbow a green-shaded electric lamp cast a bright light on the papers beneath his hand. The chief wrote neatly and carefully, and when the door opened and Grew came softly in he did not lift his head.

"Mr. Treves to report, sir."

"I'll see Mr. Treves immediately."

"Very good, sir."

Dacent Smith raised his head.

"Oh, Grew, please ask the gentleman who is in the other room to wait a little longer."

"Very good, sir."

Two minutes later John found himself alone with the chief.

Dacent Smith motioned him into one of the deep, leathered-covered arm-chairs, opened a silver box of Egyptian cigarettes, and pushed it towards him.

"Well," he questioned, wheeling his chair and looking at John much as an astute physician might look at a patient; "I can see by your expression," he went on quickly, "that you have something of importance to report."

"I think so," said John.

"Well, what is it?"

"In the foyer of the Savoy to-night, sir, Mrs. Beecher Monmouth" —an almost imperceptible change of expression occurred on Dacent Smith's smooth features—"Mrs. Beecher Monmouth," continued John, "passed a slip of paper into my hand. I assumed at once that the paper was meant for either Manners or Cherriton, and, obeying your instructions, I delivered it at once."

"You memorised it first?"

Dacent Smith's tone was almost sharp.

"It was very short, sir. I can remember it exactly."

Dacent Smith pushed a pencil and block of paper towards him.

"Perhaps you had better write it down immediately," he said. "If you visualise it in writing you will be less likely to have forgotten or misplaced a word."

John rose, and bending over the desk wrote the exact words of the message Mrs. Beecher Monmouth had conveyed to him. When he came to the word *Imperator*, Dacent Smith whistled softly.

"You have done very well, Treves," he said. He suddenly looked into John's face. "You must better your acquaintance with Mrs. Beecher Monmouth."

"I have an appointment with her for to-morrow night," answered John.

Dacent Smith glanced at a little gilt clock on the mantelshelf.

"I think we shall be in time!"

"That is exactly what Cherriton said," John answered.

Dacent Smith was silent for a moment.

"Treves," he said, "if the *Imperator* sails to-morrow at three o'clock by Route 28, which is their code for the North Ireland route, there will be another disaster for us."

He was silent a moment and John put a question that had troubled him somewhat.

"But if she doesn't sail at that hour," he said; "if she is suddenly delayed or dispatched by another route, won't that arouse their suspicions?"

Dacent Smith looked at him for a moment, then smiled quietly.

"Oh," he said, "we shall not be quite so obvious as that, Treves, otherwise they would come to suspect a leakage. What will occur is this: I shall communicate with the Admiralty at once, and some time to-morrow morning an accident will happen—quite a small accident—to the *Imperator's* boilers. The news of the accident will be well spread throughout the crew and the deck hands. Thus the *Imperator* will be unavoidably delayed and will not sail at three o'clock to-morrow."

He rose as he finished speaking and went quickly out of the room. When he returned he was obviously much easier in his mind. With slow deliberation he replaced himself in his chair at the desk.

"Now give me details of your interview with Cherriton."

John stated what had occurred.

"Anything else to report?" asked Dacent Smith, looking at him with a penetrating glance. "I see you have a scratch on your forehead."

"Yes," answered John. "It occurred in Hampstead; a young man attacked me and endeavoured to get my pocket-book!"

"Oh, that is rather alarming!"

"It was rather sudden," John confessed, "and he was a particularly energetic person."

"Would you know him again if you saw him?" asked Dacent Smith.

"I think I should," answered John. "He was about my own height, but more slenderly built. Rather a good-looking fellow, well dressed. He was a most energetic and audacious opponent," he continued, becoming unexpectedly expansive.

"Audacity is sometimes a fault!" observed Dacent Smith. "Just sit where you are a minute, Treves; I want to introduce you to some one."

He crossed the room and opened the door. John noticed him beckon to some one, and a moment later a young man in evening clothes stepped into the room.

Dacent Smith led the new-comer towards the hearth.

"Captain," he said, speaking to the young man, "this is Mr. Treves, who is now a member of our service."

John rose to shake hands, and found himself looking into the smiling face of a young man of twenty-eight, a young man with dark brown, daring-looking eyes, a sun-browned skin, and a dark moustache. The stranger's face was humorous, and on the lower part of his left cheek was a contused redness.

As John and he shook hands, John uttered an exclamation of astonishment.

"Why, you're the man who attacked me!"

"Well, I don't know about that!" smiled the Captain, cheerily; "it looks to me as if the attacking was mostly on your side."

"I must say," John continued, "you put up quite a good fight, but I don't quite see the point. If you were acting on behalf of the Department, why did you attack me?"

He glanced at Dacent Smith, and the great man undertook an explanation. "The whole thing was a slight mistake. Your new acquaintance, known to us as Captain X., was under my orders, his avocation to-night. He saw Mrs. Beecher Monmouth shake hands with you. He also observed you—and he says, very neatly—put something in your inner breast pocket. He had never seen you before, but he naturally jumped to the conclusion that you were in league with this particular fashionable lady, whom he had been sent to watch, hence his mistaken attack on you."

John turned again to his late antagonist.

"I am sorry if I hurt you!" he said.

"You did hurt me abominably," retorted Captain X. "I am not much of a pugilist and that half-arm jolt, or whatever you call it, has my sincerest admiration."

"The luck was on my side," returned John politely.

"And the misdirected energy on mine," smiled the Captain.

Dacent Smith moved to the table, took up a sheet of paper, folded it, and handed it to Captain X.

"Now," said he, "we will return to business."

At nine o'clock the following evening John found himself in a lady's boudoir, a room heavy with the odour of Russian cigarettes. The neat, capped foreign maid who had ushered him into the apartment had removed herself, closing the door softly behind her.

The room was not large, and every effort of a somewhat exotic taste had been put forth to create an atmosphere of intimacy. It was a room, as it were, planned and arranged for secret meetings. The carpet was thick; a while polar bear rug extended itself from the hearth, and beyond the hearth, running along the wall, was a divan covered in heavy silk of Chinese blue. A Chinese *kakemono* of brilliant colours—red, orange, azure, green, and gold—covered the wall behind the divan. The general air of the place was one that did not appeal to John in the least. He did not care a button about exotic boudoirs. Neither did he care for Mrs. Beecher Monmouth, who to-night was wearing a Chinese overgown as brilliant and sumptuous in hue as the *kakemono* that covered the wall.

She had been seated on the divan when John entered. She rose now and came towards him, with the pink light softening the cold splendour of her beauty. There was no doubt about her beauty—John was prepared to admit that even at this second meeting.

"You bad boy to be so late!" breathed Mrs. Beecher Monmouth, squeezing his fingers in hers. She drew him towards her.

The moment was a delicate one for Manton. What Treves's relations had been with this woman he could not guess. But it was his business to find out. It was indeed his business to find out many things about her. For months the Intelligence Department had held her in suspicion, but Dacent Smith's most brilliant assistants had failed to make headway in her case. She was slippery as an eel—quick-witted, cunning, daring and resourceful. In that moment, as she drew John towards her, she suspected a ruse. But there was no ruse. She looked up, her brilliant eyes searching him.

"Have you nothing for me?" she whispered.

There was only one thing to do, only one safe course to take, and John took it. He, as it were, plunged, and risked the consequences. He put his arms about her shapely shoulders and pressed a kiss upon the upturned lips.

"No, no! I didn't tell you you could kiss me!"

"You said something very like it!" laughed John.

"You are a bad, daring boy."

"Faint heart never won anything worth having," returned John.

Mrs. Beecher Monmouth returned to her divan and disposed herself comfortably. "You bad Bernard, you must sit in that low chair at once, and tell me all you have been doing lately!"

She lifted a cigarette case from a low, ivory-topped table. John took one, noticing that they were the excellent cigarettes Treves had been in the habit of smoking.

"Tell me what you have been doing."

John mused, and the woman went on:

"Do you know, you looked rather handsome last night at the Savoy." She paused and became coyly and softly wistful. "I dislike handsome boys; they are so conceited as a rule."

"If I can keep her talking like this for a while," thought John, "I shall not get into deep water!"

There was a silence, during which the lady luxuriantly smoked her Russian cigarette. Then she looked at John with her slow, low-lidded smile.

"Talk," she commanded.

"I prefer to hear you talk," said John. "Tell me what you have been doing lately—to-day, for instance."

The lady pondered.

"Oh, to-day the Ogre gave a luncheon party."

John guessed that the Ogre was her unprepossessing husband.

"The Ogre gave a luncheon party, and among others we had Lady Rachel Marlin, a delightful chatterbox. Her husband's in the Navy, you know. I could listen to her talk for hours."

"I don't doubt it," thought John.

"After tea," resumed she, "I went to my Red Cross work."

John was wary. The fact that she did Red Cross work surprised him, but possibly Treves had been aware of the fact, and it would be unsafe for him to express his surprise.

There was silence for a moment until John hit on a safe question.

"Do you go to the same place?" he inquired.

"Oh, yes, the Officers' Hospital, you know. They are such dear, delightful fellows."

She told him no more about the Officers' Hospital, and he put another question.

"What have you done this evening?"

"I have been boring myself to death until you came. And now you make poor me talk and don't entertain me in the least!"

Suddenly she lifted her head.

"I hope you aren't in one of your moods?"

"Oh, no," said John, quickly. "What makes you think that?"

She looked at him long and steadily. He sustained her gaze; her brilliant, hard beauty smote his consciousness again.

"Do you remember how awful you were at first, Bernard?"

"I suppose I was pretty awful," answered John, wondering what Treves had done to earn himself that character.

Suddenly Mrs. Beecher Monmouth ceased her scrutiny and broke into a laugh, a long tinkle of laughter that showed all her fine teeth.

"What a boy you are," she said. "Do you remember that night when you swore and tore about this room like a madman?" She laughed again, as though in memory of a scene that had been grotesquely ridiculous. Somehow, in that moment John felt his instinctive dislike of her intensify. He saw her as an utterly cold-blooded traitor to her country. Only forty-eight hours earlier she had slipped into his hand information that had been intended to doom a great ship to disaster. The slip of paper that had so astoundingly come into his possession had in itself constituted a vile blow at the safety of England. And here was the woman who had safely engineered that atrocity, who had acted as an intermediary in Germany's pay. And this same woman was smiling at him in her Grosvenor Place boudoir, surrounded by all the luxuries of life, the wife of a politician of some eminence, who had only recently been in the running for an under-secretaryship.

The thought flashed into John's mind—was Beecher Monmouth, M.P., also a traitor? He did not know. But he was prepared to risk a good deal to find out.

Once more he turned his attention to the woman before him.

"It was rather weak of me," he said, "to act the way I did."

"It was as good as a melodrama," replied she. "You said you were ruined, and swore you'd end everything! I forget whether it was to be the river or in some less pleasant manner. Called yourself a traitor——"

"Traitor!" repeated John—he wanted to know more of this.

"Melodrama again," responded Mrs. Beecher Monmouth. "However, you calmed yourself in the end. You became your own delightful, foolish self again."

"Thanks," said John, and for the life of him he could not help saying aloud, "and you were able to twist me round your pretty fingers!"

She looked at him with one of her quick looks.

"Now, that is delightful of you to say pretty things to me. Do you know," she continued, leaning towards him, "you have improved immensely—you are quite changed! Before you really came to us," she adopted a note of seriousness, "you were really too dreadful for words. You raved against the army, that had treated you so abominably, and yet would not throw in your lot with us. Oh, you were very difficult, *mon ami!*"

"And now?" inquired John.

"Oh, now, you are quite another man."

"I'm glad you think that," said John aloud, and to himself he added, "my clever lady, you never spoke a truer word in your iniquitous life."

"The change in you is so marked," went on Mrs. Beecher Monmouth, "that Captain Cherriton actually doubted your loyalty to us. He regarded your escape from Scotland Yard authorities as so sudden."

"Ah," protested John, "but I was mistaken for another man."

"Of course, I know that, you silly boy! But Cherriton could not rest satisfied until he had discovered that there actually existed a person called John Manton, and that you had really been mistaken for this personage."

John made a mental note that in Cherriton he had an adversary of no mean order.

"I hope," said he, "now that Captain Cherriton has discovered my story to be true, he won't suspect me again."

"As for that," responded the lady, "he suspects his own shadow. But you are very high in favour just at the moment."

"His favour is worth having?" probed John.

"We shall discover that," said Mrs. Beecher Monmouth. Her tone suddenly became fervent, almost exalted. "After the war there will be great things for us all. Now is the time to sow; then will be the time to reap the harvest!"

The expression of her face had changed. A dark, fierce light seemed to illumine her features.

"We shall win yet! We are winning now, but the end will be swift!"

"The end of some people," thought John, "will be devilishly swift!" He was thinking of Manners, of Cherriton, and of the lady before him.

"What do you think will happen?" he inquired.

"They will come here, of course," she retorted, suddenly standing erect beside the divan and speaking with fiery and passionate intensity, "they will come here—my people!"

"Your people?" interjected John, quickly.

"My people," droned she, with a lift of her head. "You didn't know that before? But you are one of us, and I can trust you now."

"But everybody thinks you are an American," observed John, recalling what Dacent Smith had told him.

"Quite true—they do think that, and for convenience sake I am an American—a rich American who married"—she lifted a scornful lip and pointed towards the door—"who married the Ogre."

"Were you working for the—the cause when you married him?" inquired John.

But the sudden flame that had animated her appeared to die away; she became once more her beautiful exotic self.

"I have worked for the cause since— —" she stopped.

She, as it were, returned to earth.

"Bernard," she said, when she had smoked a few minutes in silence, "I have something to show you."

She rose, crossed the room, and unlocked a buhl cabinet. A moment later she returned to John, and handed him an envelope. Within was a closely written letter beginning: "Dearest Alice."

As John glanced at the writing Mrs. Beecher Monmouth came behind him, and laid her manicured finger-nail on the bottom four lines of the first sheet.

"That is all you need read," she said.

The four lines at which she pointed ran:

"If you think Treves has the courage for the task I will take your word for it—he shall be the man!"

CHAPTER X

John looked up quickly.

"Is this from Captain Cherriton?" he asked.

Mrs. Beecher Monmouth shook her head.

"From a far greater one than he," she answered slowly.

John pricked up his ears, then flashed a glance at the contents of the letter. But Mrs. Beecher Monmouth was very quick; he caught only the words, "secret session," and "ready by the twenty-eighth," when Mrs. Monmouth dexterously laid her white hand over the writing and drew it from his fingers. She folded it and placed it carefully in the bosom of her dress. She wore evening dress beneath her gorgeous Japanese rest gown, and John noticed the coquetry with which she concealed the letter from his view. He was young enough to be affected by her beauty, and was yet old enough to suspect she was playing a part—was, in fact, seeking to entangle him for the benefit of the cause. He put her down in that moment as a passionate, unscrupulous, dangerous woman, to whom adventure was the very breath of life. Moreover, he doubted her statement that she was German. She was certainly not his idea of a woman of Teutonic nationality.

Her arm that had been resting upon his shoulder still remained there. The lady's handsome face was very close to his; he could see deep into her smiling eyes, and was not comfortable under the closeness of her scrutiny. His resemblance to Bernard Treves was striking, but it was not perfect enough, he feared, to deceive the watchfulness of a woman who had evidently been closely intimate with that young man. He endeavoured to break the intensity of her gaze by leading her back to her chair.

"Well," she whispered tenderly, "have you nothing to say to me?"

"There are a thousand things I would like to say," returned John, promptly. "Let me light you a cigarette." He struck a match and placed one of her buff-coloured Russian cigarettes in her fingers. As he held the light, Mrs. Beecher Monmouth spoke on a new note of seriousness.

"Bernard, I have been kindness itself to you."

John assured her that she had.

"When the others doubted you I clung to my belief in you."

"You have been wonderful!" said John.

"You are changed, Bernard."

"That's impossible," answered John, "where you are concerned." He again experienced the sensation—a common one with him these days—that he walked upon the edge of a precipice.

"I have shown my confidence in you."

"You mean," proceeded John, "you have spoken up for me to the great personage who wrote the letter."

"Yes. Are you grateful?" inquired she, looking at him quizzically. She had disposed herself upon the divan in a graceful, languid poise.

"I am more than grateful," said John. "But, tell me, who is this great personage?"

The lady's laughter sounded musically in the little pink lighted room.

"Oh, my dear Bernard," she protested; "that comes much later."

"I suppose," John said, feeling that a bold plunge was worth while, "the personage is the head of the German secret agents in England?"

"What makes you think that?"

"My dear Alice, you would not stand in such awe of anyone less important than that." For some minutes—since the time he had caught sight of the letter, in fact—he had resolved to call her "Alice" at the earliest opportunity. He was playing a part. He had taken up another man's love affair at an unknown state of development—a dangerous thing to do. However, the duel between them, he believed, was to his advantage. Mrs. Beecher Monmouth had made a false step. She had already revealed to him the existence of a high secret power—a power far above and beyond Cherriton and Manwitz.

"Alice," he said, suddenly, drawing his chair a little nearer and laying a hand on her arm, "tell me who is the Great Unknown?"

"Patience, patience, Bernard. You will hear, all in good time." She lifted his hand from her arm and pushed him gently away. At the same moment there came a low knock at the door. A discreet pause followed before Mrs. Beecher Monmouth's foreign maid, in cap and white apron, entered.

"The master's returned, ma'am."

The girl spoke in a low tone, intended for her mistress's ear alone, and immediately went out, closing the door behind her.

"Sit over there," commanded Mrs. Beecher Monmouth, waving John towards a chair at the hearth. "Sit over there, and be very good."

John moved to the hearth. He wondered if Bernard Treves had known the Ogre, or if an introduction was to take place. The awkwardness of the situation was solved for him a moment later, when the door behind him opened. In a slender strip of mirror on the opposite wall John saw the reflected figure of Beecher Monmouth, M.P. The pink light softened a little the bilious yellow of his skin. But he was still an unprepossessing object, with his bald head, his long, pointed nose, and his thin-lipped mouth.

Mrs. Monmouth rose as her husband entered, and went towards him with hands outstretched.

"William, darling," she exclaimed, "how nice of you to come home so early. I must introduce you to Mr. Treves."

John rose and bowed. Beecher Monmouth put a large bony hand in his. He had just returned from the House of Commons, and looked weary and old; he looked every one of his sixty-four years. John wondered whether he ought to stay or not, but Mrs. Beecher Monmouth solved the situation by holding out her hand.

"You must come and see me again, Mr. Treves." Her tone was almost motherly. He shook hands with her, and saw her move towards her husband and slip her arm through his.

Husband and wife were standing together as the maid conducted John downstairs.

"What a monument of treachery and deceit she is," thought John, as he stepped out into the starlit night.

In the meantime Mrs. Beecher Monmouth had pressed her ungainly husband into a deep arm-chair, had commanded that whisky and soda should be brought, and was already holding the match that lit his cigar. Beecher Monmouth watched her with admiration in his tired eyes. He was prepared to sell his soul for her, and was never weary of telling her that he was the luckiest man in the world to have won her love.

"And what did my William do to-night?" she inquired, softly, when the whisky and soda had been placed at his side, and he had helped himself to a somewhat liberal dose.

"A most boring evening," said Beecher Monmouth. "Irish question!"

"And you saw no one interesting?" asked she.

"I saw Brackston Neeve in the lobby," answered her husband. "There is some talk of a military expedition to — —. I don't know whether it will come off or not. The Cabinet, I believe, discussed it yesterday."

"What did Brackston Neeve say?"

Beecher Monmouth took a sip of whisky.

"Why should I bore you with stupid politics?"

"They aren't stupid to me," she said. "You know every tiny bit of your political life interests me intensely." She settled herself in a low chair beside him. "Now you must tell me everything Brackston Neeve said. He is in the confidence of the Cabinet, is he not?"

Her husband nodded.

"He has the confidence of several members of the Cabinet."

"Tell me everything, William...."

Half an hour later, when Monmouth had finished his cigar and whisky, he rose wearily, kissed her, and went to his room. Mrs. Beecher Monmouth waited until he was safely out of the way, then, going to the telephone on the buhl writing-desk, rang up a number.

"Is that Doctor Voules?" she inquired.

At the other end of the telephone a deep voice answered in the affirmative.

"May I call upon you at eleven o'clock to-morrow?" inquired Mrs. Monmouth.

"Is it important?" asked the voice.

Mrs. Beecher Monmouth, in the solitude of her room, smiled slightly.

"I shall leave you to judge of that," she replied.

"Very good," answered the voice. "I shall expect you at eleven precisely."

On the following morning Mrs. Beecher Monmouth, quietly, but expensively, dressed, presented herself at the hotel bureau.

Three minutes later the lift door closed upon her and she was wafted swiftly upward to the third floor. A page boy conducted her along a corridor, opened a door, and departed.

The apartment into which she had been shown overlooked the Haymarket. Decorations of white and gold caught Mrs. Monmouth's vision. Seated at a desk from whence he could look down upon the busy life of the street below was a broad-shouldered, elderly man, who laid down his pen as his visitor entered.

Mrs. Beecher Monmouth hurried towards him.

"It is so good of you to see me, doctor," she exclaimed, effusively.

"Oh, not at all. I am charmed to see you," he answered. He moved a little farther into the room, so that prying eyes from the building opposite could not observe him; then, with an air of great gallantry, he bent over Mrs. Beecher Monmouth's hand and laid his lips upon it.

"You will sit down and tell me your news," said the doctor.

Mrs. Monmouth accepted the offered chair.

Doctor "Voules" was of middle height, sturdily, but not heavily, built. He carried himself well, holding his head high and looking squarely and masterfully before him. His head was round, his strong, heavy-jawed face was clean shaven, and his wide mouth drooped at the corners. Both physically and intellectually the doctor was a formidable figure, but the harshness of his countenance was belied by a surface air of politeness—a politeness which appeared to be assumed, and which sat ill upon him. His air, despite his efforts of concealment, was one of lofty authority.

"You will tell me your important news," he said quietly.

"I don't know that it is important," admitted Mrs. Monmouth, "but my husband heard accidentally in the House of Commons last night that there is talk of an expedition to — —."

Voules's eyebrows moved very slightly.

"I shall be grateful to know everything your husband heard."

Then Mrs. Beecher Monmouth told him exactly, word for word, all she had managed to worm from her husband.

"He considers, then," inquired Voules, "that the expedition is to become an accomplished fact?"

Mrs. Beecher Monmouth nodded.

"Did your husband learn anything else in regard to this most interesting little adventure?"

Mrs. Monmouth shook her head.

"Ah," exclaimed Voules, "it would be most useful to us if you could learn the name of the officer who is in command of the expedition. You will keep that in mind?"

Mrs. Beecher Monmouth assured him upon that point.

"Now, in regard to your protégé, Mr. Treves," observed the doctor. "This young man, I understand, is very well connected, and is the son of Colonel Treves?"

Mrs. Monmouth nodded.

"My information is that his disappearance from the British Army was somewhat rapid, and that fact, together with his propensity for drugs, gradually brought him into our service. I should like to see him," went on the doctor, "to judge for myself; but in the meantime I can make much use of him. I shall take you at your word and give him important duties to perform."

"Thank you," observed Mrs. Monmouth. "That is extremely kind of you, doctor."

Voules, who had seated himself, rose now and held out his hand.

"My compliments to you upon your excellent work."

Two minutes later, with much politeness, he accompanied her out of the room, along the corridor, and saw her into the lift.

When he returned to his own room, he opened the door of an inner apartment and summoned a thin young man, wearing tortoise-shell-rimmed spectacles. The young man was clean shaven and was possessed of a somewhat small and receding chin, which gave him a foolish aspect. He was not foolish in the least, however; he was, on the contrary, extremely fox-like and alert. The doctor's politeness vanished as he confronted the young man.

"Baumer," he commanded, "come into the other room, please." He crossed to his desk near the window overlooking the street, and seated himself. The young man entered and stood at his side, awaiting instructions. "You will make a note," said the doctor, "that a Mr. Bernard Treves is to come to my house to-day week."

"Very good, Excellenz," answered the young man deferentially. He began to write a note in pencil on a small writing block he had produced.

"You will also," went on the doctor, "inform Hauptman Rathenau that I wish to see Mr. Treves's dossier again."

"Yes, Excellenz; but if I might be permitted to suggest so much, Lieutenant Treves, whose family is well known, would be a safer person to use for purposes of association with the officers at Fort Heatherpoint."

"But our excellent Cherriton was educated at Oxford," said the elder man. "He is to all outward seeming an Englishman."

"Nevertheless, Excellenz," Baumer insisted, "I feel we should be safer to employ an Englishman. There is much freemasonry among the English, and there is always danger, Excellenz, that some one who knew the real Captain Cherriton may meet Herr Rathenau."

"But Heatherpoint," said Voules, "is one of our key positions. You forget that, Baumer."

"No, Excellenz, I remember it perfectly."

His superior was silent for a moment, then said, quietly, "I have decided that Cherriton shall do this work; he has greater experience. This time our movements must be all perfect. Our staff work here, Baumer, must be even superior to the staff work in France. We must in no degree underrate our enemies." He was silent a moment, pondering the great scheme that had grown in his brain months earlier—the scheme that was to strike a blow at the very heart of England. His orders were to restore new confidence throughout Germany in the failing U-boat campaign. Minutely, piece by piece, he had worked out his daring and masterful plan. The success of his country in discovering the sailing of British ships; the strength and equipment of our distant expeditions; the amount of munitions and arms being manufactured—these things were in the daily routine of espionage. But General von Kuhne was no believer in defensive operations. He, like his friend Bernhardi, was a disciple of Clausewitz—a believer in offensive warfare. To strike, to strike hard and unerringly, after minute preparation, was his ideal of strategy. Already, for many weeks, he had been placing his pawns ready for the great coup. Cunningly and with infinite patience he had prepared for the great blow that was intended to send a shudder through the British Isles.

CHAPTER XI

The little clock on Dacent Smith's mantelshelf chimed the hour of seven.

"I am as empty as a drum," exclaimed Captain X. His slender figure occupied one of the Chief's deep armchairs. He was smoking one of Smith's cigarettes, and his handsome face and audacious-looking eyes were upturned as he watched the smoke ascend. "How long have we been here, Treves?" he inquired.

"Three hours," answered John. He too occupied one of Dacent Smith's deep chairs and smoked his Chief's cigarettes.

"What about asking old Grew if he knows anything," continued Captain X— —. He leaned over and pressed his thumb upon the electric bell push. Almost immediately, and quite noiselessly, the door opened and Dacent Smith's big-boned manservant came into the room.

"Look here, Grew," said the Captain, twisting his head to get a view of the tall servant. "When do you think the War Council will break up?"

"I couldn't say, sir," answered Grew, looking at him with a wooden expression.

"You mean if you could, you wouldn't," returned the Captain. "But I would like to tell you, Grew, that both of us are most devilish hungry. Can you tell us anything about food?"

"I have orders to serve dinner at 7.30," answered Grew.

For three hours John and his companion, acting upon orders, had been waiting in Dacent Smith's room. The Chief had been called suddenly to a meeting of the War Council, and had not returned.

"I expect there are big things afoot," observed John, glancing at the other.

"It's a bit unusual," answered the Captain, "for him to stay so long. Perhaps he has ferreted out something new, and is communicating what he knows to the mighty ones."

He suddenly turned and looked close at John.

"How do you like our sort of work, Treves?"

"There is nothing to beat it," John answered. "My only trouble is that I am apt to lose my temper. Somehow I cannot stomach spies, but traitors always make me see red."

The Captain looked at him with smiling eyes.

"Mrs. Beecher Monmouth. The Chief would never trust me there. She is too beautiful by far, eh, Treves?"

John agreed that Mrs. Monmouth's beauty was undeniable.

"In my opinion," went on John's companion, "the Department ought to put her out of harm's way. But the Chief knows better. He has ordered supervision of all the letters she posts, and she posts a good many."

The door opened at that moment and Dacent Smith himself came hurriedly in. He apologised politely for his absence. The fact that he was head of a great department, that he was indeed a great man, never weighed with him in regard to his subordinates. Socially he treated them all as his equals; only in matters of discipline was he superior. He laughed as he looked at his depleted cigarette-box, and then seated himself at his desk.

With a brisk movement he switched on the light.

"I have had three hours of the War Council," he said, speaking to both Treves and the Captain. "Now, Treves, what is the news?"

John told him that Mrs. Beecher Monmouth was in communication with a person whose name was unknown to him; this person was evidently of great importance to the German secret service, and was considering the employment of John in a great undertaking.

"Who is the great unknown?" inquired Dacent Smith.

"I don't know, sir," John admitted.

The elder man tightened his lips.

"Mrs. Beecher Monmouth's acquaintances are becoming increasingly interesting to us, eh, Treves?"

"I believe so, sir," said John.

"We have been a little late in supervising her letters," said Dacent Smith, looking across at Captain X. "However," he said suddenly, turning the conversation, "that is a matter outside Treves's duties. I have other and more important work for both of you. This afternoon," he went on, "I have submitted a number of reports to the War Council, showing that certain of our defences are in a sensitive condition. Something is occurring, and news is leaking out at a serious rate." He was speaking particularly to John. But it was evident that he wished Captain X. to listen to the conversation.

"There is a leakage of news from certain fortified zones on the South Coast. In the case of some of the lesser forts it matters not a brass farthing what the enemy discovers, but at other places—well," he continued, "it has been decided this afternoon that a department is to direct its special attention to the South Coast. Both of you gentlemen will resume uniform almost at once. You will like that, eh, Treves?"

"Very much indeed, sir."

"The War Council," went on Dacent Smith, "was inclined to treat my fears a little lightly, but I am sure I am right. There are secret operations preparing against us on the South Coast, which are of a greater magnitude than anything that has yet been attempted by German espionage. I want you"—he suddenly rose and took John's hand in his—"I want you, Treves, to put everything into this—all your shrewdness and all your tact. You will need every quality of nerve and mind in the work I am going to entrust to you. And believe me," he said, lowering his voice a little, "matters are very serious indeed. We are out against a secret enemy, who has of late increased his power amazingly. There is some one—a new power—directing German espionage in this country, which is a real menace to us. Up to now we have done very well, but at present, I will quite frankly admit to you, our position is delicate in the extreme. I dislike preaching," he concluded in a lighter tone, "but I think you know what I mean."

John, who had gripped his hand cordially, answered simply, "Yes, sir; I think I appreciate the danger."

The clock on the little mantelshelf chimed the half-hour. Grew knocked at the door.

"Dinner's ready," exclaimed Dacent Smith. "Come this way, and I'll show you how a miserable old bachelor lives."

CHAPTER XII

On the Saturday following John's first experience of his Chief's excellent bachelor cuisine, two men sat in a little, barely furnished room, four hundred feet above the sea. There was no view from the single window of the little apartment, the one-story building of which it formed a part was deeply embedded and concealed between high grass-covered mounds. Both men were beyond middle age, one of them, in fact, wearing the gold stripes of a naval commander, was over sixty years of age, a trim-bearded, well-preserved officer, drawn for war service from the reserve.

Lieutenant-Commander Grieves was chief naval officer attached to the fort. His companion, Colonel Hobin, was ten years his junior—a sharp, nervous, over-strung little man. Hobin held the reputation of a first-class officer; he knew every yard of Heatherpoint Fort, which was his present charge. His big guns were as children to him, and in regard to his subordinates he was a strict disciplinarian, with a reputation for fairness both to officers and to men.

At the present moment he was consuming marmalade, which he took from its jar with a dessert-spoon and spread on thick bread and butter. There were none of the refinements of home in the mess-room at Heatherpoint. A tablecloth existed, and a limited number of knives, forks, and spoons. The chef of the fort was a gloomy looking individual who had joined up at Liverpool and plain and good was his motto.

"I don't like it," exclaimed Hobin, suddenly. He was pouring the Commander another cup of black-looking tea. "I don't like the look of things at all."

"Nor do I," said the Commander, "but the responsibility is yours, and I think you did well to communicate with the powers that be."

"The powers that be will do nothing," complained Colonel Hobin; "they never do."

"If things are wrong at all," said the old naval lieutenant, "somebody in the fort's wrong, for I'll bet my hat nobody can get in and out without us knowing it."

"That's what is really troubling me," said the Colonel, the frown deepening on his brow. "It's damnable, Grieves, to think that we are being outwitted. I have turned every man in the fort inside out, and they all seem to me honest as the day."

"Wasn't one of the men in the lower fort reported to have a foreign accent?"

"He was," answered the Colonel, with a bitter laugh, "and I had him up and put him through a third degree examination, with the result that his accent turned out to be nothing more dangerous than an Irish brogue. He's as loyal as I am, and when I mentioned the fact of the signal book I believe if I hadn't been in uniform he would have hit me."

"If we were one of those tin-pot forts over there," returned the Lieutenant-Commander, jerking his thumb contemptuously in a certain direction, "I wouldn't mind, but we really count in the defences."

"We are the heart of this system of defence," returned Hobin tartly, "and yet we go and lose a signal book. If it was only that," he went on, "I might have thought there was carelessness in it, but there are other things, queer things, Grieves, that I cannot formulate into words even to you. I put it all before the authorities. Whiston listened as politely as he always does, and said he'd speak to the Intelligence Department about it, but nothing will be done."

"They'll have to do something."

"They won't," said Hobin. Colonel Hobin was constitutionally inclined to pessimism, despite his ability. "They won't," he said. And at that moment the door opened, and a young lieutenant, who had that day joined the battery, entered the room.

"Good evening, sir," said the young man to Colonel Hobin.

Hobin nodded grumpily. The young man drew out a chair, seated himself, and reached for the bread and butter. Hobin, from the head of the table, handled the teapot.

"Weak or strong?" he demanded of the new-comer.

"Weak," answered John Manton, who had been at Heatherpoint a matter of four hours, and was taking his first meal in the fort.

The Lieutenant-Commander pushed the marmalade pot towards him, and John began to spread it upon his bread and butter, not quite so thickly as his Colonel had spread it a minute or two before.

Everything was in order in regard to John's presence at Heatherpoint. Dacent Smith had arranged the whole matter, and for the first time in his life John Manton, who had once before been on the way to an officer's uniform, found himself of commissioned rank.

And for once, Colonel Hobin was mistaken in thinking that the War Office and Intelligence Department had left him entirely neglected.

"Well, how do you like Heatherpoint, Mr. Treves?" inquired the old Lieutenant-Commander genially.

"So far as I have got," answered John, "I am delighted with the chance to be here." He spoke truthfully.

"When you've had six months of it, and been through the winter," said the Colonel grimly, "with your wind-gauge showing seventy miles an hour for weeks on end, and the lighthouse siren never stopping booming, I am afraid you won't be in quite the same cheerful mood."

"I am cheerful by nature, sir," said the young man, tucking into the marmalade. He ate heartily, and by the time he had finished the Colonel was smoking a cigar.

Lieutenant-Commander Grieves filled his pipe, lit it, and, with a nod at the Colonel, sauntered out to his quarters. For the first time John was alone with Hobin. For some minutes there was silence, then the Colonel spoke.

"You will take the leave book to-night, Treves. Ask Parkson about it."

"Very good, sir," John answered.

"You can go now, if you like," said the Colonel. "Get Parkson to show you the run of the place before parade in the morning."

At this point John rose mysteriously, opened the door into the corridor and looked out. Then, to the Colonel's surprise, he closed it again, and came quietly back into the room. From the inner pocket of his coat he took a long, narrow, yellow envelope, which he handed to Hobin.

"What's this?" demanded the Colonel. He tore open the envelope and began to read with furrowed brows.

When Colonel Hobin had perused the official-looking letter a second and a third time, his brow cleared; he lifted his eyes and looked at John with a new and keen interest.

"So you are from the Intelligence Department?"

"Yes, sir."

"I had no idea of that."

"My transfer was effected as quietly as possible, sir, with a view to arousing no suspicion. The letter is merely my credentials from General Whiston."

The Colonel nodded.

"Judging from this," said the Colonel, "General Whiston has an extremely high opinion of your gifts."

John tried to look as modest as possible.

"I am a great believer in luck, sir," he said, "and up to now I have had plenty of it." He was thinking of the saving of the *Imperator*, which had brought him so many laurels from Dacent Smith.

"I hope you'll bring luck to me," said the Colonel. "I can promise you I need it." He was delighted that the powers that be had really sent help, despite his disbelief in them. His eyes were still upon John. He liked the young man's frank expression, his cheerful and easy manners and the bold poise of his head.

"A good-looking, heftily-built youngster," thought he. "I only hope he is as shrewd as he looks active."

"Now, I suppose," he said aloud, "you want me to tell you all the trouble?"

"I should like to hear of anything, sir, that has aroused your suspicions," said John.

"That's a tall order," answered Hobin. "Everything has aroused my suspicions, and yet, if I put it into words, it may look like nothing to you. Have you ever had the sensation, Treves," he said, "that things were going wrong around you, and yet you could not lay your finger on a thing that is definitely wrong?"

"I have felt that way sometimes," admitted John.

"That's the way I feel now," returned the Colonel. Then, quite briefly, he gave John particulars of the loss of a signal book, which, however, might have been due to carelessness. Other things he told John were also mere surmises and sensations. "I must explain," he said, "that this fort, and Scoles Head opposite, are key positions in our South Coast defences. If we were incapacitated, the enemy would sneak in to — — and wreak the devil knows what damage. Given a big enough concentration of submarines, he could probably get fifty to a hundred ships — —"

"It's hardly likely," John answered, "that he will ever be able to sneak in."

Hobin was silent for a minute, looking John over carefully.

"Would it surprise you to hear that we have already been incapacitated?" demanded the Colonel suddenly.

He thrust out his chin truculently as though challenging John to doubt him.

"How was that, sir?"

"For an hour one morning last week the whole eastern side of Upper Fort was out of action. I've been a gunner for thirty years, Treves, and until now such a thing has never occurred in my experience."

"Could it have been an accident, sir?"

"In normal times," answered the Colonel, impressively, "I would have said yes; now I say, no! Three of the guns, numbers one, six and eight, in this battery"—he jerked his head towards the south—"went wrong suddenly. A cleaning squad was at work on number one, and discovered that the gun could not be handled at all. It was just after daylight in the morning. You know how perfectly these six- and nine-inch guns are swung?"

John nodded.

"A child can swing them like a toy cannon. My own boy's often done it," went on the Colonel. "Well, on this particular morning the guns would not elevate. Just lay inert, like dead masses of metal. Everything was in order, both in the gun-chamber and engine house. But the guns wouldn't budge, and for an hour this whole upper fort was out of action. If the enemy had tried to rush us at that time, we could have done nothing! I was not quite so jumpy as now. Not quite so many things had happened to arouse my suspicions, and I blamed Ewins."

"Who is Ewins, sir?"

"Our chief gunner."

"Did Ewins discover what was wrong?" John asked.

"Neither Ewins nor any of us," answered the Colonel. "What happened is a mystery to us all. Ewins was in bed when the thing occurred, and, knowing how jealous he is of his gun, one of the cleaning squad called him. He came out of his hut half dressed. I hear from Parkson that he was in a blind rage, and felt his gun all over, as a mother may feel for a bruise on her baby; but he could make nothing of it."

"I'd rather like to see Ewins," said John, "if it can be managed."

"He is on duty now," responded the Colonel. "Come along and make his acquaintance. But, for Heaven's sake, don't run away with any idea that

Ewins is a wrong 'un. Ewins is the best gunner on the South Coast, one of the old rule of thumb school. He knows nothing of trajectories or curves, and hardly ever looks at the wind gauge. But he has made ninety-eight per cent. at a submarine target doing nine knots."

"What was the range, sir?"

The Colonel told him, and John opened his eyes in surprise.

"Come along," said Hobin.

Together they left the mess-room, crossed a narrow, asphalted pavement, ascended a short ladder and came upon a gorgeous view of the ocean and the blue waters of the Solent. Beyond, to the right, lay England, an irregular coast-line, with swelling hills, green in the foreground and blue in the distance. In the middle of the picture, to the right, rose the tall tower of Ponsonby Lighthouse. The tower gleamed white in the bright sunshine. Colonel Hobin led the way along the edge of a grass-covered cliff, and presently, below him, John observed the long muzzle of a six-inch gun camouflaged scarlet, blue and green.

"That's Ewins's special gun," explained the Colonel. "You'll see he has the place of honour."

The green cliff-top sloped stiffly here, and beneath him John could see the big, circular iron gun platform, and below it the ladder leading into the gun chamber. On a parapet beyond the gun, and on the very edge of the cliff, a sentry paced back and forth, his outline picked out sharply against the blue of the sea that murmured faintly four hundred feet below. At the open breach of the gun itself another soldier was at work, a man who was long and thin, and a little grey at the temples. He was delicately wiping certain shining parts of the weapon with an oiled rag. As the Colonel's feet, followed by John, smote the iron platform, the soldier drew himself erect and stood at attention.

"This is Ewins," said the Colonel to John. John greeted Ewins with a friendly smile. Until that moment he had doubted him. Only a few days earlier he had met one traitor in Mrs. Beecher Monmouth, and as he and the Colonel approached the gun platform he had been wondering if in Ewins he was to meet a second.

Ewins was thin-faced, with a weather-reddened skin and clear, brown eyes. He was a man in the late forties, a typical old soldier. John, looking at him, wondered if it was possible that he could have been corrupted, but somehow he found it difficult to suspect the man.

Colonel Hobin made an excuse and left the two together.

"You are in a grand position here, Ewins," said John.

"Fine, sir," answered the soldier. His accent was British through and through. John gave him permission to carry on, and Ewins closed his breech with a heavy click.

"The Colonel has been speaking very highly of your gunnery."

Ewins looked up quickly, with an expression of pleasure in his eyes.

"Has he, sir?" He paused a moment and hesitated. "It makes a great difference being under him, sir; he sort of brings it out, if you know what I mean; puts you on your mettle."

John made a mental note of his admiration for the Colonel.

"I heard about your trouble last week, Ewins."

"You mean Tuesday morning, sir?"

"Yes," John answered. "What was the trouble after all?"

Ewins looked perplexed.

"It beats me fairly, sir. There was nothing wrong when they called me — that is, there was nothing wrong after I'd been here a minute or two. You know how she works, sir." As he spoke he almost with a finger raised the great muzzle of his weapon, then made a neat sweep to right and left. "Well, she just lay here like a dead thing."

"I suppose the explanation would be simple enough if we only knew it," answered John.

Ewins shook his head.

"I don't like it, sir. I was pretty wild that morning, thinking some of these young recruits had been messing about, but the same thing had happened to number six and eight." He pointed to a lower platform, beyond where the sentry was passing. "They went wrong that same morning," he continued.

"And got right again in the same mysterious way?" inquired John.

"Yes, sir."

"You don't think any of your cleaning squad had a hand in it?" inquired John.

"No, sir; I talked pretty straight to them, but it wasn't them."

"Perhaps you have an enemy in the fort, Ewins?"

The old soldier smiled.

"I don't know about that, sir," he said; "but everybody seems pretty friendly with me. I have been here a long time, sir."

"So I hear," said John.

"I don't think anybody in the fort, sir," Ewins went on, "would do a dirty trick on me like that. You see, sir," he said, in a voice of intense seriousness, "it put us out of Action."

John was silent for a moment. For the first time the full gravity of what had happened struck his consciousness.

"I'll swear it wasn't an accident," continued Ewins, emphatically. "Old 'Crumbs' said it was; but he don't know anything about guns."

"Who's 'Crumbs'?"

"I beg pardon, sir; I meant Private Sims, the baker."

"He said it was an accident?" pursued John.

"Yes, sir. I lost my temper that morning, and when I come here and found how things were, I gave one of the squad a bit of a push."

"Was 'Crumbs' one of the squad?"

"Oh, no, sir; he come in to bring me a lump of cake." Ewins looked sheepish a moment. "You see, sir, I am partial to cake, and he generally hands me a bit at odd times. He was in the gun chamber when I got here, sir, looking for me, with a bit of cake in his hand."

"But it was five o'clock in the morning!"

"It was new cake," said Ewins; "he'd just baked it."

"But you weren't supposed to be on duty."

"No, sir," answered Ewins.

"Wouldn't 'Crumbs'—Private Sims—know you were off duty?" probed John.

Ewins smiled again.

"He don't know much about soldiering, sir; they never do."

John had further talk with the chief gunner, which talk grew more and more technical as Ewins noticed John's interest in his work. But after a good many questions it still seemed to John that "Crumbs" walking about with cake at five o'clock in the morning showed an excessive benevolence. He felt he wanted to make the acquaintance of "Crumbs." And before going back to the Colonel in the mess-room, he looked in at the bake-house, a single-storied building next to the kitchen.

"Crumbs" was in a white apron and a white cap when John entered and found him at work. The bake-house was dark, the air warm and fragrant with a scent of freshly-baked loaves. "Crumbs," with flour on his eyelashes, and a heavy, drooping moustache, also powdered with flour, turned as John entered. In his hands he held a big iron tray of newly-baked loaves. John introduced himself. He felt that every step he made must be made with infinite caution.

"You've got a fine bakehouse here, Sims."

"Yes, sir; not so bad."

"I hear you are a master hand at cake making."

"Well, not exactly," deprecated "Crumbs." "I can hardly say that." He placed his tray of bread on the table.

"Sergeant Ewins tells me he's very fond of cake," went on John.

"Crumbs's" eyes moved quickly. The momentary, fleeting glance he cast at John was unobserved.

"The sergeant has a sweet tooth, sir."

"So have I," answered John, with a smile. "Perhaps you will make a note of that, Sims."

Sims smiled. John noticed that his complexion was sallow, that he was a loosely built, shambling man of forty. There was nothing in the least suspicious about him. No trace, so far as John could gather, of a foreign accent. He went out of the bakehouse in a dissatisfied frame of mind.

The mystery of the guns was still a mystery.

* * * * *

Next morning, at parade, John ran his eye along the men of the battery until it rested upon "Crumbs." The man, with his sallow complexion and glassy eyes, struck him as looking vacant and somewhat foolish.

"You are either that, my friend," thought John, "or most devilish cunning. I wonder which it is?"

He made it his business during that day, and the days which followed, to acquaint himself with every member of the battery. Nothing, however, occurred to arouse his suspicion or to give him the slightest clue to the untoward things that had happened. He wrote a letter to Dacent Smith reporting matters, and on the afternoon of the third day he decided to go into Newport for an afternoon's recreation. Colonel Hobin granted him leave instantly—and then John changed his mind, and decided not to go. He had no reason for staying in the fort, other than that he wanted to be on the spot as much as possible. He took a book from the badly-equipped fort library, and went to his room. Here he flung himself on the bed, and read for an hour or two. Save for the never-ending moan of the wind and the grind of the wind-gauge, the fort buildings were very quiet. Colonel Hobin, Parkson, and another officer were on duty, a subaltern was on leave, and in the four bedrooms that ran along the corridor John was the only occupant. He was lying, deeply absorbed in his book, when something made him turn his gaze towards the door. To his amazement, he saw the latch lift without noise. A moment later the door moved cautiously open, and "Crumbs," in white cap and apron, came softly in. For a minute the intruder did not see John.

"Well, Sims, what is it?"

"Crumbs's" mouth clicked shut. The start he had received caused his head to jerk.

"What do you want, Sims?"

"Crumbs" smiled under his black, flour-speckled moustache.

"It was the cake, sir," he said. "You told me you were fond of cake, sir, and I just put a cake in the mess-room for you."

John rose from the bed.

"Is there nothing else you want?"

"No, sir, thank you," answered "Crumbs," moving towards the door. John noticed, as he went, that his nose had been flattened at the bridge, as though at some time or other a heavy blow had fallen upon it.

"I only wondered," John went on, "why you came into my room."

"Merely to tell you about the cake, sir."

He went out, closing the door quietly behind him. When the door was shut between himself and John, he drew himself suddenly erect, and listened for a moment, then moved quickly away down the passage.

CHAPTER XIII

"'Crumbs' is the man," thought John the moment he opened his eyes next morning. During the night he had been awake for hours pondering the situation, and this was the decision he had arrived at. He decided, however, to say nothing of his suspicions to Hobin or to anyone else until "Crumbs" had further committed himself. Possibly, after all, he was mistaken; only time could tell. The first thing he did, however, when breakfast was at an end, was to write a note to Dacent Smith, asking that Private Sims's history might be discreetly inquired into.

"I think Private Sims is not quite what he seems," said John, concluding his letter. Nevertheless, if "Crumbs" was the suspicious character John believed him to be, he possessed an extraordinary talent for hiding his guilt.

John had pursued his investigations with such closeness during the past days, he now felt that the time had come when he might reasonably seek a certain amount of relaxation.

Therefore the morning of the tenth day saw him briskly descending the long steps cut in the face of the cliff to the lower fort. Here, immediately beyond the fort gates, a hired car awaited him. Manton stepped into the car after answering the challenge of the sentry, and drove down the long, winding road. A second sentry challenged him at the foot of the fort road, and thereafter the car bowled merrily along until it reached the gates of Colonel Treves's house at Freshwater.

John was wondering what he should say to the old gentleman. During the past weeks nothing had created a deeper impression on his mind than the pathetic figure of Bernard Treves's father. The old man, the soul of honour, cursed with a worthless son, appealed intensely to the sympathetic side of John's nature. John had learnt something of Bernard Treves's recent life from Dacent Smith. Following the discovery that the young man had been associated with Manwitz and Cherriton, he had been kept in a nursing home in strict confinement. An attempt had been made to cure him of his drug habit, with the result that he had suffered an utter physical collapse, and now was lying seriously ill. John, in discussing the matter with Dacent

Smith, had mentioned the old Colonel, and the deception that had been practised upon him.

"When the time comes," the Chief had answered, "you can either reveal your real identity to Colonel Treves, or not, as you wish. In any case, I rather doubt if his amiable son will appear on the scene again; that is a matter entirely for the military authorities. From what I hear," Dacent Smith continued, "the old Colonel hasn't much of this life before him, and if he learnt the truth about his son I know exactly what would happen. He would not be able to face it. Either death would mercifully carry him off, or——" John nodded, "or," he thought, "he would seek the death he once offered me." John saw now that the deception that had been practised upon the Colonel at the instigation of his friend, General Whiston, and Dacent Smith, was possibly the kindest thing that could have happened.

At the door of the house, Gates, the elderly butler, appeared in answer to John's ring. For a moment the servant paused wide-eyed, staring at the erect figure in uniform on the threshold.

"Why, Master Bernard!" he exclaimed, "I didn't recognise you for a minute. Come in, sir; I'll get your luggage."

"There isn't any luggage. Is—is my father in the library?"

"Yes, sir."

"How is he, Gates?"

"Just the same as usual, sir." Then the old servant forgot himself for a brief moment. "He'll be beside himself with delight, sir," he said, "to see you like that, back again in the Army, an' all."

John moved to cross the wide hall, but Gates followed him instantly.

"Perhaps I'd better break the news to him, sir; it's a little sudden like."

John followed him, and when the elderly butler knocked at the baize-covered door of the library a minute later, he heard Colonel Treves's voice from within. Gates went into the room and closed the door behind him. The old Colonel was seated in his deep chair near the hearth.

"I beg your pardon, sir," said Gates, crossing and standing before him, "but Mr. Bernard has returned."

Colonel Treves, who held a book on his knee, laid down his big reading glass on its open page, and lifted his head slowly. There was a stern light in his old faded eyes.

"I won't see my son, Gates!"

"Pardon me, sir," protested the old servant, "I think you would like to see him."

Colonel Treves rose to his feet, felt for his stick, and began to move feebly across the room.

"He is no son of mine, Gates," he said, as he went. "You can tell him that. A liar and a humbug," he said. "Always a liar and a humbug. No soul of truth in him, no honour——"

But Gates, the faithful servant of thirty years, knew his master well. He made no attempt to argue with the Colonel, but moved quietly to the door behind which John was waiting, and whispered, "Come in, Mr. Bernard."

John entered, and crossing the soft carpet laid his hand on the old Colonel's shoulder. The Colonel turned quickly, flinging up his head in indignation, then something took place on his face that touched John to the heart. The old firm lips quivered a moment.

"Is that you, Bernard?" he asked. He came nearer, peering at John, looking at the upright, uniformed figure. "I can't believe it," he added.

"It is true, sir," said John. "I received a commission a month ago."

"Take my arm, boy," said the Colonel, suddenly; "lead me back to the chair."

John led him across to his deep chair, and Gates softly went out of the room. When the Colonel was seated, he fumbled for his strong glasses, and put them on with fingers that shook visibly. Once again he looked John over from head to foot.

"It's the good blood that tells," he said after a long pause. Suddenly he broke into a laugh. "Do you know, Bernard, boy," he said, "a minute ago I was telling Gates you were no son of mine. You see, I thought you had broken your promise; you broke it so often before."

"That may be, sir," answered John quietly, "but this time I managed to keep it."

He permitted John to help him into his chair at the hearthside, and John, at his bidding, rang the bell.

"Gates," said the Colonel, when the old servant entered, "serve tea up here; I and my boy will have it together."

"Very good, sir."

"Now, Bernard, boy, tell me your news!" demanded the old soldier, when Gates had left the room.

John gave a sketchy, vague account of his doings during the past weeks.

"And so you are with Colonel Hobin. You must give him my kind remembrances; we met thirty years ago, when he was a subaltern at Aldershot. He had the making of a good soldier, I remember." He talked on, on general matters, and all the while John felt that his mind was solely occupied with his pride and satisfaction at seeing his son in uniform once again. In his excitement and pleasure he forgot two letters that had reposed on his desk for two days, waiting for John. Finally, he remembered them. "I must give you your letters, Bernard."

"Thank you, sir," answered John, "I'll get them myself, if you tell me where they are?"

He found the letters on the Colonel's desk, and excused himself for reading them. The first letter began: "Dear Bernard," and the first sentence ran: "You bad, bad boy." John knew in a moment that it was from Mrs. Beecher Monmouth, and skimmed the four closely written pages casually.

"*Have you seen the Great One yet? ... The Ogre is always in the House of Commons now ... I am utterly alone ... I wonder if any fine, handsome young man is thinking of sending me a hundred Russian cigarettes, the same as the last.... Next time you come, you must not be nearly so bold....* —Yours, ALICE."

"A very satisfactory letter," thought John, "if I had happened to care two straws about her." A vision of Mrs. Beecher Monmouth's brilliant beauty came before his eyes. It seemed strange to think that this woman, in the heart of London society, was a traitor, using her gifts of fortune and beauty for the nefarious purpose of ruining her own country, but such was indeed the case. What had been the original cause of Mrs. Beecher Monmouth's treachery, John did not know; only afterwards was the full truth made plain to him.

He opened the second letter, which was in a handwriting unknown to him. The note was from Captain Cherriton, to whom he had given this address when he left London.

"DEAR TREVES," ran the letter—"*Will you please call at Rollo Meads one day next week, Tuesday for preference, at five in the afternoon? I shall be there, and you will meet a new friend, Doctor Voules, who will supply you with what you want.*" (He was referring to the tabloids Manwitz had been in the habit of supplying to Treves.) "** Our old friend,**" went on the letter, "*who formerly* *supplied you, you will regret to hear, was taken ill, and has gone away to the coast for a time.*

"*Yours very truly,*

"JOHN CHERRITON."

John folded this letter carefully and placed it within his pocket-book. A specimen of Cherriton's handwriting, he inwardly decided, would be useful to Dacent Smith. Half an hour later John took his departure, and the old Colonel accompanied him to the door of the house.

"Good-bye, my boy," said the old man, gripping his hand at parting, "come again soon"; then he lowered his voice so that Gates, who was waiting at John's hired car, could not hear, "Bernard, boy," said the Colonel wistfully, "when you are tempted to go a little wrong, just keep in mind that I am believing in you."

"Very good, sir," John answered, "I won't forget that." He stood at salute a moment, then ran down the steps and sprang into the car.

"Good-bye, sir," said Gates, the old butler.

"Good-bye," cried John as the car whirled out of the avenue.

When John reached the foot of Heatherpoint Hill, and began to ascend the long slope towards the fort, it was already seven o'clock. The sun lay low in the west, and there was no wind.

"Fine visibility if there was any shooting for Ewins," thought John.

The car halted before the first sentry.

"Friend," said John.

"Pass, friend," answered the man.

A minute later, from his seat in the car, John was able to see the south shore of the island, and obtained a momentary glimpse of a strip of sand below, which was accessible only to those within the area of the fort itself. Looking down into the little bay three hundred feet below, John was caught with admiration by the mirror-like blue of the water, the languid white roll of the waves. The little beach, as always, was deserted, or at least, John thought so in the first moment. But a second glance showed him that a soldier was strolling about with apparent aimlessness down below. The man was smoking a cigarette, and in the clear evening air John could plainly see the white smoke. So much he saw, when the man was lost to view.

In the fort, a minute later, John caught himself wondering what soldier it was.

"Evidently somebody who is fond of his own company," thought John. He went up to Commander Grieves's look-out. The old naval officer was at the long telescope. "May I have a squint through that, sir?" John requested.

"By all means, youngster, by all means," returned the old man; "here you are." He swung the telescope, and John found that, to his chagrin, he could see nothing of the man on the strip of beach below.

"What do you want to see?" asked Commander Grieves.

"I want to look sharp down from here to the south," John said. "Some one from the fort is walking down there, and I'm wondering who it is."

"You can't see with this; I'll lend you my Zeiss," returned the Commander. He took out a pair of binoculars, and handed them to John. "We do not cover that bit of shore," said Grieves, "either with the guns or with the searchlights. It's of no importance, and isn't navigable for anything drawing more than three feet of water."

John took the binoculars, and thanked him, then went to the cliff edge. Here, moving with particular caution, he began to focus his glasses. When definition seemed to be right, he leaned carefully forward, and surveyed the beach below. The soldier was still there. After pacing with apparent aimlessness back and forward, he had seated himself on the smooth strip of sand. At the present moment the khaki figure was occupied in placing a pebble on the sand at arm's length. He placed a second small stone next to this, then made a span with his fingers, and put a third pebble in a line with the first and second. He made another span, and placed down a fourth stone and a fifth beside it. His operations were steady and systematic. He was absolutely absorbed with his work. John, from that cliff top, watched him for a full five minutes; never once did the soldier raise his head. In khaki uniform, at that distance, he might have been any soldier at the fort. Finally, however, when he had finished his operations, which had grown more and more interesting to John, he rose and looked at his handiwork upon the smooth sand. Evidently he had completed his task, whatever it was, for he turned and continued his aimless strolling. This time he was pacing towards the fort, and as he turned he lifted his eyes, and swept the cliff in a swift, embracing glance. In an instant John had recognised the sallow, upturned face of "Crumbs."

For a full ten minutes he waited, holding himself back. At the end of that time, however, he again cautiously approached and looked down. Below him spread the bright golden sands, a few chalk boulders were scattered here and there, and the waves continued to roll and break languidly as before.

The figure of "Crumbs" had now vanished from the sands. A steep, winding path ascended the cliff to the fort, and it was upon that path that John again saw Sims. It was a good twenty minutes' walk from where "Crumbs" was to the fort itself, and John, after watching him for a minute, lowered his glasses, rose and made his way back to the mess-room.

"Collins," he said to an orderly, "bring me the leave book."

When the leave book was in his hand he ran his finger quickly down the list of names.

"Pte. Sims, eight o'clock," he read.

Sims was on leave until eight.

"I'll wait and investigate," thought John, "when he is safely in his quarters."

He went to his room after that, took the cartridges out of his Colt automatic revolver and examined the weapon closely. Having reloaded the pistol, he slipped it into his hip pocket.

At eight o'clock, when John passed across the asphalt pavement between the officers' quarters and the kitchen, he was able to observe Sims, who was fond of his bake-house, sitting in the open doorway of the bakehouse itself, innocently reading the morning's paper. He appeared not to be aware of John's departure, and continued to read.

Manton, in the meantime, made his way towards the sentinel-guarded wire entanglements. A tall, double ladder, spanning the entanglement, here permitted exit on to the cliff edge behind the fort. The ladder was a temporary affair, drawn in always at night, thus making the fort, with the aid of the sentries, impregnable from the rear.

The sun was low in the west when John reached the expanse of sand whereon "Crumbs" had occupied himself. Once upon the shore, it was the simplest matter in the world to trace "Crumbs's" path. He walked briskly, following the man's footsteps, full of a keen desire to know what "Crumbs" had been doing. No ordinary purpose, thought John, had been at the back of "Crumbs's" operations. Nevertheless, an ordinary observer watching, as John had watched, would have entertained no suspicion at all.

"Perhaps," mused John, as he followed "Crumbs's" irregular footprints, "I am a fool for my pains! He may be the mere aimless nonentity he seems to be." He remembered that "Crumbs" was known to be a collector of shells, that he spent a good deal of time searching for specimens upon the foreshore. A baker and a conchologist are incongruous mixtures at any time. Especially were they incongruous on that coast where shells are almost non-existent. Keenly interested he drew nearer to the spot whereon "Crumbs" had occupied himself, but the smooth sand was undisturbed save for the man's heavy-footed indentations.

John's spirits instantly fell. There was nothing upon that spot which in the slightest degree could arouse his suspicions. The sand was smooth and firm, with round, sea-eroded pebbles plentifully scattered here and there — the usual pebbles that lay in thousands upon the beach.

"After all, I was a fool!" thought John.

He could see quite clearly the impress of "Crumbs's" body as it had lain upon the ground. And as he stood looking upon this impression he observed that "Crumbs" had made what might be called a crude pattern with pebbles — a row of parallel lines. John was able to make out, in all, three separate lines of stones.

For a long minute he remained looking down upon these innocent-seeming pebbles laid out with childish regularity. Then gradually his first suspicions returned. His attention ran along the orderly row of little stones — a third and a fourth time.

And suddenly a vivid light blazed in his eyes. He uttered an exclamation under his breath.

"Great Scott! so that's it."

His whole mind focused upon the pebbles; he began to speak in measured tones.

"Dot-dash-dot-dash; dash-dash-dash."

As the words left his lips on the solitude of the sands, he was conscious of a quick thrill of excitement. The stones laid thus innocently held a sinister meaning spelt out in the Morse code. Two pebbles lay together, then further to the right an isolated pebble, then again two pebbles.

"Dash-dot-dash," John interpreted.

The message was quite a long one. With a glance at the cliff edge—he knew that "Crumbs" was safely in his quarters—John took out his pocket-book and made a faithful copy of "Crumbs's" laborious message.

When he had copied it all down he made his way back to the fort, pondering upon the significance of his discovery. For whom was the message intended? Both Hobin and Commander Grieves had told him that the possibility of any enemy signalling from the fort, or to the fort from outside, had been completely eliminated, and had said, "We should instantly see any light that might be exhibited by an enemy."

"And yet," thought John, "our ingenious friend, 'Crumbs,' seems to have thought out a plan which evades every one of their precautions."

The ingenuity and simplicity of "Crumbs's" plan struck him with astonishment. It was clear to John that "Crumbs" regularly placed his innocent-looking messages on the sands, to be subsequently taken up by a confederate who came ashore from a submarine in the darkness.

"Cunning isn't the word for him," thought John, as he hurried towards the fort.

CHAPTER XIV

A few minutes later in his own room and by candle-light he set to work to find a meaning for the arrangement of little pebbles "Crumbs" had placed upon the foreshore. A dozen times he went over the dot-dash lines in his pocket-book, and each time the hidden meaning intensified in clarity. Finally, he began to write with a sudden vivid and passionate interest.

The first word defined was "Oberst." Then he continued slowly and carefully: *"Mistrauish und aufgeregt. Neue Minen karte in Händen des Capitans. Nicht möglich es sofort zu finden. Von R. ist nichts zu hören. Ganze geschichte schwierig. Bitte um antwort. — S.*

"So, friend 'Crumbs' is a German after all, and an educated German at that," he exclaimed under his breath.

Then he took his pencil and began to translate the message. The result in English was as follows:

"Colonel suspicious and nervous. New mine chart in hands of naval commander; impossible to find it at once. No news of R. Matters difficult. Answer this. — S."

John looked up with a grave face. Almost for the first time he felt a doubt. In that moment he almost doubted even Dacent Smith's power to cope with such subtlety, such ingenious co-ordination as this.

"Crumbs" was a spy actually in the heart of a vital fort, a spy who was possibly one of a score, or a hundred, busy upon the South Coast at that moment. John felt oppressed by a consciousness of dark agencies planning evil. Here was no romance. Here was real, hard, solid fact; War. Sims was an item in this warfare, one of a chain, of which Manwitz, Cherriton, Mrs. Beecher Monmouth, and the great unknown himself were all separate links.

For some minutes John paced the narrow confines of his room.

Who was R. from whom no news had arrived? A sensation that calamity and failure was possible bore in upon him. He had made a discovery truly, but would that discovery mean the frustration of the mysterious attack that was impending? He did not know, he hardly dared to hope.

"If Heatherpoint Fort were out of action," Colonel Hobin had said, "and if Scoles Head were similarly out of action, there might be the devil to pay."

John realised as he paced his little room with "Crumbs's" message in his hand, that an attack by sea was planned. Otherwise why the mention of the new mine chart? And if an attack by sea was intended on the great naval port of ... Scoles and Heatherpoint must be first put out of action. After that, the boom which ran across from Ponsonby Lighthouse to ... must be overcome.

He looked again at the message.

"This must be got to Dacent Smith at once," thought he; "and in the meantime 'Crumbs' must be watched."

He placed the message carefully in his pocket-book. Then, a new thought having struck him, he hurried out and sought Sergeant Ewins. The sergeant occupied one compartment of an old railway coach, which had been turned into huts for the men. Ewins was lying on his bunk when John entered, reading a Sunday paper by the light of a fort candle as thick as a man's wrist.

"I want to have a word with you, Ewins," said John, sitting on the edge of the chief gunner's bunk, which had formerly been a railway seat. "Can you tell me," he went on, "if it is possible for anyone to make a landing on the south shore, there? I mean in the bay below the look-out."

"It's possible, of course," Ewins answered, "but risky."

"You don't think it possible," inquired John, "for a submarine to lie out there in the bay and send a small canvas boat ashore?"

Ewins shook his head.

"You've forgotten our minefield—a submarine could not pass it, sir."

"No, I haven't forgotten that," answered John; "but suppose the Germans know where our mines are?"

"Then they'd know more than we do, sir," answered Ewins. "Nobody in the fort knows that, except the Commander, and perhaps the Colonel."

"The reason I am asking you," went on John, "is that I have discovered something and want to give you an opportunity of coming down on the shore with me."

"To-night, sir?" inquired Ewins.

John nodded.

"I suppose, Ewins, it seems fantastical and impossible to you, but I have a theory that the Germans intend to bring a boat ashore there. In my opinion, they have been there before to-night."

Ewins's eyes opened wide.

"Do you think that is so, sir?" he asked in a voice of deep amazement. Then his eyes brightened. "I'd like to come with you, sir, if you think there's any likelihood of that sort of thing."

"I don't only think it, I know it," said John. "It may not be to-night, because of the full moon, nor to-morrow night. But some time or other, and maybe soon, I am prepared to bet my hat that a German will land from the sea. He will land, Ewins, in the bay below us, within a quarter of a mile of where we are now sitting."

The manner in which Ewins took this information filled John with satisfaction. The old soldier was spoiling for a fight. For four years he had had nothing better to shoot at than a target, and he was longing for a chance of real action.

Nevertheless John's fear was correct, for that night and the next night the moon shone brilliantly, and nothing happened on the shore. "Crumbs's" message lay unread in the bright moonlight. The third night, however, the sky was overcast.

But by a sudden, swift turn of circumstances John was not there to see what happened.

Manton's record on "Crumbs's" secret signal had been taken with the utmost seriousness by Dacent Smith, and on the afternoon of the third day, when John was alone at tea in the mess-room, an orderly thumped along the passage.

"A gentleman to see you, sir," said the orderly.

"What's his name?" John asked.

"Captain Sinclair, sir."

John rose, and a minute later Captain X. stepped into the little room. Captain X. was in uniform, and John noticed that he wore the Mons ribbon and the D.S.O.

"Surprised to see me, eh?" exclaimed the young man, gripping John's hand heartily; then dropping his voice, "I'm here from the Chief. Is it quite private here?"

"Quite," John answered, "but I would rather take you into my room."

They went along the passage to John's bedroom. John seated himself on the bed, and Captain X. or Sinclair occupied the only chair.

"The Chief's thoroughly stirred up," said Sinclair, plunging into his subject without preliminary. "He has passed on your information to me. I must say you seem to have all the luck, Treves. A signal on the sands, eh? That beats everything for cunning. I have heard of clothes being hung out in the Morse code, and Morse smoke signals from a chimney—by the way, do you think your chap Sims signals with smoke from his bakehouse?"

John shook his head.

"I have spent hours looking at his chimney," he said. "It was the first thing I thought of when I began to suspect him, and it was only an accident which made me get on to his real game after all. I knew any kind of flash signal was out of the question here."

"Neatest thing they've done yet, eh, Treves? I must say this sort of thing makes the fight full of zipp and go," he said. Then he looked at John with a commiserating eye: "I am going to dash your spirits, old chap."

"Well, get on with it," said John.

"I am going to pick up the plums you have shaken off the tree."

"How's that?"

For answer Sinclair drew an envelope from his pocket. John recognised the colour and shape of the envelope in a minute. He read the short, typed letter with gathered brows, then struck a match and destroyed it carefully. The letter contained an order from Dacent Smith that John should surrender his position at Heatherpoint to Captain X., and was to resume work immediately against Cherriton, Dr. Voules, and Mrs. Beecher Monmouth.

"It's rough luck, old chap," said Captain X., "but I expect that before this big movement is finished you will have as much chance of adventure as I shall."

"I hope so," said John. "But I was looking forward to the result of 'Crumbs's' signal. Last night the moon shone out of pure cussedness."

Captain X. sprang up to the window and looked out.

"It's clouding up to-night, old chap," he exclaimed joyously, "and you'll be away for the fun. Hallo!" he said. His eyes were lowered and were fixed upon a man in shirt-sleeves in the doorway opposite. "Is that 'Crumbs'?"

"Yes," said John, "but don't let him see you looking at him. I am not so sure that he hasn't spotted something."

"He'll spot something in a day or two," said Captain X., coming back from the window, "and in the meantime the Chief's orders are to leave him a long rope."

John's orders from his Chief were that he should report to Colonel Hobin and leave Heatherpoint immediately. He began to change his clothes, and talked to his companion at the same time.

"You can rub acquaintance with 'Crumbs' while I get out of the fort," he said. "He mustn't see me in mufti. I shall spend a night in Newport, and call on Dr. Voules to-morrow morning."

"Who do you think Voules is?" asked the Captain.

John shook his head.

"I shall know more about that to-morrow," he said.

When he was ready to go he shook hands cordially with his companion. He always felt older than Captain X., though their ages were the same. Captain X.'s audacity and joy in life amused John. His colleague always put so much zest into everything he did.

"I should advise you," he said, gripping the Captain's hand, "to use Ewins if you want any help on the beach to-night. He is an old soldier, and I should think, if an awkward moment arrived, you could rely on him."

"Thanks," said Sinclair. "This is a new game for me. I have never had the chance of angling for a German submarine commander before. but I expect there'll be one ashore here to-night, eh, Treves?"

"Somebody comes ashore," responded John, "and reads those signals."

He went out and sat in the mess-room for a few minutes, leaving Sinclair time to occupy "Crumbs'" attention while he slipped away from the fort.

CHAPTER XV

The situation at Heatherpoint was exactly to the liking of Captain Sinclair. He realised, from what John had told him, that "Crumbs" was no mean antagonist, and he was feverish to make the spy's acquaintance. But the manner in which he strolled into "Crumbs's" bakehouse before John's departure was the most casual in the world. One of Sinclair's chief gifts was an innocent and infectious smile, and under the most trying of circumstances he was always cheerful. With this smiling cheeriness of manner Sinclair possessed, as is often the case, a fair share of astuteness.

"It smells good in here," he said, putting his head into "Crumbs's" warm atmosphere.

"Crumbs," who was kneading dough at his board, turned about.

"Don't mind me," said Sinclair cheerfully. He stepped into the bakehouse and held a good-humoured conversation with "Crumbs." He spent a quarter of an hour in cheery garrulity, and when he went away, "Crumbs," from the darkness of his lair, watched him stride across the asphalt yard towards the officers' quarters. The man's eyes narrowed as he recalled that Sinclair had been peering at him out of John's quarters a little while earlier. When his work was finished that night "Crumbs" cleaned himself and had a chat with Ewins, who was smoking a pipe on the step of the old railway carriage that formed both men's quarters in the upper fort.

"Who's this new captain we got?" Private Sims asked.

"Don't know," answered Ewins. "He's done his bit, seemingly." He was referring to Sinclair's Mons ribbon and the D.S.O.

"We seem to be getting a lot of changes lately," pursued "Crumbs." He had removed the flour from his eyelashes and moustache, and his lean, sallow, discontented face and glassy, strange-looking eyes struck Ewins as particularly unpleasant. Sims was generous in handing cake and so forth whenever chance occurred, but he was not liked in the fort. The other men could not get the hang of him, and when he rose presently and shambled away into the fort buildings, Ewins, who was expecting every minute to be called by Sinclair, was not sorry.

For an hour or two that evening "Crumbs" pottered about. He gossiped in the kitchen, had a talk with the sergeant controlling the leave-book, found his way into the mess-room, and complained to Parkson, who was adjutant, on the quality of the flour being supplied from outside. After that the Colonel met him in the corridor, where he had no right to be, near Sinclair's bedroom. And, as the Colonel was the one man in the fort, outside Sinclair, who knew the truth about him, he questioned "Crumbs" somewhat sharply.

"What are you doing here, Sims?"

"I have just been in, sir, to complain about the flour to the adjutant. I wasn't thinking," he went on, with a perfect semblance of an absent-minded air, "I wasn't thinking, and I came here instead of going along to the right— —"

"You ought to know the run of the fort by this time," said the Colonel, and passed on.

It was an hour later that Sims, who had made a shattering discovery, sat in his cubicle of the railway compartment, with the door locked, and penned a rapid letter. He wrote fluently, in the manner of a man whose education has been thorough and efficient. His lips twitched slightly as his pen sped over the paper. There was a tense expression upon his sallow face, and he pulled nervously at his long, drooping moustache.

At the head of the letter he put no address.

"*Dear Doctor,*" he wrote, "*our plans are threatened. The new officer here, Lieutenant Treves, has been watching me closely for the past week. He has cross-examined Ewins about the guns, and evidently knows something. To-day a second officer has arrived, a Captain Sinclair. I doubt him also. They both suspect me. But my important news is that to-night I secured my first opportunity of going through Treves's belongings. I was able to open his dispatch-box, and among other papers of no importance, I discovered a letter from Cherriton, with whom he has apparently some association. The letter was signed by Cherriton, which clearly showed me that Treves is playing both for and against us. I have suspected him for days. I implore you, doctor, to probe this matter. If you hear no more from me you will know that things have gone wrong. I beg of you to act drastically and immediately.—S.*"

When "Crumbs" had finished this letter he read it carefully through and avoided blotting it, so that there could be no trace of its existence. When the letter had dried he placed it in an envelope and addressed it to "Dr. Voules, Rollo Meads, Brooke."

It was the custom at Heatherpoint for the fort letters to be sent to Freshwater post office every night at seven precisely in a locked bag. "Crumbs," with his letter in his pocket, hovered about the orderly-room until the bugle began to blow seven. He then hurriedly followed the orderly into the mess-room, where the adjutant nightly locked the bag with his key. Lieutenant Parkson was in the act of locking the bag when "Crumbs" shambled into the little room with an apology. He handed his letter to Parkson, who dropped it in and locked the bag.

CHAPTER XVI

John decided to walk into Freshwater, and then take the train to Newport. As he made his way along the road from Heatherpoint, carrying a small handbag, a red bicycle came towards him.

"Are you going to the fort?" he asked the telegraph boy.

"Yes, sir."

"Anything for Treves?"

The boy nodded.

"Lieutenant Treves, sir."

A minute later John had torn open an envelope containing a telegram, which ran:

Come to me at the Gordon Hotel, Newport. Shall be there this evening. ELAINE.

Elaine's wire came to him as an utter surprise, a surprise that was tinctured with pleasure. He had never forgotten her since their first, and only meeting. He had indeed thought of her a hundred times, recalling her as she stood in the little room in Camden Town. Without doubt she was the most beautiful woman he had ever seen.

During the past weeks every moment of his time had been occupied, and there had been no possibility of carrying out his promise to visit her.

As he walked he drew out her telegram and read it carefully through, possibly for the sixth time. The wording brought to him a measure of comfort; he felt, somehow, that she was not in so distressed a state of mind as when he had received her former wire to Bernard Treves.

"I shall see her within an hour," thought John, as he stepped into a train at Freshwater. But as the train drew nearer to Newport his high spirits evaporated; he began to argue that Elaine Treves was outside his sphere of work. Dacent Smith had impressed upon him the intense seriousness of the German menace on the South Coast; no private considerations, John told himself, held precedence of the duty that lay before him. Elaine Treves was a victim of the innocent deception he had been obliged to practise. But it was not his fault that she was an extremely beautiful woman, and that she believed him to be her husband.

At the Gordon Hotel, a small quiet, specklessly clean building, John entered the hall, and found Elaine herself descending the stairs. For a moment the girl did not notice him, and John was free to observe the daintiness of her costume, the slender dignity of her figure, and the quite astonishing beauty of her grey, long-lashed eyes. The note of pathos that had been apparent when he first met her was now not so marked. She struck him as serious, but not depressed.

Elaine had descended the stairs to the vestibule before her eyes met his.

"Oh, Bernard," she exclaimed, and instantly took his hand in her gloved fingers. "But you can't have come in answer to my wire?" she went on.

"No," said John; "I came on other business."

"You are not angry with me?"

"No; why should I be angry?" asked John.

"Because I wired to you," said Elaine. "Let us go upstairs, Bernard. The sitting-room's empty; we can talk there."

She led him up to a little, parlour-like apartment, with a gay carpet, and a circular table in the middle of the room. Here she closed the door and stood with her back to it, looking up into John's face. Her eyes searched his closely. Her splendid beauty, the wistful expression of her face, a certain shy girlishness, all appealed to John's feelings. He found it difficult to sustain the searching gaze lifted to his.

Suddenly Elaine drew in a deep breath.

"Bernard," she whispered, "you are different."

John turned away.

"Yes," he answered, quietly, "I suppose I am a little different."

"Ever since the last time I saw you I have felt it," went on Elaine. "I have thought much of our last meeting," she added.

"So have I," John answered lamely, not knowing exactly how to handle the situation. They were seated now on opposite sides of the hearth, and Elaine was taking the hatpins out of her hat with pretty feminine gestures that held John's attention.

"I was only going a lonely walk," she explained, "when I met you, but I won't go now; we'll have tea here together. You will notice," she went on, placing her hat on her knee and piercing it with her long hatpins, "that I have not scolded you for failing to write to me."

"I am sorry," said John, "but I have been tremendously occupied."

"I guessed," said Elaine, "that you were at home with your father. I am so glad of that, Bernard; I used to feel," she went on, hesitatingly, "that you were not treating him well, and that his indignation against you was—was—" she hesitated a moment—"well—justified."

John had been observing her closely.

"Why did you wire for me, Elaine?" he said, using her name for the first time.

Elaine looked at him, and then away. The colour rose to her cheeks, a delicate colour that enhanced her beauty.

"I don't know," she said. "I got a little frightened, I think. You see, your friend, Captain Cherriton, began to call on me rather regularly."

John pricked up his ears.

"Did he cross-examine you about me?"

Elaine shook her head.

"He scarcely mentioned you."

"Oh, I see," said John, suddenly enlightened; "he came to force his unpleasant attentions upon you. Is that it?"

Elaine was silent a moment. She was thinking how well John carried himself. The husband she had known, neurotic and nerveless and irritable, now appeared before her clear-eyed, calm and more manly than she had ever believed him to be. She felt herself drawn to him, as she had felt herself attracted on that last meeting in London. Her nature was quick and ready to forgive.

"I had to forbid him the house in the end, Bernard."

John sat suddenly erect.

"Was he impudent to you?"

The sudden lowering of his brows and tension of his figure caught Elaine's interest.

"Then you do mind, Bernard?" she asked quietly.

"Of course I mind, when you are insulted," he returned. "Or, rather, I ought to mind."

For, like a blow, the thought suddenly struck him that he himself was treating her with gross injustice. It was one thing to deceive, in a good cause, Colonel Treves; it was another thing to deceive this young and beautiful girl, who was another man's wife. And he, John Manton, was standing in that other man's shoes.

John's situation at that moment was as delicate as any situation in which he had yet found himself. It was an easy matter to confront Manwitz and Cherriton, and even Mrs. Beecher Monmouth, in the character of Bernard Treves. It was not so easy to present himself in that character before Bernard Treves's wife. The thought that had occurred to him at their first meeting came again into his mind; at any moment he might make a false step. An unlucky turn of phrase, a lack of knowledge of some incident in their mutual past, might instantly betray him. For Elaine Treves, despite her striking beauty and her intense femininity, was quite keenly alive and intelligent.

They took tea in the hotel, and after the meal John suggested a walk in the town. Elaine readily assented, and together they explored the quaint side streets of Newport. If matters had been different, if John had accompanied her in his own character, and had not had to act a part that was extraordinarily difficult, he would have been in the highest of spirits.

Already he had remarked upon Elaine's air of distinction. She knew how to dress, how to put on her hat, how to make herself in all respects a delightful picture of girlish attraction. John knew nothing of feminine economics, or he would have been aware that her fashionably smart costume and that pretty hat she wore had cost almost nothing at all, and had been mostly the work of her own hands.

During the walk they stopped and looked into a quaint curiosity shop. John admired a set of old Chippendale chairs and a pair of inlaid duelling pistols. He and Elaine were standing close together as he spoke, and he felt her slender, gloved hand laid delicately on his arm.

"Bernard!"

"What is it?" asked John.

She was looking up into his face, a pleased expression in her fine grey eyes.

"Your taste seems to have changed utterly."

"Oh, I don't know," said John. "I—I—perhaps my taste has matured——"

"You used to hate all old things."

John was looking down into her face, that appeared to him now as the most beautiful in the world. He made no answer to her remark, and Elaine went on:

"You look at things so differently, Bernard."

"In what way?" John asked.

"I don't know," answered she. "I have a sort of queer feeling, Bernard, that you are yourself, and yet there is something that has occurred to make you different."

John felt that the discussion was drifting in an awkward direction.

"Do you know what I think?" he remarked.

"What do you think?" asked Elaine, as they walked together.

"I think I ought to do something to make up for all the bad times—er—I have given you in the past."

She was silent, walking along gazing before her.

"They were bad times, some of them, Bernard," she returned, quietly. She moved a little nearer to him as they walked. "But I have always felt," she went on, "that it was not really you. I feel that—that the unfortunate habit you had contracted, the—the——"

"I understand," John intervened.

"I believe now," went on Elaine, "it was not really you. You were not responsible, and I always hoped that some time, when you had conquered yourself, you would become different."

She paused a moment, and John felt her arm slip through his. It was strange, but his pulse-beat quickened at this quiet manifestation of her growing feeling towards him. He felt that, somehow or other, she was being drawn towards him, that she was, as it were, shielding herself under his protection. And yet, all the time, the situation was an impossible one. He had no right to permit advances of this sort; the deception he was practising upon her was utterly and completely cruel. What would have happened, he asked himself, if he had suddenly faced her and had said: "I am not your husband, I am not Bernard Treves—but John Manton? The man you believe me to be—your husband—is a drug-sodden and hysterical degenerate, a soldier who has been guilty of treachery to his country."

His thoughts switched back to the necessity of turning the conversation. He could feel the warmth of her arm resting upon his own.

"Let us talk of cheerful things," he said. "For instance, that is a very pretty hat you have on."

"Do you like it? I made it myself."

"Yes, I like it," responded John, appearing to look at it with the critical eye of a husband. "Of course," he said, "it is quite easy for a hat to look well where you are concerned."

Elaine was frankly pleased.

"Why are you flattering me, Bernard?"

"That wasn't flattery. If I set out to flatter you, I should talk in quite a different way to that."

"Do you know," she went on quickly, "when I met you in the hotel my heart was beating terribly. I was afraid you might be angry!"

"How could I be angry?"

"I don't know," she said; "but sometimes, Bernard, you used to be so dreadfully angry at the things I did."

Somehow the recollection of these things appeared to sweep over her, for she drew her hand away from John's arm.

"I thought we were going to talk of cheerful things," John reminded her. He began to draw her attention to the quaintness of the streets, and managed, until their return to the hotel, to keep her mind fully occupied with trivialities.

When they reached the little sitting-room at the hotel, he rang the bell and ordered dinner to be prepared for two at seven o'clock.

"May we have it here in the sitting-room?" he asked the waiter.

"Certainly, sir," answered the man.

Elaine, whose air of constraint had quite vanished again, went to her room, took off her hat, and put on an afternoon blouse. When she returned to the sitting-room John noticed her little attempt to dress herself for the evening.

"I thought you'd like to see me in something smarter for dinner," she said. "Do you like it, Bernard?"

"It could not be better," said John. Inwardly he was saying: "I like everything about you; I like your fine, dark hair; I like your frank, beautiful eyes, and your honesty and your simplicity, and the fact that you are a girl and yet a woman. What I do dislike, however, is the fact that you have a waster of a husband, and that I have no right to be here this minute standing in that waster's shoes."

They sat down together at the round table in the middle of the hotel'
parlour. The waiter, a gloomy individual, in tired-looking dress clothes and
in a white shirt that should have been washed a week earlier, lit four pink-
shaded candles, served the soup, and went away. Soup was followed by
fish and an excellent entrée. John, looking over the top of the pink-shaded
candles, saw a brightness in Elaine's eyes. He had been talking gaily keeping
the conversation away from anything personal, and telling her anecdotes
that made her laugh. And all the time, although he was not aware of the
fact, he was drawing her towards him, fanning the flame of love that the
real Bernard Treves had never kindled. She was experiencing new feelings
towards this man whom she believed to be her husband. The shifty look in
his eyes that she had disliked in the past had vanished. The Bernard Treves
who sat before her looked frankly and keenly into her face. He was not in
the least intimate; he was, indeed, somewhat aloof, but this very quality of
aloofness puzzled and attracted her.

By the time dinner was cleared away and the cloth removed, Elaine was
completely at her ease. Her old fear of offending her husband had totally
vanished. She could not understand her own feelings and began to take
herself to task for having been hard with him in the past. When Bernard
Treves had persisted in his habit of heavy drinking and drug-taking, she
had been obliged to make a stand. She had done everything she could to
win him to better ways. But when to these habits he had added violence and
other cruelties towards herself, she had informed him that until he made
some effort to control himself she could not live with him as his wife. It was
characteristic of her, as it is sometimes characteristic of gentle people, that
firmness lay beneath an unaggressive exterior. She had kept her word. But
to-night, for the first time, she began to doubt the justice of what she had
done. She told herself that she had been hard on Bernard Treves, that she
ought to have clung to him, however low he sank.

CHAPTER XVII

John, who had deposited himself on a chair at the hearth, lit a cigarette, and was consuming it with a good deal of satisfaction. He had never in his life partaken of an evening meal that had given him so much satisfaction; even the funereal and shabby waiter seemed to him a creature of delight, and the little room in the hotel—he would always remember it as an apartment brightened by the eyes of Elaine Treves. It was not usual for John Manton to be led away, but to-night, for some minutes, he let his senses toy with impossibilities. He permitted himself to forget the existence of Bernard Treves. And when the waiter left the room, and Elaine rose and came towards him, he made no effort to avoid her approach, as he had done once or twice earlier in the evening. She stood beside his chair and laid her hand on his shoulder. John looked up and saw that her face had grown serious.

"I want to make a confession to you, Bernard."

"Let it be a cheerful confession," smiled John.

"I was mistaken, after all."

"It's easy to make mistakes," returned John.

"I ought not to have sent you away from me," said Elaine.

John thought a moment, then observed quietly:

"Perhaps I deserved to be sent away."

"Do you remember, Bernard, when you came to Camden Town after you had seen your father?"

John, naturally, did not recollect.

"I do not recall it very clearly," he said.

"When you—you——" She broke off, and again, as she had done in the street, she moved a little away from him. A wave of aversion towards him appeared to sweep over her. "When," she went on, "I told you that we could not be together again until—until——"

"Until I could behave myself," John put in.

Elaine nodded slightly in assent.

"I thought that I was doing right, and when you said you'd never forgive me I still held out. I wonder, Bernard, if you will forgive me?"

"Of course I'll forgive you," returned Manton, magnanimously. He would have forgiven her anything. He could not believe her capable of anything which would need forgiveness. She came to him again and stood before him, looking down.

John, out of politeness, that she should not be standing when he was seated, stood up, and suddenly he felt Elaine's hand in his.

"Bernard," she whispered, "you care for me still— —"

"I care for you more than ever I did," said John. He tried valiantly to slip his hand from hers.

"You love me, I mean?"

Elaine's face was upturned; there was a wistful expression in her fine, grey eyes, and there was something more than wistfulness. John could see it shining there. Inwardly he was conscientiously cursing the Fates that had placed him in this impossible position—and yet outwardly he was glad. He was thrilled and happy that this situation had arisen. Then his thoughts took a turn, and his spirits sank. The love he saw shining in her eyes was not for him, but for Bernard Treves. He put away her hand and moved back in his chair.

"You do love me, Bernard?" she whispered again.

"Yes," John answered. He was convinced that there was no other thing for him to say.

"And you'll forgive me for sending you away?"

John nodded.

Elaine went on again: "It was wrong not to let you stay with me. I had no right to do it; after all, a wife has no right to act as I did."

"Why think of it and worry about it now?" said John, attempting to strike an ordinary tone of voice.

"But I want to make everything straight between us, Bernard."

John led her to a chair, and she seated herself. He tried to turn the conversation, but this time he failed. Elaine felt a growing desire to wipe away all misunderstandings between them.

"I have still my confession to make, Bernard."

"What is it?" inquired John cheerily.

There was a silence for a moment—a silence that John felt to be momentous, that rendered him uncomfortable. Then Elaine's words came to him, uttered in a low tone.

"I never loved you till to-night, Bernard!"

John was conscious of a sudden and exultant thrill.

"Is that all your confession?" he asked.

Elaine nodded. Her hand was in his. John lifted it to his lips. Then recollection came to him; he drew himself erect, standing away from her.

"It's getting late, Elaine," he said. "I ought to be going." There was something vibrant and new in his voice that caused her heart to beat violently. "You see," John went on, somewhat clumsily, "I have important work to do to-morrow."

But Elaine had not loosed her grip of his hand. She suddenly hid her face on his shoulder; he could feel her arms about him. For a minute, what was to John an awkward silence, subsisted between them, then Elaine spoke again:

"Why should you go, Bernard?" she whispered. "I was cruel to you, but I did not wish to be cruel."

"You are never cruel," protested John. "Don't think of it any more."

His situation in that moment was the hardest that Fate could have possibly imposed upon him. Here was the finest woman he had ever met— young, beautiful and ardent, with her arms about his neck, whispering love to him. She was speaking to him as a wife to a husband whom she loves, and all the time he was not that husband. And, to complicate matters, he felt now that the love she was prepared to offer was not offered to the other—to Bernard Treves—but to himself alone.

"Bernard," she murmured, "at the back of my heart, through all those black days, I whispered always that some time I should be happy."

"I am sure you'll be happy," said John. "It will not be my fault if you are not." He drew in a deep breath. "But to-night—I must go; I—I am very busy; I have many things to do to-night. Confidential work." He lifted her hand, bent and kissed her slender white fingers. "Some day I'll explain."

A minute later he was gone.

*   *   *   *   *

The gloomy-looking waiter, who had served dinner the night before, informed John that the only way to arrive at Brooke was by hired pony-trap or by bicycle. Choosing the latter method, John, early in the morning, hired a bicycle, visited the hotel, and said good-bye to Elaine.

"You'll come back to me this evening, Bernard?" whispered she as she kissed him good-bye.

"This evening," said John. "I had no right to let her kiss me," he continued inwardly, "but, after all, it's part of the deception, part of the character I am obliged to play." Nevertheless, he felt uneasy as he rode the winding and hilly path to Brooke. The night before he had played his part valiantly and well, but he felt that in regard to Elaine tremendous difficulties were ahead.

It was eleven o'clock when John reached the road which led to the empty, forlorn line of shore at Brooke. He could see the sea ahead of him, a grand expanse of blue ocean. He passed quaint Brooke church on his left hand, and suddenly slowed up near a large solid-looking dwelling, overgrown with creepers. Here was Rollo Meads, with a strip of garden in front. As John neared the dwelling he noticed a gardener at work. Something in the quiet and homely exterior of the house made him for a moment think he had made a mistake, but as his hand fell upon the gate the gardener lifted his face, and John recognised the pallid countenance and close-set eyes of Conrad, the manservant who had first admitted him to Manwitz's house in St. George's Square.

Conrad informed him that Dr. Voules was in and was awaiting him.

"Now," thought John, as he followed Conrad to the front door, "matters may begin to move again." Dacent Smith had for some time been groping towards the identity of Dr. Voules, and John realised that in being permitted to undertake the work he was now upon he was being trusted and favoured by his Chief. He resolved, in his interview with the doctor, to exercise the most extreme caution, and to play the part of Bernard Treves with the closest simulation.

There was silence as John stepped into the hall of Rollo Meads. The servant preceded him along the passage, knocked on a door, then entered, and vanished, leaving John alone. Conrad emerged a minute later, and summoned John towards him.

"Will you please go in, sir."

A moment later John found himself in a good-sized morning-room, with two windows overlooking a lawn and a garden. The room was heavily furnished with a long oak table in the middle, and half a dozen massive dining-room chairs surrounding it. At the head of the table Doctor "Voules" was seated. He wore a markedly English-looking tweed suit, but his thick neck, his circular head, and heavy jaws showed him to be not quite the amiable retired doctor he pretended to be. Seated on Voules's right hand were two men, deeply sun-tanned. One of the men wore a blond beard, and looked frankly and honestly at John. The other was a fair-haired man, with a supercilious-looking expression. John put both down at once as naval officers. Standing at the fire-place, in uniform, was Captain Cherriton. The air of the room was heavily impregnated with the smell of cigar smoke. Cherriton was smoking a cigarette, but Doctor Voules held in his powerful mouth a long, black cigar. He flashed a keen scrutiny upon John as the young man stepped into the room and closed the door behind him.

"You are Mr. Treves, eh?"

John assured him that he was.

"You will take a seat," said Voules, pointing to a vacant chair upon his left hand. "These are two friends of mine," he said, indicating the blond-bearded man and the supercilious younger man, "Mr. Sharpe and Mr. Rogers."

"I am pleased to meet you," said John, making a swift mental summary of each man's appearance.

"I am glad to make your acquaintance," responded the blond-bearded man, and his accent was so thoroughly German that it would have betrayed him anywhere. The other man appeared to speak no English at all, for he merely nodded.

"Sit down, Cherriton," commanded Voules, and Cherriton, who was lounging at the hearth, came and seated himself at John's side.

"I am in the thick of it," thought John. He wondered what was to occur, what attitude Voules would take towards himself, whether Voules would regard him as of consequence, and of possible use, or would he fail to trust him.

"You are no longer in the army?" Voules inquired, looking into John's face with cold grey eyes. It was his custom to examine personally such men as were brought to him; he had infinite belief in his own powers of judgment, and in many ways he possessed a shrewd and penetrating mind. His infinite confidence in himself, however, sometimes led him into mistakes. He believed, as he looked at John, that he was examining a weakling, and a drug-taker. Cherriton had supplied all information as to Bernard Treves's unstable character and habits, and though Voules was a little surprised to find the young man healthy and vigorous looking, he was deceived by the manner in which John avoided his eyes; he was still more deceived when John, cleverly resting his elbow on the table, permitted his sleeve to fall back so that Voules could see pinpricks on his wrist, the sort of wound that is left by a hypodermic syringe used for administering morphia and cocaine

Voules's sharp eyes instantly fell upon this tangible evidence of the drug habit. He was quite satisfied with the evidence of his own eyes.

"You are no longer in the army?" he repeated.

"Well, as a matter of fact," John said, after a moment's hesitation. "my father has used his influence, and I am to be restored to my commission."

Voules's eyes widened a little.

"Indeed," he remarked. He appeared to consider this change in John's circumstances for a moment, then he put out a hand and laid his heavy fingers on John's sleeve. "You have told this news, eh——" he paused a moment; "you have told this news to Alice?"

For a second John hesitated; he did not realise who Alice was; then he remembered her as Mrs. Beecher Monmouth.

"No," answered John, "I have not told her yet, but I intend to write and tell her to-night."

"Ah," said Voules, "you think she will be pleased?" The intensity of his gaze increased. John saw quite plainly a doubt in his eyes. "You think she will be pleased?"

"I am sure of it," said John.

"And why?"

"Because I can be of more use, doctor."

"We have a very high opinion of the lady in question," said Voules; "we have every reason to trust her."

"I hope you will have every reason to trust me," John said.

Voules looked at him silently for a minute.

"I hope so," he announced. "We shall make it worth your while to serve us." He paused for a moment, and glanced at Cherriton. "Cherriton has already told you," he said, "that when the Day arrives, when the success that is bound to come, has been given to us, we shall not forget our friends in England." He suddenly turned away from John, and looked at the blond-bearded man on his right. His voice seemed to deepen in tone, and he began suddenly and rapidly to speak in German. "What is your opinion of our young English friend here?" he rapped to the blond-bearded man.

"I cannot judge of him, Excellence."

Voules went on still in German:

"Manwitz and Rathenau have each testified to his usefulness; he is also in the hands of a lady who can well supervise his doings."

The blond man fingered his blond beard, sliding it through his hands.

"Excellence, let me say, may I not suggest a certain reserve in our conversation, in the circumstances."

Voules laughed for the first time. John noticed that his teeth were strong and well kept, and that his laugh was not at all pleasant.

"Our Englander," he said, "understands not one word of German. We may speak freely, Muller. Is it not so, Rathenau?" He turned quickly to Cherriton.

"Yes, Excellence," answered Cherriton, with his contemptuous curl of the lip. "Not one English officer in a thousand knows half a dozen words of German; our friend is no exception."

"He is well controlled by the particular lady mentioned?" inquired Voules.

Cherriton smiled.

"Quite, Excellence; even if she cared for him in the way he believes she does, she would still watch him like a cat."

"True," said Voules; then again turned to John and spoke in English. "My apologies to you, Mr. Treves," he said, "for speaking in German, but my friends here speak no English."

"I don't mind in the least," answered John. He did not in the least, and as he had understood every word it made no difference.

"In regard to your reinstatement in the army," went on Voules, "I offer you my felicitations. You will be able to help us even more than in the past, and I may hardly say that the reward will be in proportion to the work done. If you are stationed in London we can find work for you in London. If, on the other hand, you are returned to your regiment, then you can also help us. The treatment you have received at the hands of the army, Cherriton tells me, is abominable. You are quite honourably acquitted of allegiance to your nationality. I tell you this, that you may have no inner qualms; in serving us you serve the cause of Kultur. Is that not so, Cherriton?"

"Yes, Herr Excellence."

"Kultur," thought John; "Kultur, that stabs in the dark, that murders children and women; that calls might right. Kultur that takes a man sodden with drugs and turns him into a traitor to his country; then, having made him commit crimes against his fellow-countrymen, has the audacity to tell him that he is acting the part of a man of honour! Some day," thought John, a sudden blaze of fury burning through him, "you, Voules, will be taught a very different culture from that." Aloud John said nothing, but merely sat nervously in his chair, fidgeting with his collar, and clasping and unclasping his hands upon the table—an excellent imitation of the real Treves.

"Is there anything you would wish to say?" inquired Voules.

John looked guardedly at the two men who sat opposite.

"Please go to the window," commanded Voules.

The two men rose obediently and crossed the room. John dropped his voice.

"I understood," he said to Voules, "that I was to receive"—he stopped, looked into Voules's face, then turned his eyes away.

"Rathenau," Voules commanded, "ring the bell."

Cherriton rang the bell, and a moment later Conrad entered the room.

"The packet, Conrad, for Mr. Treves."

Conrad went out and returned a moment later, carrying a small white packet. He handed it to Voules, and Voules passed it to John.

"Thank you—thank you!" exclaimed John, taking it quickly. He knew the packet contained cocaine, and he slipped it carefully into his pocket.

"You will report to us wherever you are?" inquired Voules.

"Wherever I am," answered John.

"Great matters are pending," responded the doctor; "soon you will be of use to us. In regard to finance," he added, after a moment's pause, "you will write to our Captain Cherriton." He rose and gripped John's hand. "You will have no cause to regret your association with us, I can assure you of that."

"Perhaps you'll have some cause to regret your association with me," thought John, as he looked into the heavy jowled face.

Five minutes later he was out in the road, bidding good-bye to Captain Cherriton, who waved a careless farewell to him.

"We shall meet soon again," said the captain.

John nodded, leapt on to his bicycle, and rode briskly down the road.

CHAPTER XVIII

On the following evening, at eight o'clock, John Manton presented himself at Dacent Smith's apartment in Jermyn Street. He had hurried to London in answer to a wire, telling him to report himself personally. Elaine, who had made the journey with him, had gone on to her rooms in Camden Town. The door of Dacent Smith's suite of rooms was opened by Grew, who conducted John immediately to the great man's apartment. As always, when John visited his Chief's abode, the speckless cleanliness of the stairs, the glitter of varnish and brass reminded him somewhat of the interior of a battleship.

His superior's own room was orderly as usual, and Dacent Smith himself, who occupied a deep leather-covered chair at the hearth, rose and greeted him with a cordial handshake. The elder man was in evening clothes; he was, as always, plump, ruddy-cheeked, bright-eyed, and cheery in manner. His politeness struck John in marked contrast to the gruffness of Doctor Voules. These two men, Voules and Dacent Smith, heads of two great secret armies, were conducting a duel for supremacy. They were totally different in character and calibre, and John (perhaps he was prejudiced in the matter) was prepared at any odds to back Dacent Smith to win.

"Help yourself to a cigarette, Treves."

John took a cigarette, and seated himself in a chair opposite his Chief. For a moment there was silence, then Dacent Smith, who had been watching the ascending smoke, looked at the younger man with the faintly humorous light that sometimes animated his vivid eyes.

"I am glad to see you alive, Treves. You have had one of the narrowest of escapes."

John expressed his surprise.

"I wasn't aware of any narrow escape, sir."

"Perhaps not," said Dacent Smith, "but yesterday morning, when you went to Voules's house, you literally walked into the lions' den. Fortunately, however, you were successful in preserving a whole skin."

"I had no sense of anything adventurous happening during that visit," John returned, full of curiosity.

"I'll tell you exactly just what did happen," Dacent Smith continued. He rose, went to his desk, and drew a letter from one of the drawers. "Read that letter," he said, "and see what your chances would have been if it had arrived at Voules's house before you did."

"Who wrote it?" asked John, looking at the single initial "S" at the end of the sheet.

"Your amiable friend, Crumbs," answered Dacent Smith. "He discovered Cherriton's letter in your dispatch case."

John lifted his eyebrows in intense surprise.

"I had no idea that letter was discovered, sir. I took every precaution against discovery, and should have destroyed it, but it appeared to me a specimen of Cherriton's handwriting might be useful to you in the future."

"It will be useful when we come to stop his activities," answered Dacent Smith. "In the meantime its discovery by Sims very nearly resulted in your career coming to a sudden end. You can imagine the situation, Treves," he went on, "if that letter had arrived at Brooke when you were in Voules's house. For their own sakes, Voules and the others would never have dared to let you go. However, the letter never reached Voules, for Sinclair had it out of the locked bag at the fort five minutes after Sims deposited it there."

"It's a lucky thing for me," John said, handing back the letter to his Chief, "that Sinclair acted the way he did."

"Devilish lucky, Treves." Dacent Smith rose, placed the letter in a drawer in his desk and returned to his seat at the hearth.

"Now, Treves, as to Voules. Who is he?"

"He is some one in authority," answered John. "There is no doubt of that whatever."

"What is his appearance?"

"He is a heavily-built, bullet-headed man, between fifty and sixty. I should judge him to be used to exercising autocratic authority over others. When I reached Rollo Meads there were also present in the house two Germans, who gave me the impression of being naval officers. The fourth member of the party was Captain Cherriton, whose real name is Rathenau, as I discovered owing to the fact that they spoke German, which Cherriton believes I don't understand."

John continued and detailed fully his interview with Voules. He described his receipt of the cocaine tabloids from Conrad and his exhibition of the bogus five little wounds on his wrist, which had convinced Voules that he was a victim of the drug habit. When he had concluded Dacent Smith's lips tightened.

"You acted very shrewdly, Treves. I will see that Voules and his little party are kept under observation. From your description, I can tell you exactly who Voules is, Treves," he said. "We have suspected his identity for some time. Until two months ago Voules was General von Kuhne, in command of a corps of the Fifteenth Army. He is a Badenser, born and reared in Constance. Our investigation department informs me that he is credited by the enemy with great ability. In character he is instinctively aggressive; a fighter imbued through and through with the offensive spirit. It is to General von Kuhne that we owe our present awkward predicament on the South Coast. Outwardly nothing is wrong, but our department knows that Germany is preparing a heavy blow. We are contending against something new, big, and masterful; something that has been arranged and planned for months. How far General von Kuhne's plans have matured I do not yet know. We are so far, Treves, only groping towards knowledge. My reports tell me that at least eight forts on the South Coast are being subtly tampered with in one way or another. You have seen yourself the masterly manner in which Sims managed to work his will at Heatherpoint.

"Sims's dossier," he went on, "reached me in full only to-night, and is a further instance of an effective German trick. Sims's real name is Steinbaum. He is a Hamburg Jew, who emigrated to America in 1912. We cannot trace him from then until 1915, when, with the German naval attaché at Washington, Captain Boy Ed, he made an attempt to blow up the Pittsburg bridge works. He escaped the American police, and vanished. The next step in his career was when he landed at Liverpool from America. He was already a German spy, and enlisted in our army under the name of Sims, a baker by trade."

"I suppose," inquired John, "the idea of arresting Voules and his immediate confederates is outside our plan?"

Dacent Smith nodded. He put his finger-tips together, and remained thoughtfully silent for several minutes.

"No; it would not do," he said, as though desirous of convincing John of the correctness of his judgment "If I were to lay Voules, and a dozen of the others whom we know, suddenly by the heels, we should damage our chances, possibly irretrievably. You see, if we did that, we should be removing our special avenues of information. By arresting the spies we know, we should lose the great mass of information we manage to glean from them, and at the same time should be obliged to continue the fight against other agents whom we do not know. Do you follow me?"

John nodded. "I confess it never occurred to me in that light, but I can see the force of your argument."

"We always stand to learn something from Mrs. Beecher Monmouth, by secretly reading all her letters," continued Dacent Smith, "but if we arrest her we lose that advantage. Then, again, their present scheme in the South may be so far advanced that it will work to fruition by itself, even if we remove a dozen individuals. General von Kuhne is, of course, the keystone of the whole business, and when the time comes we shall get him— —" he paused a moment, and looked quizzically into John's face—"or he will get us!"

"He will have to rise pretty early in the morning to get you," thought John, genuinely impressed by his reasoning. Nevertheless, he inwardly admitted that Kuhne was an antagonist well fitted to measure swords even with Dacent Smith. Always, in these short interviews he obtained with his Chief, John felt himself drawn anew to the head of his department. Manton had no doubt whatever of Dacent Smith's ability, his intelligence was keen as a sword-blade, and swift as that same blade in the hands of a brilliant fencer. For all that, it seemed strange to John, as he sat in the well-furnished, neatly-ordered, bachelor apartment, to think that this quiet, well-groomed, middle-aged gentleman was the head and heart, the chief nerve centre, in fact, of the greatest defensive force in the country.

"Now," said Dacent Smith, when he concluded his observations, "is there anything at all troubling your mind, Treves, anything you'd like to get off your chest, for instance?"

John looked at him quickly, wondering if his keen eye had detected anything.

"Well," he confessed, "as a matter of fact, there is something that bothers me a good deal."

"Pass me another cigarette," said Dacent Smith, "and let me hear it."

John handed him another cigarette, and hesitated.

"Go on," urged his Chief.

"Well, I should like to report, sir," John said at length, "that my personal position has become—well, peculiarly difficult during the past few days."

"Do you find your work disappointing?"

"I am keener on my work than ever," John answered.

"What is it, then?"

"Well," confessed John, "to be precise, I find I am getting rather entangled with a lady." His tone was serious, and Dacent Smith took the statement gravely.

"Mrs. Beecher Monmouth, do you mean?"

John shook his head.

"Mrs. Beecher Monmouth is rather pressing whenever I meet her," he said, with a deprecating smile, "but she is not the lady in question."

"Who is the lady?"

John was silent; he found a strange diffidence in tackling this subject. It was a matter of some difficulty to state exactly what was the situation between himself and Elaine. Dacent Smith waited, and then tapped the arm of his chair with his finger, which was his only manner of showing impatience.

"Come, Treves, who is the lady?"

"Bernard Treves's wife, sir!"

"Oh! And wherein lies the particular awkwardness?"

"Yesterday she came down to the Gordon Hotel in Newport to see me, and stayed the night there."

"Was that awkward for you?"

"I'm afraid it was, sir. It seems," went on John, "that there was a disagreement between her and her husband, which ended in the lady refusing to live with him until he improved his habits."

"A very proper and spirited attitude to take," responded Dacent Smith.

"That is my opinion," said John, "but, unfortunately, she has decided to forgive her husband."

Dacent Smith suddenly sat erect.

"You don't mean she has made any untoward discovery?"

"Oh, no," said John, "she accepts me absolutely. And so far as I know she has never experienced the faintest doubt. But the awkwardness comes in through the fact that she has decided to forgive her husband and take him back again!"

Dacent Smith looked at the younger man for a minute, then whistled softly.

"By gad, Treves, yours is certainly a difficult path."

"I am glad you see it as I do, sir."

"Devilish difficult—and what's the lady like? Is she young and pretty?"

"She is about twenty-three years of age," said John, "and—and, well pretty doesn't quite describe her. She has dark hair and grey eyes. She is rather above the average in height. She——" John hesitated and stumbled. "I am no connoisseur in these matters, sir, but in my opinion she is an unusually beautiful girl."

Dacent Smith looked at him squarely.

"And that, no doubt, intensifies your difficulty, eh, Treves?"

"Well, my position last night," he said briefly, "was more than awkward." A sudden note of irritation found its way into John's voice; he could not have himself explained why he felt irritation. "The situation was wrong altogether. I felt I had no right to pass as Bernard Treves. It is one thing to deceive Treves's father in a good cause, or to deceive everybody else, but it is quite another matter to trick a young, good-looking woman the way I had to deceive Mrs. Treves. It doesn't seem to me to be playing the game, sir."

"You mean," inquired Dacent Smith, quietly, "the young lady made advances to you, she forgave you, and offered to live with you again as your wife, and you, being a man of honour, felt the situation keenly? Tell me, Treves," he went on, with a new interest in the matter, "what is she like? Her mental equipment, I mean?"

"She is very feminine, and by no means a fool," explained John. "I evaded her last night, but she came to London with me to-day, and is waiting for me this evening. She knows Cherriton and Manwitz. Cherriton, as a matter of fact, has been paying her undesirable attentions." John, who had been looking at the hearth-rug, suddenly lifted his face. "That's the whole situation, sir, and I don't feel that I can go on deceiving her."

For a long minute there was silence in the little room. Dacent Smith's little gilt clock on the mantelpiece chimed the half-hour.

"We're in deep waters here, Treves," he said slowly and seriously. "I can see only two ways out of it. One is that she should be restored to her undesirable husband."

"If," said John, "Treves is cured of his drug habit, I suppose that would be the right thing to do." Even as he spoke a feeling shot through him that was quite definitely antagonistic to this idea. He felt jealous and utterly resentful at the thought.

"He isn't cured, and shows no likelihood of being cured," answered Dacent Smith. "My last report is that he tried to break out of the nursing home, and very nearly got away. He is in the condition where he would give his very soul to get drugs. No," he said, shaking his head, "we'll leave Bernard Treves in his present isolation. In surrendering his personality to you he is making some slight restitution; he is unconsciously doing something for his country. We need waste no pity on him. So far as we are concerned, Treves does not count."

"What if Treves had actually managed to escape, sir?"

"In that case 'Voules' and the rest of them would be down on you like a ton of bricks, but we need not at present anticipate a calamity of that sort. Now in regard to Treves's wife, when you see her to-night, give her my compliments, and say I should like her to call here one afternoon this week. I think I can then ease the awkwardness of your position in regard to her. I have an idea at any rate."

Half an hour later John made his way out to Camden Town, and rang the bell of 65, Bowles Avenue. Elaine herself opened the door and offered him a smiling welcome.

CHAPTER XIX

In the soft illumination of the white and gold dining-salon of the Golden Pavilion Hotel John found himself completely at home. Two days had passed since his visit to Elaine, and he was again at work under the ægis of Dacent Smith. He had chosen a quiet table in the corner, had selected the dishes for his dinner, and was leaning back in his chair surveying the brilliant scene with an appreciative eye. The Golden Pavilion Hotel is famed alike for its refined and luxurious furnishings, its band, its cuisine, and its exclusiveness. The head waiter, who looked like an archbishop, advanced soundlessly over the rich carpet, and stood at John's elbow.

"I beg your pardon," said the man, in a low, smooth voice, "but the lady at the table beyond the second pillar, sir, would like to have a word with you."

John raised his head and glanced in the direction the man had indicated. He had already seen Mrs. Beecher Monmouth, and had made a special point of concealing the fact. He rose now, however, and moved across the room between crowded tables.

Mrs. Beecher Monmouth, seated with a party of friends, flashed a brilliant smile at him when he advanced.

"Oh, you poor lonely creature," she exclaimed, as she placed her jewelled fingers in his. "I saw you moping in your corner," she continued, when a waiter had brought an extra chair and John had accepted an invitation to dine with her party, "and took pity on you; don't you think that was nice of me?" She looked at him with a long, deep glance, conscious of her striking beauty. Her beauty was of the instantly arresting order. The fact that the art of coiffeur and cosmetic enabled her to heighten her charms was all in her favour where men were concerned. Quite, as it were, by accident, she now laid her fingers on John's sleeve.

"I must introduce you to my guests. My husband you already know."

John bowed slightly towards Mr. Beecher Monmouth, whose evening clothes intensified the sallowness of his complexion. John noted the parchment-like character of his skin, the tired look in his eyes, and the manipulation of his thin hair to create the effect of youthful plenty. He was an old man striving hopelessly to look young. Mrs. Beecher Monmouth turned her eyes from her husband towards the slender figure of a woman at her right-hand side.

"Lady Rachel," she said, "may I present Mr. Treves." John bowed again, and Lady Rachel Marvin smiled at him graciously. She was a woman of slender figure, with exceptionally large, long-lashed eyes. Her neck was long, slender and white, and she wore diamond ear-rings, which scintillated as she moved her head. Her age was probably thirty-five, and she was, in appearance, distinctly aristocratic. Her voice was thin and high-pitched, and she talked incessantly.

The third member of Mrs. Beecher Monmouth's party was a fat woman of fifty, the wealthy wife of a colonel in the gunners. Any woman assessing the jewels Mrs. Pomfret Bond wore would have known that she was wealthy, and that she was determined other people should know it. She was a foolish, vulgar woman, and John, looking at her, realised almost immediately that she would be as wax in the hands of Mrs. Beecher Monmouth. But it was to Lady Rachel Marvin that John turned his attention. "Did you know the Seventh Division has been moved from Aldershot?" she was inquiring, looking at Beecher Monmouth.

"No," said the elderly man, "we don't hear anything in Parliament, Lady Rachel."

"I heard it only quite by accident," babbled Lady Rachel. "You know my cousin, Derrick, is in the Coldstreams; you remember Derrick?" she said, turning her big eyes upon Mrs. Beecher Monmouth, "I have told you so much about him."

Mrs. Beecher Monmouth smiled brilliantly and nodded. Lady Rachel then went on to explain that it was Derrick who had told her of a new gun being tested at Woolwich. Derrick had been on the G.H.Q. Staff, "and," went on Lady Rachel, "he is almost as mysterious about it as his friend Commander Loyson is about the new cruiser—the *Malta*, which has just been put into commission at — —"

"Is there a new cruiser being commissioned at — —?" inquired John, sliding into the conversation. He was so apparently interested that Lady Rachel looked at him with a pleased expression on her somewhat foolish face.

"I am afraid, Mr. Treves, I ought not to chatter about it. But being behind the scenes, and knowing so many people one naturally picks up little bits of news here and there. It is quite easy to piece the bits together. I have not heard anything actually about the new cruiser," she said, "the *Malta*, I mean, but from things Commander Loyson said to Derrick, and from other things I have heard, I can assure you it is something wonderful."

John, listening to her chatter, wondered how much of this information she had, out of sheer vanity, passed on to Mrs. Beecher Monmouth.

Lady Rachel Marvin certainly knew a great number of people, and her social position gave her many chances to pick up exclusive information. Her silly, butterfly existence consisted in flitting from one drawing-room to another. Here she exchanged such gossip as she had been able to collect from her equally frivolous friends. As John listened to her he realised that such women as Lady Rachel are a real source of danger to the nation.

When dinner was at an end Lady Rachel went to speak to some friends at another table, and the minute she had gone Mrs. Beecher Monmouth turned her attention solely to John, ignoring Mrs. Pomfret Bond and the "Ogre."

"Naughty boy," said Mrs. Beecher Monmouth under her breath. "Why have you never been to see me?"

"I have been in the Isle of Wight visiting my father," answered John promptly.

"I know that," answered she; "therefore, and because you sent me those Russian cigarettes, I intend to forgive you! Now, you must come and see me soon," she went on, "there are many things I want to talk to you about."

"I should like to talk to you about quite a number of things," responded John in the same intimate tone.

"When can you come?" asked she.

"Any time you like."

"Not to-morrow, the 'Ogre' will be at home then," she said, in a voice too low for Mr. Beecher Monmouth to catch. "Don't you think he is looking very old and worn?"

John glanced at Beecher Monmouth's glazed countenance and tired eyes, and even at that moment the elderly politician was looking adoringly at his wife, admiring the richness of her hair, the fine contour of her shoulders, and the brilliance of her complexion. John felt almost sorry for the befooled and weary Member of Parliament, who had sold his old age and his happiness into the bondage of this woman.

"Come to tea the day after to-morrow," said Mrs. Beecher Monmouth, and John accepted the invitation with alacrity.

Two days later when he presented himself at five o'clock in the afternoon at Mrs. Beecher Monmouth's residence in Grosvenor Square, he was ushered immediately into the lady's boudoir.

He had seen that room only in the illumination of the pink-shaded electric light, now he saw it again in daylight, and found it even more luxurious than he had imagined—the white polar-bear rug, the brilliant-hued Chinese *kakemonos* hung on the wall behind Mrs. Beecher Monmouth's divan, the long gilt-framed mirrors, and gilt-legged chairs all conspired to create an atmosphere of sumptuous richness. Mrs. Beecher Monmouth in an afternoon gown which gave her almost a slender and distinguished appearance, was seated in a low arm-chair. Lady Rachel Marvin occupied the divan, and John, much as he disliked this foolish ox-eyed woman of fashion, was obliged to admit that she had disposed herself gracefully upon the cushions. The third guest was Mrs. Pomfret Bond, who was delighted to be in that society, and talked as much military gossip as she could to show that she, too, was in the swim.

When John had been cordially received, and had accepted a cup of tea and a fragment of bread and butter, he seated himself at the foot of the divan and entered into conversation with Lady Rachel. Under orders from Dacent Smith he had come there with that express purpose.

"We have been talking of the dreadful news, Mr. Treves," said Lady Rachel, biting a slip of bread and butter with long sharp teeth.

"You mean the sinking of the *Malta*?" inquired John.

"Yes, how appalling it is," said she. "I heard it before it appeared in the papers."

"It's one of the worst disasters we have had for some time," responded John; "a new ship costing a million pounds of public money, and two hundred fine lives."

Mrs. Pomfret Bond spoke up indignantly.

"I can't imagine how the Germans find out about our ships. We're supposed to have an Intelligence Department. Why don't they put a stop to this sort of thing?"

"I expect they do the best they can," remarked John.

"But one always has to reckon with spies," said Mrs. Pomfret Bond.

"Of course," said John.

"But the *Malta* was a new vessel," observed Mrs. Beecher Monmouth; "how could they find out when she was to leave — —?"

"The Germans must have found out," intervened Lady Rachel, claiming the conversation again, "for no submarines had been in those waters for weeks, and they had been swept for mines the day before. I know this for a fact."

John looked at her keenly. That afternoon he had had a long conversation with Dacent Smith in regard to Lady Rachel Marvin. The fact that she had, two days ago, mentioned the *Malta* during her irresponsible chatter at dinner, had aroused a suspicion in John's mind that possibly the disaster which had happened to the new cruiser had been directly due to her foolish vanity—to her ineradicable desire to obtain social distinction by revealing to her friends her superior knowledge of what went on behind the scenes. This idea, as he sat in her presence now, listening to her talk, grew in strength, and at the first opportunity that occurred, he drew Mrs. Beecher Monmouth aside. He knew that he was venturing upon very thin ice in putting questions to her.

"Well, you bad boy," whispered Mrs. Beecher Monmouth, "why have you been trying to flirt with Lady Rachel?"

John had seated himself on a low Turkish stool at her side.

"How could I see Lady Rachel when you are in the room?" he answered, gallantly.

"If you only meant it," responded Mrs. Beecher Monmouth, "I'd give you two pieces of sugar in your next cup of tea!"

"Lady Rachel cannot hold a candle to you," affirmed John.

"You mustn't be hard on her," returned Mrs. Beecher Monmouth. In the afternoon light the "Ogre's" wife looked scarcely twenty-five, a remarkably beautiful and imperious woman. Even John was obliged to confess that no fault existed in her passionate and somewhat sensuous beauty. For her part, Mrs. Beecher Monmouth was so used to admiration that she accepted John's flattery as a matter of course. Bernard Treves, she told herself, was one of the strings to her bow, and quite the nicest-looking boy of them all. "You mustn't be hard on poor Lady Rachel," she said; "she is such a dear, delightful chatterbox."

"Lady Rachel seems to know a good deal about the *Malta*."'

Mrs. Beecher Monmouth turned her eyes and fixed her gaze swiftly upon him; then she remarked, quietly:

"One of her relations is a big-wig at the Admiralty."

"That fact, and what she picked up from other of her naval friends, enabled her," said John, "to give a guess at when the *Malta* would leave — —"

Mrs. Beecher Monmouth became suddenly very still.

"How did you know that, Bernard?" she asked.

John observed a hardening of the line of her mouth.

"I merely put two and two together and assumed it," he said. Then, quietly daring, he leaned forward, unobserved by others in the room, and seized Mrs. Beecher Monmouth's hand.

"Is it true?" he questioned.

She looked at him a long minute, and then smiled, but there was a cruel light in her eyes.

"It is true," pursued John.

A silence followed; then Mrs. Beecher Monmouth inclined her fine head very slightly. John was dexterous enough not to slide his hand away from hers too soon. The aversion he felt from her made him remove it as soon as he reasonably could. Then he drew in a deep breath.

"I see," he said, in a low voice, "she told you when the *Malta* was to sail."

And though Mrs. Beecher Monmouth was too cautious to admit the fact, John knew in his heart that it was absolutely true. Lady Rachel, exercising her silly desire for gossip, had been tricked into imparting this fatal information. Because of this she was, John believed, just as much responsible for the sinking of the *Malta* as if she herself had discharged the torpedo which wrought its doom. She was, in fact, an unwitting traitor to her country. And John, as he moved from Mrs. Beecher Monmouth's side, felt a certain implacable animosity towards this vain society woman, with her wide eyes, her high-pitched voice, her elegant aristocratic poses.

Nevertheless, he was politeness itself as he drew her towards the window.

"I'd like to have a word with you alone, Lady Rachel," he said.

When they were out of earshot of Mrs. Beecher Monmouth and Mrs. Pomfret Bond, John lowered his voice, and looked down into the big, long-lashed eyes.

"You were speaking a few minutes ago, Lady Rachel," he said, "of the *Malta*."

Lady Rachel smiled and nodded.

"I think," went on John, "I ought to inform you that I am a member of the Intelligence Department!"

"Oh, are you really?" exclaimed Lady Rachel, looking at him with a sudden vivid interest. "I have so often wanted to meet some one in the secret service. I think you all so splendid!"

"I am glad you appreciate us," John answered dryly; "perhaps, Lady Rachel," he went on, "you would like to know more about our department?"

"I should love it dearly," said she, with an expression of delight on her weakly pretty features.

"Well," said John, "if you care to accompany me to my office in a few minutes, I will present you to my Chief. He has already expressed a wish to meet you."

Lady Rachel looked puzzled for a moment.

"Perhaps I know him, Mr. Treves. I may have met him in society. I suppose I mustn't ask his name?" she added mysteriously.

"No, don't ask his name," answered John.

Ten minutes later Lady Rachel Marvin was seated beside John in a taxi. The vehicle glided out of Grosvenor Place and passed Green Park.

"Why are you looking so grim?" observed the lady. as John leaned back with folded arms.

"I am thinking of the *Malta* and of the two hundred fine fellows who were drowned yesterday."

CHAPTER XX

It was six o'clock when John stepped out into Dacent Smith's bachelor room. His Chief was seated at his desk, deep in work. John closed the door and crossed the room.

"Well?" asked Dacent Smith, raising his head and still sitting with poised pen at his desk.

"I was right, sir, in regard to Lady Rachel Marvin. The information that sunk the *Malta* was conveyed by her to Mrs. Beecher Monmouth two days ago."

"You don't mean she intentionally conveyed it?" exclaimed Dacent Smith, rising and looking at John in amazement.

"Oh no, sir, not at all; she conveyed it with no intention to do harm, and only out of an inveterate habit of gossip."

Dacent Smith drew his brows together. His expression was more stern in that moment than John had ever seen it.

"A damnable habit of gossiping," he observed forcibly. "Well, what have you done, Treves?"

"I have brought the lady with me, sir, thinking you would wish to act at once in regard to her."

Dacent Smith nodded in approbation.

"Send her in to me, Treves, and wait outside."

John went out of the room, and Dacent Smith moved to the mantelshelf and looked for a moment at the photograph of a girl of eighteen, a girl who looked scarcely more than a child. He was still at the hearth when Lady Rachel was ushered into the room by John, who closed the door and left the two together. What took place between Dacent Smith and the woman whose foolish vanity had sunk the *Malta* John did not know, but he was able to guess pretty well, for twenty minutes later Dacent Smith opened the door and summoned him into the room.

"Come in, Treves."

John entered and found Lady Rachel standing near his Chief's desk. Her face was white, her nose unromantically red; she had been crying. On Dacent Smith's desk lay a letter in Lady Rachel's handwriting.

DEAR BOB, it ran, *I have had a sudden breakdown in health. The doctors inform me I am to go to Pitt Lunan Hydro for at least four months. I may not even be well enough to return to town even then. Forgive me, Bob, for not being able to say good-bye, but I am obliged to hurry away at once.*

Your devoted wife,

RACHEL.

As John entered the room Lady Rachel Marvin folded this letter, placed it in an envelope, and, still standing, addressed it to her husband, "Lieutenant-Commander Marvin, H.M.S. — —, Southampton." She closed the envelope and accepted a stamp from Dacent Smith.

Dacent Smith broke the long silence that followed.

"Treves," said he, "Lady Rachel leaves Euston for Scotland to-night by the seven o'clock train."

"I don't want to go to Scotland!" intervened Lady Rachel petulantly. "I dislike hydros intensely; I think them absolutely detestable places!"

Dacent Smith watched her for a moment with unrelenting eyes, then spoke in a tone there was no mistaking.

"Lady Rachel, you will take the train for Scotland to-night. You will then stay there the full period my department has prescribed for you." Lady Rachel flashed a rebellious look at him, but Dacent Smith continued in his unyielding tones: "Failing this, you will find yourself, I can assure you, in a place far more 'detestable' to you than even the most uncomfortable of hydros!"

He turned to his desk. For a moment Lady Rachel wavered, then, seeing from his attitude that resistance was hopeless, she lifted her head and went haughtily out of the room. John escorted her to the street, helped her into a taxi, and saw her drive away after a flash of her big eyes that was meant either to consume him with fire or to freeze him to death; he did not know which. When John returned his Chief was standing at the mantelshelf. The expression of sternness had entirely left his face. In his fingers he held the photograph of a charming girl, scarcely more than a child. For a minute he was silent, his eyes upon the figure in the silver frame; then he held up the picture and showed it to John.

"This is my niece, Treves," he said quietly.

John took the photograph and inspected it critically.

"An extremely pretty girl, sir."

Dacent Smith nodded.

"She is just eighteen, Treves. She became engaged to young Rashleigh, gunnery lieutenant on the *Malta*." His tones deepened in intensity. "That was four days ago—and to-day Rashleigh is dead. He was one of the finest fellows who ever stepped. And, in my opinion, he and two hundred others lost their lives solely because Lady Rachel Marvin could not keep her mouth shut. My niece, who is still only a child—you can see for yourself what she is like, Treves"—for the first time his voice shook with emotion—"my niece is at home lying in a semi-conscious condition. The doctors tell us that her reason is threatened—and all this because a silly woman babbled about things that didn't concern her!"

The man who was one of the greatest powers in the country was still holding the photograph in his fingers, his eyes fixed pitifully upon the delicate girlish beauty of his niece. He replaced it slowly on the mantelshelf, then, turning, stood looking before him, his hands clenched at his side. The sternness of his lips at that moment revealed to John all the hidden strength behind his kindly exterior; he was stirred to the depths. And suddenly he flashed a look at John and struck his open palm with a clenched fist.

"If I had my way, Treves," he said between tense lips, "if the powers that be would make me autocrat for a week, I'd treat these fool women as traitors. An unguarded word," he went on, "is, in my opinion, just as much an act of disloyalty in time of war as an insult to the flag or the army. If the public only knew it, we have lost ship after ship, and possibly thousands of men, as a result of vain gossip in clubs, trains, shops and smart drawing-rooms. On Saturday we lost a cruiser worth a million. Young Rashleigh died, and two hundred splendid sailors, because Lady Rachel Marvin must have her afternoon's social success! What do you think of it, Treves?"

John was thinking of the tragedy of it all—of the desolated homes—the two hundred homes where sorrow stalked that day. He was thinking of the sweet-faced, broken-hearted girl, hovering on the verge of sanity.

"I'd like to wring Lady Rachel's neck!" said John, swept out of himself.

"I could tell you a score of such cases," said Dacent Smith. "In one case a present of a hundred cigarettes and a silly woman's curiosity meant one of the greatest disasters that has occurred to us since the war began." He suddenly stopped, pulled himself up, and became normal in tone. He was fully himself again, the keen, resourceful man of action. "Now, Treves," he said, "we must get back to business. Lady Rachel Marvin has been a valuable 'feeder' to the enemy. She is now out of action, however. I regard," he went on, "Beecher Monmouth, M.P., as also dangerous. Is that your opinion?"

"My opinion," said John, "is that Beecher Monmouth is not disloyal, but, as he is wax in his wife's hands, his political position makes him dangerous."

"You don't believe he could keep a secret from her?"

"From what I've seen of them both, sir, I should doubt it."

Dacent Smith went to his desk and made a note on his writing pad. "I will write a note to the Home Secretary. I think we can get rid of Beecher Monmouth without arousing suspicion. Now, Treves, in regard to the sinking of the *Malta*—we are a little bit at sea in this matter. Mrs. Beecher Monmouth and her accomplices have out-manoeuvred us. In some manner or other she managed to get her information to Germany, or to a German submarine commander, eight hours after picking up the facts from Lady Rachel Marvin. We want to know how she managed to do this, Treves."

He crossed the room as he spoke, and took a sheaf of papers from his cabinet of drawers against the wall. He handed the documents to John. John observed that the sheets were thin and almost transparent, and that each sheet had been written over in indelible pencil.

"You have in your hand," explained Dacent Smith, "intercepted copies of all Mrs. Beecher Monmouth's letters since the fifteenth of last month. That is," he added, "all the letters she has sent through the post. You will notice among them three advertisements—all jewellery for sale."

John glanced at the pile of letters in his hand. There were among them orders to tradesmen, half a dozen letters to a dressmaker, showing the great care with which Mrs. Beecher Monmouth apparelled herself; and two letters written and posted to her husband. These last were interlarded with extravagant expressions of affection and love. But it was the third advertisement, addressed to a famous daily paper, that held John's interest. This ran:

"Lady wishes to sell privately a pearl and platinum pendant, perfectly-matched pearls, surrounding Orient pearl of splendid lustre.—Apply Box A3656."

John closely examined this advertisement, and the other two, which were similar.

"Do you think she is in debt, sir?"

"Beecher Monmouth's a rich man," answered Dacent Smith, "with big interest in the timber business. However, one never knows what an extravagant woman may succeed in spending. I think it may be worth your while, Treves, to follow up the trail of this advertisement. I want you to apply yourself assiduously to the cultivation of this lady for the present. And keep well in mind the fact that, though her letters show nothing, she is yet conveying news regularly to the enemy."

CHAPTER XXI

Two evenings later Mrs. Beecher Monmouth's Spanish maid came to the door of her mistress's boudoir, knocked, and entered quietly.

"Doctor Voules is here, madam."

"I told you, Cecily, I was not at home!" said Mrs. Beecher Monmouth. "I don't want to see Doctor Voules—I don't want to see anybody!"

"But, madam," protested the maid, "it would be impossible to refuse to see Doctor Voules!"

Something took place between mistress and maid—an exchange of glances—which seemed somewhat to alter Mrs. Beecher Monmouth's mood of irritation.

"Very well, Cecily, let him come up." And when Cecily had departed to summon Doctor Voules, Mrs. Beecher Monmouth went to her low Turkish table, lit a buff-coloured cigarette, and stood with her back to the hearth, smoking somewhat more rapidly than usual. A knock came at the door, and Doctor Voules entered. He strolled into the apartment with his shoulders well back, his heavy chin thrust forward, the smile that sat so ill upon his harsh face was well in evidence.

"My dear Mrs. Monmouth, my felicitations!"

Mrs. Beecher Monmouth took the gloved hand languidly and turned away.

"Don't felicitate me on anything, Doctor!"

"But the *Malta*!" protested the Doctor. "That was a superb stroke for the Fatherland! It is not often I am lavish of praise."

"You are certainly not a woman's man!" retorted Mrs. Beecher Monmouth, flashing a look at him.

"Your beauty is apparent to me, as it would be to a much younger man, I can assure you of that, my dear *gnädige Frau*," said Voules.

"I am not talking of beauty—I am talking of moods," replied she. "You observe nothing of my disturbance!"

Doctor Voules, who did not believe in moods, who never permitted such weakness in his subordinates, pressed his lips tightly together.

"You will be good enough, *gnädige Frau*," he commanded, "to be a little more precise and explicit. Something has occurred, no doubt, to ruffle your temper." He went to a chair at the hearth, seated himself, asked permission to smoke, and lit one of his big, black cigars.

Mrs. Beecher Monmouth looked at him squarely for a moment.

"Of course, my personal sufferings are nothing to you! It is nothing to you, for instance, that my friend, Lady Rachel Marvin, has vanished!"

Doctor Voules lifted his eyebrows.

"In what manner has she vanished?"

"She is one of the most useful friends I have ever had," returned Mrs. Beecher Monmouth, "and has suddenly disappeared without leaving me a note or a line."

Doctor Voules drew his brows together.

"Refresh my memory, please, in regard to this lady."

"She is the foolish little chatterbox who provided me with all the information I needed in regard to the *Malta*," retorted Mrs. Beecher Monmouth curtly.

Doctor Voules suddenly became all attention.

"And you mean, *gnädige Frau*, that this lady has vanished?"

Mrs. Beecher Monmouth assured him of the fact.

"No one knows," she went on, "where she is. She was my most intimate friend. I had put all my hopes in her, Excellenz! Then, to add to my vexation, my husband has been suddenly and unexpectedly appointed to a Government commission of inquiry in Ireland. He is delighted, of course; it is an honour for him. Then, again," went on Mrs. Beecher Monmouth, "Mrs. Pomfret Bond, who was in the habit of telling me everything she knew, who was always scraping up bits of gossip that were of use, is— —"

"Has she vanished also?" inquired Voules, suddenly rising.

"No," returned Mrs. Beecher Monmouth, "but she has become mute as a fish. My opinion is that she has been warned not to talk, and that I have at last become a suspected person!"

Voules looked at her and shook his ponderous head.

"No, no! Your position, *gnädige Frau*, is too secure for that; also you are too clever."

"I am not a fool," answered Mrs. Beecher Monmouth, "but these things disturb me!"

"Your love of the Fatherland, your belief in final victory, will sustain you. You lose your friend, Lady Rachel Marvin, but to a woman of your beauty and position nothing is impossible. You shall get other fools—is it not so? England, *gnädige Frau*, is full of fools!"

He moved across to her and took her hand firmly in his.

"Soon you shall have your reward. I will promise you my very best efforts. You will wait yet a little while longer. My plans," he added quietly, "are shaping themselves with the perfection of clockwork. Enormous things have been done, my dear *gnädige Frau*, in the last few weeks, and disaffection now, even from you, would destroy the harmony.... Remember your sentiments towards these people!"

"I remember them well enough!" answered Mrs. Beecher Monmouth. She was still standing at the hearth, and looked steadily before her as she spoke.

"Good!" exclaimed Voules in his throat. "We will now come to the purpose of my visit. You shall have your part in the big work afoot. I assure you there are bigger things than the sinking of the *Malta*! For instance, on the twenty-eighth we shall strike a blow that will not rapidly be forgotten by these English!"

He suddenly snapped his teeth together and drew tight his lips; a gleam of ferocity lit in his hard eyes.

"These English!" he exclaimed between his teeth. "Their arrogance maddens me! It is a torture to me to live among them, concealed thus as a civilian! I am maddened by their complacency!" he went on, "their calm! Nevertheless, we shall strike deep this time! Your work, *gnädige Frau*," he said, speaking in the tone of masterful authority that was his real habit, "your work is not difficult. On the twenty-fourth I request you to go to Heatherpoint Fort. It is fortunate that your husband is away. You can thus go to the Isle of Wight ostensibly for a holiday. While there you will make the acquaintance of the adjutant of Heatherpoint, who visits regularly the — — Hotel in Newport. My report is that this young Lieutenant Parkson is susceptible to beauty. You, *gnädige Frau*," he smiled his hard smile, "are, indeed, beautiful enough to engage the attention of one far less susceptible!"

"What do you wish me to do with this particular susceptible man?" inquired Mrs. Beecher Monmouth, with slight sarcasm.

"You are to engage the young man's attention, and his affections."

"You appear to forget, Excellenz, that I am a married woman of social position!"

"I do not forget, *gnädige Frau*; but your complaisance on that account will be more than ever flattering. The young man in question will not be able to resist the charms of the beautiful and wealthy society woman who is—to fall in love with him!"

Mrs. Beecher Monmouth smiled, and spoke with a touch of irony.

"I am your servant, Excellenz!"

"You are the servant of the Fatherland," answered Voules gravely, "and all I require is that this young man, Lieutenant Parkson, shall not be at his post in the fort on the night of the twenty-eighth. How you will succeed in keeping him away from duty is a matter for your own discretion—I have the fullest confidence in you. Captain Cherriton undertook the work, but the young man in question neither drinks nor gambles. Cherriton's efforts ended in complete failure. Moreover, our agent inside the fort has been strangely silent of late. We have received neither signal nor message from him for some days. If you play your cards neatly with Parkson, you will possibly secure an invitation to tea at the fort mess."

He went on and gave her a rapid sketch of Steinbaum, otherwise known as "Crumbs." The silence of "Crumbs" during the past few days had puzzled and disturbed him.

"We have made a number of arrangements in regard to Heatherpoint Fort," he concluded, "and it is absolutely essential to our purpose that no guns should be fired from that spot."

His eyes suddenly lit up. He was thinking of his great scheme, which was hourly drawing nearer fruition, and, on parting, he gripped Mrs. Beecher Monmouth's hand in his.

"*Gnädige Frau,*" he announced, "glorious things are shortly to occur!"

When he had gone Mrs. Beecher Monmouth seated herself in a chair and stared thoughtfully into the fire. She was conscious of a sense of doubt and uneasiness. General von Kuhne was a soldier of long training, masterful and aggressive. His gift of organisation, his theory of attack was always excellent—nevertheless, he was not subtle, he was not sensitive to the importance of little incidents. The sudden disappearance of Lady Rachel meant nothing to him, aroused no suspicion in him, and yet...

CHAPTER XXII

In pursuance of Dacent Smith's instructions, John presented himself at the massive doors of 289, Grosvenor Place, two nights later. He had pondered much upon those three advertisements, and the more he considered the matter, the more Mrs. Beecher Monmouth's desire privately to sell her jewels struck him as unusual. It was not usual, he told himself, for a woman of Mrs. Beecher Monmouth's position to dispossess herself of jewellery through the medium of advertisements in a newspaper. There are half a dozen firms in Bond Street alone, of proved honesty, any one of which is willing to make purchases of this kind.

John rang the bell, and the butler presently drew open the door.

"I am very sorry, sir," the man began, "but madame is not at home."

John expressed his complete surprise. He was, however, not in the least surprised, and had planned his visit with the sole object of finding Mrs. Beecher Monmouth away from home. For a minute he hesitated, looking doubtfully at the butler.

"Can you," he inquired, "tell me if Mrs. Monmouth's maid is in. I have a message to give her for her mistress."

"I can take any message you wish, sir."

"Thank you, no," said John, smiling at him; "what I have to say is—is rather personal to Mrs. Beecher Monmouth."

"Very good, sir," answered the sedate servant, and bowed. "Will you kindly step into the morning-room."

John went into the morning-room, moved to the window and looked into Grosvenor Place, out over the broad smooth road to the high brick wall surrounding the royal gardens. A few minutes elapsed, and then Cecily, Mrs. Beecher Monmouth's maid, came quietly in.

"You wish to see me, sir?"

John turned.

"Yes, Cecily." He looked into her face, noted her bead-black eyes, her olive skin, and the slight tendency to a moustache at the corner of each lip.

"Cecily," he said, "I have really come to ask your advice on a little personal matter." Cecily looked at him with an unreadable expression on her sullen countenance. "I want to give Mrs. Beecher Monmouth a present," went on John. "A little matter of a pair of pearl ear-rings. Can you tell me if she is fond of pearls?"

"Pearls, monsieur; oh, no!" Cecily shook her head. "Rubies or emeralds, yes, monsieur, but pearls, no."

"Oh," resumed John, "she doesn't care for pearls then?"

Cecily shook her head.

"She says they are insipid, monsieur."

"Perhaps she is right, Cecily, but in that case," he said, "I shall have to think of something else. Thank you, I am much obliged to you." He slipped a pound note into the woman's hand.

"Thank you, monsieur."

"Perhaps," John probed delicately, "madame is not fond of pearls because she has so many?"

Cecily was folding her pound note.

"Pearls do not suit madame; she never wears them. She has none at all, monsieur, only one pearl necklace, a wedding gift from her husband. She, however, never wears it."

John appeared to think.

"Surely, Cecily, I have seen her wearing a pearl pendant?"

Cecily shook her head again.

"No, monsieur, never. Madame has no pearls."

John laughed.

"Well, in that case, it must be emeralds or rubies."

"Emeralds or rubies," responded Cecily, "madame is most fond of them."

Three minutes later John was out of the house and hailing a taxi. As he relapsed back into the cushions, he fell into thought. "There is certainly," thought he, "more in these advertisements than meets the casual eye. Mrs. Beecher Monmouth detests pearls, she has none, never had any—and yet advertises them for sale!"

A quarter of an hour later, when John stepped into Dacent Smith's room, the elder man glanced quickly up from his desk.

"Well?"

"In regard to those three advertisements of jewellery," answered John, "inserted in the newspaper by Mrs. Beecher Monmouth, I should be glad, sir, if you would have them decoded."

Dacent Smith raised his eyebrows slightly.

John narrated what had occurred at his private interview with Cecily, and Dacent Smith was instantly of the opinion that Mrs. Beecher Monmouth's harmless advertisements were a matter for closer scrutiny. In the first place, he telephoned to his department and ordered that inquiry should be instituted at the newspaper office as to any earlier advertisements which may have been inserted in the paper by Mrs. Monmouth. If the three advertisements were a code message the intelligence decoding department would find its task vastly more easy if a considerable batch of advertisements in the same code were submitted. A brief code message, as John was now well aware, is always difficult to read. The longer the message, the easier is it to decipher.

The department's search at the newspaper office resulted in the finding of no less than sixteen earlier advertisements inserted by Mrs. Beecher Monmouth. In each case, only a box number was given, therefore the lady's identity never became public.

"It looks as if you are on the right track, Treves," said Dacent Smith, when this information was conveyed to him on the telephone.

Half an hour later Dacent Smith, again at the telephone, took down the decoded first advertisement, the one wherein Mrs. Beecher Monmouth had advertised a pearl pendant for sale. John's chief wrote it out carefully, and handed the slip across to the younger man.

"There is your advertisement, Treves," he exclaimed. There was a grave ring in his voice. John took the slip of paper and read:

"Note of Warning.—New standard eight thousand ton ship purposely advertised by shipping authorities here as fitting out at —— is a 'Q' ship, armed with six-inch guns, torpedo tubes are being fitted. Further news in next message."

John looked up from the pencilled lines. He saw in a flash the exact purport of the message. Mrs. Beecher Monmouth in pretending to advertise a pearl pendant was in reality sending a message to Germany to the effect that a certain vessel then building was a decoy ship, one of the famous vessels which had done so much to break the back of the submarine peril. John could easily realise how swiftly that news would reach Germany. Automatically the paper would reach Holland within two days. Any neutral ship might carry copies, and Berlin's Naval Department would possess the information a few minutes after the daily paper containing Mrs. Beecher Monmouth's advertisement reached Dutch soil. Every German spy in England who read the newspaper would receive the news on the morning of its insertion.

"I think for cunning that beats everything," said John, handing back the paper to Dacent Smith.

"They have been preparing this sort of thing for years," answered Dacent Smith. "But I am willing to admit that Mrs. Monmouth has this time stolen something of a march on us.

"Every one of her advertisements is being decoded, however, and every one, I have no doubt, will convey information of this nature. On the other hand," he said, "we have not yet learnt in what manner she communicated with the submarine that sunk the *Malta*, That must have been a much quicker communication. I shall leave it to you, Treves," he said quietly, "to find out what that method is. You will have to learn much more of Mrs. Beecher Monmouth than we know already. The fight is quickening between us. And the big fight which von Kuhne is planning in the Isle of Wight is not quite so indefinite to us as it was. The date at least is in our possession. And by then," he went on, "all the carrion will have wended their way there, even our friend, Mrs. Beecher Monmouth, will be there by then." John looked at him in sudden surprise.

"I thought she was seldom out of London, sir."

"That is the fact," answered Dacent Smith; "it is also the fact, however, that from the twenty-fourth of this month she has engaged rooms at a select boarding house in Freshwater. She is going to Freshwater," he added ironically, "to recuperate after an arduous London season!" He looked meaningly at John. John understood the significance of that look. The carrion were gathering. By the twenty-eighth all von Kuhne's active forces would be drawn to the Isle of Wight. Mrs. Beecher Monmouth, in taking rooms at Freshwater, was acquiring a residence in close proximity to Heatherpoint Fort. John wondered what her particular manoeuvre was to be. He put that question to Dacent Smith.

"We shall know all in good time, Treves," answered his chief. "You yourself will be in the Isle of Wight by then."

A few minutes later John bade good night to Dacent Smith. Being free for that evening, he took the tube to Camden Town. Here, at Bowles Avenue, in the quiet little street, he knocked once again at the door of Elaine's residence. He had not visited Elaine for nearly a week, and he knew that for some days to come he would be deeply occupied with Mrs. Beecher Monmouth, so he wished to make the most of the present opportunity. Twice during the past week Elaine had written him short notes asking him when he could come to visit her. There had been nothing in the notes to convey the idea that she wished him urgently to come. He was surprised, therefore, when Elaine, in answer to his knock, drew open the door and recognised him with an expression of infinite relief in her grey eyes. She was dressed prettily, quietly and inexpensively as usual. John, comparing her appearance with the brilliant beauty of Mrs. Beecher Monmouth, realised that Elaine's attraction lay just as much in her fine and upright character, in her intense feminine gentleness and loyalty, as in her beauty itself.

She took John's hand in hers, drew him into the little passage, and quickly shut the door.

"Bernard," she whispered, resting her hand on his shoulder, and looking up into his face, "I am so very glad you have come!"

She drew his face down to hers and kissed him as she had never kissed him before. There was something that was almost passionately fervent in her embrace.

"I have been so afraid for you, Bernard," she murmured.

John released himself. He felt the extreme awkwardness of the situation.

"What made you afraid, Elaine?" He thought at first that an over-vivid imagination had been running away with her, that some feminine mood had made her fear for him. Then he remembered her beliefs as to his character. The man she believed him to be was a weakling with will undermined by drugs, a nervous, overstrung neurasthenic; capable of drifting into all sorts of trouble and embarrassments.

Elaine led him into the little parlour, lit the gas and drew down the blind. John noticed again that something troubled her mind. She appeared to look at him strangely and thoughtfully. And, for an instant, for a fleeting space of time, he feared that she had penetrated the secret of his identity. If this was the case, all his castles in the air would in a minute come toppling about his ears.

"Why are you looking at me so anxiously, Elaine?" he asked, assuming a casual tone of voice.

"It is because of Captain Cherriton, Bernard; he has been here to-day, and has been asking questions about you."

"What sort of questions?" John asked quickly.

"He asked me if you had been at Heatherpoint Fort lately. He himself has been down at the Isle of Wight and he appears to have found out something about you that disturbs him terribly."

John made the best effort he could to play his difficult part.

"Well, Elaine?" he questioned, "did Captain Cherriton tell you the particular cause of his disturbance?" He was smiling slightly as he spoke, treating the matter airily. Nevertheless, inwardly he was deeply perturbed. If Cherriton suspected him, and communicated his suspicions to Voules and his confederates, John knew that the position for himself would be one of infinite peril. He had experienced one fortuitous escape from discovery owing to the interception of "Crumbs's" letter to Voules, but he could hardly hope that fortune would again favour him.

He questioned Elaine closely, and learned that Cherriton had definitely heard of his presence at Heatherpoint Fort at a time when he was supposed to be working in the interest of Voules. This knowledge, John knew, would confirm all Cherriton's suspicions the minute it was discovered that "Crumbs" had been trapped and had vanished from the fort.

However, it was not in John's nature to meet trouble half-way, and for the present he was happy to be in Elaine's radiant company. Elaine, for her part, had much to say to him; in the first place, she detailed all that had occurred in an interview she had had with Dacent Smith. The great man had treated her with marked courtesy, and had, without revealing John's true identity, enlisted her services in much the same manner as Mrs. Beecher Monmouth acted for his adversaries, Voules, Cherriton, Manwitz, and company. Elaine had undertaken the work in the idea that she could thus protect from danger the man she loved, whose name she believed she bore.

John listened to her narrative with the deepest interest, and gradually the wonderful subtlety of Dacent Smith made itself manifest. The great man had promised to relieve him of his awkward predicament in regard to Elaine, and the manner in which he had accomplished his promise was simplicity itself. Elaine was to permit—within limits—the advances of Cherriton, and was to pretend to keep her "husband" at a distance! The neatness of this plan filled John with admiration. He felt instantly much freer with Elaine. The delicate moment when she had offered to resume marital relations with him would not immediately occur again.

For some minutes after Elaine had ceased speaking John held silence—a doubt had come to him.

"Elaine," he said, earnestly, "Captain Cherriton is far more dangerous, perhaps, than you know." He rose, and, pacing back and fore, with an anxious face, warned her that the man was one who would stop at nothing to attain his ends. Elaine listened patiently; then, on a sudden, quick impulse, flung her arms about his neck.

"Bernard," she whispered, "don't you know I love you, my darling? All those minutes that you have been pacing up and down there in raging jealousy——"

"Jealousy!" echoed John.

"It was jealousy, Bernard," she smiled, happy in the possession of his love. "All the time I have been adoring you and loving you more and more. Bernard," she whispered, "I am to pretend not to care. But you will know in your heart, won't you, that I am yours always?" She drew her face away from his and looked deep into his eyes. "You know that, dearest?"

"I know it," said John, looking back at her.

"And you love me as I love you?" questioned she.

He had never seen her so beautiful as in that moment, with her face upturned to his, her cheeks flushed, and her eyes offering him her love. He was standing in another man's shoes, and at that moment those shoes pinched him to the point of anguish. For a fleeting moment he was tempted to fling all prudence to the winds and confess everything. Then the recollection that she was a married woman smote him like a blow. Whatever happened, she could never be his. Very gently and tenderly he held her from him.

"You can't doubt me, Elaine," he said, in a low voice. "Nevertheless, I think Dacent Smith is right; you ought to pretend not to care for me, for just a little while—anyway, until the great contest that is now beginning between our department and Cherriton and his confederates is at an end."

He led her back to her chair, lit a cigarette, and made an effort to give a humorous description of his life during the past few weeks. He told her of Sinclair, of "Crumbs," of his adventure and his visit to Voules; everything, in fact, except his real identity and his arrest in mistake for Bernard Treves.

As his narrative unfolded, Elaine's eyes widened in amazement and admiration.

"I had no idea you were so splendid, Bernard."

"But I am not splendid. I am not telling you that I am splendid."

"Of course you are not, you silly boy; you are trying to make out you are nothing at all. But I shouldn't love you as I do if I couldn't read between the lines. Oh, Bernard, what an idiot I have been about you. I used to think — —" she paused and looked away.

"You used to think awful things of me," continued John, "that I took drugs, that I consumed whisky by the half-bottle, that I was a brute both to you and to my old father."

"Yes," said Elaine slowly. "I used to think I — —" Then suddenly, and with the inconsequence of woman, she broke off and covered her face with her hands. She was crying softly and steadily. It was not John's business to comfort her. The only man who had the right to do that was the drink-sodden neurotic, who was still a prisoner in the nursing home. Nevertheless, in less than a minute John was kneeling before her.

"What is it, Elaine?" he asked in passionate anxiety. She looked at him with eyes bright with tears.

"It is the past, Bernard; I can't understand it. Those days, long ago, lie like a pain in my heart, always. You have grown so different. It is cowardly and mean of me to think of it, but I love you, Bernard, and I cannot bear to think there was a time when you were not as now." She paused for a moment, and a shadow, a twinge of agony crossed her face. She looked at John with affrighted eyes, then spoke in a low voice. "That night when you struck me, Bernard!"

John felt the blood quicken in his pulses. Some time in the past Bernard Treves had struck her. How and under what circumstances he could not guess. He turned away his head, so that the sudden rage which blazed in his eyes should not be visible to her. For a moment he was silent, then collecting his senses, he said quietly, and still without looking at her:

"Elaine, I swear that if in the past I ever raised my hand to you, ever was cur enough to strike you, then I know nothing of it. I have no memory of such a thing," he went on, speaking the truth.

"I tell myself that, in those early days, you were not yourself," conceded Elaine.

"I want never to recall those days," said John. "If I ever acted as you say, I must have been mad." He suddenly turned towards her. And all his passionate desire to protect her, the deep love he had grown to feel for her seemed in that moment to animate his face. "Elaine," he said, "promise me you'll forget it, and never think of it again?"

"Never again," answered she. She slid her arms about his neck and drew him towards her. For a minute he forgot his compact with himself. But presently his self-possession returned to him. He fell back a pace, and, lifting her hand, kissed her fingers, and once again assumed the light conversational tone.

"We are comrades now, Elaine," said he, "both working against Voules and his myrmidons." He turned and looked at the little clock on Elaine's mantelshelf. "Hallo!" he exclaimed, "I must be off; I am on duty to-night."

He felt that it was safer to go, and five minutes later he was at the door of the house.

"Remember, Elaine," he said, looking down at her in the dim little passage, "any time you want me, if Cherriton offends you in any way, ring me up at the Golden Pavilion Hotel."

CHAPTER XXIII

One evening, a week later, when darkness had fallen, John found himself in Grosvenor Place, pacing unobtrusively in the shadow of the russet-brown brick wall which surrounds the royal garden of Buckingham Palace. He was watching a taxi which was waiting before the broad door of Mr. Beecher Monmouth's residence. Some minutes passed before John, from his discreet vantage ground, observed Mrs. Beecher Monmouth herself, a vague, befurred, silk-clad figure in the distance, descend from her house and enter the vehicle.

The lady's taxi sped away, and John lifted his attention from the door of the house to the first floor. Here a chink of light from two windows showed him that Mrs. Beecher Monmouth's maid, having attired her mistress for the evening, was still busy, either in the bedroom or Mrs. Beecher Monmouth's boudoir.

"When Mademoiselle Cecily puts out the light and goes downstairs, I'll make a dash for it," thought John.

For a quarter of an hour after that he waited patiently in the shadow of the royal wall. Then first one light, and then another, vanished behind the first floor curtains of the house across the road. John gave Cecily sufficient time to descend to the housekeeper's room, where she usually spent the evening. At last, however, with something of alacrity and a quickened pulse-beat, he crossed the road. He was the veriest amateur as a burglar, but his cause was the best in the world, and in less than a minute he had slipped a small Yale key into the hall door. He had possessed himself of that key from Mrs. Beecher Monmouth's handbag earlier in the evening, and he knew she would not miss it until her return from her dinner-party at the Savoy.

The key moved noiselessly in the lock. No drama at all accompanied his entry into the lofty, deeply-carpeted hall. The light was dim, the hall deserted, and when John had soundlessly closed the front door behind him, he hurried forward and ascended the carpeted stairs, two steps at a time.

From the servants' quarters in the lower regions he could hear voices faintly. No other sounds came to him, and in less than a minute after he passed the front door he found himself in Mrs. Beecher Monmouth's intimate boudoir. Here he cautiously closed the door behind him, turned the key in the lock and switched on the light. Everything was as usual, save only that on every previous visit to that room Mrs. Beecher Monmouth, brilliantly gowned, brilliantly beautiful, and always amiable to himself, had been his chief centre of interest. To-night, however, it was not Mrs. Beecher Monmouth he desired to cultivate, but that lady's belongings.

He was there under Dacent Smith's instructions to search for clues which would enable John's chief of department to check her flow of information to the enemy. For not yet had John been able to discover in what manner, within eight hours, she had been able to communicate with the submarine which sank the *Malta*.

John, standing with his back to the gold and white boudoir door, surveyed the room with a slight sense of bewilderment. It was difficult to know where to begin. Nevertheless, he did begin, and during the quiet minutes that followed he made a close search for documents in every possible hiding-place he could discover. His care and patience, however, met with no reward; he found nothing of the slightest significance.

When John had thoroughly exhausted the possibilities of the boudoir and had found nothing, he opened the door which communicated from that room directly into Mrs. Beecher Monmouth's spacious bedroom. He had never viewed this apartment before, and he was much impressed by its gorgeous furnishings, its shining brass twin bedsteads, its white French furniture and deep carpet of pale grey and rose colour.

Having quietly locked the second door of the room which opened into the passage, he began a rapid search, taking care to replace everything as he found it. Mrs. Beecher Monmouth would probably not return until half-past nine, and he felt that if he could complete his business quickly he would be able to slip downstairs and out of the house before being observed.

Cecily was the only person likely to disturb him, and he had already thought of a plan which might secure his safety in this event. In regard to Mr. Beecher Monmouth, John felt completely at ease about him. The "Ogre" had, a fortnight ago, been neatly transhipped to Ireland as a member of a Government commission of inquiry. Dacent Smith, with the aid of the Home Secretary, had brought this about without arousing Monmouth's suspicions.

The fact that Beecher Monmouth adored his wife, and had desired to take her with him, had created something of a difficulty, but Dacent Smith had overcome this point in his habitual neat manner.

"No; I don't think I need worry," thought John, glancing at an expensive clock of ivory and silver which adorned the dressing-table. "I shall be safe for another half an hour at least."

Mrs. Beecher Monmouth's bed was covered with a rich eiderdown covered in purple satin. John seated himself upon this sumptuous covering and rubbed his chin thoughtfully. He had been twenty minutes in the bedroom of Mrs. Beecher Monmouth, and had discovered nothing.

He noticed now a door, with a crystal knob, which opened into a wardrobe, which was a small room in itself. Here Mrs. Beecher Monmouth's numerous costumes hung in rows. John caught a glimpse of a shelf containing a score of pairs of boots, shoes and slippers. Beneath this shelf was a big tin box, a black japanned box, which immediately engaged John's attention.

The lock was a simple one, and John had it open in a moment. Then the disappointment that had been growing on him intensified, for in the box was nothing but Mrs. Beecher Monmouth's costly sables laid away for the summer. A reek of camphor assailed his nostrils from the folded furs. He was about to close the box, when the idea occurred to him to run his hand down the sides. A moment later he was glad of this impulse, for from the bottom of the tin he drew up a small, strong-looking cash-box.

He rattled the box, and was able to detect a faint rustle from within. Carrying the dispatch case, which was something under a foot in length, he went into the bedroom. Once again he seated himself on the purple eiderdown and tried all his keys. None of them fitted the dispatch box, which was protected by an unassailable Chubb lock.

John contemplated this lock for some minutes with an unfavourable eye, then he took out a heavy steel tool he had brought with him. It took him less than two minutes to wrench open the lid. Within the box, completely filling its interior, were neatly folded and tightly packed letters and papers.

John's interest quickened mightily as, opening one of the letters, he discovered it to be in German.

The note-paper was of the flimsy description, almost tissue paper, in fact. John, examining it closely, observed with a certain degree of interest that the paper had been folded very small indeed, evidently for facility in transmission.

As he sat on the edge of the bed, with the open box on his knee, and this letter in his hand, he swept Mrs. Beecher Monmouth's large and expensively furnished room with his glance. There was a deep silence in the room, and between the rise and the fall of the traffic noises outside, John could hear the light ticking of the little ivory and silver clock on the dressing-table. He was not occupied with the silence, however, but with the contents of the letter, which he read rapidly, eagerly, and with swiftly augmented interest. Written purposely small in a firm, foreign hand, the missive, which was to Mrs. Beecher Monmouth, ran, in German:

"DARLING ALICE,

"*Your loving letter reached me only yesterday, and I am hastening to answer it by the usual channels. I am still jealous. You tell me your husband is very old, but one of the solaces to my captivity here is the English newspapers, which we are allowed to read, and yesterday, in one of the picture papers, I observed Mr. Beecher Monmouth's photograph. He is not so old as you pretend, and though his face assures me that he will never win your heart, yet still I am jealous. It makes me laugh to think of you as the wife of an English politician, a member of their stupid Parliament! I wonder if in society you ever meet the Duke of Thule and Lord Harrisgrove. I recall our beautiful happiness in Washington together. You loved me then, I believe, more than you do now.*"

The letter ended with expressions of endearment, and was signed "Kurt von Morgen."

As John read the signature his lips tightened. In great haste he ran his eye over the handwriting of at least a score of other letters, each one of them in the same handwriting, that of Kurt von Morgen, a German Cuirassier officer, a young aristocrat who had been captured on the Western Front six months earlier. He knew that Count Kurt von Morgen was a prisoner in the — — camp for officers. And as he handled the flimsy sheets of paper he wondered consumedly how the young man had managed to convey these letters to Mrs. Beecher Monmouth.

A word in another letter by von Morgen caught his eye:

"*I am glad you have met General von Kuhne,*" said the writer. "*Kindly convey to him my compliments, and tell him his nephew, who is a prisoner here, is well and happy. His Excellency's presence in England means much. I throb with interest to know what will happen. But perhaps, Alice, meine herzliebste, I shall soon be free, and shall soon see you! Preparations for my escape are going better than ever. I have for my servant a very intelligent fellow from the Black Forest. Do not let your English 'Ogre' love you too much. Think of me always and the little week when you were my wife at Palm Beach. I kiss you behind the ear.—KURT.*"

A smile crossed John's face as he finished reading this amorous missive.

"Here," thought he, "we get a pretty complete clue to Mrs. Beecher Monmouth's earlier history before she came from America. It shows also where Mrs. Beecher Monmouth's affections are really centred."

John had already read enough to know that these letters must be delivered as swiftly as possible into Dacent Smith's hands. One or two had slipped to the floor as he scanned them hurriedly. He bent down to pick them up, and saw very neatly written on a slip of paper the key of the code which Mrs. Monmouth had used in her newspaper advertisements. As Smith's department already knew this code, the discovery was not of much importance, but on another sheet of paper which also lay on the rich rose and grey carpet he discovered a second code with its accompanying key. His attention fixed upon this with swift intensity. He had at last made a discovery of importance, and he became suddenly animated by the hope that his department had hit upon the manner of Mrs. Beecher Monmouth's swift communication with the enemy. He reached out, took up the slip of paper—and then suddenly became still. For an instant he remained motionless, his mind working with lightning rapidity. A sound had come to him from Mrs. Beecher Monmouth's boudoir, a soft impact of footsteps upon the thick carpet.

John could scarcely believe his ears. He had carefully locked the door of the corridor boudoir when he entered the room. As a further protection, he had left the key in the lock. And now this sound! He was still on his hands and knees, and very slowly he turned his head. At that instant the boudoir door opened towards him, and a man enveloped in a heavy tweed overcoat and wearing a soft grey hat stood in the aperture. At sight of John on his knees near the bed, the new-comer stopped dead and stared with wide-amazed eyes.

John leapt to his feet. Mechanically, at the same moment the figure at the door removed his grey hat, and the thin hair, the parchment-like face, and the thin, sharp nose of Mr. Beecher Monmouth stood revealed. Moved by his passionate desire to be with his wife, the elderly politician had unexpectedly hurried from Ireland to spend the week-end in London. Beecher Monmouth's expression was one of simple and complete amazement. He blinked two or three times; then, suddenly recovering himself, drew shut the door behind him, and stood with his back to it. His sallow face grew pale with swift kindled hate and rage.

"Mr. Treves," he demanded, drawing in a sharp breath, "what are you doing here? Are you here with my wife's knowledge?"

"No," answered John frankly. "Your wife hasn't the faintest idea that I am here."

"You mean you came to the house in her absence?"

John felt it was necessary to tell him something near the truth.

"I suppose you have a right to know that I came here in her absence. I came without her knowledge—let myself in with a key and locked the doors outside there, so that I should not be disturbed. How you got in I don't know."

"I got in through my own bedroom which is beyond the boudoir," retorted Beecher Monmouth icily, amazed and further enraged at his calmness.

"Oh!" said John. "There must have been a door I didn't lock. Well, to get along with my explanation—"

Beecher Monmouth drew away from him; mechanically he drew off his overcoat and threw it to the floor.

"Young man," he shouted, his face suddenly turning from white to scarlet, "what are those letters there?" His eyes fell upon the opened cash-box lying on the bed. He rushed to it and took it up. "What were you doing with this?"

"I was breaking it open," answered John.

Beecher Monmouth fixed upon him bewildered and stupefied eyes. Then he hurried across the room and put out his hand for the bell. John, however, was too quick for him; he leapt forward and flung his arms powerfully about the lean, elderly figure.

"You mustn't ring that bell," he said in a low, tense voice. "I am here on very particular business, and there must be no disturbance whatever."

"Will you let me go?" shouted Beecher Monmouth, his face contorted with rage. "Let me go!"

"Certainly," said John, stepping with his back towards the bell. Beecher Monmouth eased his collar, which had been disturbed. He put his hand to his thin, neatly-ordered hair. He was breathing heavily.

"You'll drive me mad. Have you come here to rob me, or——"

Then his mood suddenly changed. The one passion of his life welled to the surface. If John was there intending to rob him he cared little. There was one thing only that could really strike at him deeply, and that was his wife's love and fidelity.

"Look here," he said, suddenly pulling himself together, "tell me that it is not an assignation; that you are not waiting for my wife."

John looked at him and was silent for a surprised moment; then he said, quietly and solemnly:

"I swear I am not waiting for your wife. I am here on far more serious business, and, as for your wife, I neither care, nor have I ever cared, anything about her."

Beecher Monmouth's eyes took on a visible expression of relief; his gaze travelled away from John and looked about the room. Once again his glance fell upon the disorder of letters upon the bed. He made a step forward and, before John could stop him, picked up one. John saw his head jerk curiously as the first words smote his eyes. "Liebste Alice." His gaze went to the date of the letter. It was scarcely a fortnight old! He read a few lines of the German missive, which he understood, then he lifted his eyes to John.

Never in his life had John seen a man alter so in a moment as Beecher Monmouth altered in that moment.

"Do you know what these letters are?" he asked in a jerking voice. "Do you understand German?"

John nodded.

"Yes," he said. "I have read several of them."

Beecher Monmouth took out a silk handkerchief and wiped his brow. Then he bent down and slowly gathered a handful of the letters. But before he could read another, John placed a friendly hand on his shoulder. He was moved by the tragedy that was about to strike this elderly man, who seemed so ill able to bear it.

"Mr. Monmouth," he said, "it is only fair that you should know all the truth. I can see no other way out."

"What is the truth?" asked Monmouth in a dazed voice.

"I am here," John answered, "on behalf of our Intelligence Department, to make a search of your wife's belongings."

"Intelligence Department!" echoed Beecher Monmouth.

"Yes," John said; "and I am afraid it will be my duty to take away all the letters in this room. In the meantime, however, I am prepared for you to study them at your leisure."

"What do you mean?" asked Monmouth. "Intelligence Department— —"

"You will learn everything from the letters, which you can read if you wish—on condition, of course, that you give me your word of honour as a gentleman to destroy nothing. Also you will remain indoors, within call, until I have communicated with my chief of department."

Beecher Monmouth put a shaking hand over his brow.

"Yes," he said, "I suppose I understand what you say. I feel very much bewildered."

"Would you like to read the letters?"

"I have read one; I must face the others."

"You will give me your word of honour to destroy nothing?"

"Yes." His voice was low, almost inaudible.

John, pitying his utter desolation, stepped quietly out of the room, and, leaving the door open, seated himself in the boudoir. He had been there perhaps three minutes, when Beecher Monmouth looked in at him. His expression was utterly tragic.

"I should like to close the door, Mr. Treves, if you don't mind."

"Certainly," said John. He was something of a judge of men; he had accepted the elder man's word, and for ten further minutes he remained seated.

During that time Beecher Monmouth stood alone in his wife's brilliantly decorated bedchamber, and strewn about the rose-grey carpet lay the letters which meant the end of all happiness, which for him meant tragedy and darkness unutterable. He went down on his knees, and, with shaking hands, gathered up the strewn sheets. Then, dropping into a low chair near the dressing-table, he read, one after another, Kurt von Morgen's amorous letters to his wife. And in reading he pieced together, bit by bit, his wife's dark past. For the first time her utter shamelessness became known to him. And then, gradually, through the tragedy of his own wrecked life, he saw something that filled him with horror. He learnt, bit by bit, that his wife was not only faithless to him, but was faithless to his country as well. The woman he had adored and had sold his happiness to was a traitor—either that, or a spy in the enemy's pay.

As these things swept over him in great waves he clasped his hands to his head and swayed back and forth in a very agony of horrified shame. Presently, like a man in a dream, he rose and walked unsteadily across the floor. Quite neatly, and with a sort of mechanical carefulness, he had replaced all the letters and documents back in the box, and now, carrying the box under his arm, he went unsteadily over the carpet. He drew open a drawer of the little cabinet near his bed, and took out a beautiful plated ivory-handled Colt pistol. Then he took in a deep breath, assured himself that the pistol was loaded and clicked it shut again. He moistened his lips with his tongue, looked at the weapon for a moment with dazed eyes, and slipped it into his pocket. This done, he turned, and with steps that were steady and resolute, crossed the room and drew open the door of the boudoir.

CHAPTER XXIV

There was a strange light in Beecher Monmouth's eyes as he stepped into the outer apartment. He was a man who irrevocably and finally had made up his mind.

"Mr. Treves," he said, "I hand these into your care. You have discharged your duty very well indeed. I think the letters will be of great service to your department." He uttered the words tonelessly and his manner puzzled John, who took the box, and then observed that Monmouth's hand was outstretched.

"You carried out your duty honourably and well."

Their hands touched and John noticed how icy cold were the other's fingers.

"I hope, sir," he said, in a sudden rush of pity for the utterly broken and deluded husband, "I hope you will forgive my seeming harshness of a few minutes ago."

"Certainly, certainly," said Beecher Monmouth dully. He appeared grateful that John had shaken him by the hand. "You can tell your chief that I feel no animosity and that I shall keep my promise not to leave this house. Whenever you return you will find me here."

"On behalf of the department I think I can say," remarked John, "that you will suffer as little inconvenience as possible."

"Thank you," said Beecher Monmouth. "This discovery is for me, as you can well understand, a tragic one." He paused a moment. "In any case," he added, "you will find me in my wife's room when you return."

John took the japanned box and bowed slightly. He was quite sure that Beecher Monmouth would make no attempt to escape. He was also quite sure in his own mind that no charge would be brought against him. The case was clearly one of a duped and shamelessly deluded husband who had unwittingly aided his country's enemies. For a moment the elder man appeared to hesitate on the point of making some further communication, then, turning slowly on his heel, re-entered his wife's room and shut the door.

Beecher Monmouth's unfortunate advent had delayed John longer in the house than caution allowed. He made haste now to repair the tactical disadvantage, and the moment the door closed upon the elder man he emptied the letters from the box into his overcoat, hurried out of the room and down the great staircase.

In two minutes he reached the front door, which he drew open upon the darkness of the night. He inhaled a deep breath of relief. His task had been accomplished; in another moment— —

Then he stopped and stood stock still upon the top-most step—exactly opposite him a taxi had drawn to a halt. A light laugh floated up to him, and Mrs. Beecher Monmouth, shimmering in silk and jewels, alighted briskly! She was the last person in the world John at that moment desired to see, still if she had been alone John believed that he could have still escaped unobserved. She was not alone, however. With her were two men in evening clothes, and as the little party of three crossed the pavement John made out that the heavily-built, thick-necked figure who had helped her to alight was Doctor "Voules," and that the taller figure who walked upon her left hand was Captain Cherriton.

Cherriton's keen eyes had recognised John in an instant, and almost simultaneously Mrs. Beecher Monmouth uttered an exclamation.

"Why, Mr. Treves!" She ran lightly up the steps, holding out her hand in greeting. "I had no idea you were coming to-night."

"Nor had I," said John. "I came upon the impulse of the moment."

"But you knew I should be out," protested Mrs. Beecher Monmouth.

"That is true," John admitted; "but as you were not going to a theatre I expected you would be back early."

"That was very nice of you; now you must come in again." She laid her hand lightly on his arm and shepherded him back to the wide hall.

"Where is the butler?" Mrs. Beecher Monmouth, sweeping the empty hall with her eyes, turned in surprise upon John.

"I don't know," said John; "I think he's downstairs."

"But surely some one was here to let you out?"

Cherriton and his Excellency von Kuhne had both entered the hall. His Excellency pushed shut the big door, and as John heard the latch click a curious sensation of finality seized him. On several occasions in past months he had been in tight situations. He had been in an awkward position, for instance, half an hour earlier, with Beecher Monmouth. The situation, however, which now held him in its grip was in point of danger beyond anything he had yet experienced. He knew that coolness and sang-froid and daring were the only weapons with which he could fight against the three national and ruthless enemies who stood about him in the dimly lit hall. He had shaken hands with Mrs. Beecher Monmouth, and, avoiding a direct answer to her last question, he now turned to von Kuhne and held out his hand.

"How do you do, doctor?"

"I am very well," answered his Excellency in his thick voice. He looked steadily into John's eyes. Manton could read nothing in his expression, and he gave his attention to Cherriton.

"It is a long time since we met, Cherriton!"

Cherriton bowed. He made no effort to shake hands; nevertheless his manner was not openly hostile, rather was it sharply and keenly watchful.

"Quite a long time," he answered.

John, looking again into the captain's cold, light blue eyes, his pale shaven face with its bony contours, his cruelly-turned mouth, thought him even more unpleasant than he had formerly believed. He was willing to grant, however, that Cherriton carried himself with an air, that he was a powerful, big-boned, tall, well-set-up fellow.

His own eyes and Cherriton's remained engaged for the fraction of a second, then Mrs. Beecher Monmouth's voice broke the tension.

"Come, come," she exclaimed, "we mustn't stand in the hall. I'll ring for Duckett to bring us something upstairs, and in the meantime you shall each have a cigarette in my boudoir."

"I don't like cigarettes!" said von Kuhne curtly.

"Then you shall smoke one of your black cigars," concluded Mrs. Beecher Monmouth, flashing at him one of her brilliant smiles. She rang the bell, and when the butler appeared, commanded him to bring wine and glasses upstairs.

Mrs. Beecher Monmouth began to run up the wide carpeted staircase. John noticed that she wore grey shoes with scarlet heels, and that her stockings were of dark red silk to match her dress. She ascended half a dozen steps, then turned, noticing that John had begun to frame an excuse. He wanted to get away before she reached her boudoir, before she could enter her bedroom where her husband awaited her. The meeting between these two which was imminent was not one which John wished to witness. He waved a farewell hand, uttered conventional apologies and made to go.

Mrs. Beecher Monmouth, however, would hear nothing of it. She ran down the stairs, took him by the arm, shook a finger in his face, called him a "bad, cruel boy," and led him upstairs.

Cherriton and von Kuhne closed in behind.

The boudoir was empty when Mrs. Beecher Monmouth entered and switched on the lights. In a swift survey of the apartment John noticed the rifled dispatch-box on a gilt-legged chair where he had left it. Very swiftly and dexterously he whipped off his light overcoat and threw it over the box, hiding it from view.

Mrs. Beecher Monmouth, who wore extensive *décolletée*, with a small tiara glimmering in her perfectly arranged dark tresses, permitted John to relieve her of an opera cloak of grey silk brocade. She stood for a minute displaying herself in perfect consciousness of her striking beauty. Her arms and shoulders, perfectly modelled, were white as marble. There was a challenging light in her brilliant eyes as they sought John's. She was one of those women who look best at night, a flower that bloomed best in artificial light.

John's mind, since their entrance into the room, had not, however, been occupied either with her beauty or his own personal danger.

He was thinking only of a sound he had heard some minutes earlier, at the moment he had drawn open the front door. The sound, like a distant crack of a whip, had reached him from the interior of the house. Only now did that sound gather to itself significance.

Sudden doubts assailed John. In that room behind the closed door Beecher Monmouth had seen his own doting attempts at love mocked and laughed at; he had read the passionate letters of her real lover, Kurt von Morgen. She had betrayed not only her husband but her husband's country.

What if Beecher Monmouth strode in among them? At any moment the door of that silent room might fly open.... John could conceive Monmouth in a frenzy, rushing into the room and putting his lean hands about that white, bejewelled throat. The situation tingled with terrible possibilities.

In those tense and throbbing moments John felt a kinship between himself and the deluded man beyond the closed door of the bedroom.

Cherriton, he was certain, suspected him, and would take the first opportunity to cross-examine him as to his visit to Heatherpoint Fort. Nevertheless, he was determined to escape from that house with Mrs. Beecher Monmouth's incriminating letters, and with the newly-found code. He was not afraid of Cherriton; he feared neither the tall German's subtlety of wit, nor his strength of arm. His sole feeling indeed towards this unpleasant enemy was one of infinite antagonism. He knew the time was bound to come, possibly at any minute, when he and Cherriton would enter upon open conflict.

The butler came into the room bearing a large silver tray, decanters and glasses. General von Kuhne lit one of his big black cigars, and seating himself, drank a glass of champagne. The butler went out of the room and closed the door noiselessly behind him. John and Cherriton each accepted from Mrs. Beecher Monmouth's hands a whisky-and-soda. John felt Mrs. Beecher Monmouth's eyes steadily upon him. A faint shadow of doubt seemed to flit across her face and then vanish. With an almost imperceptible movement of her head she beckoned him towards her, and seizing a moment when Cherriton and von Kuhne were in conversation, she said to him in a whisper:

"Why did you come to-night, when you knew I should be out?"

John had been expecting the question, and was prepared.

"I knew you would be out," he said, looking deep into her eyes; "but I expected you'd come in again!"

"What do you mean, you enigmatical boy?" Then feeling that she had read his mind, she added: "Do you mean—you came because my husband was away?"

John smiled at her.

"Don't you think that an excellent reason for coming?" he asked.

This struck her as an extremely amusing remark. As always she was conscious of, and confident in, the potency of her beauty. She laughed and tapped him on the shoulder with her fan.

"I don't believe you love me," she uttered almost soundlessly, shaping the words with her lips.

"Don't you?" said John.

"Did Cecily let you in?"

"No," admitted John.

At that moment a knock fell upon the door of the room, and in answer to Mrs. Beecher Monmouth's summons, Cecily herself entered.

"I beg your pardon, madame," she said, "but the corridor door of your room is locked."

"Locked, Cecily?"

"Yes, madame."

Mrs. Beecher Monmouth saw no significance in the fact.

"In that case, Cecily," she said, "you may come through this way."

"Thank you, madame." Cecily, in her black dress, white cap and apron, and high-heeled shoes, crossed the carpet. She reached the second door of Mrs. Beecher Monmouth's bedroom and opened it. Nobody but John was watching her. As the maid pushed open the door she gave a violent start, stood stock still, then uttered a loud and terrified scream.

"Madame! Madame!" she called, turning a frantic face and wide-staring eyes at her mistress.

"What is it?" cried Mrs. Beecher Monmouth, springing swiftly to her feet.

The four of them were now standing staring blankly at Cecily, who was leaning against the door-frame covering her eyes with one hand and waving an arm frantically towards the bedroom.

Mrs. Monmouth hurried towards her, but it was John who first succeeded in reaching the door. From the threshold he looked into the room. All the softly-shaded golden lights were full on. And half lying, half sitting on the bed he saw the figure of Beecher Monmouth. The inert form was reclining upon its side on the rich purple counterpane. One arm hung over the edge of the bed towards the floor. On the floor itself lay the politician's ivory and electro-plated pistol, one barrel of which had been discharged.

John rushed into the room and looked close into the ashen grey face, but even before he reached the bedside, the very stillness of the prone figure had told him the truth.

*　*　*　*　*

The knowledge that had come upon Beecher Monmouth that night had marked the end. And with a courage for which few would have given him credit, considering his weakness, he had taken arms against a sea of troubles. His political life, his ambition, his hopes, the love that he had lavished, had all vanished in a flash. Kurt von Morgen's letters had told him everything, had revealed a sink of iniquity and duplicity such as he had never thought possible. The blow had been too heavy for him to bear. A younger man might have sought relief in vengeance upon the woman who had betrayed him, but he was not of that spirit. He could think of one way only, one act only which could extricate him from his tragic position.

Innocently for months and years he had been a traitor to his country. Unwittingly he had been supplying to the scheming, brilliant woman whom he adored, all the knowledge that came to him in virtue of his position in Parliament. In doing this he had himself become a criminal. No court of law could, or would, punish him. That he knew. But with all his weaknesses he was a loyal Englishman, and in thinking of the tragedy that had been wrought by his doting folly, he resolved to act manfully at the last.

Monmouth left no word, no scrap of writing, no murmur of complaint against the woman who had betrayed him, and as John looked into the waxen face that looked old, even beyond its years, he felt for the dead man a genuine and deep sense of pity.

"After all," thought he, "he has chosen the only way out!" He looked up from the face of the dead man, and saw Cherriton's eyes brooding upon him narrowly. And all through the ensuing excitement he could feel Cherriton's eyes following him keenly, spying upon every movement he made. As the minutes passed John realised that the Captain not only suspected him of playing a double game in regard to Heatherpoint Fort, but he suspected him also of the murder of Beecher Monmouth.

John wondered what would happen when the ravished dispatch-box was discovered. And the thought came to him that, despite the tragedy that had occurred, Beecher Monmouth's return had been a useful circumstance for himself and his department. For when Mrs. Beecher Monmouth found that her lover's letters and the code had disappeared she would instantly jump to the conclusion that her husband had discovered them. Having made this discovery, his despair at her duplicity would account for his self-destruction.

Soon after the finding of the body the servants were summoned from below, but no one had heard the fatal shot.

Von Kuhne, who was disturbed and annoyed, showed an urgent desire to take himself off. He was gone, accompanied by Cherriton, by the time the police appeared.

When the police were in full possession of the situation John himself took leave of Mrs. Beecher Monmouth. She was standing in her boudoir, her face deathly white, her usually scarlet lips bluish in hue. John noticed that her hand, as she touched his, was ice-cold. His feelings were of intense detestation towards her, and he found it difficult to be even conventionally polite. As to offering her words of comfort or condolence, that would have been the merest mockery. He was amazed, in bidding her good-bye, to find that there were tears in her eyes. She was an astounding woman. Beecher Monmouth had destroyed himself solely because of her unutterable depths of treachery. She had never loved him; she had incessantly betrayed and duped him, and yet she could still shed tears for him!

John went away pondering upon the mystery of the eternal feminine.

CHAPTER XXV

John's work of that night was commended highly by Dacent Smith. For his discovery of the japanned box had put the department in possession of Mrs. Beecher Monmouth's code and a score of letters evidently part of a secret correspondence conducted with a camp for officers, and with Kurt von Morgen, whose "plans for escape were progressing nicely"!

The great man commended this achievement. But, like John, he felt pity for Beecher Monmouth, who had fallen so easy and gullible a victim to his wife's treachery. In regard to Cherriton's suspicions of John he took a serious view.

"I think, Treves," he said, leaning back in his chair, "we shall have to remove Cherriton from the scene. He appears, from what you tell me, not to have confided his suspicions of you either to Mrs. Beecher Monmouth or to von Kuhne. It is unfortunate that he chanced to be appointed by von Kuhne to watch Heatherpoint. But I don't think we can blame Lieutenant Parkson for letting out the fact that you were for a brief period attached to that fort. Nevertheless the position is one that must be handled swiftly and effectively."

He suddenly smiled at John.

"You have done very well up to now, Treves," he said. "But I should not like your career to be suddenly cut short when there are big things ahead. We have safely got rid of Lady Rachel Marvin in Pitt Lunan Hydro, where she can enjoy the company of other fools of her own sort, and will be unable to endanger any more of our forces by loose gossip." He paused, then went on: "The virtual suspension of the Habeas Corpus Act was a god-send to us in the handling of dangerous social fools like Lady Rachel. We could do still more than we do at present, Treves, if every one who knew of suspicious persons or suspicious gossip would only let us know. If members of the public would take the trouble to write a letter to their favourite newspaper the information would always reach us, and would enable us to keep watch on a good many suspicious characters who would otherwise escape us."

"The trouble is," said John, "the members of the public do not understand either the power of the German spy system in this country or the wideness of its extent."

"Exactly," nodded his chief. "Who, for instance, would suspect Mrs. Beecher Monmouth, the beautiful and wealthy wife of a well-known member of Parliament? But, to my mind, persons like Lady Rachel Marvin are just as dangerous to us as the actual German spies who pick up their information."

John went away from Dacent Smith's bachelor abode that night full of intense curiosity as to what Mrs. Beecher Monmouth would do in the immediate future. If, however, he thought that the death of her husband would check her activities he was speedily disillusioned. For immediately after the funeral of the late politician, Mrs. Beecher Monmouth, looking beautiful in her widow's weeds, departed for the Isle of Wight. The funeral of Beecher Monmouth had been an impressive public affair, and there had been much commiseration for the tragically bereaved young widow. It was only natural, therefore, that after so terrible a shock she should wish to withdraw herself from the public gaze. Rooms were engaged at an hotel at Newport, and Mrs. Monmouth, in deepest widow's weeds, made the journey accompanied by her maid Cecily.

She arrived at Newport on the twenty-fourth of the month, and the proprietor of the hotel, who knew of her bereavement, received her with a grave and discreet cordiality. He himself showed her to the parlour which had been allotted to her, and assured her that he would do all that was in his power to make her stay as quiet and reposeful as he possibly could.

Mrs. Beecher Monmouth thanked him cordially. That night she dined in the retirement of her little parlour, but on the following evening it was discovered that her chimney smoked a little. She therefore decided to take her dinner in the public dining-room. As the chimney in her sitting-room had never smoked before, the proprietor of the hotel was a little puzzled. Nevertheless he prepared for her a table in a quiet corner of the dining-room downstairs. Here, accompanied by Cecily, her confidential maid, who placed her chair for her and then departed, the newly-bereaved widow took her meal. The only other diners in the room were four young officers, who sat at a table in an opposite corner. Mrs. Beecher Monmouth, in her simple and costly black dress, immediately engaged their attention. They respected her sorrow, however, and, despite the evident admiration of one of them, who thought her possessed of the most beautiful profile he had ever seen, Mrs. Monmouth did not encounter from the young men a single glance.

When dinner was at an end she rose gracefully, and, carrying her novel, went upstairs to her apartments. When the door had closed upon her the four young officers became animated in a surprising manner.

"By gad!" exclaimed one, "she's a dashed fine-looking woman, and young, too."

"A dashed sight too young for Beecher Monmouth, I should think," remarked another. "What a rotten thing to happen to her. I wonder what made him shoot himself."

They speculated upon Mrs. Beecher Monmouth and her tragedy for some minutes, then rose to go.

In the meantime Mrs. Beecher Monmouth had reached her sitting-room. Strange to say, the fire no longer smoked. She turned swiftly to the sallow-skinned Cecily.

"Cecily!"

"Yes, madame."

"Go downstairs and find out which of those young officers was Lieutenant Parkson, of Heatherpoint Fort. You know how to find out?"

Cecily looked at her knowingly.

"Yes, madame."

Presently Cecily returned.

"Lieutenant Parkson, madame, was the one with the black hair and the little black moustache who sat facing you."

"Thank you, Cecily," said Mrs. Beecher Monmouth. "Did you discover when he was coming again?"

"He and his friends have engaged the same table for to-morrow night, madame."

"Thank you." Mrs. Beecher Monmouth lit one of her Russian cigarettes, flung the match into the fire, and, relapsing into a chair at the hearth, began to smoke quietly. "I shall dine downstairs at the same time to-morrow, Cecily," she said.

"Very good, madame."

The next night the four young men were already seated at their table when Mrs. Beecher Monmouth entered the old-fashioned dining-room, followed by Cecily. This time Lieutenant Parkson caught the full view of Mrs. Monmouth's beauty for the first time. Her fine eyes met his, lingered for a moment, then turned away. After that the young man watched her during the entire meal. He watched her as she moved away. She carried herself superbly.

For some minutes, unheeding his companions' conversation, Parkson looked at the vacant place she had occupied. He remained absorbed in thought until something gleaming caught his eye on the carpet, within a yard of Mrs. Beecher Monmouth's vacated chair. Parkson saw this object, left his seat, and discovered it to be a small gold cigarette-case.

He took it up quickly and examined it with a good deal of interest. On the gold surface of the case the letters "A.B.M." were outlined in small rubies. For a minute the young man hesitated, holding the article in his hand; then suddenly he made up his mind what to do. He determined to seize advantage by the forelock.

Excusing himself to his friends, Parkson hurried out of the room. He had determined upon a course which would enable him to make her acquaintance. The single glance Mrs. Beecher Monmouth had rested upon him when entering the room gave him courage. At the door of No. 9, which was her sitting-room, he knocked quietly. A low voice bade him come in.

Then Parkson, embarrassed despite his boldness, stepped into the room.

"I beg your pardon for intruding upon you, but I think you dropped this cigarette-case in the dining-room."

Mrs. Beecher Monmouth looked at him, then at the case, and came quickly to her feet.

"Oh, yes," she exclaimed. She accepted it from his fingers and smiled at him, looking steadily into his eyes. "I am so grateful to you," she said. "I cannot," she lied, "tell how I came to drop it!"

Parkson bowed, and was moving towards the door.

"Not at all," he murmured.

"You know, the servants," went on Mrs. Beecher Monmouth, "are sometimes so dishonest in these hotels."

"Quite so," answered Parkson clumsily. Then he noticed that Mrs. Beecher Monmouth had opened the cigarette-case and was holding it towards him. There were four buff-coloured cigarettes in its interior.

"Won't you give me the pleasure of accepting one of them? I am afraid it is the only reward you will permit me to offer you, Mr. — —"

She paused, looking questioningly at him.

"My name is Parkson."

Mrs. Beecher Monmouth uttered a pleased exclamation; her face wreathed itself in smiles. For a devastated widow she looked at that moment particularly light-hearted.

"Oh, how very nice that is. Then you must know my cousin, Captain Cherriton?"

"Yes," said Parkson; "I've met him a number of times here." His tone conveyed to her swift intelligence the fact that Captain Cherriton was not high in his favour. She looked at him seriously.

"I am afraid he was not the best of company for you."

At that moment Cecily, who had been conveniently absent from the room, entered with coffee upon the tray.

"You will please bring another cup, Cecily. I am sure Captain Parkson——"

"Lieutenant Parkson," corrected the young man.

"Lieutenant Parkson will join me."

Five minutes later Lieutenant Parkson was comfortably seated in a chair on the opposite side of the hearth. He was consuming one of Mrs. Beecher Monmouth's buff-coloured cigarettes, and was very much at home drinking some of Mrs. Beecher Monmouth's after-dinner coffee. After the first few minutes he gathered together his natural self-possession. He was generally at home where women were concerned, and he was intensely susceptible to feminine beauty. At that particular moment he was flattering himself that he was making a good impression upon this rich and beautiful young widow. It occurred to him that she was, in the circumstances, unduly cheerful, but he attributed this to his own good company. The fact that Mrs. Beecher Monmouth had cunningly put him in this frame of mind was, of course, unknown to him. His own social position was quite a modest one, and this *tête-à-tête* with a woman of Mrs. Monmouth's importance and aristocratic connections flattered his vanity.

"Do you know, Mr. Parkson, I don't look upon you as a stranger in the least. You are a friend of my reckless cousin, and, therefore, we are in a sense mutually acquainted."

"It is very nice of you to say so," acknowledged Parkson.

In her amiable presence he began to grow expansive, until suddenly Mrs. Beecher Monmouth, as it were, appeared to recollect her tragic widowhood. She dismissed him very neatly, but before he went away they shook hands, and she thanked him again. He could feel her fingers warm, vibrant, and vital in his. Her brilliant eyes held his for a moment; then she permitted him to depart.

Cecily came into the room when he had gone.

"You can take away the cups, Cecily," said Mrs. Beecher Monmouth, "and to-morrow night, in addition to coffee, you will provide whisky and liqueurs."

"Very good, madam."

"Glasses for two," announced Mrs. Beecher Monmouth.

Within four days of her arrival at her hotel Mrs. Beecher Monmouth had completely enchained the susceptible young officer. Parkson was amazed at his own success, yet perhaps not so much amazed after all. He began to see himself as a newly fledged Don Juan, a dog, a daring and romantic fascinator of women.

CHAPTER XXVI

One afternoon, when Colonel Hobin's permission had been obtained, Parkson invited Mrs. Beecher Monmouth to tea at Heatherpoint Fort. It was only occasionally that ladies were allowed to enter the fort gates. Mrs. Beecher Monmouth, however, was a well-known woman, and her recent sorrow won for her every one's commiseration. In sending her the permit to enter the fort—a slip of yellow paper, rubber stamped, and with Colonel Hobin's signature scrawled at the foot—Parkson apologised for the roughness of the fare he would be able to offer her.

Mrs. Beecher Monmouth had been deftly angling for an invitation to the fort from the moment of her arrival.

Upon the next afternoon she attired herself with special care, and, when ready, made the eleven miles journey to Heatherpoint in a hired car.

She smiled graciously at the first sentry to halt her vehicle at the foot of the wide road leading to the fort gate. At the tall iron gates themselves, which clanked noisily open when her pass had been inspected by the guard, Mrs. Beecher Monmouth was conscious of a slight tremor. The sensation of being behind closed gates—for the gates clanked immediately shut upon her entrance—filled her with a sudden throb of fear. The abrupt movements, the expressionless faces of the guard also disturbed her. She had ventured a great deal in her work on behalf of the German secret service, but this was the first occasion where she had, as it were, stepped deliberately into the jaws of the lion. Her quick eyes took in all her surroundings; the cliff rose abruptly to her left; the muzzle of a six-inch gun peering out over the Solent was visible twenty yards away upon her right. A sergeant, still holding her pass in his hand, looked at her inquiringly.

"You wish to see Lieutenant Parkson?"

"Yes, please." Her heart was still beating swiftly. She had not foreseen that the gates would be clanged ruthlessly shut behind her.

The sergeant turned on his heel.

"Will you come this way, madame?"

He began to ascend steep ladder-like steps laid against the face of the cliff. Mrs. Beecher Monmouth followed the grim khaki-clad figure.

"Please, not quite so fast," she entreated, and paused for breath.

Three hundred feet below her, looking almost straight down, she could see the blue waters of the Solent shining in the sunlight. Tiny white-crested waves fell languidly into the little bay, with its jutting pier that before the war had been thronged with holiday-makers, but which was now empty and deserted. Beyond the pier, three miles away, on the mainland promontory the tower of the Ponsonby Lighthouse gleamed beautiful and white.

"What a lovely view, sergeant."

"Yes, madame."

"But in winter it must be very cold up here."

"Yes, madame."

He was standing eight or ten steps above her, eyeing a tangle of barbed wire which covered a green hill slope, with indifferent eyes. He did not approve of visitors to the fort, especially ladies. What did ladies want climbing ladders and nosing about in places where they were not wanted; they were never allowed to see anything important. And as for the so-called view, they could get a better one at the Shakespeare Monument a little farther along the downs. This was Sergeant Ewins's opinion as he conducted Lieutenant Parkson's visitor up the steep steps to the little well-hidden mess-room at the cliff top, and even Mrs. Beecher Monmouth's unparalleled beauty and charm failed to win a smile from him. Parkson, who had been on duty until that minute, came running towards them as they entered the small asphalted courtyard. Mrs. Beecher Monmouth, her eyes shining, her breath coming quickly with the exertion of the ascent, clasped his hand in hers.

Parkson dismissed Ewins and apologised briskly for not being able to receive her at the fort gates.

"I was on duty till this minute. Our colonel's a bit of a martinet."

"Is he not popular?" asked Mrs. Beecher Monmouth in the low intimate—we two are alone in all the world—voice she knew so well how to use.

Parkson opened his eyes wide.

"Good Lord, yes; he's most awfully popular. He is just, you see, and the men always appreciate that."

He led his visitor into the single story building, and along a passage toward the little mess-room. Here Mrs. Beecher Monmouth seated herself in the only armchair—a cheap wicker article—and surveyed the room with smiling, but intensely receptive eyes. In a flash she took in the bare boarded floor, the trestle table, the colonel's cigar box on the mantelshelf, the Admiralty chart of the Solent which covered the end wall and lastly, the old piano, which was the worst treated instrument in the Isle of Wight.

Parkson bustled about at the tea-table, and Mrs. Beecher Monmouth presently turned her attention upon him.

"Will anyone come in and disturb us if I help you to make the table a little more presentable?" she asked.

"I'm afraid they will," Parkson answered. "But I managed to choose a time when only one officer is likely to come in."

"Is he old and grumpy, or young and nice-looking like you?" Mrs. Beecher Monmouth looked at him with raillery in her fine eyes. She was helping herself to marmalade, and was making the best of the thickness of the bread and butter, and the strong tea Parkson had poured out for her.

"Oh, he's a dashed sight better looking than I am," admitted Parkson modestly; "his name is Sinclair, an old regular officer."

"I am sure I shall not like him," said Mrs. Beecher Monmouth.

It was fully a quarter of an hour before Sinclair made his appearance, and then the tea was nearly cold. He came in, and was introduced to Mrs. Beecher Monmouth. Looking at his lean, handsome face and audacious eyes she could have sworn that she had seen him somewhere before. As a matter of fact, his appearance was vaguely familiar to her because one of Sinclair's earlier duties that year had been to watch her at little dinner parties at the Savoy, Carlton and Ritz Hotels.

"I think we have met before," probed Mrs. Beecher Monmouth, furrowing her brows, and fixing her gaze on Sinclair's face.

"I am afraid I have not had that pleasure," replied Sinclair, who could act the part of smiling fatuity to perfection. He was thinking how well she looked in her widow's weeds, and how extraordinary cheerful was her manner, considering the tragedy that had recently befallen her.

Parkson and Mrs. Beecher Monmouth soon left the mess-room, and immediately they were gone Sinclair rose from the table, hurried to his room, and wrote a code telegram to Dacent Smith.

Mrs. Beecher Monmouth is here. What action shall I take?

Two hours later his Chief's answer came.

Take no action. Treves handling the matter.

While Sinclair was writing his telegram Mrs. Beecher Monmouth had accompanied Parkson out into the asphalted yard. Only certain limited areas of the fort were open to friends of the officers. "I am afraid it is very feminine of me," exclaimed Mrs. Monmouth as they passed the bakehouse door, "but I should so love to peep inside."

"By all means," responded Parkson, showing himself indulgent to feminine curiosity.

She tripped across the yard, and peered into the half darkness of the bakehouse. She was carrying out her instructions, which were to find out what had become of Sims, but even the astuteness of Dacent Smith himself at this moment would have failed to detect guile in the girlish innocence of her expression as she looked into the face of the red-haired Scotch baker who had succeeded Sims. She examined the great tray of newly-baked loaves, uttered feminine exclamations of astonishment and admiration at all she saw, and finally smiled sweetly into the face of the dour Scotch corporal.

"I suppose you have been here ages and ages, Mr. Lyle?"

"No, madam, it's no more than a month since I came."

Parkson, who had listened good-humouredly, awaited her at the door, and as they crossed the asphalt together Mrs. Monmouth questioned him as to the baker who had preceded Lyle. She put her questions deftly, in a manner that would arouse no suspicion.

"Oh, no, Sims isn't at the front." He looked at her for a moment with fleeting doubt in his gaze, and decided to say no more about Sims. But Mrs. Monmouth's keen eyes interpreted his expression of reserve. He knew something. She smiled inwardly. What he knew she, too, would know.

"I am afraid we must stop here," Parkson suddenly said, "I am not allowed to take anyone beyond this barbed wire."

"Do you never allow visitors to go there?"

"Never," answered Parkson emphatically.

Mrs. Beecher Monmouth turned her resplendent countenance upon him. There was a vivid colour in her cheeks; the rich curve of her lips glowed scarlet.

"How wonderful it all is—and, I suppose," she went on, looking at him with what he and any other man would have believed to be admiration, "you are watching and waiting, all day and all night—waiting for the enemy?"

"Something of the sort," answered Parkson wearily. "You never know; he may come any time."

"Do you expect him?"

They were at the top of the steps which led to the lower fort, the superb panorama of Alum Bay, the Ponsonby Lighthouse and the English coast lay at their feet.

"I can't say that we expect him any longer," answered Parkson, naturally, "but we live in hope!"

"I suppose the fort is very strong?"

"I expect it's capable of doing its bit," Parkson answered judicially.

"I suppose you have made it much stronger in the last few months— since the Germans began to do badly on the Western front?"

Parkson looked at her quickly, and she broke into a little musical laugh.

"How silly I am!" she exclaimed. "I am talking just like a man. That comes of living with a Member of Parliament."

This was the only reference she had made to her husband, but she made it in a tone which was intended to convey to Parkson that Mr. Beecher Monmouth was completely and irrevocably dead, and that being a young and vital woman, she, on her part, could not be expected to mourn his loss eternally.

They descended the steps together, and, in pretty timidity, she laid her fingers upon his arm. In Parkson's short career of gallantry he had never felt so much a man of the world as at that moment.

When the steep descent had been made, and they were upon the level of the lower fort, Mrs. Beecher Monmouth expressed much interest in the view that was to be obtained from that level. But Parkson shook his head, and explained that no visitors whatever were admitted to the lower fort.

Failing in that project, Mrs. Beecher Monmouth turned her eyes upon the tall barred gate which cut her off from the world outside. Parkson explained to her with a masterful smile, that, until he gave the word, she was a prisoner in the fort.

"You can test it, if you like," he said; "all you have to do is to walk to the gate and try to get out."

It was nearly six o'clock, and Parkson was due upon duty at seven.

"Look here," he said, "I have just time to show you out of the fort the other way, across the links. I'm afraid you'll have to go up the steps again."

Mrs. Beecher Monmouth, however, showed herself quite willing to make an ascent to the upper level. She was interested and delighted in everything she saw.

At the top of the cliff, with the short green turf underfoot, old Lieutenant-Commander Greaves met them, and saluted, and went to his eyrie, his glass-covered look-out with its great swivel telescope.

"What a delightful old naval officer!"

"He is," returned Parkson, "and as keen as mustard."

His companion put a few deft questions; it was as though she put out invisible tentacles, groping for matter that could be valuable.

Before they reached the confines of the fort Parkson led her to the cliff edge, to the exact spot wherefrom Manton had looked down upon Sims busy upon the sands. Far below them lay the quiet little bay—there was scarcely a ripple upon the blue sunlit water, and the waves rolled and fell languidly with a musical cadence.

Mrs. Beecher Monmouth seated herself beside Parkson and admired the view. She was clever enough not to force the pace; he was already entangled in her meshes, but he was not yet completely helpless. Aforetime she had conquered and wrought the undoing of men far subtler than Parkson.

"What a lovely, lovely bay, Mr. Parkson!"

Parkson admitted the beauty of the bay. He told her that it was within the area of the fort, and that it was not accessible to the public, and that there was only one way of approaching it by a narrow path descending the chalk cliff. Then quite insidiously and with incredible dexterity she led him round to talk of Sims. Months later, when Parkson recalled that conversation, he was totally unable to account for the manner in which she had achieved a return to this subject. Sims, the lank, cadaverous and bead-eyed Sims—who was really Steinbaum and a German spy—what had this man to do with the beauty and splendour of the sunlit evening? Why should his existence interest the tragically bereaved young widow, the society woman, who Parkson truly believed had fallen in love with himself? "Heart taken at the rebound," the young man quoted in fatuous gratification. He felt delighted to think that old Greaves had seen him in company of this lovely widow. He wanted the ancient naval officer to think him a dog, and when he and Mrs. Beecher Monmouth rose and passed between attentive sentries out of the fort into the downs, Parkson helped the lovely widow up certain steps, out through certain areas of barbed wire, by taking her arm in his. He wondered if old Greaves, in his glass look-out, was watching them—old Greaves saw pretty much everything that went on in the upper fort. But on this occasion it was not Greaves, but Captain Sinclair who watched him—watched every movement they made from Greaves' glass-encompassed tower.

"What do you think of that friend of Parkson's, Commander?" asked Sinclair, as Parkson and his guest passed finally out of the fort.

"She's the best-looking woman I've seen here since the war began," responded Greaves. "When I was a young man," he went on wickedly, drawing at his pipe, "I always went in for widows. There is always so much more to 'em."

"In this case," Sinclair answered, "the widow seems to be bearing her sorrow pretty lightly!"

"Old husbands are soon forgotten by young wives," observed Greaves philosophically. "When I was in Minorca, in the old Benbow, in '72 or '73," he began, and told Sinclair with never-ending gusto one of his somewhat highly-spiced stories of youthful adventures of his midship days.

In the meantime Parkson conducted Mrs. Beecher Monmouth down to her waiting motor-car. They descended the steep hillside, and Parkson still helped her on every occasion. The hired Ford car had been turned in the narrow road. Parkson, with a glance at his watch, helped her into the vehicle, daringly stepped in beside her, and placed the dust-cover over both their knees.

"I can have a five minutes' drive with you and get back by seven," he announced.

"But I didn't invite you, Mr. Parkson."

"Your eyes invited me," he returned audaciously, and under the dust-cover he slid his fingers towards hers.

There ensued a palpitating moment, then Mrs. Beecher Monmouth turned her radiantly beautiful face slightly towards him; under long, curved lashes she gave him a sidelong glance. Then, so that the chauffeur should not overhear, she whispered, framing the words with her lips:

"You bad, bad, naughty officer!"

But she did not remove her hand, which was now enclosed in his.

Parkson thought it a lucky chance that she had discarded her gloves. Parkson, in fact, was green enough to trust her absolutely. He was, indeed, the veriest babe in her hands. Her face was full towards him now. She was smiling, exhibiting her splendid teeth, and looking deep into his eyes. Her black hat and widow's weeds added only to the brilliancy of her complexion, to the scarlet richness of her fine lips. There was something in her gaze, in the warm intensity of her regard, its lingering softness, that utterly swept away Parkson's self-possession. He leaned toward her and dropped his voice.

"If it wasn't for the sentries there on the hill-top," he murmured, "I'd kiss you now!"

"Bad boy," she said with her lips.

She had a way of talking with her lips and uttering no sound that concentrated attention on her sensuous charms.

Parkson's five minutes in the car seemed to him five minutes of heaven. He was completely and utterly enamoured—and as to the future, the future seemed to blaze before him in radiant and glorious romance. He wondered how far he could go—he had never seen a woman like her. Beautiful, feminine, coy, loving.... What a blind idiot, thought he, Beecher Monmouth must have been to shoot himself.

"When shall we meet again?" he whispered, as he alighted from the car at the end of the fort road.

"I'm afraid I shall have to meet you again soon, you naughty boy!"

She put out her supple white hand, adorned only with a wedding ring. Parkson seized her fingers and impressed a fervent kiss upon them.

As the car swept away, Mrs. Beecher Monmouth turned and waved a little handkerchief in farewell.

CHAPTER XXVII

When Mrs. Monmouth reached the hotel in Newport, something over an hour after bidding Parkson farewell, Cecily awaited her in the little sitting-room.

"Are you ready, madame, to dress for dinner?" asked the maid.

"Yes, Cecily, and I shall dine here to-night."

She went into the bedroom, and Cecily disrobed her. During this ceremony the girl hesitated once or twice on the point of speaking, then refrained.

"Well, what is it, Cecily? What is it you want to say?"

"It is something important, madame, that has occurred."

Mrs. Beecher Monmouth turned and opened her eyes in interrogation.

"What, for instance?" she demanded.

Cecily, who was at the wardrobe, took out her mistress's evening skirt.

"To-day, madame, when you were away, I made acquaintance of one of the men at Heatherpoint Fort——"

"Ah!" ejaculated Mrs. Beecher Monmouth, suddenly interested; "so soon—that was clever of you."

"He told me, in regard to Sims, madame, he merely left the fort——"

Mrs. Beecher Monmouth nodded indifferently; she was disappointed.

"Is that all you learned, Cecily?"

"No, madame. I learned also that Lieutenant Treves, who was supposed by us to be staying with his father, was, however, at that time acting as one of the officers at Heatherpoint."

This was the first Mrs. Beecher Monmouth had heard of John's presence at the fort. She was at first inclined to disbelieve it. Then, when Cecily proved circumstantially that the statement was true, Mrs. Beecher Monmouth felt inclined to dismiss the matter as of no moment. If Treves had been at Heatherpoint, he was there evidently with the knowledge of von Kuhne, and possibly was acting in von Kuhne's interests, and, for her part, she was not in the least inclined to doubt John—he was one of her admirers. A more resourceful and more attractive man than Parkson, and, nevertheless, equally a victim of her charms. She flattered herself she could do a great deal with Bernard Treves. As for his attempting to deceive her, that seemed out of the question. She pointed out to Cecily that Treves's stay at Heatherpoint Fort did not mean that the young man had betrayed the German secret service, which was rewarding him so handsomely.

Cecily, however, had a further and more serious statement to make.

"When I am suspicious, madame," she said, "I am thinking not so much of Mr. Treves's visit to the fort——"

She was at Mrs. Beecher Monmouth's back now, hooking her dress, and a silence fell.

"Well?" demanded her mistress shortly.

"I am thinking, madame," went on Cecily, "of the night of Mr. Beecher Monmouth's death."

She paused again, but her mistress made no remark, and Cecily went on:

"On that night, madame, when I had folded away your things, I took a skirt into the housekeeper's room to brush. While I brushed it I talked with Mr. Duckett, the butler, who was also there. There was no ring at the front-door bell, madame—and yet when I returned to your bedroom there was a light there."

"You left it on before you went down, Cecily!"

"No, madame, I turned it off. I was very surprised to see the light, as I knew you were out, madame, and I—I——"

Mrs. Beecher Monmouth turned and scrutinised the maid's sallow face and bead-like eyes.

"You looked through the keyhole!" she said.

"Yes, madame."

"And saw my husband, who had come back unexpectedly."

"No, madame; I saw Mr. Treves. Mr. Beecher Monmouth had not come home then; and Mr. Treves, madame, was standing near your dressing-table with a small box in his hands."

Mrs. Beecher Monmouth flashed an intense glance upon her.

"What sort of box?"

"A black box, madame, the one you kept among your furs."

Mrs. Beecher Monmouth's hand suddenly leapt out and gripped Cecily's wrist. Her voice grew low, little more than a hissing whisper.

"What are you saying, Cecily? What was Mr. Treves doing?"

"I don't know, madame."

Cecily twisted her arm, attempting to free it.

"Please, madame, you are hurting my wrist!"

Mrs. Beecher Monmouth thrust forth her face—her brilliant eyes had grown hard as agate.

"Why did you never tell me this before?"

"I thought, madame, you knew he was there."

Mrs. Beecher Monmouth relaxed her grip; she stepped back a pace or two and threw up her head.

"God in heaven, what a fool you are!"

"It was natural I should think that," protested Cecily, recoiling a step or two.

"Natural! You idiot!"

"He came in with your key, madame."

Mrs. Beecher Monmouth stared in utter amazement.

"My key?"

"Yes, madame; I saw him fling something under the table, and found afterwards it was your key. He must have taken it from your bag, madame, when he visited you in the afternoon."

Mrs. Beecher Monmouth suddenly twisted on her heel and began to pace the room. The truth had smitten her like a blow. Wild thoughts surged through her brain. All these long months she had believed herself tricking and duping Bernard Treves—her business in life was to trick, dupe, and mould men to her own ends, to the ends of the Fatherland, to the imposition of its monstrous Kultur upon the world—and now this man, this handsome, drug-sodden weakling had out-manoeuvred her! She had spun a web for him, had toyed with him, expended her charm upon him, and all the time he had been secretly and darkly laughing in his sleeve. Instead of a friend and a tool, he had been an astute and daring enemy!

Enemy—that was the word. An enemy of infinite danger to herself, to von Kuhne, to Cherriton, to Manwitz—to them all. An enemy to the Fatherland! An enemy to the great, crushing blow that was about to fall upon those arrogant and high-stomached English!

Her concealed letters, that meant everything, that exposed everything, had been found—not by her husband—but by this cool and steel-nerved, subtle-witted enemy—this young man who now, from that evidence, could piece together all her life-history.

As this thought flashed into her mind, she saw her own immediate jeopardy. She lacked nothing of courage; and, being a woman, it was not her own physical peril, nor the wrecking of von Kuhne's plan, that struck her deep—it was not this, but her own vanity that was stricken. She had made many advances to Bernard Treves—she had given much. And, as she thought of the past, a murderous and implacable hate blossomed in her mind against John. An instinct to seize something and rend it to shreds grappled her. She longed to slap Cecily—first on one side of her sallow face and then on the other. She would have liked to take Cecily's arm and twist it until the woman yelled with pain.

But as these things were not permissible, she sat down and wrote a fiery and vitriolic letter to General von Kuhne. She cared nothing now for von Kuhne's authority; they were all in danger. This pleasant, amiable young Englishman had obviously acted against them from the very first. They believed him to be a drug-taker and a discredited English officer with a grievance. And all the time he had been something utterly different.

She wrote this news to von Kuhne, and poured her contempt upon him. She knew these things would hit the chief of the German service between the eyes, and she revelled in the thought. And all the time her intense and passionate nature dwelt upon the thing that must befall Bernard Treves. How much information Treves had conveyed to his department she did not know; but this she knew, that von Kuhne and his myrmidons would effectually stop his mouth. The dark corps of espionage would add another death, another extinction to its secret crimes.

When Mrs. Beecher Monmouth had finished the letter, she closed it, addressed it to Godfrey Manners, Esq., and handed it to Cecily.

"You will take this to Mr. Manners now, and ask him to deliver it to Doctor Voules first thing to-morrow. The doctor is in London to-day, but he will return in the morning. Tell Mr. Manners that the letter is of the utmost importance."

"Very good, madame."

Mrs. Beecher Monmouth detained her a few minutes, questioning her as to Treves's visit on the night of Beecher Monmouth's death; then permitted her to go.

When the maid had departed, Mrs. Beecher Monmouth stood before the little mirror on the hotel dressing-table. "Tricked, duped and fooled!" she murmured.

Then, catching sight of the pearl and emerald pendant John had given her, she snatched it violently from her breast and hurled it into the hearth. It would have given her infinite pleasure at that moment to have murdered John by slow and excruciating torture. Her thoughts were still seething, when the dejected hotel waiter knocked at her door and announced in plaintive tones that dinner awaited her.

CHAPTER XXVIII

Next morning, at twelve o'clock, Doctor Voules sat at the big oak table in his dining-room at Brooke. He had arrived from London in the morning, and was busy consuming a heavy lunch.

The brightness of the day before had vanished; a heavy driving rain was falling. From the single window of the apartment the doctor could obtain a view of drenched foliage in his garden. And, sharp to the left, as one stood at the window, a view of the sea, grey and restless beneath a leaden sky, was visible.

The doctor ate stolidly, grinding his food in heavy, powerful jaws. The only other occupant of the room was Captain Cherriton, who lounged in a chair at the hearth and read a morning newspaper assiduously. Beside him, on the floor, lay four or five other morning news-sheets.

For many minutes, save the drive of the rain and the chink of Voules's knife and fork, no sound broke the stillness of the room. Then Voules turned his chair, took out a cigar and lit it.

"The barometer is falling, Rathenau," he said in his grating, imperious voice—quite another voice from that which he assumed as the bland Doctor Voules.

"It is going down steadily, Excellenz," answered Cherriton.

"Good," returned the elder man. "We must have unsettled weather for the twenty-eighth—eh, Rathenau?"

"It is much to be desired, Excellenz."

The twenty-eighth—it was always the twenty-eighth with General von Kuhne. With machine-like precision his forceful mind returned again and again to that date—the date which was to mark the consummation of his work. The blow, the subtle, heavy blow at England's heart—the blow planned, schemed for, and ordered; the great destruction that had originated in his martial and ruthless mind.

"Things go well, eh?"

"Quite well, Excellenz," Cherriton answered promptly, for as yet he had not found courage to mention to the general his suspicion of Treves. He was not yet positive that Treves had betrayed them, and, in the meantime, he had resolved to say nothing. Rather would he wait and watch, seeking for tangible proof of duplicity on Treves's part.

These thoughts were passing through his mind when a knock came at the door, and Conrad entered to clear away the luncheon things. In his hand he carried a salver upon which lay a single letter, addressed to Doctor Voules, and without a stamp.

The doctor took up the letter.

"Herr Manwitz brought it from Newport, Excellenz," said the servant in German.

"Tell Herr Manwitz I will see him presently, and remain out of the room until I ring for you."

General von Kuhne had recognised Mrs. Beecher Monmouth's handwriting. He began to read almost casually; then, suddenly, his interest intensified, and as he read the lines of his heavy face grew hard, firm and implacable. His colour rose; he eased his collar about his throat and bit heavily upon his long cigar.

Cherriton, noticing his agitation, noticing the blazing wrath that illuminated his face, watched him with anxious eyes.

Suddenly von Kuhne sprang to his feet.

"Stand up!" he bellowed, looking at the younger man with an expression of utter ferocity. "You blind, thick-witted fool!"

Captain Cherriton's pallid features were flushed, an angry light lit in his eye. He opened his mouth and was about to speak, but von Kuhne swept the words out of his mouth with a savage gesture.

"Speak no words to me, you — — but read that letter!"

He thrust Mrs. Beecher Monmouth's closely-written sheets into the younger man's hands.

"Read that!" he roared, "and see to what pass you have brought us!"

Cherriton began to read, and as he read the colour left his face. Von Kuhne hurried to the bell and jangled it savagely. Conrad precipitated himself into the room in a state of nervous agitation. He was used to authority, but he had never yet known a bell to ring with such violence.

Doctor Voules's face turned towards him did nothing to dissipate his alarm.

"Tell Herr Manwitz to come here this instant," roared Voules.

"Very good, Excellenz." He paused a moment, then added: "Mr. Bernard Treves is here, Excellenz. Shall I also tell him to enter?"

Doctor Voules drew in a deep breath. He turned slowly and looked into Cherriton's eyes.

The stillness that ensued was intense and portentous. The glance that passed between Voules and Cherriton was one of infinite meaning. Voules's expression of ferocity moderated; he turned his eyes again to the intimidated Conrad standing in the doorway.

"How long has Mr. Treves been here?"

"A few minutes only, Herr Excellenz. He came in after Herr Manwitz."

"Very good, Conrad! You will take particular care Mr. Treves does not leave the house, and you will in the meantime send Herr Manwitz to me."

"Very good, Excellenz."

"You understand my order in regard to Herr Treves?"

"Yes, Excellenz. He is not to leave the house."

General von Kuhne nodded and turned on his heel. As the door closed upon Conrad, his implacable eyes once more sought Cherriton.

"The letter you hold," he began, making a stiff gesture towards Mrs. Beecher Monmouth's missive, which Cherriton was still studying—"the letter you hold in your hand convicts this man completely. His treachery to us, his espionage"—he paused a moment—"may bring upon us the utmost disaster. In failing to discover his duplicity you have shown yourself no less than a sheep-headed fool!"

"Herr Excellenz!" protested Baron von Rathenau, drawing himself up, a flush of colour animating his dull pallor.

"I am your superior officer!" countered von Kuhne. "It is, fortunately, my privilege to speak plain words to you; it is equally my privilege to command your obedience. You have failed in regard to this young man, Bernard Treves. From the first hour of his contact with Manwitz he has clearly tricked you both!"

"May I venture to remind you, Excellenz, that he tricked you also?"

Von Kuhne lifted his fierce and truculent gaze.

Cherriton was neither intimidated nor silenced.

"He tricked you, Herr Excellenz, the day of his first visit here. You announced to me then that you were satisfied. You observed upon his wrists the punctured marks which proved him, as you said, Excellenz, to be addicted to the injection of drugs."

Von Kuhne waved these objections aside.

"I based my opinion upon his dossier provided for me by you and Manwitz." He began to pace the floor, with his hands behind his back, his head thrust forward in deep thought. "This affair, Rathenau," he said at length, "this discovery grows more and more sinister. It is clear to anyone not utterly a fool that every step of yours and Manwitz has been dogged for many weeks past. What this young man knows of our plans we shall never learn; what he has confided to his authorities we can only guess. One thing, however, is certain: whether he knows much or little, his activities must cease." He paused and looked full into the younger man's face. "Do you gather my meaning?"

Cherriton bowed.

"I understand, Excellenz."

Von Kuhne continued to pace the carpet.

"I shall rely upon you for effective measures."

At that moment a knock fell upon the door, and Conrad ushered Herr Manwitz into the room, and closed the door upon him. The big, fat man, with his swarthy, pouched cheeks, his bristling black moustache and iron-grey hair, bowed deferentially to von Kuhne.

"You desired to see me, Excellenz?"

Von Kuhne walked to the table, took up Mrs. Beecher Monmouth's letter, and handed it to him.

"Read that!" he said curtly. He spoke in German, and used the commanding tone of an exalted German officer speaking to a subordinate. Manwitz read the letter from end to end, and as he read the colour receded from his cheeks, his heart-beat quickened in growing apprehension. As the import of the letter grew plain to him, his apprehension amounted almost to terror. The thought that Treves was a member of the English secret service filled him with infinite dread. He had never in his most suspicious moments conceived such a thing as possible. Treves, the neurotic, the weak-minded drug-taker! The man who had shown cowardice in the face of the enemy, and had narrowly escaped court-martial! Was it possible that this good-looking, feeble fool had been at one and the same time a steady-nerved, watchful member of the English Intelligence Department? Even now, as he read Mrs. Beecher Monmouth's plain words, he could not credit them. Nevertheless he was afraid—mortally afraid—for his own skin. The Tower of London and a firing squad had always loomed at the back of Manwitz' mind as a thing of infinite menace. The English were so peremptory in these matters—no talk, no fuss; merely a firing squad and oblivion! He possessed none of Cherriton's cold and brutal courage. And the thought that his own name was written in the tablets of the English secret service, the knowledge that his every movement may have been watched by a skilful English spy, sent a tremor through him that was visible both to von Kuhne and Cherriton.

"You discovered this man!" said von Kuhne, thrusting out his chin and fixing his cold gaze upon Manwitz.

"That I admit," answered Manwitz; "but I am prepared to swear that he was indeed what I thought him to be. I took the utmost care, Excellenz, and it was long before I trusted him. His information, Excellenz, enabled us to sink the *Polidor*."

"That is quite true, Excellenz," Cherriton said, suddenly puzzled.

"And in regard to his habits," went on Manwitz, "I have seen him many times under the influence of drugs, with all the symptoms, Excellenz, which I was careful to study—dilation of the pupils, irritability, fear of imaginary enemies——"

Von Kuhne waved his hand, but Manwitz persisted.

"Excellenz, he must have changed greatly, if he is, indeed, the man mentioned here!"

"You fool!" von Kuhne thrust at him; "of course he is the same man! We are speaking of Treves, and no other!"

"He must have changed, Excellenz!" protested Manwitz. "Treves, as I knew him, would never have had the nerve to act against us. I impressed upon him, Excellenz, what the punishment for treachery would be, and he values his own skin above all things in the world."

"Perhaps almost as much as you value yours!" added von Kuhne, with a sneer of contempt. "I have to warn you, Manwitz, I shall expect you to act decisively and without reservation! The Fatherland requires that this man who has betrayed us shall expiate his treachery! Do you get my meaning?"

"Yes, Excellenz."

"You will understand," he said, looking from one to the other, "that I am speaking officially and in my capacity as director of intelligence. You will obey me"—his eyes turned towards Cherriton—"as though we were upon the sacred soil of the Fatherland!"

He was standing at the table, resting one hand on the cloth. He spoke as a judge pronouncing a sentence, and in the eyes of von Rathenau and Manwitz he was, indeed, this. They took orders from him as inferior officers receiving orders from a general of division. "The removal of this man is an act of mere military justice. My orders are that you, Manwitz, and you, Baron von Rathenau, administer this just sentence!" He was passing what amounted to sentence of death on Bernard Treves. In doing this he felt no qualm, no sensitive doubt whatever. If he had occupied an English town in his true character as a German general in command, he would have put to death a hundred persons for not a tithe of the crime that John had committed against him. In sentencing John to death, in appointing Cherriton and Manwitz his executioners, he was carrying out what to him was a just, even a moderate law. He had been brought up to slaughter; he had been taught from boyhood to crush the Fatherland's enemies. To intimidate by frightfulness was the highest German ideal. He was a typical military German—that is, a typical cold-blooded murderer. He crossed to the bell now and jangled it again—this time not quite so sharply.

"My orders," he said to Cherriton, over his shoulder, "are to be carried out as expeditiously as possible. I leave the method in your hands." He turned his eyes upon Manwitz. "I shall expect you to co-operate in the work, Manwitz!"

At that moment Conrad presented himself in the door-way.

"Tell Mr. Treves to come in," said von Kuhne.

Two minutes later John entered the room. His erect figure, his clear eye, instantly caught von Kuhne's attention; every one of the German's suspicions was in that moment doubly confirmed. For a moment von Kuhne felt inclined to draw his pistol and shoot Manton down where he stood, but by a powerful effort he assumed his suave "Doctor Voules" manner.

"Come in, Mr. Treves," he said. "We have seen very little of you of late."

John came into the room and shook hands with Manwitz. He had not seen him for some time. Manwitz's hand was cold and flabby to the touch. John felt the atmosphere tense and electrical; he knew in some subtle way that Voules' smoothness of tone was a veneer to hide other and deeper feelings. The eyes of the three Germans seemed to watch him with unusual closeness. He instantly jumped to the conclusion that Cherriton had been conveying his suspicions to von Kuhne. The thought that Mrs. Beecher

Monmouth's suspicions had been aroused was the last thing that would have entered his head.

He stayed for some minutes talking upon general topics. He had come in answer to a summons from von Kuhne, and was surprised that the German had given him no definite instructions. On behalf of Dacent Smith, John had already gathered a good deal of data about the approaching operations. He knew more than a little of the great blow Germany was preparing, and he felt a little puzzled that von Kuhne appeared to have upon this occasion nothing for him to do.

"You must come again," said the German; "we will have a further talk." He glanced at Cherriton. Cherriton understood the meaning of the look.

"Which way are you going, Treves?"

"Oh! I shall cycle back to Freshwater," John answered. "I promised my father I'd stay a night with him."

"That's exactly my way back," answered Cherriton.

"It is my way also," added Manwitz, "but I'm afraid you'll have to leave me behind, as I have no cycle."

The upshot was that a few minutes later, in a pause between two heavy downfalls of rain, John and Cherriton set out and cycled away together from Voules's residence.

John and Cherriton cycled side by side. It was John's plan to spend the night with Treves's father. He was fond of the old soldier, and in deceiving him was merely carrying out his chosen part. He was playing a dangerous game in his country's interests. And the first man to applaud his actions would have been the fine old soldier, whose own son had proved so utter a disappointment. Therefore John felt no compunction in the deception.

He knew that infinite caution was required of him, and that the shrewd eyes of Captain Cherriton were always upon him. He knew that at any moment "Voules," or Cherriton or Mrs. Beecher Monmouth might stumble upon the knowledge of his true identity. In that case not only would his utility to Dacent Smith come to an abrupt end, but his own chances of escape from his enemies' ruthlessness would be hardly worth contemplating. He was surprised to find that, as he and Cherriton rode side by side, the tall German talked more volubly and affably than usual. He seemed to have forgotten his suspicions of John, his peculiar attitude in Doctor Voules's room had vanished. He questioned John cheerfully as to his recent movements, and, when John evaded his questions a little too obviously, he rallied his companion, suggesting that he was a gay dog, that he was neglecting his wife and bestowing his attentions elsewhere.

John looked at him keenly upon the mention of Elaine's name, but he could read nothing on the German's pallid, heavy-boned face. Nevertheless, as he rode, and as they drew near to Freshwater, John became aware that his companion had been pumping him with a good deal of subtlety. He was trying to find out something—what that something was John could not guess.

They rode up a long hill together and came in sight of the sea. The view was magnificent, despite the lowering clouds and the rain, which had begun to fall again. Upon their right hand, sloping towards the sea and the white cliffs, lay a wide expanse of down, broken by small coppices and clumps of gorse. There was an old grey stone farm-house, with farm buildings, in the distance and in the middle of the down, near a clump of trees, were two single-storied labourers' cottages.

Cherriton drew John's attention to these buildings.

"I want you to come and have a look at that little place, Treves," he said, in a casual tone.

"What is its particular interest?" asked John.

"It has a particular interest for me," Cherriton answered, "because I have rented it furnished for six months. It is a delightful little place, and just the sort of bachelor abode to suit me." He turned his light blue eyes and looked with what might have been called frankness into John's face. "I hope you'll give me the pleasure of being my guest there one of these days soon. Doctor Voules is lending me Conrad for servant, and I shall be able to make you fairly comfortable."

"Thanks," said John; "I shall be pleased to come."

"Why not come and have a look at it now?" continued Cherriton. "We can't ride across the heather, but there is a path, and we can push our bicycles."

"Thanks all the same," said John, "but I am afraid I cannot spare the time."

"I can give you a very decent peg of whisky," said Cherriton, quietly.

John, playing the part of Bernard Treves, smiled.

"I am afraid I must keep off the whisky, as I am going to see my father," he answered adroitly.

After that Cherriton pressed him no more. Presently, however, he slackened his pace.

"This is where I get off," he said. He dismounted, and John also alighted. "Why not come in until the rain is over?"

"I don't mind the rain," said John.

Cherriton turned and pushed his bicycle through the gap in the stone wall. He was still scheming with all his thoughts to get John into the secluded cottage. A new thought came to him.

"By the way," he said, "has your friend Manwitz been able to give you any of the tablets you used to be so anxious about?" He paused a moment, looking John steadily in the eyes, "or have you managed to break the habit?"

John detected something in his tone which caused him to move warily.

"I have had nothing from him for some time; and, as for breaking that sort of habit, it isn't so easy. What made you ask that?"

"Merely the fact," answered Cherriton, cunningly, "that I think I can give you what you want."

John had already detected that the other had a strong reason for getting him into the cottage, and, though at first he had made up his mind to accept no invitation, he now saw that he was liable to fall into a trap. For if he declined to come to the cottage for the tablets, which were a mania with Treves, he would without doubt deepen Cherriton's suspicions. Therefore, acting the part of Treves, he broke into a laugh.

"Well, if you put it like that," he said, "I suppose I must come."

Five minutes later he followed Cherriton through a gate in a low stone wall, crossed the patch of ground before the cottage, and entered the single-storied building. The house was silent and deserted. John discovered that the place, formerly two workmen's cottages, had been knocked into one, and furnished for the purpose of letting.

The room in which John stood was low, and a gate-legged table occupied the middle of the apartment. There was an old-fashioned fireplace, three or four chintz-covered chairs, and chintz curtains. From the window John could obtain a distant view of a grey sea and a leaden sky.

"It's not over cheerful in here, is it?" said Cherriton. "I think we had better have a fire." He put a match to the fire, then took whisky and glasses from the cupboard. "One peg won't hurt you," he remarked, pouring out a drink for John. "While you are drinking, I'll look for the tablets."

He stayed in the room for some minutes after that. John noticed that he poured himself a stiff dose of whisky, and drank it down with only a moderate addition of water. He gave John the impression of a man who is strung up to a high pitch of tension. He was restless and walked the floor, explaining to John that he intended to spend the rest of the summer and the autumn there.

"I have a good deal of writing to do," he said, "and Dr. Voules wants me to be near him. It's not a bad little place this, is it?"

"Not at all," said John.

Cherriton went out of the room into a bedroom with two windows, one of which looked over a deserted-looking yard, with a covered well at the further end. He stood at the window, gazing out into this yard, with puckered brows, for several minutes. Then he began to open and shut drawers in the dressing-table, making a considerable noise.

He came into the sitting-room a few minutes later and apologised to John, saying that he must have made a mistake about the tablets.

"I can find no sign of them," he said, "but you must come again, and I promise to have some for you."

John, who had been watching him closely, suddenly rose from his chair and confronted him.

"Look here, Cherriton," he demanded, "what's your game?"

Cherriton's face took on a stony expression

"What game?" he demanded.

"Why are you so deucedly restless?"

Cherriton broke into a laugh.

"It's your imagination. I am not in the least restless; I am only worried that I have dragged you here for nothing. Have another whisky?"

"No, thanks," said John, this time firmly. "I must be pushing along." He happened to be looking into Cherriton's face as he said this, and something took place on the other's face that startled him—a flame of something like ferocity lit up in the German's eyes, then instantly vanished. After that, however, he made no further attempt to detain John. He came to the end of the little cottage garden as John went away, and watched him as he mounted his bicycle and rode away towards Freshwater. Then he returned to the cottage, closed the door behind him, and, dropping into a chair, took out Mrs. Beecher Monmouth's letter and read it carefully from end to end.

He was still in his chair at the hearth half an hour later when Manwitz knocked at the door, and came in.

"Come in, Manwitz, come in!" said Cherriton, rising. Manwitz had halted in the doorway, and was slowly drawing off his mackintosh. There was a mute expression in his eyes. Cherriton, reading his expression, pointed to a chair at the opposite side of the hearth.

"Sit down, Manwitz; nothing has happened yet; our friend is spending the night with his father, but he has arranged to come over here to see me to-morrow."

Manwitz took a handkerchief from his inner pocket, and mopped his brow.

"It is terrible, Herr Baron! His Excellenz affirms that he has been watching us from the beginning, but in that case how can he explain the sinking of the *Polidor*?"

"The time for explanations has gone, Manwitz. Treves's discoveries, whatever they are, must not be permitted to check the great work his Excellenz has put his hand to."

For some minutes after that there was silence between the two men; then Manwitz spoke, easing his collar about his fat throat:

"His Excellenz impressed upon me, Herr Baron, the business of Mr. Treves is of the utmost urgency."

"That is understood," Cherriton answered grimly. "But His Excellenz has no wish that I should play the fool and expose myself to unnecessary danger. His Excellenz can rely entirely upon my discretion—and our united capacity to carry out his command, eh, Manwitz?"

Manwitz smiled and nodded, but entirely without enjoyment. Cherriton's coolness in face of the terrible duty that lay before them filled him with both terror and envy.

CHAPTER XXIX

At six o'clock that same evening Colonel Treves issued from the front door of his fine Tudor residence at Freshwater, and made his way down the drive. The weather had cleared, there was a golden light in the west, and the Colonel, wearing a tweed suit, walked briskly towards the lodge-keeper's cottage. He told himself that he had come there entirely upon business— merely to give the man certain personal orders. The truth of the matter was, however, that he could no longer stay in the house. He was expecting his son; he was looking forward to meeting his boy Bernard with a keener and happier interest than he had felt for many years. During recent months all his old love for his only offspring had returned. He was an old man, and the son who for many years had disappointed him had now grown to be a real Treves, and a man of honour. A smile flitted across his fine, kindly face. He believed that he had at last discovered the reason of Bernard's altered behaviour. The boy who had been tragically cashiered from the army, who had, indeed, been almost proved guilty of cowardice in the face of the enemy, had righted himself; and not only had he won the confidence of his superiors, but he had been entrusted with delicate and difficult duties.

When Colonel Treves reached the lodge-keeper's single-storied abode, he held the man in conversation for some minutes, but his eyes turned incessantly towards the sloping road that led past his gate. When at last he saw a khaki-clad figure on a bicycle, he turned to his elderly employée:

"Adams," he said, "is that Mr. Bernard coming along?"

"Yes, sir," answered the man, after a minute or two's scrutiny.

When John reached the drive, the Colonel was at the gate to meet him.

"Well, Bernard, boy, so there you are," he exclaimed, gripping the young man's hand. "I just happened to be doing a little business here with Adams, and caught sight of you. Come in, boy, come in. How do you think Mr. Bernard's looking, Adams?" he said, turning to the old servant.

"He's looking fine, sir," answered the man. "I've seldom seen him looking so well."

"Leave your bicycle with Adams," said the Colonel; "you can take me up to the house. I am not quite so brisk as I used to be." And he slipped his arm through John's and went up the drive, talking happily and cheerfully as he went. John had always felt drawn towards him; it was impossible for him not to feel admiration and pity for this splendid old fellow. He experienced a sense of pleasure that his visit could give the old man such genuine delight.

"Now, Bernard, boy," said the Colonel, "I have a word to say to you before we go in the house. I have a surprise waiting for you there, but before we go in I want to ask you one thing?"

"What is it?" John asked quietly.

"It's this, Bernard, boy; you haven't been trusting me. You haven't relied upon me as a son should rely on his father."

"In what way, sir?"

"You'll find that out, Bernard, boy, when we get indoors," said the Colonel enigmatically.

John questioned him closely, but he could learn nothing, and presently Gates, the old butler, drew open the door, greeted John with a smile, and took his hat and gloves.

"Your suit-case arrived this morning, sir," he informed John. "I have taken it to your room."

"It's the south room, Bernard, boy," intervened the Colonel; "it's the first time you've had the honour of sleeping in the room that used to be your mother's. But this is a special reunion, Bernard. I had to do something to mark the occasion."

He took John's arm again, and together they ascended to the library, the room in which John had first made his acquaintance. There was something on the Colonel's mind which gave him pleasure, and filled him with an air of humorous mystery.

"When you've seen who's in the library, Bernard," he said, as they drew near the green baize-covered door, "you'll understand what I mean about trusting me better in the future."

He drew open the door.

"Come in, Bernard, boy; come in."

John followed him into the big, handsome apartment, with its mullioned windows and its fine view of the sea. There was some one standing by the hearth with back to the fire-place, and John suddenly caught his breath and stood still. Elaine Treves was there, smiling at him, and as he entered the room she came forward, holding out both hands in greeting.

"Bernard," she exclaimed, a light of happiness radiating her gentle beauty; "you didn't expect to find me here, did you?"

John's surprise was complete. Thoughts of Elaine had been with him during the greater part of his ride, but he remembered Treves's secret in regard to his wife, the fact that he had always kept his marriage from his father's knowledge. He was therefore astonished to find Elaine installed under her father-in-law's roof. She looked very much at home, and John wondered consumedly how she had managed to come there. He also foresaw new difficulties for himself; nevertheless he was delighted to see her, her freshness, her beauty, her winning confidence in himself all tended to please him. It took him very few minutes to observe that her presence brightened Colonel Treves's home amazingly. It was obvious to John that she had already won her way into the old fellow's heart, and as Elaine reached up and shyly kissed him, the Colonel smiled upon them both with an air of infinite benevolence.

"Now," exclaimed Colonel Treves, rallying John half an hour later, when Elaine had gone to dress for dinner. "Now do you see why I asked you to trust me?"

"I think I do," said John, somewhat awkwardly.

"Here, you young rascal, you go and marry a charming girl, who would bring credit and honour to my family, and you hide her away from me, pretending all the time that I am the strict and cruel father. That shows how greatly you misunderstood me, Bernard boy. Why, if I had chosen a wife for you myself, I couldn't have made as good a choice as you made in marrying Elaine. She's been here three days, Bernard, and already I feel towards her as to my own daughter. I always feared you would make a fool of yourself in marrying." He paused and looked at John with his dim eyes. "Sometimes, Bernard boy," he said, with a touch of wistfulness in his tone, "I cannot understand the change that has come over you, the improvement. But it's the good blood coming out, eh—the Treves blood. I always hold that blood tells, and in your case my conviction has been proved more than right. Now, Bernard, how long can you stay with me this time?"

"Only to-night, sir, I am sorry to say."

"Come, come," protested the old Colonel, "I'd expected a week at least." As he spoke the door opened, and Elaine entered the room dressed for dinner. For the first time John saw her in evening apparel. Her dress was of an inexpensive pale yellow material, muslin or silk, John did not know which, and did not care. Her dark hair was beautifully coiffeured, her cheeks glowed with colour, and there was a light of happiness in her eyes.

Colonel Treves glanced at the clock on his desk.

"Why, it's nearly seven!" he exclaimed. "I had no idea it was so late. I must run away and change. You'll want to get out of those puttees, Bernard," he said, glancing at John.

"Thank you," said John. "I am in the south room, sir?"

The Colonel nodded, and John, wondering exactly where the south room might be, went out of the library. He walked along the corridor, and chanced upon a house-maid.

"Which is my room, please?" he said.

The housemaid preceded him along the passage, and opened a door, switched on the electric light.

John thanked her, and found himself in an imposing bedroom, beautifully furnished in the French style. His suit-case had been unstrapped and was upon a stand at the foot of the bed. Laid neatly out upon the bed itself were his clothes for the evening. A fine apartment, thought John, and at that moment a knock fell upon the door.

"Come in," he called. The door opened quietly, and Elaine stepped into the room. She advanced across the room in the most natural manner in the world. There was a light in her fine grey eyes, and she was visibly and quite frankly delighted to be alone with John. John, for his part, saw in a flash the awkwardness of the position chance had imposed upon him. In his sudden surprise in finding Elaine under Colonel Treves's roof he had overlooked a *tête-à-tête* of this kind. He had indeed hardly had time to think of the matter at all.

"Bernard, are you really pleased to see me?"

"Delighted," John answered, wondering what other word he could use, for, as a matter of truth, he was delighted and appalled at the same time. He felt that the situation involving him would require the utmost finesse, if he meant to escape satisfactorily. His own nerves were strung up to a high pitch of tension, and it came as a surprise to him that Elaine should act as though their presence together in that stately sleeping apartment was the most natural event in the world.

"Do you like my dress, Bernard?"

She came towards the glittering dressing-table and turned slowly for his inspection. Her attitude, her confidence were exquisitely attractive to John. Her wifely anxiety to win her husband's approval was the prettiest thing he had ever seen. And once again the splendid rich duskiness of her hair, the gentle glow of her cheeks, the fine contours of her well-turned lips, and the fairness of her skin won his admiration. But it was not this, it was in no sense her radiant and girlish beauty that had evoked John's feelings. Mrs. Beecher Monmouth possessed beauty, but she lacked utterly the frankness and generous natural trust, the appealing femininity, in fact, which is always potent in the winning of a man's love. For it was love, and love only that John felt for this girl who was Bernard Treves's wife, who was nothing to him, and could never be anything.

To ease the situation he told her lightly that her dress suited her to perfection.

"You said when we first met, Bernard, that this primrose colour suited me best, so I put it on to-night."

"Only to please me?" asked John.

Elaine nodded.

"Of course I like to please your father, too, Bernard," she went on. "I think he is wonderful; just the beau ideal of a fine, upright soldier. I cannot understand how you could ever have doubted his generosity."

"I didn't doubt him," John answered. "I only misunderstood him, and acted like a fool."

"But in regard to our marriage. If you had told him months ago, I am sure he would have been just as pleased as he is now. Why didn't you, Bernard?"

"I don't know," John answered. "But I am sure he would have been pleased if I had been sensible enough to trust him."

Elaine seated herself upon an ottoman, an old-fashioned circular piece of furniture which decorated the middle of the apartment. For a minute she let her eyes wander over the refined luxury of the room, then said quietly and thoughtfully:

"So this used to be your mother's room, Bernard?"

John drew in his breath slowly. "Yes," he answered, and, as he spoke, he felt suddenly and acutely the falsity of his position. He was upon dangerous ground, and he felt again intense dislike at having to deceive this woman, who was everything in the world to him.

"I think it was so dear of your father," resumed Elaine thoughtfully, "to let us have this room." John cast a swift look in her direction. "He could not have paid us a greater compliment," Elaine went on.

She was entirely absorbed in her thoughts. To her it was the most natural thing in life that the Colonel should honour his son and his son's wife by allotting to them this fine apartment. In doing so he was tacitly informing the young couple that Elaine in her turn was to be the lady of the house. But so far as John was concerned, Elaine's quiet acceptance of himself and of this fact filled him with consternation. He felt himself enmeshed and hopelessly bewildered. This was not his room only, but Elaine's. It had not entered his mind to look into the wardrobe; he had not even noticed the pair of ladies' gloves which lay upon the dressing-table. But now as he turned away, so that Elaine might not read his glance, his eyes fell upon her gloves for the first time. A moment of acute crisis had arisen. Nevertheless he still fenced, peeking a way out of the situation.

"I cannot understand," he said, "how you managed to get into touch with my father after all."

Elaine laughed brightly.

"I have been wondering when you would ask that, Bernard. It was all owing to the old butler, Mr. Gates. He came to 65, Bowles Avenue. It seems that you gave that address once at the Savoy Hotel in case Mr. Dacent Smith sent for you suddenly. Gates went to the Savoy to find you, to give you a message from your father, and the Savoy people gave him my address. I answered the door to Gates myself, and in the course of his inquiries about you, I told him who I was. He had never heard of me before and was very much surprised. Naturally, when he came back here, he told your father."

"I see," said John, "and my father invited you here?"

Elaine nodded.

"Not only invited me, but he has been absolutely charming to me."

"I don't see anything very extraordinary in that," returned John.

"Oh, but I might have been the most horrid sort of creature. He knew nothing whatever about me."

"He only needed to look at you," John answered, "to see that—that I had made an ideal marriage."

"I have made him tell me everything about your boyhood, Bernard."

John winced. He had no wish to discuss a boyhood that was naturally a blank to him.

"I believe I know more about your schoolboy days than you do yourself," smiled Elaine.

"I shouldn't wonder," said John with a smile.

Despite himself, against caution and his better judgment, he was beginning to enjoy the scene. He was still at the dressing-table, and in the depths of the mirror he could see behind him Elaine's reflection, a delicate and beautiful picture, seated on the ottoman behind him, looking at him with admiring and loving eyes, believing in him, and trusting him.

"Bernard!" Her tone was low and intimate.

"Yes."

"Come and sit beside me."

"Oh, I don't know whether I can," said John; "I've—I've got a letter to write." He was quick at inventing excuses.

"You can't care much for me, Bernard, if you bother to write a letter, after not seeing me for so long." She rose and came towards him. He felt foolish and awkward when she took his hand in hers, led him to the ottoman and seated him beside her. "Tell me what you have been doing all these long days."

"Oh, all sorts of things," John answered.

"Did you ever think of me?"

"Often," John answered, truthfully.

"Have you been loving me? Look into my eyes and say it, Bernard."

John turned his face towards hers. He saw love in her eyes; love that was offered to himself alone; and as he sustained the radiant tenderness of her gaze a wild impulse came to him to cast discretion to the winds. He hovered on the verge of telling her frankly and bluntly that he was not her husband. Nevertheless he longed to tell her that she was the one woman in all the world for him, that she had won his deepest love, and that he was prepared to break down all barriers, to risk everything if— —. Then suddenly he caught himself up. His lips were sealed. As an honourable man, even if he admitted his true identity, he must not utter his love.

"Why are you looking at me so strangely, Bernard?" There was a puzzled and anxious light in her eyes.

"Was I?"

"You suddenly drew your brows together and looked at me so furiously that I thought I must have offended you."

"You could never offend me."

"I don't think you love me after all." She was holding his hand in hers, looking wistfully up into his face. "Do you?"

John slid his fingers away from her touch and rose. He began to pace the floor uneasily. As always, he was seeking a way out, racking his brains for a solution. But there was only one method of escape, and that lay in sudden and ignominious flight.

"Look here, Elaine!" he said, suddenly and brutally. "It has occurred to me that I ought to go away again to-night, immediately after dinner!"

She rose and looked at him with startled eyes. John went on, clumsily:

"Something important has turned up!"

"Oh, but, Bernard, that would be too cruel. I have hardly seen you!" She came to him quickly and laid her hands on his shoulders. There was entreaty in her fine eyes, upraised to his. "You'll stay just to-night," she implored, wistfully, "just for my sake."

John put her away from him almost roughly; his voice was hoarse and low.

"It's impossible, Elaine!"

She stood for a moment regarding him with steady gaze. A long, tense silence lay between them. Then she spoke, quietly, and with a dignity that somehow wrung John's heart.

"Then all your protestations of love for me mean nothing at all!"

"They mean everything," said John, in the same low tone.

"And yet you repulse me as if you hated me?"

"I don't mean to act cruelly."

"If you had any regard for me at all, you'd stay. It isn't the first time, Bernard, that you—you've humiliated me!"

John looked into her face that had grown suddenly tragic. He saw in a moment how completely justified she was in her attitude. He had protested his love for her only a few minutes earlier, and had then snatched at something that must have seemed to her the thinnest of excuses for hurrying away—for leaving her.

"If you loved me really, Bernard, you'd stay." Her voice was very low. "However, I have suffered the humiliation of your refusal. I shall not make the same mistake again." She turned and walked slowly towards the door. John saw that she could scarcely restrain her tears; her head was uplifted— she was superb in her dignity. For the life of him John could not refrain from striding a few paces towards her.

"Elaine!" he implored, in a voice that rang with emotion. "Don't misjudge me. And as for humiliating you, I'd do anything in the world rather than do that! Look here, Elaine, you think I don't love you?"

She turned quietly and looked at him.

"I have every proof of it! In London you refused to stay with me; it is the same here. Your words say one thing—your actions another!"

"You will be able to make some excuse to your father for not occupying the same room with me——"

In that moment, with her face pale, her head erect, a strange light in her eyes, she was more than ever beautiful. In John's eyes she was the fairest and finest-looking woman that ever breathed. Something made him put out his hand and grip her fingers.

"Elaine!"

She strove with surprising strength to release herself.

"No, Bernard, don't!"

Then John's elaborate and well-sustained defences fell. He forgot everything in a sudden wild rush of passion.

"I don't love you, Elaine?" he cried.

"You never loved me——" she began. And in that moment John's arms swept about her. He forgot everything—the world faded. He and the fairest of women—the woman of his love—were together, and he was kissing her as he had never kissed any woman.... Elaine's weak protests faded; astonishment swept over her, and gave place to a wonderful and radiant happiness.

"My God!" breathed John; "if you only knew how much I loved you!"

"Bernard—Bernard—Bernard!" she whispered. Then, to her infinite astonishment, John wrenched himself free; he put his hands to his brows, and fell back several paces, like a man who has received a stunning blow between the eyes.

"Elaine," he said, with clenched fists, his face suddenly pale, his eyes wild—"forget that I held you in my arms! Forget what I said! Forget everything!" His voice rose almost to a shout.

A moment later he had rushed out of the room, and had drawn the door behind him.

CHAPTER XXX

Almost as John closed the door of the south room Gates began to strike, in rising and rhythmic cadences, the great dinner-gong that stood in the hall. The elderly butler turned as John halted at his side.

"Is that the dressing-bell, Gates?" he asked.

"No, Mr. Bernard, the dressing-bell went at the usual time, sir."

John looked at him in surprise. He had heard nothing. During that scene in the room upstairs, when he had lost possession of himself, the sound of the bell had passed unheard. John felt no wonder at that; even now his thoughts whirled through his brain. His temperament was naturally cool, equable, and determined. Never in his life could he recollect having completely forgotten himself, as he had forgotten himself with Elaine a few minutes earlier. The power of love, indeed, had reduced him to the common standard. His nerve, his self-possession, his swift power of decision—all the gifts, in fact, that commended him to Dacent Smith, had deserted him in a flash. For a brief moment—for a space of a moment—he had forgotten everything, save the fact that he loved a woman.

He stood now thinking of these things, and was amazed at the blind passion that had seized him. He began to condemn himself bitterly and savagely. His deception of Elaine stood before him as a monstrous thing. The thought that he occupied another's man shoes, and had thus led her to pour out a love which she would have otherwise concealed, struck him as a criminal proceeding upon his part. He was obliged to confess to himself that he had dallied with the situation, that he had not acted firmly enough. On the other hand—a small voice whispered this—his deception of Elaine was not his fault; he had not wittingly deceived her. He had, indeed, acted all through as an honourable man. This last thought gave him a certain amount of comfort as he crossed the great hall and entered the drawing-room. Colonel Treves was the sole occupant of the room, and was standing with his back to the white marble fire-place, his hand resting on the stick he used as support. John noticed that in evening clothes the old man looked more imposing and distinguished than ever. The Colonel drew out his watch.

"Where's Elaine?"

John explained that he had left Elaine upstairs a few moments ago, and presently Elaine, a little pale, came into the drawing-room. No glance passed between her and John. With a courtly air, Colonel Treves advanced towards her and crooked his elbow.

"May I have the honour?" he said.

Elaine slipped her arm into his. In her pale primrose dress, with her well-coiffeured dark hair emphasising the whiteness of her neck, she looked scarcely more than a child. John noticed with admiration that her head was held erect. She smiled and talked graciously to the Colonel as he led her into the dining-room and placed her upon his right hand. For John there was no smile.

Just as the south room and the drawing-room were strange to John, so also was the dining-room. He seated himself opposite Elaine at the head of a long gleaming white table. Gates moved from place to place softly and noiselessly. Colonel Treves, who was happier than he had been for years, made a perfect host. His happiness intensified John's own loneliness. A sensation of being a pariah came upon him; he felt that he would have given ten years of his life to be actually sitting there in the flesh as the real son of the fine old man who headed the table.

As to Elaine, and his relations with Elaine, he dared not let his mind dwell upon that subject. He was attempting to indicate by his attitude his complete contrition for what had occurred. He tried to catch Elaine's eye. She looked at him, but there was something enigmatical in her expression that he was unable to understand. Her good breeding was such that to the outward eye—to the Colonel's eye, in fact—their relationship was exactly as it had been before, and yet John knew that a barrier had risen between them.

Elaine maintained her air of stately reserve during the rest of the evening, and at ten o'clock, when she rose to go to her room, the Colonel politely conducted her to the door. As he closed it upon her he turned and looked towards John.

"You are a lucky man, Bernard!" he exclaimed.

He came slowly across the room, using his stick, as was his general habit.

"I hope some day, my boy," he said, "when this place is yours, Elaine will reign here as graciously and be as well beloved as your dear mother was."

"I am sure she will, sir," answered John quietly.

The old man slid his arm through his.

"You shall take me up to the library. We can smoke there, and make ourselves comfortable."

In the library that night John heard much of Colonel Treves's past history, much of the family history, of the man whose identity he was wearing, and the more he heard of Bernard Treves the more he realised what a complete and utter waster that young man was. Often of late he had thought of Treves in the nursing home, and wondered what were the conditions of his detention there. Dacent Smith was always reticent upon that point. The sinking of the *Polidor* through the agency of Treves had been a black and irredeemable crime. A time was bound to come when the young man must answer for that piece of black treachery against his country. Looking at the matter in the most charitable light, John regarded Treves, as evidently Dacent Smith regarded him, that is, as a feeble, will-less creature, whose reason had been unseated, at any rate temporarily, by the drugs which were a mania with him.

The fact that Manwitz and Cherriton had plied him with these drugs showed only the bold unscrupulousness of the German methods. The German Intelligence Department had used Bernard Treves, and had moulded him to its purpose as though he had been of wax. And had not Dacent Smith brilliantly substituted John for Treves, untold disasters would have ensued.

"Bernard!" The Colonel's voice startled John out of his thought. "Bernard, I have seen Gosport lately."

John wondered who Gosport might be.

"Yes," went on the Colonel. "I was hasty with you, but I have made everything right. I have made up my mind to leave everything to you after all. What do you say to that?"

"It is very generous of you, sir," John answered. He knew that it was utterly impossible that a penny of the Colonel's possessions should ever be his.

"No, no, it is only right," responded the Colonel. "You have married well. You have rehabilitated yourself in every way, and I find you more what a Treves should be every time we meet." He suddenly gripped John's hand in his. "You have given me great happiness, Bernard, and one of the reasons I made haste to change my will is that the doctor has given me rather a bad report of myself. I don't think you'll have to put up with me for very long, Bernard!"

"Don't say that, sir!" answered John, quickly and impulsively.

"I fear it is the truth," said the Colonel; "but I can face the next world with a far better grace than I could have done a year ago."

He was thinking of the fine old house and the properties which a year ago might have fallen into the hands of a worthless son. Now, as by a miracle, that son had become a man—a man of honour—and a Treves. The two things were synonymous in the Colonel's eyes, and the future, whatever it might be, however soon darkness might come, held for him no terrors.

It was after eleven that night when the Colonel went to his room.

"I'll sit up and write a few letters at your desk, if I may, father," said John, after escorting the elder man to the door of his bedroom.

He went back to the library, shut himself in, and dropped into a chair at the hearth. What Elaine was doing, what were her thoughts, he could not guess. He wondered if she was waiting for him, expecting him to come and ask for forgiveness. Perhaps some time in the dim future, when the whole truth was told, she might forgive; but for the present he knew that nothing he could do would right him in her eyes.

He sat in the arm-chair, dozing and thinking, until dawn came.

When the breakfast gong rang next morning Elaine descended and found the Colonel alone at the table. The old man looked disturbed, but in no way depressed.

"You will have to content yourself with me, Elaine," he said, "now that Bernard has deserted us again. He left me a note saying that important business has arisen, and ran away before I was down. But of course," added the old man as an afterthought, "you know all about it."

Elaine inclined her head, and said nothing. Colonel Treves put out his hand and laid it on her slender fingers.

"When the war is over, you and my boy Bernard will live here together, and be as happy as crickets."

"It is very, very dear of you to say so, father." Sudden tears glistened in her eyes. She clasped the Colonel's old, frail fingers in hers. In that moment it seemed to her that he was the only friend she possessed in the world.

So far as John was concerned, Elaine dared not let herself think. The strange scene in the south room had burnt itself into her brain. John's tremendous anxiety to get away from her, together with the undoubted fact that he loved her, was bewildering beyond solution. The thought that her husband had reverted to the drug habit had long been discarded. None of the symptoms that had marked him in the early days of their marriage were present—he was as another man in her eyes. She loved him—she was afraid, and she was bewildered. Every post that came found her anxiously awaiting a letter from John. But none came; two eventless days passed. But upon the evening of the second day after John's departure a dramatic mischance that had been impending—that had, indeed, been inevitable from the beginning—occurred.

Elaine had made her way alone into the grounds. Her mood was one that called for solitude, and in the quiet of the long, fir-treed avenue, the drive which led from the mansion to the road, she found the seclusion she needed. The evening was clear, and through tree-stems the ocean, glassily blue and empty of shipping, spread to the far horizon. The scene was calm, reposeful—everything, in fact, a troubled spirit could require.

Presently, however, the entrance gate at the end of the drive was pushed open. A young man in a green felt hat and wearing stiff Sunday clothes came into the drive and walked slowly forward. Elaine, as the stranger drew near, noticed that he was a youth, little more than twenty, wearing a service-rendered badge. The young man wore his green hat slightly on one side— his complexion was fresh, his cheeks ruddy, and his general expression one of amiable stupidity.

Elaine glanced at him and was about to pass, thinking he carried a message to the house, when the visitor halted in his walk and sheepishly lifted his hat. As he halted he drew from his pocket a crumpled, rather grimy-looking envelope.

"Is that Colonel Treves's house, miss?"

"Yes," said Elaine.

"I've got a letter for there, miss," went on the young man; "it's addressed to Mrs. Treves."

"There is no Mrs. Treves," Elaine answered; then quickly remembering, she smiled the gracious smile that was always so attractive to John. "I'm Mrs. Bernard Treves."

The young man handed her the letter, and instantly Elaine's casual air vanished, for the address was in her husband's handwriting, and had been scrawled hurriedly in pencil.

She tore open the envelope and read the single sheet of notepaper within.

DEAR ELAINE, ran the note, *I want you to give the bearer of this ten shillings. Then, if you can, and as soon as you can, you must raise ten pounds and let him bring it here to me. General Whiston and a person called Dacent Smith have been keeping me prisoner here. The suggestion is that I am* non compos mentis. *I don't know whether my father's in it or not, so on no account mention this letter to him. Whatever you do, don't fail me; I have been suffering the tortures of the damned here. The young man who brings this can get to me, and there is a nurse here who can help me to get away if I can get hold of ten pounds. Remember this, Elaine, you are my wife, and I hope you aren't siding with my father against me. I can't stand the torture of being here any longer, so I look to you to act quickly. You can act quickly enough when you want to. I am nearly off my head with being deprived of the medicine I used to take. The bearer of this would get into trouble if found out, so don't forget to treat him well.*

Your affectionate husband,

BERNARD TREVES.

As Elaine slowly read this letter for a second time the colour fled from her cheeks. Her heart-beat quickened almost to suffocation—she could make nothing of it.

Her eyes travelled to the head of the missive and read:

"St. Neot's Nursing Home, Ambleside Road, Ryde."

"St. Neot's Nursing Home—St. Neot's Nursing Home." Under her breath she uttered the words in a dazed, stupefied fashion.

It seemed impossible that her husband, who had been with her only forty-eight hours before, could be incarcerated there. Then the strangeness of the letter! ... She read it again, shrinking instinctively from its tone. Here was her husband as she had known him from the beginning—querulous and domineering.

For a minute she wondered if there had been some extraordinary and unexplainable mistake, but she knew his handwriting. Nevertheless, with a great effort to steady herself, she looked into the face of the messenger.

"If you will come to the house," she said, "I shall be pleased to give you something for being so kind as to bring this to me."

"Thank you, miss."

"Are you one of the servants at St. Neot's Home?"

"No, miss. I work for the dairy that supplies them."

Again Elaine glanced at the crumpled letter in her fingers. There was no possibility of forgery—and yet how came it that Dacent Smith should wish to detain her husband? She recalled that the brilliant Chief of the secret service had had nothing but praise for Bernard.

Again she looked quickly into the young man's face.

"Have you seen Mr. Treves lately?"

"I saw him this morning, miss."

It seemed ridiculous to put the question, to dally still with the idea of forgery. Nevertheless, she put it.

"Could you describe Mr. Treves to me?"

"Yes, miss. He's a good-looking gentleman. Tall, dark hair——"

"Thank you," said Elaine, interrupting him—and her last doubt vanished.

Something had happened to Bernard since yesterday morning, since his departure from the house without saying good-bye to her. He had evidently been seized and incarcerated in the nursing home against his will. Yet, even now, as she strove to accept the fact, her instinct rebelled against it. The thing seemed so motiveless, so utterly outside the natural order of events; and Bernard must have been seized almost immediately after he left his father's house, for she noted that his letter was dated the day before.

She again questioned the young man.

"How long has Mr. Bernard Treves been at St. Neot's Nursing Home?"

"The first time I saw him there, miss, was about two months ago, when he asked me to get him something at a chemist's; but he must have been there more than a month before that. I should think, miss, he's been there going on for three months or thereabouts."

"Three months!"

"About that, miss."

Elaine looked at him with widened eyes. The thing was impossible and incredible. Nevertheless, she dared not let the matter rest where it was. She decided to act, and to act instantly. As yet no suspicion of the truth had dawned upon her.

CHAPTER XXXI

At the very hour when Elaine received the strange letter signed "Bernard Treves," a letter which awoke all her defensive feminine instincts, John occupied a chair in the little mess-room at Heatherpoint Fort. The occasion was one of deep and portentous significance. At the head of the table, where Mrs. Beecher Monmouth had so recently taken tea with Lieutenant Parkson, General Whiston was seated in state. His big, commanding figure bulked largely in the chair usually occupied by Colonel Hobin. Beneath the General's eyes was a map of the South Coast defences—an elaborate, minutely particularised map, which in a layman's eyes would have been almost undecipherable.

The General held a blue pencil over a particular section of the Solent; his eyes, however, were fixed upon the countenance of a naval captain who sat at his left hand, a little farther down the table. Opposite the naval captain was Colonel Hobin, and next to Hobin sat old Commander Greaves.

John occupied an insignificant position next to Greaves, and near the end of the table there was a vacant chair.

"Is there no possibility, Captain," inquired General Whiston, speaking to the naval officer, "of altering the mine-field in the time at our command?"

Before the naval officer lay a small Admiralty chart of the Solent clustered with a multitude of red crosses.

"Well," he said, deliberating upon the situation, "this is a pretty elaborate field, and it would take us quite two days to make an effective new arrangement. Of course, we could mine the free channels, but that prevents us coming in."

He went into technical details.

General Whiston cast a glance at John.

"You are quite sure your friends Voules and Company intend to strike on the twenty-eighth?"

"All the evidence I have been able to get points to that, sir," answered John promptly.

"The twenty-eighth is the day after to-morrow," put in Greaves.

"Mr. Dacent Smith," said John, "had an idea that the attack might be postponed, but he has now come round to my view."

As a matter of fact, John had that day amply convinced his chief that the German blow was to fall on the date originally prescribed. Since leaving Colonel Treves's house, and since his embarrassing interview with Elaine, John had made certain valuable discoveries, all of which pointed to the imminence of the German attack on the South Coast defences. With infinite subtlety von Kuhne had managed to institute nefarious schemes in a dozen different directions. The night of the twenty-eighth had been marked out in the German general's mind with the clockwork precision which was a second nature to him. And John believed that nothing would shake his resolution. Mrs. Beecher Monmouth's particular work of the early part of that night was to see that Lieutenant Parkson was not at his post. All her potent charms were to be expended to that end. That she would succeed in her task was, in von Kuhne's and the lady's own eyes, a foregone conclusion. As to Manwitz, he was to be mysteriously occupied with certain men of his Majesty's forces whose business it was to operate the boom between Ponsonby Lighthouse and Windsor Fort. Cherriton's particular duty upon the eventful night John had not been able to discover. The tall German still occupied the isolated cottage he had recently taken on the Downs near Freshwater. Since John's visit to the cottage he had not had further meeting with this particular formidable enemy.

In thinking of his visit to the cottage, however, John was conscious that the man's attitude upon that day had been singular in the extreme. What had been in Cherriton's mind he did not know, and he was, of course, totally unaware that sentence of extermination had been passed upon him. It is no stretch of imagination to say that in visiting the cottage he had, without knowing it, walked within the very shadow of the grave.

"Friend Cherriton is no mean antagonist," thought John, pondering upon the German's personality as he sat in the little mess-room.

Now that the great blow was so soon to fall, Dacent Smith—an unusual circumstance with him—had left his post in London and come to the Isle of Wight. General Whiston and Captain Throgmorton, who respectively commanded the counter military and naval measures, found the pleasant, keen-eyed Chief of Intelligence an invaluable ally. His intuitive knowledge of the German character proved to be of the utmost assistance. He had been studying Germany and the German secret service for twenty years, and what he did not know about Teutonic psychology, chicanery and guile, was not worth knowing.

Dacent Smith, however, never made the mistake of under-estimating his enemy. Von Kuhne's blow would, he conceded, be a well-wrought and scientifically delivered attack. There was one slight thing, however, which von Kuhne had possibly overlooked—he had possibly overlooked the important fact that the Isle of Wight is after all an island, and that in gathering his forces upon this particular portion of His Majesty's dominions he was isolating himself from chances of escape in case of failure.

Dacent Smith thought a good deal upon this subject during his first day at Heatherpoint Fort. But when he presently resumed his chair at the end of the table in the little mess-room, opposite General Whiston, his pleasantly good-humoured face showed nothing of the intense mental activity within.

General Whiston lifted his eyes as Dacent Smith took his seat.

"Well, have you found out anything else for us?"

"Nothing," answered Dacent Smith, "except further confirmation that von Kuhne will make his attempt the day after to-morrow. He has disposed his forces with a good deal of ingenuity. This end of the Isle of Wight is at present dotted with amiable Britishers who happen to be Germans!"

A curious smile flitted across the face of John's Chief.

"It must have been very gratifying," said he, "to Captain Cherriton, Manners, and von Kuhne to say 'British subject' to our good-looking policeman as they stepped on board the boat at Lymington. Manners, so I hear, was the only one of a dozen who came that way who showed the slightest trace of nervousness. I think we shall have to reckon, General," he concluded, "upon von Kuhne providing something pretty forceful and daring!"

The naval captain whose eyes were still occupied with the chart of the Solent, lifted his keen gaze. "Something in the nature of our own adventure at Zeebrugge and Ostend, do you think?"

Here he turned his red-starred chart face downwards. On its back were twenty or thirty neatly-pencilled lines.

"That," he said, pushing the chart towards Dacent Smith, "is my forecast of what is going to happen in this area during the next forty-eight hours. If your date is correct, I think my forecast will be pretty well right. What do you think, General?"

Throgmorton's incisive, clean-cut features turned towards Whiston.

"I think it's a devilish clever piece of work!" answered General Whiston, generously.

Dacent Smith's eyes lifted from the pencilled forecast. His vivid gaze rested for a minute in admiration on Throgmorton's handsome, well-wrought features.

"Some day, young man," thought he, "you will be ruler of the King's Navy."

He pushed back the chart towards the naval officer; then turned towards John.

"You can go, Treves," he said, "with the General's permission."

Whiston nodded.

John saluted and withdrew from the room.

As Manton passed out into the asphalted courtyard he met Chief Gunner Ewins.

"Well, Ewins," he said, "what about your wife's dangerous illness?"

"She wasn't ill at all, sir. I can't make it out—I've just got a letter from her to-day, saying she's as well as ever she was."

"Of course, she never sent the wire," explained John.

"Who could have sent it?" said Ewins, looking at John with puzzled eyes; "it's a silly sort of joke to play on anybody, sir."

"Very silly," John admitted. "It looked as if somebody wanted to get you out of the fort for a day or two. That's why the Colonel wouldn't grant you leave. He didn't think you were playing a trick on him. He thought some one was playing a trick on you. How are your guns, Ewins?"

"Nicely, sir, thank you," answered the chief gunner. "But I'm sorry we've missed our nine-inch practice this week."

"You won't miss much by that," John answered. "You'll shoot as well as ever when the time comes."

He knew how soon the time would come, though Ewins did not.

John descended the steps of the fort, took his bicycle, and, with due observance of ceremonies, passed through the great gate that had recently all but intimidated Mrs. Beecher Monmouth.

An hour later, John, still pedalling steadily, descended the winding road into Brooke. At the outskirts of the village he placed his bicycle against a gate, climbed into a field, and, by a detour, made his way to the back of Doctor Voules's house. In the darkness he walked softly forward under the shadow of the doctor's garden wall He had made only a few paces when a voice came to him out of the gloom.

"Who's that?" demanded the voice, in a guarded whisper.

"Treves," answered John. "Is that you, Watson?"

"Yes, sir," came the answer.

John drew himself to the top of the garden wall and looked down upon a corporal in uniform.

"Anything happened?" John asked.

"Yes," answered Watson; "three men came to the house after dark, stayed a little while, and went away again, sir."

As a matter of fact, half an hour earlier Doctor Voules and two tall young men had stealthily mounted the wall and entered the house by the back way. Corporal Watson had been concealed in the garden and witnessed this visit, and Voules's and his friends' departure in the same stealthy manner.

"They are evidently trying to give the impression that the house is uninhabited, sir," the corporal amplified.

John, who had climbed into the garden and was standing by him, gave a few further instructions as to Voules's abode, presently mounted his bicycle and rode away. Three quarters of an hour later, in a small clump of trees on the heather-clad cliff-top near Freshwater, he spoke to another soldier. This man, with three others, had been detailed to watch Cherriton's cottage.

"The captain's been in his cottage all the evening, sir," said the man to John, "and the big, fat man's been with him."

Having satisfied himself as to the whereabouts of Cherriton and Manners, John cycled on and entered the Freshwater Hotel. Here he put through a trunk-call to Newport. When he had been connected with a particular number he inquired into the telephone:

"Is that you, Gibb?"

"Yes, sir," came the answer.

"Do you know who is speaking?"

"It's Mr. Treves, isn't it?"

"Yes," John answered.

Having satisfied himself that he was in touch with the gloomy-looking waiter at the Newport Hotel, he put a discreet inquiry. He had parted with certain Treasury notes to the benefit of the gloomy waiter. The waiter, thereafter feeling himself a small but important wheel in a piece of vast machinery, made himself busy and active in John's service.

"Is anybody at home, Gibb?"

"She's not been out all day, sir, and went to bed immediately after dinner. She told her maid that she had a lot to do to-morrow, and asked to be called at eight."

These details were, for the moment, enough to satisfy John.

"You know where to ring me up, Gibb, if anything exceptional occurs."

John, having concluded his duties for that day, pedalled slowly back to the fort. The night was overcast, the air close, and as he led his bicycle up the long white road to the gates, he could hear the waves softly falling at the foot of the cliffs in the bay below him. No other sound broke the stillness, and when the outer sentinel suddenly barred his path and a challenge rang out on the close air, John was startled out of a mood of dreams.

He passed the second and the third sentries, a wicket in the great gate of the fort opened and admitted him, and, having reported himself to the Colonel, he went straight to his room. For the better part of that night his mind occupied itself with the momentous doings of the morrow. The cloud that had gathered itself about that end of the island was about to break. What would happen to himself and others on the morrow he could not forecast. But one thing he knew—the long, hidden contest between Voules and Dacent Smith would reach its culmination. Each man, with his pawns, had manoeuvred, moved, finessed and counter-moved. The subtlety of Dacent Smith had been pitted against the precision and military skill of von Kuhne. What was to be the end? John did not know, and at that moment his mind was only secondarily occupied with the point; he was thinking, not of to-morrow, but of yesterday, of his interview with Elaine, of his abrupt separation from her, of his apparent brutality and harshness.

He wondered at himself, that he, a capable, alert and non-sentimental young man, an individual who had withstood the seductive blandishments of Mrs. Beecher Monmouth, he wondered to find himself deeply and passionately in love with a girl whose knowledge of artifice was of the slightest. Elaine's genuine trust in him, her belief in his integrity, her delight in the improvement in his character, all helped to enchain John's deepest affections.

As he lay now in the quiet and darkness of his room, he felt he dared not let his mind dwell upon the future. He had tricked and duped Elaine, and some day she would be bound to find him out.

What would happen then? What would happen when she learned the truth?

"There is nothing for it," John pronounced suddenly and emphatically. "I must tell her myself—I must confess the whole thing from the beginning."

Having arrived at this decision, he saw himself making the confession, though he could not see what her attitude would be. He could visualise, always standing between them as an impassable and sinister barrier, the man whose identity he had borne for so many months. Bernard Treves—his *alter ego*, his *doppel-gänger*—had become what he had probably been from the first—his evil genius. From the very first he had disliked Treves; he had later grown to despise him. The man was contemptible beyond words.

At this point John took himself resolutely in hand—or, rather, he thought he took himself resolutely in hand. What really happened was that he put away thoughts of Elaine, hiding them courageously and tenderly in the deeps of his mind, for the sole reason that to think of her, to think of the hopeless situation between them, meant nothing but misery and bitterness.

At eight o'clock, when John appeared in the little mess-room, Colonel Hobin was alone at breakfast, at the head of the table.

"Well, Treves," he said, "if your predictions are right, this is going to be the day of our lives!"

"I think I am right, sir," John answered.

"We shall see," answered the Colonel. "Pass the marmalade, please."

John passed the marmalade. He noticed the Colonel's hand was steady—none of the nervous irritability that characterised him usually was apparent—and the old soldier's eyes had taken on a new masterful expression of command—the countenance of a good captain on the bridge in face of a great oncoming storm.

CHAPTER XXXII

The portentous day, the twenty-eighth of the month, passed at Heatherpoint Fort with no untoward incident whatever. There was a difference, however; there existed an atmosphere of tense expectancy. Something was afoot, for doubled sentries held all points of vantage along the cliff-tops, doubled sentries guarded the fort gates, and the barbed wire entanglements at certain other places. All leave had been stopped, and at midday, when Lieutenant William Parkson asked for leave for very urgent personal reasons, he was astonished to find that the Colonel had grown totally immovable.

"If you would let me go from eight o'clock till ten, sir, I should be satisfied. I assure you, sir, it is most important."

It was indeed important in Parkson's eyes. But though rebellion surged in him there was no possible means of getting out of the fort that night without the Colonel's pass. Only one person, in fact, left Heatherpoint Fort that evening. This person happened to be John Manton. General Whiston uttered final words of advice as the young man took his departure.

"If you are successful, Treves," he said, "you will be probably back here before the dust-up begins."

"I hope so," said John. He saluted and clattered down the flight of steps to the main gate.

It was still light as he cycled swiftly away along the white road. A smile curled the corner of his mouth. The work he was upon was exactly to his liking; there was something in it of danger, and something of finesse. When John had cycled for half an hour he looked at his watch.

"Parkson's appointment with her," he said, "was for seven o'clock. I wonder how she intended to handle him?"

He mused upon Parkson, and admitted that the young man would be as wax in Mrs. Beecher Monmouth's adroit fingers. He recalled Mrs. Beecher Monmouth's long, black record, her superlative daring, the manner in which she had expended her great personal gifts and keen intelligence in the service of the enemy. He thought of the *Malta*—of the two hundred fine lives sacrificed upon her information. And at the thought his lips tightened, his smile vanished, and the face that Dacent Smith always knew as good-humoured and pleasant to look upon, grew hard and forbidding.

Darkness had fallen by the time John turned off the Newport road towards Brooke. He did not light his lamp, however, but this time rode straight through the village and alighted at Dr. Voules's house. The doctor's residence was completely dark. No light shone from any of the windows. John advanced to the door and placed his fingers on the bell. He rang twice, but no answer came to him, no sound of footfall reached him from the interior of the house. Then, noticing that the door was slightly ajar, as if left purposely, he entered the hall, and in complete darkness walked along towards the room at the end of the passage, which he remembered as Voules's dining-room. He had advanced but ten paces when a door opened quietly in the darkness, and a low voice came to him.

"Is that you, Billy?"

John was silent for a moment. He had braced himself for an intensely violent scene. Now, in a flash, he realised that there were new and exciting possibilities. Nevertheless, caution animated his entire conduct.

In regard to Mrs. Beecher Monmouth he did not know that she had discovered his association with Dacent Smith; he was not aware of the lady's sentiments of bitter antagonism, of virulent hatred towards himself. He was to learn these things later. But at the moment he felt there was little danger of stepping into a trap. The beautiful woman whispering to him from the darkness awaited William Parkson, not Bernard Treves or John Marton.

"Is that you, Billy?"

Her voice came to him again in a tense whisper.

"Yes," answered John in a tone low as her own. She drew wider the door of Voules's dining-room.

"I told you to come straight in, Billy. Why did you ring the bell?" she admonished him, lifting her voice to a more ordinary tone.

"Oh, I don't know; I forgot," answered John.

"Come in——" Her hand groped forward and took his. She drew him into the heavily-curtained darkness of the dining-room and closed the door.

"We mustn't light up till eight o'clock, Billy," she whispered.

"Why not?"

"It's a fad of mine."

Then she put her face close to his; she let her smooth, firm hand glide about his shoulder as she drew his face down. She kissed him firmly on the lips.

If John had been easy to deceive, that kiss would have deceived him. He would have believed absolutely and implicitly that its fervour and passion were genuine.

"I thought," she whispered, her cheek close to his, "that you would not be afraid of the darkness."

"Oh, I won't be afraid," responded John in her ear. He could have laughed—the situation was throbbing with exhilarating possibilities.

"I was afraid you would be late, or wouldn't be able to come."

"You knew I'd come," said John.

He groped his way towards the hearth, holding her hand in his.

"Won't you sit down?" he asked.

"You sit down." She forced him into Dr. Voules's comfortable chair, then seated herself on its arm, and slowly smoothed his hair with her hand. She lowered her face and pressed it to his. Her rounded cheek was firm, cool and satin smooth.

"You can stay with me quite, quite a long time," she whispered.

"Thanks," mumbled John; "that's awfully good of you." He squeezed her hand. He could understand what would have happened to Parkson at that moment—Parkson already enamoured, flattered to think of a woman of her social position and extraordinary beauty flinging herself at his head.

"Will they miss you at the fort to-night, little Billy?"

"I don't know that they'll miss me particularly," said John.

"Oh, but you're so—so important there. Did you find it difficult to get away, Billy mine?"

"Not so very," John answered; "all the same, I haven't much time—I've only managed to get two hours' leave."

She drew in her breath sharply, then suddenly flung out both arms and drew him towards her.

"Oh, Billy, Billy!" she protested.

John instantly made mental note that she had in her mind a certain time during which she intended to detain him there.

"Then you can't love me," she breathed ardently. "You said you'd stay—a long time."

"Three-quarters of an hour is every minute I can stay," John said.

"Oh, but it won't matter if you're just a tiny, tiny bit late—just once in a lifetime! You don't know how difficult it is for me, Billy. I have risked everything for you! I should be ruined utterly if it was discovered that I gave you this *tête-à-tête* here at this time of night.... You must stay, Billy, until I'm ready to let you go; it will make it easier for me."

"I don't see that," protested John. "You can slip away— —"

"No, no; don't ask questions—don't say that! If you only knew how difficult it was. You won't bother me with questions, will you dear, dear Billy? And you'll be nice to me and let me get you something to drink. You bad boy," she said, after a moment's pause, "I don't believe you realise the honour I am conferring on you!"

"Oh I do—I am fully aware of it," answered John. She had risen from the arm of the chair, and had gone to the window. John heard the creak of the window blind as she drew it up upon the semi-darkness of the garden. For an instant he was startled, wondering if her movement portended some sort of signal.

As the blind ascended the complete darkness of the room sped away. He could now make out the rich shadows of her hair, and something of the outline of her fine features. Her hands in contrast with the black widow's weeds, looked unusually white.

"I thought you were fond of the darkness?" questioned John.

"I am, silly Billy." John guessed that she was wasting a coquettish smile upon the encumbering gloom.

She had gone to the sideboard, which was in shadow at the far end of the room and returning now to the middle table, placed upon it glasses, a soda syphon, and a whisky bottle.

"I must give you just a little peg!"

John heard the gurgle of liquid, and the "squirt" of a syphon. A moment later Mrs. Beecher Monmouth came across the room, put a glass in his hand, and lightly kissed his ear.

"I wish it was a little lighter," she whispered in a cooing fashion that was peculiar with her, "then I could see my pretty boy's face."

"If you did see your pretty boy's face," thought John, "you'd get the shock of your life!"

He took the whisky glass from her fingers. Silence lay between them for a moment, then Mrs. Beecher Monmouth spoke again.

"Drink," she whispered urgently.

John, who had been holding his glass in his left hand, shifted it to his right.

"Well, here's to you," he said, lifting the glass.

"Have you drunk it?"

"What else do you think?" inquired John, and laughed.

As a matter of fact he had not drunk it, for before raising the glass he had dexterously poured its contents upon the carpet. Her trick was too obvious. Parkson, blinded, enamoured by love, might have fallen into the trap, but he, John, knew his antagonist in this singular duel which was taking place in the semi-darkness. He came well armed with a knowledge of her character.

Minutes passed, during which Mrs. Beecher Monmouth held him enchained, as she believed, by her finished coquetry.

John, who had been probing about in his mind, hoping that she might divulge something useful, rose at last and stretched his legs.

Mrs. Beecher Monmouth was again at the window. He noticed that several times during the last quarter of an hour she had drifted there, as if with some intent and watchful purpose.

"Why do you keep going to the window?" he asked, suddenly and abruptly.

"I like to look out at the night."

"There's nothing much to see," returned John. "It's clouded over again, and the air is close enough to stifle one!"

"Yes," answered she.

In the gloom John saw her put up her hands to her throat. "It is enough to stifle one," she breathed, slowly and intensely.

Then John knew that big things were afoot, that she was waiting, strung up tensely to more than concert pitch. He put up his hand, pushed up the catch of the window, and opened it quietly upon the sultry night. A faint wind stirred, rustling the leaves. There was silence for a minute, then Mrs. Beecher Monmouth seemed to remember the role she was playing, slid her fingers into his and looked up into his face.

"Billy," she whispered.

And at that moment a sudden thunderous and heavily-resonant boom rent the stillness of the night.

John knew it in an instant as the detonation of a heavy gun. The door of the room creaked under the heavy vibration, the casements of the window rattled, and a red smear of light blazed against the low clouds and vanished.

Mrs. Beecher Monmouth had turned her face to the window. For an instant John saw it, tense and ecstatic in the glare of light—then darkness fell again.

And suddenly Mrs. Beecher Monmouth stood away in the dark room. The passionate sibilance of her whisper smote John's ears, like that of a snake.

"At last! At last! ... Oh, you can go now, Billy, Mr. Parkson. Yes—go, or stay! It matters not!"

"But it does matter," said John, "a deuce of a lot!"

And as he spoke the room was shaken with the detonation of a heavy gun—was again lit up with a red light. A second and a third gun was fired—one sound mingling with the other in tremendous crashing reverberation. And at each report a red glow filled the room, searching out the darkness in its most distant corners.

Mrs. Beecher Monmouth had turned towards John—in the leaping red light, amid the roar of artillery, her eyes pinioned themselves upon his. She drew nearer—peering, as it were, with all her senses, her hands clenched.

Their faces were close together when a red glare revealed his features in every lineament. He was smiling, looking down upon her with easy nonchalance. Even in the fleeting light John caught the swift distortion of her features. She made a movement in the darkness— —

In Mrs. Beecher Monmouth's entire life of daring adventure, in all her vicissitudinous career, never had such a blow stricken her as that moment. She had expected to see the good-humoured and somewhat stupid countenance of Parkson, and instead, she had seen John. She had been outwitted by the enemy whom of all others she hated most. From the very first this pleasant looking, resourceful, cool young man had outmanoeuvred her. What had happened to Parkson, and how John had managed to substitute himself for that enmeshed young man, she could not guess. She was conscious only that in the darkness her mortal enemy had received her caresses, and laughed in his sleeve.

Her tryst had been with Lieutenant Parkson, and by a manoeuvre that was a mystery to her this other had substituted himself....

John heard her move softly in the darkness, and draw in a low, sibilant breath. He was taking no chances, however, and had already stepped cautiously behind the big dining table. Here he paused for a moment, listening, then swiftly struck a match. In the orange glow of the light he saw Mrs. Monmouth's face of undeniable beauty contorted with fury. As the match flared and John put out his hand to light the lamp which was on the table, she made a strong effort to control her features. She was a woman who seldom remained long at a disadvantage. Every move in the whole gamut of feminine emotion seemed to be at her command. There had been a momentary stillness; now the roar of heavy artillery thundered again and again. The red glow from the window filled the room.

A false expression of smiling irony crossed Mrs. Monmouth's features.

"So, Mr. Treves, you have been exercising your cleverness again!"

"What I did was all in the day's work," John began; then he stepped swiftly towards the end of the table and barred the way to a certain chair upon which her long black coat had been thrown.

"No, don't go to your coat," he politely admonished her. "I am afraid I don't trust you!" He knew that ladies of Mrs. Beecher Monmouth's temperament and activities are apt to carry lethal weapons, and are not scrupulous in the use of the same. She had already made an attempt upon him with what he shrewdly and correctly guessed to be drugged whisky.

"How subtle and resourceful you are!" laughed Mrs. Monmouth. She turned and strolled with an air of indifference towards the window.

John was wondering what her next move would be. He had already made up his mind as to his own next move, when Mrs. Beecher Monmouth strode to the table, and, in a flashing change of mood, smote it sharply.

"You think yourself extraordinarily clever, Mr. Treves!"

"Oh! not at all!" protested John. He really did not think himself clever, but he was satisfied with the present position as he found it. He had taken her coat, and was holding it over his arm. There was no weapon in its pockets.

A roar of artillery again filled the room. Mrs. Beecher Monmouth's eyes blazed in exaltation and excitement.

"Do you hear those guns?"

"I can hear scarcely anything else!"

Beecher Monmouth's widow paused, looking him over, excoriating him with her fine eyes; then went on slowly and intensely.

"Well, Mr. Treves, perhaps it will surprise you and your friends to know that we have outwitted you from the beginning."

"I don't quite get your meaning," said John.

She lifted her head and laughed aloud in his face. Her mask was off. She let herself go. She swept her arm toward the darkness of the night, then looked at him with the eyes of a fiend. "Those guns you hear now mean that we are making our great attack." Her voice rose shrilly; her scarlet lips writhed. She was truly possessed at that moment. "For all your espionage and cunning we shall be able to make our way into Portsmouth. We shall deliver a blow from which you will not easily recover. Your ships——"

John moved to the end of the table and motioned towards the door.

"Thank you," said he, "that is very interesting, no doubt, but I think it is time we were going."

The fury beyond the table paid no heed. With both hands on its surface she thrust her chin towards him and spat out her words.

"Every fort on this coast has been silenced by our finesse!"

John, listening to the roar of the guns, was unperturbed.

"That was a pretty heavy one," he remarked, as the room reverberated again to the renewed crash of artillery.

"Our guns, you fool!" Mrs. Beecher Monmouth lifted her voice to a scream. "Our guns—German guns!"

John stared at her. He had never seen anything like the tornado of passion that was sweeping through her. He listened, enthralled, against his will. Nevertheless, he was master of the scene. She hated him—loathed him—because he had tricked her. She had expended charm, she had enveloped him in the sunshine of her beauty to no end. Her vanity was outraged. He had enjoyed her caresses and laughed in his sleeve.

"The boom——"

"What about the boom?" John asked.

"From Ponsonby Lighthouse to Windsor Fort the boom is not down to-night. Think of that. Your searchlights—where are they? Dark—dark—every one of them." She dropped her voice suddenly in a measured, triumphant whisper, "and our Unter-see boats are creeping in."

Even now she was beautiful, but there was something animal-like in the distortion of her mouth.

"Where, precisely, are your U-boats creeping into?" inquired John calmly.

"Into—into Portsmouth." She mouthed the name of the great harbour.

"You thought to outwit us, and we outwit you!"

John bowed. "I have only your word for it."

She paid no heed and went on. "So you see, Mr. Treves, what you get in wasting your time on me—a woman!"

His obstinate coolness maddened her, and in a wild gust of rage she crashed her fist on the table.

"You fool! You fool! You sheep's head!" she announced, elegantly. She paused a moment, breathing heavily, then sweeping round the table, snatched her coat from his arm and strode towards the door.

"There is no hurry, Mrs. Beecher Monmouth— —"

She halted and gave him a glance that would have turned Parkson to stone.

"What do you mean?" she demanded.

"I mean that our interview is not at an end!"

The menace of her eyes glittered upon him. If her strength of body had been equal to it at that moment, she would have leapt forward and strangled him with her bare hands. Knowledge of her own peril, of the Nemesis that was sweeping upon her, had not yet entered her disordered mind.

John made—in pursuance of his prearranged plan of action—no effort to stay her as she went towards the door. But as Mrs. Beecher Monmouth paused and cast a final look at him, a sudden doubt crept into her eyes. For John had gone to the window. He appeared no longer to be occupied with her. His back was towards her, and presently he lifted a whistle to his lips and blew two short, shrill blasts.

A transformation passed over Mrs. Beecher Monmouth's face that was startling. The colour flowed from her cheeks. Her lips seemed suddenly to become bloodless.

"Why do you do that?"

John turned upon her slowly. There was no pity in his eyes.

"When I did it," he answered, grimly, "I was thinking of the *Malta*, and two hundred fine fellows who died at your hands. I am thinking now of other things—of the *Polidor* and her scores of non-combatant passengers who were drowned by your machinations.... You have had a long run for your money, but at last— —"

He stopped—a sound came to him, a tramp of heavy booted men advancing in the passage. Some one pushed open the door, and a corporal—a tall, grim-looking fellow—appeared on the threshold.

"Is that you, Davis?"

"Yes, sir!"

John spoke over Mrs. Beecher Monmouth's head to the man beyond.

"This is the lady, Davis!"

"Very good, sir!"

"You will take her at once. Put her in a car and drive her to Newport to-night. I have already communicated with the Chief Constable, who has made arrangements to receive her."

He turned his eyes once more, and for the last time in life, on the beautiful woman in the doorway.

CHAPTER XXXIII

"Hallo—what's that?"

A red glare of light saturated the low hanging clouds and suddenly vanished. Close, windless air vibrated under the detonation of heavy artillery. A Sergeant, who had been concealed in the shelter of a stone wall which ran round Captain Cherriton's cottage, turned to the man at his side.

"What d'you reckon it is, Nobby?"

"It must be night practice."

"Not it," answered the Sergeant, "that's the 'nine-inch' at Heatherpoint, with a full charge!"

As the words left his lips a second crashing roar reverberated from the fort. Then, almost before Sergeant Watson could further comment upon the fact, a sound like rapid beating of a tom-tom came to them. Busy, drum-like notes, some deep and long-drawn, as if coming from the bowels of the earth, some sharp, short, and angry, took up the refrain.

"Hallo!" exclaimed Watson, amazed, "they're all at it. There's something up."

He stared at the sky, thence out to sea.

"Hallo, where's all our searchlights?" exclaimed Nobby.

"That's just what I was going to ask you," Watson answered; then instantly dropped down behind the wall, pulling his companion with him. Watson had seen a figure approaching from the road. The stranger wore mufti and a soft felt hat, and as he came stumbling and hurrying through the grass, leaping artillery flashes momentarily lifted him into view, and again plunged him into utter darkness.

Watson, with Nobby and two other men, had, under John's directions, kept a three-days' watch on Cherriton's cottage. At the present moment Cherriton himself was alone in the low, single-storied building which, from two workmen's dwellings, had been converted into an artistic residence.

Watson waited. And presently, in the silence between the roll of drumfire at the western end of the island, he could hear the fall of footsteps, and presently, through the screen of bushes, and in the light of gunfire he made out the figure of a tall young man, whose face for a moment looked familiar to him, then caused him to pull Nobby by the arm.

"Who is it, Nobby?" he asked.

The new-comer had reached Cherriton's gate and was hurrying into the little garden.

"Why, it's Lieutenant Treves!"

"What's he doing out of uniform?"

"I don't know," answered Nobby. "It's him right enough. Look again."

"He looks as if he'd had the fright of his life—I've never seen him look like that."

"Nor me, neither," answered Nobby, eyeing the figure hurrying towards Cherriton's door.

Both men watched the visitor disappear into the cottage, then discussed the matter in low tones. There was something that puzzled them about Treves's visit to Captain Cherriton—there was something that to Sergeant Watson's intelligent mind seemed altogether wrong about that visit, and yet he could not tell what.

Cherriton had been at the back window of his cottage peering out since the heavy gunfire began, and a look of triumph animated his pallid, hollow-cheeked countenance. He was startled at length by a low, feverish rapping at the cottage door. He paused a moment in thought before answering, then shifted a Mauser pistol from his hip pocket to the left hand pocket of his coat. He was a left-handed man, a fact which at certain moments of crisis was apt to redound to his advantage. With a due amount of caution he drew open the door, and the man from the threshold strode in upon him.

As Cherriton's eyes fell upon the stranger in the candle light the lines of his mouth altered.

"Why, it's you, Treves—this is a surprise!" he exclaimed. He gripped the young man's hand and drew him forward into the room.

Bernard Treves, pale, haggard, swept the room with his restless glance. His likeness to John Manton was striking even now.

"Have you got anybody here?" he asked quickly.

"No."

"Where's Manners?"

"He isn't here," answered Cherriton.

"Where is he?" Treves came forward and laid a hand on the other's arm. "I must see Manners."

"Why?"

Cherriton looked at him with sudden malice. He felt that this man who had tricked and betrayed them from the beginning, was still pursuing his deep game. However, they were playing now upon even terms. Mrs. Beecher Monmouth's information had opened wide his eyes. Moreover, a mandate had been issued. General von Kuhne had spoken....

A sickly smile crossed the visitor's pallid, handsome countenance. "It's no good trying to keep it quiet," he said; "but I must have cocaine. It's a matter of life and death with me. Look at my hands!"

He held out his hands which shook visibly.

"I don't mind saying it," he went on; "but I've been pretty nearly over the brink two or three times lately. Yesterday I tried every chemist's shop in Ryde and Newport, but I couldn't get anything."

He wiped his brow with a handkerchief. Cherriton was regarding him closely, puzzled at the change in him.

"You managed to get along without it for a long time," retorted Cherriton, looking at him coldly.

"I had to—there was nothing else for it. That damned nursing home——" Suddenly he put out his hand and laid it on the German's arm. "Where's Manners, for God's sake tell me—tell me? I must have some——"

Then he became aware of a narrowing of the other's gaze. "Why are you looking at me like that?"

The Captain laughed.

"Don't do it; it makes my blood run cold," Treves protested.

"I was thinking of your drug habit—how conveniently it comes and goes."

"Don't sneer at me, for God's sake," pleaded Treves. "I'm desperate." He walked the floor in a state of nervous tension, which would have been pitiable to witness, had there been in Cherriton any spirit of mercy. "It seems there's been a law passed forbidding chemists—you can't get cocaine anywhere," he jerked out, hopelessly.

Cherriton's dark gaze was again upon him.

"I can't give you cocaine, Treves," he said, "but if you come into my bedroom there, I'll give you something else."

Treves clutched his arm.

"What?"

"Morphia," answered Cherriton.

He led the way into a low-ceilinged bedroom at the end of the cottage, carrying the candle from the parlour table as he went. He placed the light on the dressing table near the window, took a key from his pocket, and opened a drawer in the only chest of drawers in the small room.

Treves, watching him with impatient eyes, moistened his lips and waited.

Cherriton searched in the drawer and drew out a syringe and a small bottle.

"Here," he said to Treves, "sit over on the chair near the dressing table."

Treves greedily eyed the syringe, and obediently seated himself with his back to the little mirror. The candle on the white dimity cloth of the dressing table threw its light full upon him. He watched Cherriton fill the syringe with morphia, and almost clutched it from his hand.

"Wait," said the German, holding him off, "you shall have it full."

"Thanks—thanks—thanks."

Treves watched him as a famished dog watches a bone.

"You don't know what I've suffered, Cherriton—that nursing home, St. Neot's, curse it—it's been hell!"

"You are so clever, Treves, I wonder you didn't get cocaine before?"

"My God, if you knew how I've tried."

Cherriton was standing about a yard away from Treves, with his big chin thrust forward. The expression of his face at that moment would have shot terror into his visitor's heart, if he had lifted his eyes. But Treves was busy. He was pulling back his sleeve, and in another instant he had dug the needle into the flesh of his forearm. His lips tightened as he forced the morphia into his blood. Then he slowly raised his head, a look of ecstatic happiness glowed in his eyes; he drew a deep sigh of contentment.

"A-h-h," he exclaimed.

And Cherriton, who had been standing still as a statue, still as death, moved. The veiled light in his eyes blazed into murder. With swiftness and stealth he whipped the Mauser from his pocket, aimed and fired. His shot passed through Treves's heart.... Before the reverberation had died, he fired into Treves's body a second time, and this time so near was he that the blaze scorched his victim's waistcoat. He had made assurance doubly sure, and his next quick move was to lean forward, blow out the candle, drop his pistol near the body, that had fallen heavily, and fling open the window.

Two minutes later he was speeding swiftly across the yard at the back of the cottage. As he ran a gun-flash from Heatherpoint lifted the darkness for a moment, and again he was enveloped in the surrounding gloom.

Before Sergeant Watson and his three men could reach the door of the cottage, Cherriton had vanished into a clump of trees.

"There's something wrong!" said Watson. "I'm going in." He took Nobby with him, hurried along the path, and knocked at Cherriton's portal.

No answer came. He thrust open the door and found the living-room in darkness; he struck a match, lit a candle from the mantelshelf, and held it aloft.

"Hallo, there's nobody here."

The door of the bedroom was open, and the draught—a puff of close air—from the open window beyond suddenly blew shut the front door with a crash.

Sergeant Watson was a man of steady nerve, but he did not like the crash, neither did he like the silence, the heavy, brooding silence. Nevertheless, he lifted his voice valiantly.

"Is there anybody there?" he called.

He could hear the curtain rings faintly rattling in the bedroom, but no answer came to him. Then with the candle in his hand and followed by Nobby, gripping his rifle, he went into Cherriton's bedroom. On the floor beyond the end of Cherriton's bed, near the dressing table, they could see a foot and the lower part of Treves's trouser leg.

"My God!" exclaimed Watson, hurrying forward with a fleeting glance at the open window.

The figure lying near the dressing table with a revolver near it, and a morphia syringe a little distance away, was huddled and motionless.

*   *   *   *   *

Three minutes later, Watson, Nobby and two other men stood in an open space on the downs, forty yards before Cherriton's cottage. Watson was busy rearing a tripod stand about five feet in height. When the tripod was ready Nobby handed him a lantern, which was dexterously screwed upon its apex. He struck a match, lit the lantern and flicked open a shutter.

"Stand back out of the line of light," he cried to one of his men.

Then with little scraping clicks of the lantern shutter, the single eye of light turned westward, he began to spell out a message.

Three times he gave his opening call before receiving an answer by signal lantern from behind the fort at Freshwater. Having achieved connection he patiently spelt out the following message:

"Report to officer in command Heatherpoint."

"Who are you?" came the answer.

"Watson, emergency light number 6."

"Yes, what is it?"

"Lieutenant Treves been murdered. Lying dead Heather Cottage."

The lantern at Freshwater took the message, and before signalling on said, "Repeat."

Watson, with a grim face, repeated the message and added:

"Shot by Captain Cherriton. Murderer escaped, running north by east."

CHAPTER XXXIV

John having disposed of Mrs. Beecher Monmouth returned to Heatherpoint Fort. Within the fort gates the ground quivered and vibrated. Far below him the Solent was alive with the sweeping beams of Throgmorton's cunning emergency lights. John could see flashes of fire from Ponsonby Point, from Scoles Head, and from a new secret battery beyond Windsor Fort. His time was emphatically not his own, he had received orders to leave the fort on a new mission. Within five minutes he had passed the rear defences and the barbed wire of the fort, and was out upon the downs. He sprinted forward over the short springing turf, and soon came to the cliff edge and the narrow path that descended the chalk to South Bay.

As he reached the cliff edge and looked down an amazing panorama smote his eyes. Dover lights—tremendous, blinding blue-white illuminations—floated upon the surface of the water shedding forth almost painful rays of light. The yellow of the sand in the little bay became a ghost-like floor in this radiance. Sinclair, he knew, was down there busy at his telephone, but it was not Sinclair nor the drama of the scene that occupied his thoughts; he was thinking not of them, but of a slip of paper Throgmorton had handed him bearing the message of his own death, and of Throgmorton's words, "Somebody was murdered."

"Yes," thought John, "somebody who was mistaken for me."

His mind projected itself upon the scene in Cherriton's cottage, and the thing he had suspected from the very first instant revealed itself fully. Bernard Treves had escaped in his second effort to free himself from his enforced detention at St. Neot's, and, of course, the first thing he had done was to search out the whereabouts of Cherriton and Manners in order to obtain the drugs that were a passion with him. He had gone to the cottage, Cherriton had received him, and had clearly shot him in cold blood....

John turned his mind away from the possibilities Treves's death had created for himself. After all, he was sorry. Treves's broken and enfeebled will had been too much for the young man to contend against. He had failed—death had come upon him suddenly and terribly, but perhaps, after all, it was for the best....

His thoughts turned to Colonel Treves.... As was to be expected, and inevitably the delicately beautiful vision of Elaine rose before him.... Her life of bondage was at an end.... Then John drew himself up and took himself severely to task. These thoughts were not for him. In this hour of drama, of tragedy, he must not let his thoughts dwell upon her. There were decencies, and he was a man of honour; nevertheless, in the depths of his heart, something moved, a dim obliterated ray of hope flickered into life....

To the music of the guns he continued his descent of the chalk path. Where the damp penetrated it was slippery beneath his feet, nevertheless he went quickly with steps that must have been noiseless. The path reached the beach some distance away from the scene of activity, of which Sinclair was the centre. And as John came within thirty or forty feet of the shore, he saw below him, at the bend of the path, a man crouching. The man was huddled in a sheltered corner, intent upon some occupation invisible to John, who halted and looked down upon him with some curiosity. The silent figure was in khaki, and his shoulder and half his cap were visible. He was deeply absorbed, and John was able to go forward and descend two or three turns of the path without being observed.

Presently, walking softly on the narrow path in the cliff's face, he came full into view of the stranger, whose presence was concealed by the projection of a cliff from the pitiless Dover flares.

The man was Captain Cherriton.

John was not in the least surprised to find his able and resourceful enemy crouching down working a flashlight towards a portion of the sea cut off from the fort lights.

Manton knew that the hour of destiny had arrived. The thought came to him that Cherriton's hands were stained with blood, that not an hour ago he had — —

He moved forward a pace, his face grim and set. Cherriton, still crouching, heard him, and turned, but in the gloom of that sheltered place he did not see clearly. Quick as thought, however, he turned his electric torch and flashed it full upon John's face. In the circle of incandescent light he saw something that caused him to choke with horror—that something was the face and the living eyes of the man he had murdered an hour ago.

The sight was too much for him, the light fell from his fingers. John, guessing what had happened, resolved to give him no chance of discovery. With a shout he leapt forward and flung his arms about him.

Half in terror, half in growing knowledge that he had to deal with a living and determined enemy, Cherriton struggled like a maniac. Each man put forth his entire strength. John sought to get his hands round the German's throat. Together they rocked, bumped, and swayed, and, finally, together they fell, tumbling and thumping to the sand, fifteen feet below.

For a minute each man lay still, stunned by the impact of the fall. Then John, first to recover, creeping on hands and knees, approached Cherriton and fell upon him again.

"I'm done," breathed the German, "get off me...." There was a truce for some minutes after that, during which John sat with a Mauser in his hand, and recovered himself fully.

Cherriton, who had been lying on his back in the sand, turned.

"Who are you?" he asked, staring with strained eyes into John's face.

The mystery was beyond him. Were there two Bernard Treves? He had killed, or as he would have put it, he had legitimately executed Bernard Treves in the cottage less than two hours ago. So far all was clear to him. But this other man, this replica and simulacrum of Treves, who was he? He was Treves, and he was not Treves. He continued to stare and his mystification deepened. John, feeling that the moment for explanation had come, came to his aid.

"You are recalling that you killed me in your cottage less than two hours ago?"

"Yes," began Cherriton.

"All along," went on John, "you and your colleagues have been mistaken in me. I have played the part of Bernard Treves with some success, but my real name happens to be John Manton."

Dawn came, and with it victory for the defenders of the Solent. In the last moment von Kuhne's plans had gone astray. His submarines which had intended to cause havoc among the multitude of shipping at Portsmouth had indeed passed the boom, only to meet destruction beyond. Eight submarines went to the credit of the R.G.A. and the Navy that night; eighty German marines were captured on the little shore of South Bay. And now, in the fort mess-room that had known so much of drama during the last few months, Colonel Hobin occupied his chair at the head of the table. Beside him was seated Throgmorton, the Flag-Lieutenant. Commander Greaves and John Manton were also present, grouped at the end of the room, near the window whence the dawn crept in. At the far end of the room stood Ewins, something of a hero that morning, but the time for compliment had not yet arrived.

"Bring them in, Ewins," commanded Hobin.

Ewins saluted and clattered away.

Five minutes later he returned with a squad of men who waited in the little passage outside. And Ewins ushered into the mess-room Captain Cherriton, still in British uniform. With him was the tall German naval lieutenant John had some time ago seen at Voules's house at Brooke. The last prisoner to enter the room was Voules himself, the General von Kuhne who had so industriously instituted the attack which had met with disaster.

Colonel Hobin put a few questions.

"I am an officer of the German Navy," said the tall lieutenant. "I demand all the privileges of an honourable prisoner of war."

"Certainly," intervened Throgmorton, "in your case there is no question of the death penalty."

"I, too, am an officer," began Voules in his rasping voice.

"I am afraid the fact," said Colonel Hobin, "that you neglected the formality of wearing uniform in your attack upon us will tell somewhat severely against you. All I want this morning," he concluded, "is that you should each admit your identity."

The three Germans had no objection to this.

When the prisoners had been removed Hobin and then Throgmorton gripped John by the hand—in fact, everybody in the room shook hands in the grey of the dawn that morning.

"All the luck in the world was ours, Treves," said Throgmorton.

"My name is Manton," John reminded him.

"Of course, of course—I had quite forgotten that."

John's life story was only just beginning—the recovery of his own name marked an epoch. Summer went and autumn came; the sun of Peace rose over the horizon. Letters at first somewhat formal, but later growing in cordiality, passed between himself and Elaine. Then, at last, on a certain autumn day—a red-letter day for John—he received an epistle in Colonel Treves's shaking hand. "*My dear boy,*" ran the Colonel's letter, "*I want you to come and visit me. We have been friends a long time—you have played your part well and truly. That which my poor boy failed to do, you have done in his name. You have done credit to my house and to the name of Treves. I am well again now, and shall welcome you with all my heart.*"

John did not know how it was, but a film came before his eyes as he finished reading the old Colonel's letter. And on the Saturday following, when he drove up to the Colonel's house in a hired motor, from Freshwater, the sun was setting over the Solent and yellow leaves were falling in the long drive.

Gates drew open the front door of the mansion before John alighted and conducted him straight to the Colonel, in the library. The old man, who had been standing in the window expecting his arrival, came across the room and gripped his hand. He looked into John's face, then smiled. There was conviction in his voice.

"Yes," he said. "You're a Treves in everything except name."

There was much to talk about. In the first place the Colonel spoke of Elaine always as his daughter-in-law. She had completely won his heart.

"This gives me a new lease of life, my boy," he said to John. Then the smile that was so attractive in him lit up his face. "And when that lease is run out she shall have all that is mine just as she would have had if my boy had lived." The Colonel laid his hand on John's shoulder.

"John, my boy," he said, "your attention's wandering, it isn't me you want to hear talking, so I'll take myself off now."

He went out of the room, and John, walking to the window, looked for a moment upon the autumn scene outside. Then a sound came to him, and he turned to see Elaine, radiant yet doubtful, and strangely shy—looking like spring in autumn.

For a moment John was still; then he hurried across the room and took her hands in his.

"Elaine," he whispered, "is everything forgotten and forgiven?"

Elaine lifted her eyes to his. She was ten times more beautiful at that moment than the image he had treasured in his heart.

"There is nothing to forget, and nothing to forgive, John," she said quietly.

John drew in a deep breath.

"You love me, don't you?"

"You know I do."

Again John drew in a deep breath, this time of complete happiness.

"Thank goodness," he said—"so that's all right!" Then, without more ado, he swept her into his arms. "I'm going to make mad love to you until seven o'clock," he announced masterfully.